The
Rosendorf
Quartet

The Rosendorf Quartet

A NOVEL

NATHAN SHAHAM

*Translated from the Hebrew
by Dalya Bilu*

GROVE PRESS
New York

Grove Press
841 Broadway
New York, NY 10003-4793

Published in Canada by General Publishing Company, Ltd.

Library of Congress Cataloging-in-Publication Data

Shaham, Nathan.
[Revi' iyat Rozendorf.   English]
The Rosendorf quartet : a novel / Nathan Shaham ; translated from
the Hebrew by Dalya Bilu.
p.   cm.
Translation of: Revi' iyat Rozendorf.
I. Title.
PJ5054.S3R4813   1991
892.4'36—dc20
91-6482

ISBN 0-8021-3316-9 (pbk.)

Manufactured in the United States of America

Printed on acid-free paper

Designed by Irving Perkins Associates

First American Edition 1991

10   9   8   7   6   5   4   3   2   1

The
Rosendorf
Quartet

First Violin—
Kurt Rosendorf

"Calm Sea and Prosperous Voyage." In the Germany of
today Mendelssohn's fate is no different from ours. But they
won't be able to expurgate him from the *Encyclopaedia Britannica*.

The sky is clear, golden blue. Only the sea is somber, in
Prussian blue: dark, as if last night's storm is still seething in
its depths. Foamless waves lap against the sides of the ship.
The engine plays a chord in E-flat major. It goes well with the
color blue, which is the color of yearning for the absolute. The
Masonic key of friendship.

I would like to believe that it is possible to find friends
everywhere, even in a country of low culture and so much
politics. It will be strange to play Mozart in the desert. A
gentle melancholy, not in the least "major," suffuses the
works he composed in this key—the Sinfonia Concertante for
Violin and Viola, the Piano Concerto, the String Quintet—as
if he did not trust even the friendship of those who had sworn
to be faithful to each other.

I'll write home: even the ship's engine plays a friendly note.
A little white lie. There's no point in worrying them. It would
be foolishness to write in my first letter home that already on
the way there I am worried by the dulling of my own senses.
But the fact is that I used to be as excited by travel as a boy
setting out on his first trip alone. And this time, on my way to
introduce so radical a change in my life—total indifference.
The two days I never touched the violin, because of the storm,

3

upset me more than the uncertainty about the future. A strange apathy has descended on me. I'm on my way to play in a provincial orchestra, which has been established for humane reasons, in fear for the future, and here I am sailing like a tourist on holiday, my head empty of thoughts.

Perhaps because I needed all my inner resources to take the first step—to leave home, family, friends, fatherland—and there is nothing left to mobilize for the future. My thoughts are drawn to the past. My imagination shrinks from the effort of envisaging life in the wretched town built on sand. It's hard to imagine a symphony orchestra in a kind of overgrown Mediterranean village without an opera or a cathedral.

I have never before seen a town which was founded only twenty-eight years ago. From the picture postcards it was impossible to tell. Little houses on either side of a street leading to a building with Gothic arches and a tower. And I thought: How strange—a town built around a high school.

I don't dare imagine a string quartet.

Greta said: "You'll be able to live without me. But not without a quartet."

I said to her: "I'm going there to play in an orchestra, you know."

She looked at me in concern. I hadn't even set out and already I was lowering my standards. Already I was beginning to measure myself against the standards of some remote immigrant country. As if foreseeing my deterioration she had that expression of superior disappointment on her face, that expression of resignation to facts which stemmed not from external circumstances but from her husband's character. It did not even occur to her to ask me to change my mind. She had no intention of arguing with a stubborn mule who made his rash decisions into sacred principles. Once we had made the decision to separate for an undefined period there was no point in quarreling. Quarrels would only wound without solving anything.

When I told Egon Loewenthal, the well-known writer, he

seemed quite encouraged to hear that someone like myself was also going to Palestine; it meant there was a chance of finding a cultural milieu there. But about my arrangement with my wife, I saw from his face that he doubted our chances of ever being united again. Hitler is not a passing episode which Germany will shake off sooner or later, he said. That's wishful thinking, and nothing to do with the facts. Hitler is popular with the people and the only thing capable of defeating him is an outside power. Unfortunately, no such power exists. The West will do whatever it can to humor the madman, and no prophesies of doom from the refugees will make them change their minds.

We spoke only of the political problem, although he made me understand that he could imagine a number of other reasons for a man and wife to separate of their own free wills. But he would not press me. People tell others the things that they themselves want to believe. He assumed correctly that if there were any nonpolitical problems separating me from my wife, I would keep them to myself.

Temperamental differences, like erotic problems, lie beneath the surface of definition, and there is no point in calling them by name. We shall never know how important the suppressed miseries of our past really are. It is quite possible, after all, that this sudden blunting of feeling is the normal state, which others call common sense.

The contradictions in character between myself and Greta were simple and obvious. Even a stranger could see them. The Orthodox would no doubt attribute our separation to the preordained failure of mixed marriages. For from every other point of view we were a couple whose harmony seemed assured. We are both musicians, of more or less equal stature, each in our own sphere—there was no room for competition or parasitism; we both enjoy making music, reading a good book, and devoting ourselves to the education of our daughter; neither of us is attracted to bohemian life, which can alienate a person even from himself, and neither of us possesses extreme opinions, which can undermine the firm foundations of mutual understanding. We are industrious people, who know how to work hard and save up for a rainy day, to understand each other without the need for too many words, and to beware of the kind of crude humor which may give rise to misunderstandings.

And nevertheless, there were dissonances.

Dissonances which we scrupulously avoided attributing to any difference in our formal religious affiliation. Greta defined it well. After we had become involved in a dispute about some trifling matter, from which we could on no account extricate ourselves, I intimated that she attributed my stubbornness to my Jewish origins.

"You're as Jewish as I'm Christian. We don't belong, to exactly the same degree. So why let the mob come between us?"

There was a considerable difference in our degree of sensitivity. Where artists are concerned, this can be disturbing and unbalancing.

Although she has never actually said so, I sense that Greta is repelled by my oversensitivity. If I am not mistaken, she blames it for my "failure" as an artist, too: I never had the stomach for the kind of competition in which you sometimes have to "tread on corpses," as they say. This is the reason, in her opinion, that I am not a soloist with an international reputation, but only the first violinist in an orchestra, who finds his happiness in a string quartet that performs in small halls.

It pains me that she fails to understand: chamber music is a way of life. It was not for fear of nerve-racking confrontations that I did not concentrate all my efforts on struggling to gain the status of a soloist—although, of course, I willingly abandoned chamber music from time to time in order to play violin concertos. Chamber music—it is difficult to explain to anyone who doesn't understand of his own accord—is the right compromise between the ego and a profound recognition of the supreme importance of teamwork.

I shall not ignore the fact that Greta's disappointment in me stemmed not only from my modesty, which was incompatible with her visions of the happiness in store for us: two gifted, good-looking, discriminating, diligent people, who had had the good fortune to be born in a nation capable of appreciating musical talent, diligence, and Hellenic beauty. She was also tired of trying to educate me to stand up for myself. Sometimes she would look at me in deep despair. When was I going to grow up? A man of thirty-eight, with a not inconsiderable musical career behind him—and any woman that came along, even if she was frivolous, stupid, or vulgar, could twist him around her little finger and force him to adapt himself to her moods; I was incapable of making others recognize that my status accorded me a central position, and everyone else had to revolve around me.

There is something in the above. I can add this, too: when I meet someone who abases himself or herself to me—an admirer or a girl bowled over by my good looks—I am enormously embarrassed. And I immediately look for some subject which will give them a certain advantage over me. Instead of talking about music I begin jabbering about politics, cooking, bringing up children, literature, and God knows what else.

Perhaps I really am oversensitive, afraid of making myself conspicuous—a Jewish trait inherited from my parents, and unable to stand up for my rights.

An example, of no importance in itself, may help to clarify the problem:

We have a very small apartment in Berlin, situated in a side street but near the Berlin Philharmonic, where real estate prices are high. Sufficient for the needs of three normal people. But when all three have to practice (Anna, our daughter, plays the piano), problems arise. On the face of things, these problems are not insoluble. Especially within the family circle.

When the bedroom door is closed the noise is muffled. I can play in the kitchen. The hours of the day can also be fairly divided. But while Greta—who should supposedly be the most sensitive of the three of us, for what is more vulnerable than the vocal cords?—was able to shut herself off from the world and ignore everything as if she had gone somewhere else, I—who ostensibly need nothing but a little warming up to get back into shape—was upset by the least little thing: sounds from the street, a bad mood of Anna's, a significant silence on Greta's part, anything at all. I could draw the bow over the strings and run my fingers to and fro, but the essence was lacking: concentration, inspiration, empathy.

Greta considered this morbid. At first she regarded my trips out of town to play in a friend's abandoned house as a piece of bohemian playacting. When she realized it was serious, she was deeply disappointed. She would have been happier if it had been a pose. Such exacerbated sensitivity seemed to her a mental disease. To be precise: not a mental disease, but a disease of the spirit, a kind of debility due to overfastidiousness. For this disease she also had a cure: just as one tells pale, pampered children to go out into nature and play sports, she sought to strengthen my weak spirit by challenging confrontations initiated by herself. This was a bad mistake. Although she did it playfully, I could not accept these deliberate disturbances, intended to strengthen my character, as a game in which I was compelled to participate.

Recently—too late!—she stopped. She despaired of me. Although she was very careful not to say so, I sensed that she attributed this characteristic to my "Jewish nature." We are a people doomed to have no peace of mind. We deserve to be pitied. There is no chance that we will change. Not in our generation. At least our daughter will be saved from this fate. The blood of Bavarian peasants flows in her veins.

Instead of battle drill to fortify my spirit I began to receive little examples of how a mature person masters his moods. The latter were organized displays of control over the situation. With disguised glee she would maneuver herself into embarrassing situations, in which her superior virtues blossomed. Once a quarrel had broken out over some trivial matter—who isn't dragged into such disputes because of misunderstandings or suppressed tension?—her eyes would gleam like those of a child with a new treasure: an opportunity to prove which of us was obstinate and which magnanimous. With what delight she allowed me to win an argument in which I was in the wrong! Obliquely, from Olympian heights, she would give me a shrewd look. She did not waste her magnanimities in vain. They had an educational aim. Gradually she was molding my character. I still had a chance to become a strong and optimistic creature.

I have to admit: our personality clashes did not detract from the physical pleasure we derived from one another. All the dissonances were resolved in bed. There all ended on a strong chord, and with a major cadence. Quite often we brought daily disappointments to our lovemaking and assuaged professional setbacks in each other's arms. How sweet and loving she was after she failed to get a part in *The Twilight of the Gods*! In the world of silence seething in the flesh we were completely at one. But despite our mutual ability to plunge together into a happy oblivion, which lasted as long as the act of making love, during the course of time we felt a need for temporary separation. "To renew ourselves" was the formula we agreed upon between us. We needed to miss each other for a while—the time we needed was never defined—in order to come together again and be as close as we had been in our first years together.

The political facts, too, urged us toward the same conclusion. Although at first their influence was in the reverse direction. Greta, who was strongly opposed to Hitler's ideas, felt the need to demonstrate solidarity with a Jew. But even this she did so gracelessly that there was nothing heartwarming about it. Sometimes I felt that she was exploiting even this melancholy state of affairs in order to put the record straight:

in our family there was one partner who granted patronage and one who needed it.

Huberman's offer to join the orchestra which he was about to establish in Palestine came at the right time from every point of view. I had recently been dismissed from my job with the Berlin Philharmonic, and the Rosendorf Quartet—three Jews and one pure Aryan—had no chance whatsoever of earning a living by music. In Germany we were subject to the racial laws and in other countries the quartet was not yet known. Although we had one concert to our credit in Liverpool and one in Strasbourg, which caused us considerable financial loss, and one record—a hasty and inaccurate recording—this was not enough to ensure us a decent living in another country. Nor was my performance as a soloist with the Frankfurt Symphony Orchestra enough to consolidate my position. Playing the Brahms there only one year after Szigeti was a tactical error.

Palestine seemed an excellent temporary refuge.

Greta thought it an insane idea.

"If you go to England or France, we have a chance of coming together again. Consolidate your position there (one of her favorite expressions) and we will be able to join you after a reasonable period of time."

One thing was sure: she would never go to Palestine. Not because it was a refuge for the Jews; she had no prejudices against the Jews. She had married a Jew, hadn't she, and endangered herself by denouncing anti-Semitism in public! And not because of her own musical career either was Palestine beyond the pale. She was ready to give up her ambitions and content herself with being a singing teacher and giving an occasional performance with the orchestra, if, indeed, Huberman succeeded in putting together an orchestra worthy of the name. But on no account was she prepared to risk Anna's future. "It's out of the question to take a flower like Anna and plant her in the middle of the desert," she said.

Anna showed every sign of possessing exceptional musical

gifts. At the age of fourteen she was already a mature musician. She had excellent technique, concentration, and, above all, outstanding personal expressiveness. There was no doubt that she had a brilliant career in store, if she persevered and had the right teachers.

They say there are two or three decent teachers there, but Greta, who knows them by reputation, is not prepared to recognize them as the "cultural milieu" which Anna requires. Furthermore, in her opinion a young artist of Anna's stature cannot develop without the company of young musicians of her own age.

Perhaps she is right. Germany is a place in which the talent of a young artist can flourish.

From this point of view too, the "time out" we have taken will be beneficial. Without a Jewish father on her back Anna's chances will be better.

But in Trieste homesickness attacked me mercilessly, settling like an oppressive physical entity in the cavity of my chest. The pain drew all my attention to itself and stopped me from concentrating. A necessary sacrifice, I said to myself. A serious musician has no private life. You have to accept it. Mozart parted from his mother and set out on his wanderings before he was eight years old.

On the ship I began to wonder whether our sacrifice was not in vain.

The meeting with Egon Loewenthal, which filled my heart with joy, also gave rise to an unexpected pain. He was careful not to say so, but I could see that he questioned the assumption that the Nazis would not harm a talented young girl because of her Jewish father. All he said was: "I suspect that none of us has any idea what these people are capable of."

He apparently knows something that people like me, who were merely dismissed from their posts, can only guess.

He was one of the first prisoners in Dachau.

*   *   *

I met him on the deck on the second day at sea. He recognized me. At the end of 1931 he had attended a Rosendorf Quartet concert and he remembered my face ("A face you don't forget," he said to me, as if stating a fact). He came to tell me how much he had enjoyed (five years ago!) Schubert's A Minor, a quartet of which he was particularly fond. He introduced himself in an unintelligible mumble, and I had no idea that I was talking to the famous writer, the author of *Ancient Glory*, which I had liked so much.

After I had placed him—mainly by means of his unusual manner of speech—he surprised me again. A man like him, who had known both fame and terrible trouble, was capable of being moved by the fact that I remembered a book which had not made a great impression when it came out.

"I have a particularly soft spot, like a bereaved father, for the books rejected by the public," he said with a smile.

I thought it ridiculous of him to be excited by the admiration of someone like me, who has read so few books. I too enjoy the praise of the uninformed, but the only thing capable of really exciting me is the appreciation of serious musicians. Perhaps it was the circumstances of our meeting—on a ship carrying us to a country we had not chosen. In understandable fear of the unknown.

In a number of ways his fears are more reasonable than my apprehensions. There is no symmetry: I have a steady job waiting for me, a salary, and a more or less settled life. He has nothing. (He has vague promises from an émigré newspaper in Switzerland, and some woman friend there, who earns a living as a secretary. If he keeps up a steady flow of articles, next year they will pay him a regular salary—about half of what a violinist earns in an orchestra.) I have music, a universal language, fingers in good working order, a fine violin (a Guadagnini) and a guaranteed audience (a "Philharmonic Society" has already been in existence in this godforsaken place for a number of years now). He has no assurance of finding a publisher for his books. (An author without a language is like a violinist with broken fingers.)

Regarding the salary—I asked the other passengers whether twenty pounds a month was a respectable living (if I am appointed to the position of concertmaster) and whether it was possible to manage on seventeen or sixteen (if they prefer a better violinist to me). It's silly of me to worry, I know, but in situations of uncertainty and confusion we seize on details in order to have something to hold onto. Someone said that twenty pounds a month was a fortune. But he is a kibbutz member on his way home from a mission abroad, and the way he sees things anyone who isn't hungry should be happy. The second person I asked, not without embarrassment, smiled and gave me a look full of pity. He is an Arab who studied medicine in Germany, his family are wealthy property owners, and twenty pounds is the kind of sum he sticks between the breasts of a dancer in a nightclub.

The "friendship" that sprang up at first sight between Egon Loewenthal and myself is apparently of the kind that comes into being in convalescent homes, and ends with the conclusion of the cure. It stems from the loneliness we feel on a ship carrying an ill-assorted crowd of passengers—immigrants, returning residents, government officials—who have nothing in common with one another. Both of us feel a certain bitterness at our first encounter with the inhabitants of the Promised Land. We could barely find one or two with whom it was possible to exchange a few sentences. And the only one who speaks fluent German, in a peculiar accent, is the Arab. Some of the others—the kind who never miss an opportunity to strike up a conversation with a stranger—have only pretensions to speaking German. They talk a jargon which we barely understand. "The sound of it puts my teeth on edge," says Egon. I am less sensitive. Their manners bother me more. Especially their rowdiness. And also the odious habit of beginning to talk about music the minute they discover who you are. I am also disgusted by the cordial expression that appears on their faces only after it transpires that you are not a refugee in need of their favors.

I call the delicate web of relations which has come into being between Egon Loewenthal and myself by the name "friendship," even though I have no idea if we will ever meet again on dry land. (Simple logic says we will; with the country so small and the number of German immigrants not large.) This does not mean, however, that we spend a lot of time together. On the contrary. We seldom meet. But we have no need of lengthy conversations in order to sense our mutual understanding. About Dachau, for example, he has not said a word. He let me understand for myself that the facts are not important. As for their effect on him—he does not yet know himself. It seems to me that he summed up his experience there in a single, quintessential sentence (like that pupil of Shön-berg's who wants to encompass the whole of music in a single page): "A man you did not want to know you cannot forget." About his books he never speaks at all. Perhaps he is afraid of finding out that I have not read them (a reasonable assumption). Only about *Ancient Glory*, which I myself mentioned, did he say a few words. The Prince there is a figure relevant to our times. And the moral too: it is possible to be moved to tears by sentimental music while at the same time remaining indifferent to human suffering. (Loewenthal is knowledgeable about music. In his youth he played the piano.)

Last night, after the sea grew calmer and I went to my cabin to play a little, he came with me. Music affects him strongly. He regards me as a friend because I never stay with him longer than he wishes. Greta would certainly interpret this to mean that taking my cue from the sensibilities of others is second nature to me. Escaping across the sea cannot cure a man of a fundamental weakness.

*   *   *

Greta, naturally, cannot know what I am like in the company of other women. She believes—in this she is probably no different from other wives—that modesty with regard to the physical side of love is also second nature to me. This is an assumption it would be difficult to contradict. I cannot reinforce my claims with facts that would be painful to her.

Frivolous women are drawn to me like sinners to sin. On board ship this can lead to awkward and ugly situations. Fortunately for me there are hardly any dark corners here and no privacy in the cabins. But anyone satisfied with hasty embraces has countless opportunities for enjoyment. House arrest on a ship at sea brings out in human beings, including women, all the silliness and irresponsibility latent in them. The enforced idleness makes them garrulous and reckless. Shamelessly, like people baring their bodies to the sun, they expose their most obscene qualities in public. First a few outer garments are removed, and later the thin skin of civilization, too, is shed.

There is one woman here, two or three years older than I am, apparently the wife of a well-known lawyer, who parades the deck as if the necessity of bearing the burden of her own personality alone is torture to her. Bored to desperation, she signals her availability for empty flirtations, which will end the moment she reaches safe harbor, to every ass on board. One ass, named Rosendorf, after resolving to keep away from all such nonsense, found himself standing on the deck arm in arm with the lady, which wouldn't have been so bad if he had not been obliged to listen to an emotional declaration regarding the beauty of the sea in the twilight, and its even greater beauty at night. And all for the sake of unsatisfactory embraces which make him feel contemptible and insincere.

There is another woman, younger but less attractive, who pushes up against me with her big, comforting bosom in order to practice her charms and the German she learned at a Viennese high school (her parents, who come from Galicia, spent a year there on their way to Palestine). She has very interesting stories to tell me. In Vienna she sang in the school choir. In Jerusalem she heard Huberman (and she looks at me compassionately—common sense tells her that I am not in the same class as Huberman). Her cousin used to play the violin too, but after graduating from high school in Tel Aviv he gave it up. She once read a book about Chopin, but she stops telling me about its contents when she remembers that he had been a pianist and not a violinist. She knows a few rude jokes too. And once she even hinted, extremely crudely, that the life-boats are covered up with heavy tarpaulin.

There is also a young girl from Germany who is going to work on a women's training farm. She looks at me with yearning eyes and bated breath when we bump into each other in a narrow passage. She is a charming girl, as sensitive and delicate as a Mozart minuet. In refraining from touching her I hope to atone for my deeds elsewhere; with the respect I feel for her I purify my soul from the muck.

Sometimes I think I am behaving like a boy considered a failure by his parents, who leaves home determined to prove them wrong by establishing a financial empire.

Loewenthal is a strange man. At times he seals himself off like a house with its shutters down. He listens to his interlocutor with demonstrative politeness and eyes tired to death. His good manners do not permit him to turn his back on some fellow who imagines that his own boredom is sufficient reason to impose himself on a helpless stranger. He is angry with himself for his inability to cast his manners aside.

Haydn must have listened thus to some tone-deaf aristo-cratic fiddler, full of anger against the way of the world which did not permit him to say: "Sir, you play very badly and should leave music to others." (The violinist Solomons found a saucy way to say this to King George III: "Violinists may be divided into three categories: the first—those who don't know how to play at all; the second—those who play very badly; the third—those who play well. Your Majesty has already reached the level of those in the second category. . . .")

His look, for no apparent reason growing more morose from minute to minute, casts terror into the heart of his interlocutor. On other occasions he is very affable and talks nonstop. Conversation with him is generally a strenuous mental effort. He speaks in hints, and you feel that he is putting your intelligence to the test. If you pretend to understand and smile, you will be entered on his blacklist, where all the various imposters are written down in a cramped hand. He utters half a sentence, like a man offering his companion half an apple, and pauses, until you feel uncomfortable and present him with the other half. If you have guessed right, you are his friend. If you are wrong—he has seen through you. He tells jokes with a poker face and glassy eyes. The humorless might imagine him to be bemoaning his fate. It seems to me that all the above are fences erected to defend him from pests.

He speaks of the loftiest matters as others might gossip. "The gods of Greece are rebelling," he said to a certain woman who was showing off her Latin (we were passing Crete; the sea was stormy and we were all green about the gills; it wasn't very nice to make fun of our situation, but he succeeded in giving an impression of speaking with the utmost gravity). "On our way from the West to the East, to the source of pure spirituality, we made the mistake of ignoring the Hellenic conception of beauty. And now the gods are taking their revenge." The woman smiled, but at the sight of his serious face she too put on a solemn expression and said, "There's something in what you say." Later he bellowed with laughter at her expense. I thought him guilty of intellectual sadism. I, too, saw "something" in what he said. Although I find it difficult to discuss such abstract matters with the familiarity with which one speaks of family relatives, the idea seems basically correct to me. We are traveling against the direction of history.

I have given this much thought: we are going to a country which needs manual workers and neither requires nor is capable of supporting a German writer and an international violinist (in all modesty, if Hitler had not come to power the Rosendorf Quartet would today be one of the best-known quartets in the world, on par with the Busch Quartet or the Griller Quartet, and I could have emigrated to England, France, Switzerland, or America without having to fill out forms). Here they call emigrating to Palestine "aliya." An ascent. From my point of view, and Loewenthal's, it is a decline. Almost a fall from grace.

Signs of a certain decline were already apparent to me in the following trivial episode:

Last night I was approached by a man who introduced himself as a Gymnasia teacher and informed me that it was "undesirable" to make friends with an Arab. Terror was rampaging in the country, and people might think me a Communist. I laughed in his face. The Arab doctor had explicitly denounced acts of violence. "And you believe him?" the Gymnasia teacher sneered. "You're naive. Lying to you doesn't bother them. With them it's something to be proud of."

In the end I was obliged to break off relations with the Arab doctor. When I told him what the pedagogue had said, he spoke in the same vein. I wonder if he would have dared to speak to me about the "Jewish character" if I, and not he, had paid for the drinks in the First Class bar.

I have not yet reached the Promised Land and already I have been forced to choose my acquaintances according to criteria which are against my principles. It will be a victory for anti-Semitism if we too classify people into Jews and non-Jews. Something which I have avoided doing all my life. I prefer to classify people according to their qualities of mind, drawing close to those who are close to me in spirit and rejecting those whose qualities are detestable to me. There will be Jews and non-Jews in both camps. As for the common Jewish destiny— I did not choose it, but neither did I attempt to run away from it. I was never false to myself. I did not convert to Christianity, as I was advised to do when it was still possible, in order to ensure myself a life free from worries. I am not prepared to live by the dictates of religion, any religion whatsoever. I am not prepared to give preference to a Jew over a person with whom I share similar tastes and sensibilities. It was pure chance that we were three Jews and one non-Jew in the Rosendorf Quartet. It was agreement on musical questions that brought us together. The idea of preferring a mediocre musician to his superior just because the first is a Jew is an abomination in my eyes. I will always prefer a discriminating Christian to a tone-deaf Jew.

(I had bitter arguments with Steiner, the cellist, and Bernfeld, the violist, about inviting the violinist von den Burger to join us, because we weren't sure that his style of playing suited us. I'm afraid that in the end he was accepted for the wrong reasons. Steiner thought, without daring to say so, that the addition of a man with a wide circle of acquaintances in society and an aristocratic title would be helpful to us. An extraneous consideration. And one for which we paid dearly. Von den Burger did us considerable harm. Whenever he had the melody he played it loudly and crudely. He played Haydn and Mozart scherzos—sprightly, lighthearted passages, full of joie de vivre—clumsily and gracelessly, because he related to them with exaggerated reverence, as if every piece of music composed by a German was family property, to be protected from strangers by barking. Although he disgraced us on more than one occasion, he insisted that he understood the German *volk* better than we did. Perhaps he was right. But why punish Haydn and Mozart? We should have found a second violin who did not see this role as damaging to his self-esteem, but it's difficult to find a good second violinist of Jewish descent. I seem to be contradicting myself . . . To get back to the point: I want to know first who you are, and only after that will I be prepared to hear what temple you pray in. And I am distressed by the thought that playing in an orchestra of refugees from racial discrimination will force me to submit to the notions of narrow-minded nationalists who see respect and affection for an Arab as a betrayal of Jewish solidarity.)

I told Loewenthal about my apprehensions. He surprised me by his prejudice. "You won't be able to be friends with the charming doctor, if only because he is rich as Croesus and you'll be eking out a living as a musician in an orchestra."

Is that really so? Some of my best friends in Germany were very wealthy people.

On second thought: they were wealthy Jews.

This morning, when I went up onto the deck, I was approached by Egon Loewenthal, who put his hand on my shoulder and guided me to the prow. The touch of his hand bore witness to some hidden excitement, for he is usually repelled, to an exaggerated degree, by physical contact, as if the touch of skin on skin arouses repressed emotions in him. And although he spoke ironically, with a deliberate twist to his words—"Here's the land they promised us"—it was obvious that the sight of the distant coast robbed him of his composure.

Yesterday I could already sense a certain agitation in him. I went to my cabin to play awhile: scales, exercises, and etudes to keep in shape. Egon came in, very polite, sat down on the edge of the lower bunk, and listened admiringly, with an approving smile, as if every technical trick was a challenge I had met with credit and he was affirming my proficiency with a smile of encouragement. Then he asked me to play something by Bach. Suddenly I saw that his eyes were full of tears. I stopped playing, and he retired in embarrassment.

I was dumbstruck. I would never have imagined that he could be so moved. Anyone who had experienced Dachau dry-eyed, I assumed, would not shed a tear over Bach. I, too, am capable of being moved by an inspiring work well played, but not under the present circumstances—in an iron cabin that muffled the sounds, and to the chugging of the engine, emitting a permanent E-flat and clashing with every D- and E-natural in the work. I permitted myself to conclude that Loewenthal's emotion stemmed from a different source.

It's one thing to keep a stiff upper lip when confronting those who wish you ill, and quite another to be forced into exile to a place that is supposed to be your chosen motherland. I can understand him. And the more I think about him, the better off I seem to be compared to him. He has nothing but that woman—what she means to him I have not succeeded in finding out—and an anonymous public which has not read his books. And according to what I hear, he will find a few hotheads waiting for him, too, who want to prevent German-speakers from speaking their mother tongue in public places.

When we next met, he apologized for his hasty departure. He felt uncomfortable about the sudden weakness which had overcome him.

"I wonder if this hypersensitivity will bring us much benefit where we're going," he said.

I was glad that he had spoken in the first person plural. It was a compliment. He did not speak of "exquisite tone" but of what I too regard as the most important things: sensitivity and subtleness.

His emotion infected me, too. The way he spoke was a declaration of friendship, and I had good reason to be pleased. Before setting foot in the country I was so apprehensive about, I already had one friend in it. A true friend. And so I felt as if the whole of Germany was accompanying me there.

Haifa port. A town scattered over a mountainside. An omnibus crawls uphill like a red beetle. The ship's ramp is lowered and a group of policemen and customs officers come aboard. The stevedores have dull faces and filthy clothes. The policemen wear short khaki trousers and long khaki socks exposing knees broiled as red as beets. The screeching of the cranes and the hooting of the ship are swallowed up in the human commotion. Scurrying to and fro like a swarm of ants. Carrying the luggage to the lower deck. Returning to the cabins to make sure nothing has been forgotten. Standing on the upper deck and shouting at the tops of their voices. Opposite us, behind a fence, people who have come to meet their relatives.

Violin in hand—at times like this my fears for it override everything else, and since I have unfortunately lost the strap I can't even sling it over my shoulder—I climb the stairs to the upper deck. What a cacophony! Can anyone understand anything in this din?

Egon is by my side. He is ostensibly indifferent, but some secret mechanism has begun to operate in his eyes. He is busy photographing everything: the mountain, the policemen, the people, the commotion. Perhaps he is trying to introduce some order into the chaos. Or to instill meaning.

We are separated from the possessors of British passports and returning residents. This kind of bureaucracy nauseates me. Egon is not as tense as I am. The policemen do not fill his heart with obscure terror. He has survived worse. They examine our papers and tell us to stand to one side. I feel that our fate is sealed. But Egon reassures me: all this fuss and bother has no other purpose than to justify the existence of the bureaucracy.

I envy his composure. Perhaps he really is capable of living in a world of happy abstractions. It is not Egon Loewenthal here, on his way from Germany to Palestine, with migraine and eczema, but a product of the West sailing to the East in order to confront "The Orient." Rather than seeing himself as a little Jew, desperately trying to make ends meet in a country which has no need of his skills, he imagines his existence in Palestine as a fascinating encounter between the declining philosophy of the West and the ancient sources of the East. He awaits the processes about to take place in him like a man who has plugged a kettle into a source of electricity. The boiling of the water is only a matter of time.

I will still have to take myself to task for the obsequious way I fawned over the policeman and for my pathetic attempts to strike up a conversation with him in broken English ("This violin play too in London . . ."). A further proof of Greta's thesis: anyone can intimidate me. Not all my papers are in order. (Even though the High Commissioner refused to recognize my Guadagnini as property entitling its owner to a certificate as a person of means, I was able to prove that I was not arriving in the country empty-handed.)

Here comes the representative of the orchestra—a firm foothold in a strange place. Where is Egon? Perhaps he can help him, too. He is a German Jew and must have heard of him. The man speaks English fluently, albeit with a heavy German accent. The immigration officer treats him with respect: the representative of a bourgeois institution. A reassuring sight. A German Jew on equal terms with authority.

Egon has disappeared. Has he, too, got someone waiting for him? The arrivals hall, a kind of huge hangar, is totally chaotic. But some people are trying nevertheless to introduce order of a sort and get the passengers to stand in line. I am filled with shame at the sight of my fellow Jews pushing and shoving for the sake of gaining a little time. Kleiner, the representative of the orchestra, a member of the Society of Friends, which he is busy setting up here in Haifa, really saves the situation. Amazing how one man, who knows who you are, can restore your self-confidence. A moment ago I was a helpless nonentity in an unruly crowd, and now I am myself again—Kurt Rosendorf, a man worthy of being treated with respect. (The first disappointment: Kleiner has never heard of the Rosendorf Quartet. But this does not diminish me in his eyes. I am a person of worth because I have been invited to play in Huberman's orchestra. I cannot restrain myself from telling him that I was exempted from the audition in Basel, so solid is my reputation as a violinist of the first rank. But he knew nothing about the selection procedures, and I felt that I had made a fool of myself.)

The formalities are over, and we emerge into a street flooded with sunshine. In Germany it is autumn now but here the summer is in full sway. How strange it is to suddenly find yourself in a place where all kinds of languages are spoken, not one of which you understand. Kleiner surprises me again. He speaks Arabic too (he immigrated to Palestine in 'thirty-one and has already learned two and a half languages. He began studying Hebrew in Germany, even though he was not sure that he would need it one day). I am surprised when he haggles with the porter over a few pennies. But he explains to me that bargaining is a way of life here.

The bus stop is not far and we walk behind the porter, who has loaded my luggage onto his donkey. How strange it is to be here in this mixed, Mediterranean town. For some reason it seems that all the people talking to each other are shouting at each other. Perhaps it is the guttural sounds which give me the impression of outbursts of rage. Kleiner apparently guesses my thoughts. I am not the first person he has met at the port and shepherded to the bus stop. He smiles to himself at the sight of my astonished stares. He tells me about himself. Not because it is important to him for me to know who he is, but in an attempt at reassurance: You see—it's quite possible for a German Jew to live here, in this frightening place. He has a house on the Carmel and is content with his lot. Almost all his friends are well-off Jews from Germany. They meet and listen to music on records. They are waiting impatiently for the orchestra to give a concert in Haifa. There is a movie theater with a large stage here, big enough to accommodate an entire orchestra. He is a Zionist and came to the country when Hitler was no more than the leader of a gang of hoodlums. He seems to think that he will be able to convert me to Zionism in the time it takes to walk from the harbor gates to the bus station. At least his missionary zeal does not take the form of shallow clichés, like the ones I heard from a number of the old-timers on board ship with me.

I tell him that Egon Loewenthal arrived with me, an asset to the German colony—but he has never heard of Egon Loewenthal. He excuses his ignorance on the grounds that he is a man of music, not literature. As far as literature is concerned he is stuck with Thomas Mann and Stefan Zweig. I wonder if he has any idea of what went on among artists after Hitler came to power—the frantic attempts to become as famous as possible as quickly as possible. (As a prescient poet at the beginning of his career once said to me: "One can't afford to be unknown at a time like this. It's too dangerous.")

The bus windows are covered with wire net against stones thrown by ruffians. I joke: "I ran away from a jail in order to sit in a cage." Humor is not Kleiner's strong point. He delivers a long lecture about the riots which raged here for several months. They were aimed at putting pressure on the British not to keep their promises to the Jews. Now they have subsided—because of the citrus season. But just to be on the safe side, the British are still patrolling the roads. An armed British policeman gets into the bus and sits in the front seat. I have to admit that his presence is a great relief to me. I cannot completely overcome my fear, but I say to myself that if so many men and women are prepared to take their lives into their hands by traveling in the bus, the danger cannot be so terrible.

Kleiner gives me a sum of money and an address in Tel Aviv, and parts from me with the promise that I shall be his guest when the orchestra plays in Haifa. He wants to introduce me to some of his music-loving friends.

We had spent only one hour together, but already I felt a great need for his presence. When he left, I felt abandoned. Perhaps I too was afraid of being anonymous. I needed to be known to someone, as if such an acquaintance would have the power to protect me from strangers.

From the outset of the bus ride, I can't find a common

language with the woman sitting next to me. She speaks Yiddish and my German annoys her. In her opinion every Jew knows Yiddish and if he insists on speaking German it is out of pride and arrogance. She wants me to put the violin in the baggage compartment. By holding it between my knees, to protect it from being jolted, I am trespassing on her space, which in any case takes up two thirds of the seat since I am thin and she is fat. Perhaps she imagines that I am spreading my knees on purpose to press against her hefty thigh. Egon was right: we are democrats who love the people from a distance.

The mountain accompanied us for a part of the way. Then a perspective of low hills opened up, with a view of Arab settlements in the distance. It is easy to distinguish between an Arab and a Jewish settlement. The Arab villages look as if they have been there from ancient times, planted in the earth.

The journey was uneventful. In one of the Arab villages a young boy hit the wire mesh with a broken plank, but nobody seemed unduly disturbed by this hostile act. The only intrusion on my peace of mind was the doughy thigh of my neighbor fighting for her rights. Nevertheless, I was relieved when we came out onto the coastal plain and began driving through an area of continuous Jewish settlement. I have never seen so many oranges in my life.

Late in the afternoon the sky darkened, and under this gloomy sky I felt at home. I missed the entry into Tel Aviv, since it does not look like a city at all: a flat town, with no industrial districts, no commercial center, no downtown. A few new buildings in the Bauhaus style came as a certain surprise. Under a gray sky you can imagine for a moment that you are in a workers' quarter in the suburbs of a German city. But most of the buildings are one or two stories high, in a rustic style, with red tiled roofs.

During one's first hours in a new place every detail is etched in the memory with the utmost sharpness. The smallest and most trivial facts take on significance. The chance behavior of individuals seems to illustrate the nature of the place: the cab driver who cheated me and demanded payment for two other passengers who had volunteered to assist me and rode part of the way with us; the bellboy of the pension who dawdled and let me struggle with my luggage by myself; a passerby who bumped into me and almost made me drop my violin and still had the nerve to blame me for blocking the pavement. Like ill omens at the outset of a journey. In times of stress, every mishap is a portent of the future.

I've started on the wrong foot, I said to myself. Then I smiled ironically: you jump into a stormy sea and complain because the water's cold?

Entering the Hella Becker Pension was like soaking in a warm bath. The lobby, where a few modest lamps were already lit, was astonishingly like one of those middle-class pensions on the banks of the Rhine: spotless tablecloths with embroidered hems; antique candlesticks next to a delicate vase holding a single flower; a napkin rolled up in a silver ring; padded cozies keeping teapots warm; pictures on the walls of meadows, clear lakes, and snowy mountain peaks; carved sideboards with doors which were partly wood, to hide what was nothing to boast of, and partly glass, to show off the gleaming crystal goblets; and the warm, tremulous voice of the plump little woman whose face was comelier than her body and who stood up the moment she saw me and came forward to greet me with tiny, Chinese steps.

"Herr Rosendorf."

A question and an answer at once.

The proprietress herself. A voice that rang in my ears like a forgotten melody, surfacing at precisely the moment you wanted to remember it. A typical Berlin accent that brought a lump to my throat: "I heard you in Berlin in 'twenty-nine and the Schubert was wonderful. (Von den Burger played one false note after the other, but never mind . . .) This way please."

Like firm ground underfoot. A bit of home in a foreign country.

The fact that I had forgotten my clothes brush on the ship ceased to bother me. Even the din penetrating the open window and preventing me from taking a nap before dinner (tonight I am the guest of honor) seemed amenable to a reassuring interpretation.

This din was the sound of the sea breakers, interrupted by the dance music from the terrace of a café on the beach. A screeching saxophone and an out-of-tune piano. A few middle-aged couples were revolving clumsily around the dance floor. The disturbance had a pleasing effect, too. It was nice to know that there was a petit bourgeois life going on here—with all its comforting dullness—and the shallow, popular music characteristic of it soothed me. ("Bad musicians are the most authentic representatives of the people," said Proust.)

The words of my brother (an orthodox Marxist, living in exile in Holland) came to my mind: "Wherever middle-class pleasures, which the proletariat wishes to enjoy, exist, there is a chance of a 'higher' music too. The new bourgeoisie, which has recently succeeded in liberating itself from the world of petit bourgeois ideas, adopts the idle pleasures of the aristocracy and sanctifies them."

(Walter made this pronouncement when it became clear that I was going to be a "lackey of the ruling classes." Both of us came from the same roots: bourgeoisie of the Mosaic persuasion who covered up their Polish origins. I became a musician, while Walter became a revolutionary. The expression "lackey of the ruling classes" hurt me very much, for I knew I served the most exalted values of Western culture. My brother smiled: "It's never too late to learn." And whenever we—the members of the Rosendorf Quartet—were obliged to fawn on patrons of the arts in order to get a slice of the cake, I recalled his words. Now for the first time ever, I found some consolation in them. I could say to myself: so I'm not the only grasshopper in a country of industrious ants. There are other idlers

here besides me. And there is also music for the proletariat. In
other words, I am needed here to elevate the cultural life of the
country . . .)

In my talk with Huberman the following things were also
said: wherever there is a monied public (which collects concert
programs, musical scores, and sometimes even old subscription tickets as if they were decorations and marks of distinction) you will also find the educated worker who is prepared
to forgo his regular diet of popular entertainment for the sake
of buying a ticket to a concert. With his tired back he supports
the distant walls of the concert hall and nods off reverentially
in the direction of a culture he cannot afford to acquire, to the
sublime notes of a music born out of a different pain (Huberman promised to hold special concerts for workers at reduced
prices. "They deserve the best," he said, "because they are
building the motherland").

The first supper in the new motherland was like the last supper
in the old one. Frau Becker in a black evening gown, a string of
pearls on a respectable bourgeois décolleté, and a benevolent,
hospitable smile on her face. (Kleiner said: "For the first four
days you'll be her guest. Don't offer her money and don't ask
any questions. Everything will be taken care of later.") On the
table china plates with a floral pattern in four colors, a bottle
of red wine reflecting the flame of the candle in the silver
candlestick, a single rose resting on an asparagus fern, crystal
goblets and glasses, silver cutlery, a matching salt and pepper
set, like a pair of playful, charming Baroque statuettes. How
vividly I remember the kind of details I usually ignore. Perhaps
this was so because here each object was a symbol, part of a
series of artifacts, intended to signal the presence of culture, of
the kind of people who would rise from this elegant table and
call for their carriages to take them to the concert hall. The
"family" menu too, as Frau Becker referred to it, enveloping
me in a sympathy which was, perhaps, a little too "familiar"

for my taste, was saturated with memories of Germany, not only because of the Rhine wines and the classic examples of German cuisine (the sauerkraut was a little too obvious, I thought) but because of the way in which the dishes had been prepared: the cloves in the roast and the apple tart served with filtered coffee before the brandy.

(I ask myself if I would be able to afford a meal like this on my salary, but on Kleiner's advice I thrust aside reflections liable to cast a pall on the pleasure of meeting a cultured, polite, and discriminating woman. Greta would have been proud of me: I am amazingly calm and relaxed. Not for a moment do I need to tune my strings to Frau Becker's tuning fork. She is like one of those Japanese hostesses who make it their business to guess your every wish. Her guest is her master. All you have to do is sit back and relax and allow her to perform her role.)

But the wine went to my head, while the cognac twinkled in the intelligent eyes of Frau Becker. How well she knew the weaknesses of an immigrant in a strange country! She offered her attention like a refreshing draught to a guest, who desired nothing more than to unburden his soul. Which is precisely what I proceeded to do without putting a curb on my tongue. How delightful it is to offer illuminating insights into your own personality to someone so eager to know you. (Especially after she has told you how Tel Aviv has gained in stature by your graciously consenting to join its orchestra.) Her voice was measured, melodious, and soothing, and I, complacent and intoxicated, ignored the dangers of empty boasting and fatuously mentioned compliments paid me in other places, in the palmy days of Strasbourg and Stuttgart. And she, perhaps slyly, perhaps absentmindedly, and perhaps because the sentence had been on the tip of her tongue all the time and she was unwilling to relinquish it now, even if it might sound out of place, remarked that the greatest artists are also the most modest.

How easily we oscillate between happiness and despondency! Performing artists are as eager for a kind word as a spaniel is to be stroked. How we love to hear our praises sung, even when we do not deserve them.

Frau Becker told me how moved she had been by one of our concerts. She made an effort to remember and succeeded: we played the Mozart B-flat Major, K. 458, Beethoven's Opus 18, no. 1, and Brahms's Third with the beautiful viola solo. (I made an effort to remember and failed: we had never played the program she mentioned. I would never play the B-flat Major and the Opus 18, no. 1, one after the other. Both have very strong, somber slow movements which are enormously demanding. Then I remembered who had played that program in Berlin in 'twenty-nine. I had undeservedly received praise due to others. But I was not sober enough to demand that truth be given its due.)

And afterward, thrilled by the opportunity of enjoying an intimate exchange, untainted by any suspicion of vulgar, silly flirtation with a kindred soul in a remote, foreign land—I told her about my family, and my "arrangement" with Greta. Indiscreet as some aging bachelor in a summer resort.

There is something rather agreeable in forgiving yourself after having made a fool of yourself the night before, due to a slight overindulgence in wine.

A cloudy morning with a purple-gray sea. I shall welcome the rain. There is nowhere that I have to go. I shall be able to shut myself in my room and devote myself to my violin. The long journey has probably been bad for my fingers.

I reconstruct last night's foolishness in my head. Was she smiling slyly at having caught me out, or was she perhaps an amateur collector of human foibles, enjoying the way she was manipulating me? Without her having to say a single word about herself, I had exposed all my treasures to her eyes. The family arrangement, my ambitions, and even my most secret plans. I can only hope that she is discreet. Huberman is a frequent guest in her home. If she tells him what I told her, he will think that I have come here for a short transition period, and have no serious intentions with regard to the orchestra. But what right has he got to demand that I bury myself in this godforsaken place? In one fortnight he himself is in Trieste, Milan, Paris, London, Berne, Marseilles, Corfu, Tripoli, and Tel Aviv. And whenever he has a moment to spare he spends it hovering above Europe and spinning his web over it in his dreams.

I am not comparing myself to Huberman. But there is no reason why I should see myself, at the age of thirty-eight, as a bird whose wings have already been clipped. At the bottom of my heart I am profoundly convinced: I am the victim of political circumstances. If Hitler had taken power a few years later I would today have been a well-known violinist, invited on concert tours to London, Paris, Boston, and New York. And Rosendorf Quartet recordings would be on sale all over the world.

(I wonder if peace would have returned to the family circle, too. Were recent events really exclusively to blame for separating us? There were other discords, too. Artistic jealousy, and temperamental differences. But I prefer not to think about them. I am afraid that last night I touched on these things, too, with rather broad hints. In a new place one should beware of generosity too, lest one topple barriers one would have preferred to leave erect.)

After sitting down at the little table to write my first letter home, I change my mind. In order to write letters I need absolute peace of mind. Under the influence of so drastic a change in my life I lack the clarity of thought and concentration necessary to express my emotions in writing. Especially when every word is going to be examined under a magnifying glass.

There is nothing like practicing for emotional confusion. Even scales. They're like the morning run you take to get your circulation going and wake yourself up to confront a new day. A regular daily schedule is a guarantee of mental health.

New impressions will only weary my spirit.

One last peep through the window: construction workers rolling wheelbarrows up the scaffolding of an unfinished building, a young woman pushing a baby carriage, a mule-drawn kerosene cart, whose driver is waving a bell with a sound I cannot hear—and already the violin is in my hands, my back to the sights arousing my curiosity.

The Guadagnini sounds strange, in spite of all the precautions I took during the voyage. Although the climate is humid, I can sense a dryness in the low notes. But the instrument soon finds its true voice again. Warm and sweet. And even the glissandi do not sound too sentimental, but all eloquence.

A tasty and nourishing breakfast in the company of Hella Becker. Fragrant coffee, fresh rolls, an asparagus omelet, fresh butter, and homemade marmalade. Hardly a word is spoken. Like a tranquil family waking to a new day and its duties. With what delicate tact she mentions that I started playing too early in the morning: "The guests must have enjoyed listening to you play, although some of them were perhaps not fully awake yet . . ." Not one word about how I feel in her pension. If she had asked, I should have had nothing but praise. And it wouldn't have been lip service either. I feel completely at home here. Embarrassingly at home. As if there is something slighting toward my landlady in the way I feel. I know myself—if there had been a hint of anything erotic in the ambiance of family intimacy enveloping myself and Frau Becker, I would have felt a certain shrinking. And guilt would have put in its appearance too. But since I do not feel in the least physically attracted to her—not even casually or momentarily—I feel very comfortable in her presence.

I am afraid this is not mutual.

The irony of fate: women I do not desire are attracted to me. And now I shall have to surround myself with a wall of politeness in order not to hurt her. But this will not involve any great effort. I won't be here for more than four days.

A surprising and encouraging beginning: the city quiet and

industrious, with no evident signs of tension due to the disturbances; the first day in Hella Becker's pension, on typically
German territory, calling to mind the happy, hopeful days of
the Weimar Republic; the cordial, enthusiastic welcome, the
abundance of food and the mildness of the climate; the astonishing number of music lovers waiting impatiently for the first
concert under Toscanini's baton—all these things blurred the
feeling of foreignness. And at first I was sure that I would
surmount the difficulties of the adjustment period without
being plunged from hope to despair at every deviation from
the proper order. But disappointment soon followed. I was
informed that I would not be the first violinist in the first
concert, in spite of a definite promise from Huberman. I had
come too late and Toscanini had already chosen his concertmaster. Although I resolved to take it like a man, my
dejection showed in my playing. Toscanini shot me an angry
look. I started playing properly again, with total concentration and complete compliance with his demands.

To my annoyance, I shall have to stay on for a while in the
pension, owing to the fact that I failed to state if I wanted a
room or a flat (the difference is significant). Now I will have to
wait until they find me a room, as I requested, where I can play
during the day and also give lessons. Although Hella Becker
said: "Please don't worry about payment. Leave that to me
and the orchestra management," I am determined to pay her
in full, down to the last penny. I am sorry to be so preoccupied
by financial matters, but it transpires that a musician's salary,
even a top musician, although not low, will not suffice for me
to save the fare to America if the opportunity arises.

The concert hall where we play is very bad. Construction is
still going on during the rehearsals. There is no lobby worthy
of the name. The entrance into the hall is straight from the
street. They are building some sort of partition, from wood,
but it will not be enough to block the noises from the street. I
am surprised at Toscanini for being prepared to conduct an
orchestra under such conditions.

The one bright spot is the attitude of the building workers. They agreed to work at night in order to vacate the hall for rehearsals during the day without demanding extra pay for overtime or night work. All they asked for were tickets for the concert. (Last night I got into conversation with one of the workers. He was a law student in Munich and came here before completing his studies. He is a great admirer of Mahler and Kurt Tucholsky. A strange combination, in my opinion, but understandable in view of the fact that his only education consists of interrupted legal studies. In any case, after my conversation with him I began to understand Huberman's demand for special concerts for workers.)

Hard to say anything definite about the orchestra yet. From the warming during the breaks—which can tell you something about the character of the musicians, or at any rate about their need to impress their colleagues—it seems to me that the technical standard is very high. Which is not to be wondered at when seventy-two were chosen out of five hundred (in Frankfurt an oboe player who was turned down said something shocking to me: "I'm going to die because I'm a mediocre oboe player"). But as an orchestra this is a motley collection which will require a long period of consolidation before becoming an orchestra worthy of the name. Side by side, before one music stand, sit people who have no common language even for the purposes of speech. They play the same notes, but not the same music. There is a great difference in outlook between those who received their musical education in Germany and those from other countries. Their behavior during rehearsals stands in need of considerable improvement, too. Some of them talk to each other in every pause, and in spite of the autocracy of the old maestro, the rehearsal sometimes resembles nothing so much as a dialogue of the deaf. When the maestro lost his temper and shouted the "Porca miseria!" of which he is so fond, some of the members of the orchestra thought that he wanted forte and fell furiously upon the quiet, gentle mezzo-piano in the second part of Brahms's Second.

Even the program of the first concert is not to my taste. A little long and monotonous and full of irrelevant gestures. Rossini's *La Scala di Seta*, a bow to Italy; Brahms's Second, Schubert's *Unfinished*, Weber's *Oberon* Overture; and the Nocturne and Scherzo from Mendelssohn's *Midsummer Night's Dream* in order not to deprive the Jews. A concert more suitable for an outdoor summer concert than a festive musical event with "historic significance," as they say here, with the natural inclination to inflate every "first" in an immigrant country designed by ideologues. It requires special courage to say that Toscanini's tempi, too, are not to my liking. Too fast and brisk even in places where it would be better "to let the liquor roll around the tongue," as my teacher, Karl Meyer, used to say. Over here the great maestro enjoys an understandable hero worship. He turned down an invitation to participate in the Bayreuth Festival in order to come here and conduct an orchestra of refugees "for the sake of humanity."

TEL AVIV, DECEMBER 31, 1936

My dear Greta,

This is my second letter. I still haven't received a reply to the first. I trust that it is only because of the postal arrangements that your letter has not yet arrived. People tell me that the mail to Europe leaves and arrives at set times. I will be sorry if my first letter has gone astray. I won't be able to repeat what I wrote there. The impressions are no longer as vivid as they were in those first days, and one gets used to change quickly. I wrote to you at length about the voyage and the people and the first impression of Tel Aviv, together with an initial assessment of the chances for establishing a reasonable musical life here.

One hardly feels any excitement here at the approach of

the new year, but as far as I am concerned I feel more homesick than ever. Perhaps because I remember how we celebrated last year and got drunk in a determined attempt to forget our troubles, and how afterward we behaved like a pair of newlyweds on their honeymoon . . .

In the meantime the first concert has taken place. It was written about all over the world as if it was an important event. Perhaps because a meeting between Huberman and Toscanini is regarded as political news. Both of them have extended their influence here beyond music to life itself. In my opinion it was an ordinary concert by European standards, although the playing was enthusiastic. A performance that would be regarded as mediocre in a European city, and here they hear the voice of history in it. I don't want to sound cynical, but something inside me protests when people try to use music as a means for the propagation of nonmusical ideas. But it may be that in our times everything, in some strange way, becomes political. Musicians who are regarded as possessing moral authority try to use their influence to change the world. Perhaps only people like me, who have no power, can devote themselves to music today. I am not criticizing Huberman or Toscanini, even though they preach ideas that have no chance of succeeding. The unification of Europe today, when everything is falling to pieces before our eyes! (A malicious remark I heard in this context: Huberman is devoting himself to uplifting humanity because his playing has deteriorated. In the field of public relations he has no competitors among the young violinists. . . . There are small-minded people everywhere.)

An English-language newspaper that comes out in Jerusalem wrote about our concert in provincial superlatives: "A festive and memorable occasion. The players seemed inspired and the Maestro's baton was like a magic wand calling forth tones of joyous beauty. . . ." Never mind. The more good music they hear here the more the critical sense will develop. To say that the orchestra will have to work hard before becoming a cohesive musical ensemble takes a lot of courage. It could hardly be said that I have a lot of it. I have dared to express my opinion to two or three people and that's all. It's hard to overcome the enthusiasm of fifteen thousand listeners—three thousand in the Exhibition Hall and another twelve thousand over the radio—who were all beside themselves with excitement. What can you expect of them? They've never heard a real orchestra, like the one in Berlin before they expelled the Jews from it. True, a little of the excitement infected me too—after all is said and done, a country where a Jew can feel free. . . . But I have to say I was more excited when I met Loewenthal after the concert (I am assuming that my first letter reached you, but if it didn't—I am speaking of the famous writer. Yes, he too is here, and we became good friends on the voyage) and he told me that he had decided to stay. The fact that a man like Loewenthal feels able to live here is a great relief to me. It's good to know that there are people in the vicinity with whom one can talk about other things besides music. I also met his woman friend, Hilda Moses, who said that she had met you in Berlin, about ten years ago, at the Lichtenfelds'. She said that you would probably not remember since she had not been particularly conspicuous, and you were the star of the evening. She is a little younger than us, tall, with an athletic build, a strong, honest, intelligent face, and the jaw of a boxer. Loewenthal likes strong, unsophisticated women. He's got enough brains for two.

The salary, as I wrote before, is nothing special, but not too low either. After all the doubts about the post of concertmaster were dispelled, I have enough to live on modestly, without giving up anything essential, and I am also able to save a little. In another two or three months I will be able to send tickets for you and Anna (return tickets, don't worry) so that you will have a chance to see for yourself what conditions here are like. It won't do any harm to think about it again. There are at least three good piano teachers here (two from Germany and one from Czechoslovakia) and even the head of the Kultur Bund has arrived in the country. People say, although I have not yet seen for myself, that there is also a circle of young music lovers here of a decidedly satisfactory standard. Soon I shall begin giving lessons to outstanding pupils, partly in order to supplement my income, but mainly in order to contribute toward the education of a generation of musicians who might join the orchestra in the future. (Even if they do not eventually play, they will constitute the audience after the flight from Germany is over.) In the meantime, I am still living in the pension I told you about in my first letter—owned by Frau Hella Becker, a woman who does a lot for the orchestra, and this too is a considerable saving. (Every morning we quarrel, good-humoredly, because I want to pay her and she refuses to accept the money. She should pay *me*, she says, she enjoys my playing so much . . .) But I am determined to find myself a room soon, since it makes me uncomfortable to live at her expense. Who knows how I will have to repay her when the time comes? . . .

Write to me, my dearest, and tell me everything that is happening there. Even the smallest things. Especially them. The big things reach our ears in a thousand ways. Things that aren't published in the newspapers, too. A senior official in the High Commissioner's office, who has friends in the German Foreign Office, told someone that they are very upset by Germany's unpopularity in world public opinion. Perhaps this is a sign that they are coming back to their senses.

Yours with sincere sentiments of love,

Kurt

My dear Anna,

Mother will probably tell you what I have written to her, and there is no point in repeating the same things twice. I shall only add this: in these difficult times there is only one thing that we little people can do—devote ourselves to our work and try to do it as well as we can. And the best thing that you can do now is to apply yourself to your studies. But especially not to be lazy and to practice several hours a day. The talent we are born with is only a small part of our capabilities. The ability to work hard, the patience to apply oneself to small details and not to tire of endless exercise— all these are no less important than a musical sense and a good pitch. I hope that Mother is being firm with you in this respect.

I am living in a pension next to the sea in a nice little town where all the houses are white and new and I hardly lack for anything—except for my beloved family. But I hope that in the end we shall all meet again and resume the good life we had before the barbarians gained the upper hand and bad people took power. I have not yet seen the desert, and camels only once, outside my window. They passed in a caravan carrying crates full of sand and tiny stones called "zifzif," which are used for mixing cement for building, on their humps. Here people are building while somewhere else all they can do is destroy. But we must be optimistic. Governments come and go while music endures forever. And it will accompany us wherever we go.

I am saving a little money so that we can meet soon. I have a friend here, an excellent pianist and first-rate teacher, who will be happy to teach you when you and your mother come here. Who knows, maybe one day you'll play with our orchestra and I shall be very proud of you.

Your father who misses you day and night.

* * *

A temptation I cannot resist:

In exchange for giving lessons to a girl of about fourteen I shall get a room for nothing in an apartment inhabited by three people, near the sea. The locality: a workers' neighborhood in the north of the town. A two-story building with only four families living in it. A bus station on the corner of the street. A few minutes' ride from the Exhibition Hall.

A considerable saving since the rents here are higher than a teacher's fees.

I spend a lot of time thinking about money. At least it's in a noble cause. I believe that if I can only persuade Greta to visit the country, she will agree to stay.

It's going to be a problem with the little girl. I don't have the patience to teach beginners. They told me she studied for three years with the music teacher at the school for workers' children. I inquired about him. Everyone I asked smiled scornfully, arousing the suspicion that the foundations are rotten and I shall have to begin all over again. Afterward I learned that the man in question is a brilliant fellow but incapable of making up his mind as to what he really wants to do. I wanted to ask him about the girl, but he had left the country—volunteered for the International Brigade in Spain. I was sorry that we had not met. He reminds me of my brother, more talented than me in every way, who insists on being a professional revolutionary.

I informed the family that I would give them my reply after examining the girl. I am not about to waste my time on a child with no talent at all simply to save a few pounds.

Yesterday I went over there. The place charmed me from the moment I entered the street. Little houses, secluded behind front gardens. The gardens are surrounded by wire fences or stone walls, covered with creepers. Within the walls are fruit trees—citrus, guavas, and grapevines. The entire street looks like a corridor leading to the sea. Only the sidewalks are paved. Between them is a dirt road, a playground for children.

A pair of mules drawing a cart ambled down the street. I felt as if I were in the countryside.

The house is somewhat isolated, beyond an empty field, at the end of the street. The front yard is large, and you have to descend steps to reach it. Paved paths lead to the entrance and to garbage bins in little houses with iron lids. Fresh grass peeps out between the cracks in the paving stones (reminding me of a country garden in the vicinity of Mannheim, where a relative of ours lives) and covers most of the yard, except for the basins of loose soil at the feet of the fruit trees, whose tops reach the second-story windows without hiding the view.

The room is spacious, with two windows—one overlooking the sea and the other the garden. The furniture—a bed, a table, two chairs, and a wicker armchair—is modest but well made (by the landlord himself, who is a carpenter and foreman in a contracting company owned by the local Labor Federation). There is only one obvious disadvantage: there is no separate entrance. In order to reach my room I have to pass through a hall which leads to the kitchen, the bathroom, and the two rooms occupied by the family, who apparently never shut their doors. On second thought, however, this might be for the best. If I mean to devote myself to my music it's a good thing that bringing women here would be awkward. Also, the place possesses one truly outstanding advantage: during most of the hours of the day the flat is empty. The father is out of town, the child is at school, and the mother works and only comes home in the evening. ("You can play to your heart's content, bring your pupils here, and even play chamber music," the woman said to me. "The neighbors won't object. There isn't a living soul here throughout the morning. We're all working people," she said with a pride that reminded me of my brother on the day he went to work in a factory and boasted of the hardness of his hands.)

I examined the child—an examination that filled her parents with apprehension although it was completely perfunctory. For a room like that, on the terms offered me, I would have been prepared to compromise with my conscience and teach a girl less talented than the one who held a wretched violin in strong hands and produced miserable sounds from it with a stroke of the bow that said more about her teacher than it did about her. The girl was not eager to succeed, like her parents. The whole business was not to her liking from the outset. After I came in, though, she found me less frightening than the person she had imagined. She was prepared to devote a little more than the bare minimum to her playing, and she even made touching efforts to oscillate her left hand and produce the semblance of a vibrato. Her ear is good. She corrects the mistakes made by the fingers of her left hand with a strange gleam in her eye—bright and sharp and full of a challenging curiosity—which leads me to assume that it was not only for the sake of her musical education that her parents made me so generous an offer, but for fear of what so lively a girl (she is physically well developed, sturdy, and well built, and looks eighteen although she is only fifteen and a half), who spends three out of seven evenings a week at the Youth Movement, might get into in her spare time. It was this restless look of hers, too, that made me think that she possesses latent artistic inclinations which could develop if she had the right teachers.

I put on an expression of indifferent consent for my own benefit more than for her parents—the fault of my father's education: if you've made a good bargain don't show that you're pleased—and said, "We'll have to change everything from the foundations—the way she holds the violin, the bow, the way she stands, everything . . ." They were so overjoyed that I had agreed to give their daughter lessons—as if it were evidence that she possessed some exceptional gift—that the mother offered on the spot to do my laundry too, an offer which instantly solved one of the most critical problems I remembered from my bachelor days. This delighted me to such an extent that I immediately offered to give the family the free tickets I was entitled to as a senior member of the orchestra.

I still have to bring Hella Becker to the new room, to obtain her approval (she treats me like an absentminded artist, incapable of making intelligent decisions about practical affairs), as if there might be some mysterious, hidden drawback to such a simple transaction. And right after that I shall settle down in a corner of my own for at least as long as my contract with the Palestine Symphony Orchestra Trust lasts.

A place of my own, a regular schedule, disciplined, uninterrupted playing, proper meals, the right amount of sleep, organized study of the Hebrew language (the generous landlady has volunteered to help)—all these things will put my life on a steady course, without which I should be lost.

After all this there will be only one thing missing: chamber music.

The more I play with the orchestra, the more I feel the need for chamber music. Playing in an orchestra gives you dangerous habits. In an orchestra you don't have to worry about the nuances of expression without which your playing is nothing but the correct reproduction of a series of notes and their dynamic signs.

Putting together a chamber ensemble is not a simple matter. I have already played in a number of groups and I have already had a quartet of my own and I know how difficult it is to find a group of people, even a small one—three or four—capable of that intimate understanding which turns playing together into a revelatory experience instead of an endless battle over interpretation. I am not afraid of this battle. Sometimes differences of opinion between people who have something to say only sharpen our senses. And sometimes it is pleasant to yield to a person with definite musical principles, someone who is unwilling to concede to technical limitations or the dictates of an admired teacher.

Working habits are important, too. Some people like playing entire movements from beginning to end without working on details, until the music "gets into their fingers." They see a movement in a quartet, which lasts a few minutes, as an integral unit, and the attempt to build it up from units of two or three bars seems to them a pointless fracturing. To these musicians everything depends on inspiration and fluctuations in mood, the weather, the conditions of the hall, the audience, and the atmosphere in general. These are the happy amateurs. They never get rid of their amateurism even after making music their profession. There is a charm to such music, which puts its trust in the probability that the presence of the audience will awaken some inner enthusiasm and inspire them to produce more from their instruments and themselves than what can be extracted by stubborn practicing. But there is always the danger that in certain circumstances—the accumulation of inauspicious conditions and difficulties stemming from some unknown source—the performance will be terrible, below any acceptable standard and lacking in a sense of responsibility toward those who rightly see a concert ticket as a unique and unbreakable contract. By the way, musical amateurs also tend to be carried away by their feelings—they speed up exciting passages until essential details are blurred, and linger over sweet, tender melodies, drawing them out to the point of boredom. Among such people I have to behave like some kind of traffic policeman, slowing down those who are speeding and hurrying up those who are stuck at the intersection.

And then there are the perfectionists. They dwell on the minutest details and assume that the full expression of the composer's intentions will result from the correct sequencing of well-polished details and meticulous attention to the development of the whole through the structure of the parts. They can't let a single mezzo-piano go without questioning its precise degree—is it meant to express a certain weakening of volume, or only to hint that the request for softness need not be taken too seriously? ("There's no need to take off your hat and bow in reverence to this mezzo-piano," my teacher Karl

Meyer used to say. "You're not in church. You're speaking quietly because there's no reason to whisper and no need to shout.") A rehearsal with people of this ilk can wear you out. You play half a line and become involved in a lengthy argument over every note. Over the nature of every sforzando. A gypsy tossing his head? A groan of rage? A sigh of pain? ("If only it were possible to translate the dynamic signs into exact numerical values, anyone could play Mozart," I once said to a conductor who asked me to play louder. "I'm not playing too softly. The orchestra is playing too loudly." He expressed his disapproval in a dismissive shrug. "In order to hear you the audience will have to hold their breath," he said. "That's what they come to concerts for," I replied. One of those pointless arguments invariably won by the person in power.) These people read the score as if it were written in code, full of hidden clues which need to be deciphered.

I am one of them. I don't believe in brilliant improvisations. I am willing to be swept away, but only along a clearly demarcated course. I would never let myself go except within a rational framework. I will not exceed the degree of license allowed by a deaf musician of genius in the first quarter of the nineteenth century. In his music I hear the passionate protest of a man whose deafness only sharpened the clarity of his vision with regard to the limitations on his freedom. What I know today about the absurdity of that Promethean stance vis-à-vis insignificant princelings, the idle and pampered sons of the Viennese aristocracy, does not permit me to play that pathetic rage ironically. I pay the closest attention to the slightest changes in the development of the theme and ask myself why he chose to do this and not that. I try to understand things which elude definition as well. Only afterward do I allow myself to play the entire passage straight through from beginning to end.

Working with me is not easy. At first I seem an easygoing, affable man who does not insist on his own opinions or need to be the center of attention, but the impression is misleading.

When they begin to play I show my claws. And they think that I've been misleading them deliberately. But this is not the case. I have very clear musical principles, but they can't always be defined in words. Demonstrations along the line of "I hear it like this" are not to the liking of certain musicians. Some see this style as insulting, as if they were pupils being told to imitate their teacher—a method of instruction which nobody would uphold.

The key man, in my opinion, is the second violinist.

It's hard to find someone whose playing will be a kind of reflection of yours. In other words, someone whose playing will resemble yours even in little details, but who will at the same time be prepared to play second fiddle to you on a permanent basis.

A famous quartet won't have any difficulties in finding a violinist disappointed in himself, even of quite a high standard, who will agree to improve his status by joining a well-known group. But there's not much chance of him staying on. He'll grit his teeth and play second violin until a more attractive prospect opens up. In most cases he'll play with the group for two or three years and then try to set up a group of his own. If he stays on because he failed in the attempt, he will be a bad second violinist: a man who has given up hope of improving his playing. With feelings like this he won't contribute much to the group. He may even have a negative influence. He'll be a second violinist who plays as if the part that he's playing is of no importance. There is no greater mistake.

For the sake of emphasis, you might even say that a good second violinist is one who sees his role as a vocation. He plays his part, which is sometimes boring, as if the whole composition depends on it. He plays with the modesty of a philosopher, who knows that if house painters hadn't improved brushes and paints, painters wouldn't be able to create their masterpieces. If the accompaniment were only beating time and providing harmonic fillers, it could have been dispensed with entirely. Another important virtue for a second violinist, which gives his modesty a charm often lacking in the virtuous: a sense of humor.

It will be said that these demands are excessive. But a number of the best quartets of our day possess permanent second violinists who dedicate themselves to their role with pride in their modesty. Gone are the days when Joachim would travel from place to place by himself, co-opt three local musicians, and appear with them after two or three rehearsals in a quartet which he ruled with an iron hand, with all the authority of a great violinist demanding absolute obedience in everything from his players. A method which might perhaps suffice for a few Haydn quartets and a few of the youthful quartets of Mozart. But no more than that.

Whether my demands are excessive or not, it seems to me that I have found the man I am looking for. Not before silently rejecting a number from both the second and the first violins in the orchestra: one, a very polished and even brilliant player, after I heard him backstage playing a Bach partita (it was all external, all varnish and no soul); a second and a third because of character failings; a fourth because he speaks only Hungarian; and a fifth because he has two small children and a sickly wife and is so depressed by the sudden change in his life that I am afraid he will commit suicide (I asked him what he thought of a quartet, and he looked at me as if I had fallen from the moon, or was asking him to do hard labor without pay). And then I started talking to my man and feeling him out.

His name is Konrad Friedman. He was born in a little village in Saxony. His father is a businessman, an observant Jew who sent his children to a Christian school to obtain a general education. Up to the age of twelve he was a devout Christian, to the distress of his parents. At the age of twelve he underwent a crisis. I could not understand its nature. He went back to being a Jew, with characteristic seriousness, and with the consistency of a determined young boy became a Zionist too. His father agreed to send him to the Hochschule für die

Wissenschaft des Judentums, a Jewish college in Berlin, where he discovered a particular interest in Jewish history. Music was a hobby, although his music teacher made touching efforts to promote the violin at the expense of history. When he was sixteen, the music teacher won. ("Not because of his or music's persuasiveness, but for negative reasons: I was sick and tired of the college's wishy-washiness, neither milk nor meat, and their attempts to teach me to be a German patriot while taking pride in some glorious nonexistent tradition of Judaism.") But at the Conservatory too, which he began attending on a full-time basis, he did not devote himself to the violin. He was more interested in the history of music. Fortunately, playing came easily to him. He was blessed with perfect pitch and his intellectual curiosity extended to questions of technique as well. (Build helps, too. He has very broad shoulders, a heavy head, strong fingers, and particularly long hands. The violin is very steady under his heavy chin and his left hand is free to run without strain. And if I may be permitted a note of humor: his nose is very "violinistic" too. He has a hooked nose like Paganini, and the eyes of a bird of prey, big and frightening—in this too resembling the well-known sketch of the Italian virtuoso.) His playing is a little slipshod for someone of his gifts. But this, as he says himself, is because he has never been interested in practicing for its own sake. Since he was not seeking a career as a soloist he absolved himself of vain efforts. His only real interest is chamber music (an encouraging sign).

By the way, he too is one of those who did not have to take the audition. He is one of the "locals" chosen by Huberman to play in the orchestra before the auditions began. He has not been in the country long—he arrived in 'thirty-two—and this, apparently, gave him a certain advantage. I doubt if he would have passed the strict auditions in Basel. But from my point of view this is a matter of no importance. When he came to the country he went to work as an agricultural laborer and instructor in a youth village. Before the Arab general strike he

would drive to Jerusalem in a truck carrying agricultural produce and play piano trios there with the wife of a British
official and a professor from the Hebrew University. When
Huberman arrived in Jerusalem a few years ago, he was introduced to the trio, the pride of the town. ("I was scared to
death when we played for him. We chose a passage from a
Brahms trio which we could play with great élan, and luckily
for me Huberman stopped us before we reached the first
pianissimo.") He himself thought it improper that he had been
invited to play in the orchestra without passing the audition. I
reassured him: he wasn't the only one. He laughed with
charming modesty when I offered myself as an example. There
was no flattery in his laughter. He did not yet know what I had
in mind.

I first noticed him when he agreed with me that Toscanini's
tempi were too quick and not right for Brahms's Second. After
that he dared to criticize the way the maestro worked as well.
Perhaps he said it because he found a willing listener in me.
But I gained the impression that he would not hesitate to
express his opinion even if nobody agreed with him. I like
fellows like him, free of idolatry but not out to smash legends
for the sake of making an impression either. We fell into
conversation and I discovered that as far as chamber music is
concerned, he is in my camp. He is not one of those who think
that the divine spirit is floating about in higher worlds and has
to be called down with vows and whispers. He knows, as I do,
that the divine spirit is at the tips of our fingers, in the wood,
the rosin, the strings, and the horsehair, and that you have to
work hard to get it out of there, and that inspiration is skill
which has reached the point it has reached by dint of efforts
which are no longer visible.

We met again in the youth village. I went there to visit a
friend who had emigrated to Palestine as soon as he received
his Ph.D. Owing to the curfew in the neighboring Arab town,
the last bus was canceled and I had to stay the night.

In the evening I heard music when I passed the dining room.

Out of curiosity I went up to the window, and to my surprise I saw Friedman. He was playing a Mozart sonata. Next to him at the piano sat a young girl with a thick braid in a long white dress. I went quietly into the kitchen and waited for the intermission. Around bare tables sat boys whose tired faces showed that only the knowledge that they were performing a sacred duty kept them there. The girl's playing was not inspiring. She pounded the keys with unrestrained enthusiasm and drowned out the sound of the violin, which was soft and pleasant. Friedman apparently sensed this too, but refrained from "competing." Whenever he had the opportunity he offered a demonstration of a subtler interpretation. Unfortunately, this educational example had no effect on the determined girl, whose hard, pretty face showed her to be one of those females who are not easily moved from their opinions. I liked Friedman's playing. Not that I didn't find flaws here and there. Which of us is free of them? But I was impressed by his seriousness and his modesty. And also by the fact that he obtained particularly fine tones from the lower strings. At that moment it flashed through my mind: here's the second violinist I'm looking for. A violinist who knows how to play Mozart. (Mozart, in my opinion, is the supreme test: anyone incapable of playing him with humility should keep away from chamber music.)

Another thing which impressed me was this: he made no compromises with the taste of the audience. He had the courage to play serious music to farmers, and not some scherzo tarantella with nimble fingers to enthuse the ignorant. Afterward it transpired that it wasn't a recital at all. Friedman and his friend were simply playing to themselves in the only place with a piano in it, and the audience had gathered of its own accord. (In the end, in response to a request from the audience, he played the Rondo Capriccioso, and I've heard it played better . . .)

When it was over I came out of the kitchen into the dining room. Friedman was very embarrassed when he saw me.

"Have you been here long?"

"From the Mozart."

He apologized with a touchingly childish shyness. They had not intended performing unprepared, without rehearsing (an unbecoming blush appeared on his savage face). They couldn't stop people from coming in, it was a public place, and once the audience was already there, they didn't like to stop from time to time to "go into details"—and so they found themselves "giving" a concert.

"You were fine," I reassured him. "But the young lady forgot that the word 'pianoforte' is made up of two words, one of which means softly," I joked.

Friedman not only failed to smile, but reacted to my light-hearted remark sharply, almost angrily.

He did not raise his voice, God forbid, or rebuke me; he simply stated a fact which was supposed to show me how rude I had been.

"She works in the cowshed."

He couldn't have made himself clearer. I understood: music was important, but there were other things no less so. And those that were done with dirty hands were nobler. A musician who chose to work in a cowshed was a more moral person than her colleague who did nothing but play the piano. I had heard similar things from my brother on more than one occasion.

In the morning, when we rode in the bus to Tel Aviv together, I heard an exposition of his views.

Reverentially he spoke of the girl whose name I have forgotten but whose appearance is vividly engraved in my memory. Superlatives such as those are possible only in the case of platonic love. According to him, she was destined for a great musical career (I permit myself to doubt it) and she renounced it in order to educate these homeless boys. They had hired her to teach literature and music, but she went to work in the cowshed because she realized that she would not be able to reach them unless she did the dirty work too. Such work, he explained to me, stiffens the fingers, but the damage is worthwhile when you take the end result into account. A musician is not only an "executor" of lines of notes—he is the representative of a specific spiritual world. Beethoven is Beethoven not because of his technical mastery, but because he was a humanist and a rebel. The outstanding symbol of Jewish humanism in our time is the cowshed. A musician who shovels manure in a cowshed is enriched by values unknown to those who play in an orchestra.

What holy innocence! I could not but respect it. Under the tail of a Palestinian cow one finds today the romanticism that was lost to us in Europe. Could I tell him that I know musicians of the first rank who have neither lofty ideals nor noble sentiments, and whose playing is nevertheless perfect? Didn't he know for himself that what he had just said bore no relation to the actual facts? Wagner was a scoundrel and a genius just the same. Palestrina was a wily fur trader. Gesualdo was a murderer. I know more than one musician who is prepared to tread on corpses to further his career, but when he picks up a violin the nightingales in heaven break into song. I knew that there was no point in saying any of this to him—when a man needs to believe something, the facts will not budge him from his opinion.

I could imagine what Huberman had seen in him. Noble ideas had struck a chord in his heart. When Friedman expounded his views to him, he probably thought that it would do no harm to the orchestra to have an oddity like him in it, too. Among the ill-assorted crew of immigrant musicians, whose collective despondency rose from them like a miasma over a swamp, it would be a good idea to include one person who believed in something.

It wouldn't harm the quartet either, I thought, to have one member for whom this country was not a place of unwilling exile; someone whose heartstrings were in tune as well as his violin strings—in tune with the spirit of the times and the conditions of the place.

I told him that I was about to put together a quartet. He

said: A good idea; the country "needs" one. I smiled to myself. Zionist slogans drop from his lips as if they were self-evident truths. The country needed nothing—*we* needed *it*. Others might benefit or not. If we weren't good enough to perform in Paris and London too, "the country" would derive precious little benefit from us.

"You won't have any problems putting a good ensemble together," he encouraged me. "There are some very good musicians in the orchestra."

I told him that I was still considering my selection: there were plenty of good musicians, but not every combination of four good musicians constituted a good quartet. Something else was required too, some unifying glue.

"What glue?" he inquired with naive curiosity. At the age of twenty-seven I too believed that anyone who had reached the age of thirty-eight before me had an advantage over me in wisdom.

"If I knew what glue, I wouldn't have to think about it so much."

Then I formulated my "theory" in rather extreme terms: "A quartet has to begin from the second violin." He did not understand. Or perhaps he understood but was unable to believe his luck.

"Well, what do you say?"

From his excitement I concluded that he had not dared hope.

"I'm greatly honored," he said. A childish happiness gleamed in his eyes yet immediately died down. "But I'm not good enough."

His modesty touched my heart. For educational reasons I was careful not to praise him excessively. "Leave that to me," I said. Which could also be interpreted to mean: leave it to me to guide you and make you worthy. Although that was not what I actually meant.

He was silent for a long time. His face was expressionless, but there was a question mark in his eyes.

In the end he made up his mind to speak: "I'm afraid of disappointing you."

"A quartet is not a Catholic marriage."

I thought that he was afraid of the challenge. Sensitive people, afraid of disappointment, often prefer not to put themselves to the test.

But he surprised me: "I'm still not sure that I want to devote my life to it."

I thought that he had mistaken my intentions and imagined that I wanted to set up a professional quartet which would leave the orchestra and devote itself to chamber music exclusively. So I replied: "If only we could devote ourselves to it. We shall all have to continue playing in the orchestra. The idea is to do it in our spare time, as much as we can."

To my astonishment, he meant music in general. He had still not made up his mind if he wanted to be a musician, he explained.

"Then what do you want to be?"

The long silence that followed this question was little less than insulting. It was as though he were trying to make up his mind whether I was capable of understanding him or not. In the end he said, with a certain embarrassment (to his credit, in my opinion) and very quickly, as if to get it off his chest: "Maybe I'll go back to the youth village. They need a teacher for Jewish history. And the man in charge of the plantations has left as well."

"When will you make up your mind?"

It was a provocative question, and he realized it. I was casting doubt on his seriousness. As if he was only flirting with lofty ideals.

"Now you've made things even more difficult for me."

"Well, if you decide before the end of the month, let me know. It won't be too late. I'll keep a place for you."

He sensed that I was hurt by his response and wanted to placate me.

"Who are the other two?"

"I haven't decided. Now that there are two of us, I have someone to consult."

"That would be too great an honor for me." He smiled.

I saw that I was not mistaken in him. He was clumsy but quick-witted. He realized at once that I had no intention of consulting him, and felt no resentment against me. My mocking tone did not upset him. Apparently he thought it justified: I was treating him as he deserved. I had made him a very attractive offer, and instead of being grateful he had permitted himself to express his doubts aloud.

His smile was cordial but at the same time somewhat reserved, the smile of a man prepared to laugh even at the things that he takes with the utmost seriousness. Friedman's humor was to my liking. Although later on I discovered that one had to be careful: his humor did not apply to certain Zionist principles or to Johann Sebastian Bach. Toward these his attitude was one of reverence. However, I had no doubt that we would find a common language. I would show him a few pages from the *Musical Offering* and prove that Bach himself had not lacked a sense of humor.

By the time we reached Tel Aviv I was sure of it: I had a second violin! Friedman was not offended by my speaking to him as if he had never even mentioned the fact that he had not yet made up his mind. On the contrary. He was beaming with pride. The more he thought about my offer, the happier he was. Like a child who had received a present that could be taken apart and put together again. By the time we reached Tel Aviv he had already forgotten his ambition to be a cowhand. He spoke of the future quartet as if the whole thing had been his idea in the first place.

The second one to catch my eye was the violist. From every point of view. And I wasn't the only one to be charmed at first sight. When Eva Staubenfeld appeared at the first rehearsal of the orchestra, we couldn't take our eyes off her. Such beauty could give rise to the suspicion that it was not musical talent alone which had secured her a place in the orchestra. It had been a long time since I had seen so statuesque a body, and her calm, clean-cut Aryan face was so like the faces of the frosty-eyed women on the Nazi propaganda posters.

She sits at the first stand of the violas. The location arouses my curiosity, too. Does she play so well that she has been promoted over the heads of well-known violists from prominent European orchestras? Or does her position smack of some unpleasant favoritism liable to cause friction in the orchestra? That first day I was unable to hear a single note. She is one of those people who put down their bows the minute the conductor calls a halt. Nor does she take part in backstage solo performances like many of our colleagues who stand about in passageways showing off their paces. She puts her instrument away in its case and goes out to smoke. No one dares approach her. Her expression makes it quite clear that she has no desire to chat. Only once did I catch her "warming up" backstage. It was a very cold morning, and everybody's fingers were frozen. I moved closer and listened, but she was only playing scales, without vibrato, as a kind of exercise. I stood in a dark alcove and looked at her. The casualness of her daytime clothes gave her a kind of unfeminine authority. The trousers outlined a classical figure. Long legs, not too muscular and not too soft, a wasp waist, and the flat belly of a boy. The long sweeps of the bow tautened and relaxed a wonderfully round breast. When I went up to the stove to warm my hands, she stopped playing and came to stand next to me. "That's an idea," she said, and spread long fingers over the stove. It was the longest sentence I had ever heard her say. And the only one, too. For a while I stood next to her contemplating the long fingers, which looked as if they had an extra joint. I did not dare strike up a conversation.

I cannot remember when a woman made me feel so shy.

I said to myself that there was something artificial and unpleasant about her. What made her so much better than the rest of us? But I failed to convince myself. She ignored me without any intention of putting on an act. The need for solitude was deep and natural to her. She had no intention of sending out signals of hidden distress in order to attract attention. Nor did she have any desire to offend anyone who tried to approach her. She was simply shut up in a profound ennui from which only music could rescue her. She didn't care if we didn't love her, but it wouldn't affect her if we loved her either. If anyone wanted to fall in love with this inaccessible duchess—good luck to him. Anyone who preferred a bird in the hand would keep away.

When I began to take an interest in her as a potential member of the quartet, I had a number of encouraging signs to go by. Three basic characteristics made her seem suitable: discipline, concentration, and seriousness. But nevertheless, I hesitated: to be a good violist in a quartet you need to be modest and decisive. A rare combination. She seemed too arrogant, and I was afraid that it would be difficult to point out mistakes to her, even if I were right. And perhaps her tone would be as cold and expressionless as her face? She would have good cause to assume that I had chosen her for improper reasons: I wanted to rub shoulders with a beautiful woman and found a pretext to do so. But it was precisely her stunning looks which made me hesitate. I was somewhat apprehensive about the kind of emotional involvements which only do a chamber group no good. Friedman would no doubt be afraid of her and also despise her for symbolizing in his eyes the narrow-mindedness of people who are interested in nothing but music. She would certainly not find it in her heart to respect either cowhands or the sacred cows of Zionism. I was also afraid that if I chose her, I would have difficulties in finding a cellist. I did not want to have to use extraneous criteria in my selection. If I had to reject anyone with a roving eye, I would be forced to choose the only woman cellist in the orchestra. And I already knew that I did not want her. And the one who seemed to me most suitable of all— Bernard Litovsky—was the polar opposite of Eva. He was ready to get into conversation with anyone, and any form of snobbery infuriated him.

I decided not to bring up the subject until I heard her play, but I never had an opportunity to do so. My attempts to isolate her playing from the rest of the orchestra were all unsuccessful. I am usually able to fix my attention on an individual musician and hear him within the general harmony—but not Eva. And to her credit, her playing blended into the rich, warm sound of the violas as perfectly as if she were deliberately seeking anonymity. In the end I reached the conclusion that this, too, was evidence of flawless professionalism on her part. A first-rate player in an orchestra knows that too much emotion or enthusiasm on his part can be just as ruinous to the right balance as a false note or late entry.

The way things turned out, I did not have to take the first step.

A few days ago she approached me on her own initiative and asked me if I would play the Sinfonia Concertante with her on the radio.

I was so surprised that for a moment I said nothing.

"I know I've got a nerve to ask," she said without affected modesty. "You don't know me and you haven't heard me play. But you can try. I won't be insulted if you say no."

Her cool look mocked my hasty, overingratiating "God forbid!" as if to say: wait until you've heard me play, at least.

Then she told me that the performance had been proposed by the conductor of the radio orchestra, who knew her from her student days at the conservatory. He had suggested that she play a work for a viola solo, but they did not have the score or all the instruments for *Harold in Italy*. She herself had suggested the Mozart Concertante, and when he asked her whom she would play with, she said that she would ask me. The conductor said that he would be very pleased if I agreed. He had heard me in Basel.

"Have you heard me yourself?"

"Unfortunately not."

I did not have the opportunity to bring up the subject of the quartet then. We immediately began going into technical details: fees—a set sum, since the radio was a government institution, rehearsal times, and a place where we could play with a piano accompaniment. For a moment I hesitated, wondering whether it was worth my while to perform for such a miserly fee. But I decided to agree. For two reasons: I have already been in the country for several months without performing as a soloist. I am in danger of slipping back into anonymity again. A duet is not actually a solo, but playing over the radio will be like presenting my calling card. (As far as the fee is concerned, I would rather volunteer my services to a public institution for nothing than accept so contemptible a sum. But I did not want to go into questions of this kind during my first conversation with a strange woman.) The second reason is obvious: I did not want to miss the opportunity of playing with Eva Staubenfeld. It would be a test which would tell me whether I should invite her to join the quartet or not.

"Is there a piano where you live?"

"No. And you?"

"No," I said, after considering whether to ask Hella Becker to allow us to use her piano and deciding against it. An inner sense told me that it would be wiser to keep the two women apart.

However, it didn't matter. Eva had already taken care of everything. She had a pianist friend who played at a kindergarten. We would be able to have our rehearsals there, after the children went home.

Her practicality, too, was evidence of a serious, professional attitude. The piano had been tuned a week before, and the neighbors would not make any trouble, since the building housed two shops and a lawyer's office. There was a bus to the kindergarten door. She would bring the music and the stands.

The pianist would bring coffee. And I must not be shy about changing my mind if I found that she was not good enough to play with me.

I did not change my mind.

The warmth and tenderness of her playing were like balm to my soul. Superficial musicians are apt to interpret the spirit of Mozart as one of charming frivolity. Eva Staubenfeld's Mozart is grave without being solemn. According to the style of the Sinfonia Concertante, each of us often sings as if to himself, but nevertheless a dialogue develops. The two participants have to agree between themselves when one asks and the other responds. With Eva Staubenfeld there are no problems of interpretation (the high notes on her viola are sometimes a little shrill, but this seems to be a technical problem which can be solved).

I try to avoid sentimental expressions. A kindred soul is one of them. But a more complete agreement in questions of interpretation—where to put the accent and where to take a deep breath before embarking on a new adventure—I have never yet known.

The only question I ask myself is whether to tell her this. I am afraid she won't believe me. She'll think my words are empty compliments. We shall have to play together for some time before I win her trust and she takes my admiration at its face value. But then, I imagine, I won't have to say anything. My feelings will be taken for granted. At the moment I can say only this: my silence is accepted with gratitude and respect. If I can hold my tongue a little longer, perhaps I will be able to say something, too. In all my life I have never met a person so suspicious of words, as if everything a man says requires confirmation from another source. If all human relations were like love, there might be room for such an extreme demand. Lovers expect each other to make sacrifices in order to prove the seriousness of their intentions. But all we are doing is playing a work for violin and viola together. Perhaps I'm wrong. People shouldn't play together without the kind of spiritual closeness that requires absolute sincerity and the avoidance of small talk and empty jests.

The manner in which she plays, too, is aesthetically pleasing—very erect and without any emotional postures. Everything is expressed in controlled tones and precise bowing. The fair hair cascading in curls down her neck does not participate. Her very light blue eyes send out no signals. But for the music stand in front of her, I would have said that she was looking inside herself and reporting. Inside it's apparently nice and warm—quiet and hospitable with a fire burning in the hearth. The snow and ice are all on the outside. Anyone who manages to get in will find it pleasant enough. Day to day I have to make a greater effort to maintain the silence that keeps us friends. I warn myself: if you want her in the quartet you must stop entertaining vain hopes. You must not try to gain entry except with a violin in your hands. Any other intrusion on her privacy will be the end of the quartet.

Her lack of humor frightens me a little. Violists, too, need a little humor to play Haydn quartets, when they sometimes have the boring role of setting the beat. But after two rehearsals I saw that she was not without irony. Even sarcasm. Her friend—I would not call such crude relations of give-and-take by the name of friendship—is a very mediocre pianist. I refrain from making any comments on her playing. Why should I hurt her feelings? She is doing it for our sakes after all, without asking for payment. I therefore took her contributions to our discussions of interpretation in good spirit.

"In the concert we'll do it the way you want us to," said Eva.

A slight, ironic smile accompanied this remark, which wounded the pianist so deeply that she fell silent and did not open her mouth again to the end of the rehearsal. Perhaps that was what Eva wanted. Her reaction seemed to me too aggressive, even cruel.

I saw a certain danger to the quartet. Friedman, who loves

philosophizing, can talk the hind legs off a donkey. (It took five minutes to explain to me why he played three bars the way he did . . .) If Eva ever makes any kind of cutting, ironic remark to him, he'll be insulted and the rehearsals will be full of tension. (But why cross your bridges before you come to them? Perhaps Eva only uses irony against those who do not know their place.)

Greta is right. I am an adjustable animal. In Eva's presence I have accustomed myself to keeping silent as if I have never felt the urge to speak in my life. I have even come to like this silence, which accompanies us in the bus like a private climate of our own (Eva, too, lives in the north of the town).

The other passengers give us sidelong glances. Probably because of Eva. And perhaps also because of our instruments, which help them to remember where they know us from. But sometimes I think that they regard us as a couple on bad terms with each other. We'll sit in silence all the way and when we get home we'll fight.

The journey to Jerusalem involves a certain degree of danger. But I could not back out now: did I have so little courage that I would show a woman who was not afraid how afraid I was for my own skin?

But the journey passed without any untoward events. We were driven there in an armored car belonging to the British army. Peeping at the view through the shooting apertures in the armor was an experience in itself. I only became fully aware of it after organizing my impressions in my memory in order to recount them to Egon Loewenthal and describe them in my letter to Greta.

To Greta I described it as a deed of extraordinary daring. Apparently I have not yet overcome the need to demonstrate courage. I have a real need to prove that my flight from Germany was not an act of cowardice but of human protest.

The Jerusalem which I described to Greta was slightly different from the one I described to Egon. I exaggerated a little in describing the religious sentiments which filled my heart at the sight of the Holy City. The truth is that I would not be prepared to live there unless it had a symphony orchestra worthy of the name. The radio orchestra pays government salaries to amateurs.

To Egon I told the truth. I was frightened throughout the journey although there was no real reason for my fear. (We Rosendorfs seem to degenerate from generation to generation. My father was an officer in the imperial army and won the Iron Cross, yet I felt insecure even in a steel box on wheels, even though I derived a certain security from Eva's composure.) It's good to have a close friend to whom you can tell the whole truth without feeling ashamed.

Egon was interested in Jerusalem. I could not tell him much. I had seen little of the town. But anyone could feel that it was saturated with memories.

"It's a different country," I said to Egon. "Another world."

"Tel Aviv is built on sand; Jerusalem on stone," he said.

A metaphor, not the conclusion of personal observations. He had never been to Jerusalem. He was gathering strength to go there, he told me. He was afraid that he wouldn't like it. Tel Aviv was the rough sketch of a city. You could love it or hate it. It made no difference either way. Jerusalem would not allow him to enjoy the privileges reserved for visitors. He would have to take a stand.

The Englishman who traveled with us was an officer in civilian clothes who had taken leave in order to accompany us. An agreeable character. A keen music lover and extremely knowledgeable. He could whistle entire violin concertos with amazing accuracy. Throughout the journey he spoke to me and looked at Eva. She makes an overwhelming impression on anyone seeing her for the first time who is not yet aware of the need for caution. I feel sorry for anyone who falls in love with her. Eva was not impressed by the Englishman's astonishing memory. His musical memory was only a byproduct of a profession which obliged him to photograph and store in his mind a vast number of details, she said. She guessed immediately that he was a detective. I, at any rate, was glad to meet a man like him. If the British regime was anything like him, the situation was not so bad.

The concert was a success, in spite of the orchestra. The government secretary and several dignitaries, both Jews and Arabs, were in the audience. Eva played like someone who feels no stage fright whatsoever. An audience was a challenge to her. Everything we had polished during rehearsals she now produced with greater clarity and with true feeling. Even an annoying mistake in the cellos, which confused the conductor, did not faze her. She skipped the bar they had missed with no sign of tension on her face. I no longer had any doubts. Even in Berlin I would have chosen her. She was better than Bernfeld, who is considered a top-notch violist.

I suspect it was not in my honor that we were invited to dine with the government secretary after the concert. He, too, is a pleasant, cultured man, who owns the only record we brought out in Munich. He apologized on behalf of the High Commissioner for the latter's failure to attend the concert. An exciting experience for a German Jew—to receive an apology from the highest representative of the government!

The latter event added a special weight to the part of my letter to Greta in which I attempted to persuade her that there were some advantages to coming here.

That night in the hotel, outside the door to her room, I asked Eva if she would be willing to play in a string quartet.

"What a question!" she said.

She did not even ask what quartet, whether it would be on a permanent basis, and who the others were. She opened the door, wished me good night, went inside, and with an expressionless face shut the door behind her.

A week later, in Tel Aviv, we discussed details. I suggested Bernard Litovsky and she approved with a nod of her head. She had heard him in the hall of the Herzliah Gymnasia; he had a big, penetrating tone and a long bow. I immediately adopted this descriptive phrase, so expressive of a long breath and a continuous melodic line.

Eva is sparing of words, but everything she says bears an individual stamp. She has a unique way of discussing technical details. She avoids flowery phrases and always looks for her own way of putting things. ("He plays in little blocks," she said of a cellist whose name came up as a possible candidate. I listened to him. And indeed, in his desire to beautify the sound he stresses every bar separately and loses the continuity of the melodic line . . .)

She is not happy about Friedman, but since I have already spoken to him she does not demand the right of veto.

"The first violinist is the leader, and he has the right to decide," she says.

I told her about my "theory" regarding the second violin. She accepted my decision, but was surprised that I had chosen him of all people. She suggested Vitali. I had never seen any outstanding quality in him apart from taciturnity.

It occurred to me that the contradictions between Eva and Friedman might be beneficial. In the role of peacemaker it would be easier for me to lead a quartet which, in Eva's words, had more than one "center of gravity."

I went on worrying about the choice of the cellist for a while longer. Musical questions were not uppermost in my mind. I don't know him well enough. He has a roving eye, and I still don't know whether what makes it rove is natural curiosity or lechery.

I have made up my mind: Bernard Litovsky is our man. I consulted Friedman, too, out of good manners. Friedman was not enthusiastic. He's an excellent cellist, he said, but unstable. I thought he was talking about rhythmic stability. But he clarified the point: as a human being, there was a certain weakness in him. He was easily influenced. One day he held one view, and the next day another.

"Put your mind at rest," I told him. "When he plays in the

quartet he won't have time to change his views. He'll be so busy he won't even have time for one."

He would be happy to play with Litovsky, Friedman concluded during our short conversation, but they would never address each other with the familiar *du*. This, in my opinion, was all to the good. It would preserve correct professional relations, and there was something else as well: since none of us would ever dare address Eva familiarly, this way nobody would feel that it was three of us against one of her.

"Our quartet will be composed of two handsome members and two ugly ones," he said in the end.

Friedman's ideas of beauty are rather childish. Litovsky has an attractive, manly ugliness. He is a big, strong German with a curly, expressive head. His hard, angular face looks like that of a man who has had an interesting, adventurous life. Not that I know anything about his life, but this is the impression he makes. I only know two facts about him: one, that he came first in the Budapest Competition; and two, that he succeeded in escaping to Czechoslovakia with his wife and his cello.

A face like that is a gift from God to a musician. Even when he's tuning his strings he looks as if he's listening to voices from the deep.

Litovsky weighed my offer with the sly expression of a professional politician who never forgets not to sell himself cheap. He was very pleased but checked his enthusiasm—good taste obliged him to show restraint, as if this would teach us to appreciate him more. I let him play his game, but to Eva Staubenfeld I announced: "We have a quartet!"

When Litovsky joined the quartet the problem of a place to meet was solved. He lives in a three-room apartment, on the first floor of a three-story building on Eliezer Ben Yehudah Street. His wife, Martha, a physical education teacher, is a keen music lover. She was glad to put her home—a childless home—at our disposal, and serves coffee and cookies at four o'clock on the dot. We are always made welcome there and never have the feeling that the rehearsal has upset our hostess's plans. We all like Martha, even—if I may be permitted a note of cynicism—her husband. She seems to be the only woman with whom Eva finds a common language. As far as Konrad Friedman is concerned, she treats him like a motherless child who must be looked after and made to rest and eat and dress properly. I admire women like her, who lost their looks at a very early age and already at thirty-eight or forty radiate a kind of acceptance of their fate. She has no bitterness, nor any need to prove that she possesses something of worth to take the place of the lost beauty. Her face beams with benevolence and the kind of wisdom gained by a person who has suffered from things for which nobody can be blamed. I doubt if I could live with a woman like her, but I would certainly be happy to be her son. Whenever I see her, my heart fills with pity, in addition to the deep affection I always feel for her, even though there is no proof that her husband is unfaithful to her. All I know is that after every concert there are two or three women waiting for him outside with something to say about the short solo he played during the course of the evening.

The first rehearsals were a success from every point of view. Friedman is an artist in ensemble identification. Every time he plays after someone else he is like a mirror reflection. Eva is an experienced violist who has taken the responsibility for balance upon herself. She has a soothing influence on Litovsky, whose big tone is sometimes in danger of smothering us.

There were no arguments about the division of the takings, either. Friedman hinted that he would be prepared to get less than the others. Since I knew that he was saving up to bring his father to the country, I scolded him. I told him not to talk nonsense and he almost wept with emotion.

There is some friction, but on the whole everything is proceeding as expected. Soon we'll be ready for our first concert. We shall play the Haydn "Quinten" Quartet, the Beethoven

Opus 18, no. 3, and Brahms's Third—as a gesture to Eva Staubenfeld, because of the prominent role played by the viola in the third part. The first concert will take place in two weeks' time at the Jascha Heifetz Hall.

My life is taking on a regular pattern. Rehearsals with the orchestra in the mornings, the quartet in the afternoon, three times a week, and four or five pupils, one of them really talented. In the evenings—concerts, except for Friday nights. Sometimes I have a free evening in the middle of the week when my landlady gives me a Hebrew lesson. For payment, of course. The quartet fills my life with a rich content, and it was interesting to note that we four were among the only ones to object to threatening the orchestra management with a strike if they brought new musicians to the country before raising our salaries. (For Friedman it was a question of principle and the rest of us accepted his view: Jews should not prevent their fellows from being rescued.) Once a fortnight I dine with Hella Becker, and once a fortnight, on Friday night, I am invited to spend the evening with Egon Loewenthal and his woman friend, whose character I have not yet gauged. And so I never feel the emptiness which troubles the bachelors among us on the weekends. Once a week I write to my wife and daughter. Once a month I write to my brother at the address he gave me in The Hague, although I'm sure that he isn't there. (I haven't had a reply from him yet, but I presume that in Holland, too, he is in the underground. The address is probably that of some organization affiliated with the Communist party; he appears to be moving from country to country and trying to organize resistance to the Nazis. I suppose this gives him satisfaction. Practical results are another matter.)

Hella Becker complains that I am neglecting my old friends. Now that I have acquired new friends I never have time for those who really love me. She is joking, but I know she really means it. What bothers her is not my friendship with Friedman and Litovsky; she sent a bouquet of flowers to the first rehearsal of the quartet with a card saying: "A great day in the musical life of Eretz Israel!'' The relationship that gives rise to an undignified curiosity in her is that between myself and Eva Staubenfeld.

Her jealousy of Eva is ridiculous and annoying. First, because she has no right to demand faithfulness of me, and second, because there are no grounds for her jealousy. If I tell her this, she'll think that I am apologizing, and the apology will be interpreted as a recognition of her rights. I keep quiet and carefully pick my way around the obstacles she strews along my path—hints alternatively broad and subtle—which give rise in me to nothing but pity for an intelligent woman making a fool of herself. She fixes me with sorrowful eyes for longer than I can stand, as if I still owe her a reply to a question which has not been asked.

I always manage to involve myself in situations which others seem to evade with ease. Perhaps because I am incapable of rudeness, even to the minimum degree sometimes essential for putting people in their place. And as far as Hella Becker is concerned, there is no real danger. Nothing that could happen between her and me is as frightening as the developments taking place in the house where I live. Something strange is happening to me and I don't know how to put a stop to it.

There is no one I can talk to about it, not even Egon.

In the preliminary stages, it is possible to teach someone to play the violin almost without talking. Everything can be demonstrated. At a more advanced stage, explanations become necessary. Sometimes my ignorance of Hebrew weighs heavily on me. You need words in order to give your pupil a deeper understanding of music. Technical instruction is not enough. True, today I can say a few sentences in Hebrew, but most of the time I am forced to use my hands.

This is the root of the problem.

Once I was standing behind the girl and holding her arm holding the violin with my left hand, and her hand holding the bow with my right. I wanted to demonstrate the correct way to hold the violin. Something strange happened. Her arms were stiff, as rigid as if they were frozen, both the right and the left. They gripped her body tightly and refused to respond to me. At first I thought that she didn't understand what I wanted. But in a moment it became clear that one of us was a child—and that one was me. Her left arm pressed my fingers, which were holding her elbow, to her hard, supple breast. We were standing very close to each other, and my loins were pressing up against her backside. The contact provoked an immediate response, but the girl did not recoil. I blushed, but her peachlike cheek did not change color. It was rosy with a strange delight. There was a happy smile on her lips. I was shocked. She was not embarrassed at all.

I do not mean to say that a girl of fifteen was trying to seduce me. Such things happen of their own accord. But once they happen, there is a danger of their turning into a reprehensible habit. After overcoming my embarrassment, I pretended that nothing had happened. But the next lesson she held the violin negligently again, and I saw a cunning gleam in her eye, as if she were asking me to repeat last week's demonstration again.

I was overcome with confusion. Once more, it was the girl's lack of embarrassment which frightened me more than anything else. She threw me a rather mocking, astonishingly mature, and even slightly patronizing look. The way someone sure of his own worth might look at a timid conformist afraid of public opinion. I have seen such a look on the face of a girl of about the same age once before.

It was on the tram in Frankfurt. The tram was crowded and we were standing pressed up against each other, and the same physical configuration took place. I tried to detach myself, but the other passengers pressed me against her and I couldn't move. I was afraid that she might think I was doing it on purpose until I saw—after daring to transfer my eyes from the ceiling to her profile—that she was not in the least angry. On the contrary, there was a mature, mysterious smile on her face, without a trace of guilt, and a gleam of pride in her eye. She saw no need to hide her pleasure in the miraculous power she had discovered in her buttocks. This happy smile increased my excitement, and for a while we swayed together, until I could bear it no longer. I was stunned by the tremendous enjoyment I derived from this stolen embrace. But I felt no guilt until afterward, when I was back at home.

That girl was anonymous and there was little chance of my ever seeing her again. She made me aware of a certain attraction to the sophistication of the immature—and then disappeared from my life. But my pupil is the daughter of people who trust me. For them I symbolize all that is noble and ethical and spiritual in European civilization. I see her every day. I can't stop the music lessons without an explanation.

Her name is Ruth. And in five months' time she will be sixteen. A poor consolation.

I believe that I shall be able to overcome my lust. I am an adult man and I will not allow the stupidity of the flesh to ruin my life. I must control myself. This girl is not meant for me. This forbidden fruit is not for my picking. But every week it becomes more difficult.

There is no longer any doubt in my mind that her behavior is deliberate. She knows what she's doing and she does it shamelessly. Almost impudently. And always with the same glint of excited expectation in her eyes, fearless and guiltless. You could hardly call it seduction in the crude sense of the word. It's more like a wordless invitation. A door is opened before you, and if you are not afraid, you can enter.

In spite of everything, I cannot say this girl is corrupt. There is something innocent and touching in this passionate recklessness. If I may be permitted a guess, what we have here is not a sexual attraction to a father figure; it is more in the nature of a childish infatuation with the strange and foreign.

To her I represent everything that is exotic and remote from her closed, narrow world of family and neighborhood school. I am part of the magical, exciting life that goes on beyond the horizon, where it is sometimes possible to catch a glimpse, through the window, of a passenger ship sending up smoke like a poignant signal on the skyline. For hours she can lie on her stomach, waving her legs in time to the rhythm of the lives in the translated novels she reads with passionate enthusiasm. Novels in which people like me travel from city to city to reap applause and to allow beautiful princesses to fall in love with them. Music, too, is a ticket to foreign realms for her. It seems to me that she would not permit herself to cuddle up so shamelessly to a man to whom she could talk. Let us hope that shame will return to the no-man's-land between us when my knowledge of this difficult language improves and I am able to talk to her in Hebrew. An odd idea, but nevertheless I cling to it as to a lifeline. Time is on my side. When the strangeness wears off, we shall remember our plain moral duty.

A more concrete evil may grow from the increasingly close relationship between myself and Eva Staubenfeld. To the quartet, I mean, not to me personally. Or even to my marriage. There is no danger here of falling madly in love. We rarely fall in love with women who resemble our wives too closely. Eva and Greta are made of the same hard clay typical of ambitious, opinionated women. Neither of them is the kind of female who wants a man's protection. It would never occur to them to demand a "commitment" from a man who goes to bed with them. On the contrary, they are glad when he leaves them alone after the act and does not imagine that he has acquired rights to their body.

These are only assumptions, of course. I don't know if there have been any other men in Greta's life. For a while I suspected that the experience she had when we met was not acquired in books. But I never demanded that she give me an account of her life before she met me. As for Eva, I know even less. I proceed by analogy from Greta to Eva, and I do not think that I am mistaken. And even if I am mistaken, it is of no great significance. I am determined not to indulge in frivolous, ridiculous flirtations and become embroiled in silly love affairs.

But I am not immune to another form of emotional dependence, which is liable to develop into a certain kind of love that resembles kinship. This feeling is elusive at first, but habit deepens it. Routine does not impair, but rather strengthens it. Sometimes I think it is more dangerous than romantic love. Time does not erode it but builds it layer upon layer. This is how I sometimes feel at the beginning of a theme common to the viola and the first violin. I wonder then how I could ever have played in a quartet which did not include Eva Staubenfeld. Sometimes it seems to me that I have never realized the full extent of my powers as I did on the night when I played the Sinfonia Concertante with her. (*The Palestine Post* wrote: "They played as one . . . a riveting dialogue between two first-rate musicians who know what they want to say. . . .")

I can only promise myself that as far as I am concerned, I will never take a single step that might be interpreted as an attempt to go beyond the framework of professional relations. I don't know how I would behave if she were to do anything provocative. I'm afraid that I would be as helpless as usual. At first I would be curious and unwilling to give offense, and in the end I would be carried away. You vibrate your finger on a string and are swept away by an emotion which you yourself have aroused.

These are not groundless fears. I can see worrying signs, which have increased since Egon Loewenthal began coming to our rehearsals. Lately he has been turning up rather often. Whenever he "needs to get away from the country."

He discovered us by chance. We met on the way and he accompanied me. We became absorbed in a conversation, which lasted all the way to the front door. Martha, who knew who he was, invited him in. He was as brilliant as ever in the presence of a beautiful young woman. Martha was fascinated. Friedman found an opportunity to show off his erudition. Litovsky took note of his witticisms so that he could repeat them elsewhere. We were all delighted by the interruption. Even Eva, who kept running her fingers over the strings without bowing, as if she grudged the time, was only pretending to be indifferent. She knew very well that all his fireworks were aimed at her.

Then he asked us to play.

"I'll sit far away and listen. I'll be very grateful if you ignore me."

In Litovsky's modest apartment it was impossible to sit "far away." And ignoring him wasn't easy either.

"You'll be bored," I said to him, not without a certain pride in the fact that we addressed each other as *du*. "We often stop to argue. It's not exactly a concert."

"Never mind; your process interests me, too," he said.

The rehearsal did not go well. Friedman got stage fright. As always when someone he admires is listening to us. (When Huberman came to listen to the orchestra rehearse, his hands trembled as if Huberman had nothing else to attend to but the way in which he played the important part of second violin . . .) And we refrained from stopping even when there was something that should have been clarified. I was far from pleased when he asked permission to come again, but I could not bring myself to refuse.

"Don't you find it boring to listen to a rehearsal?" I asked him.

"Not in the least. It was riveting!"

I smiled to myself. His eyes had been riveted on Eva all the time. He did not take them off her even when he was pouring himself a cup of coffee.

He said that he took a particular interest in rehearsals, which enabled him to study the work in depth. Later on, at the concert itself, he could follow the ideas in their realization. "A string quartet is a microcosm," he said, "a world, and the fullness thereof, in miniature." Then he let his imagination run wild: "It's a cell in which four people sentenced to hard labor are bound together by emotional chains; a hothouse in which flowers from a different climate are grown; an architectural structure built in time instead of space; a sterile laboratory for well-tempered human relations; four fish in a net which grows tighter the harder they struggle." And so on and so forth . . . (Metaphors jump into his head half a dozen at a time, he says; the problem is which to erase.)

He also said that he might write a book about a string quartet, and promised that we would not find ourselves in it.

"In our day," he said, "there are only two possibilities: either to alert the world to the Teutonic danger, or to write books about nothing."

"A quartet is nothing?"

"I mean something that does not belong to our times, something that could have been written about in the same way in 1837."

"Whenever I feel homesick or fed up I need Schubert," he added, and developed the idea of escaping into music "instead of escaping from here." Lately he had been suffering from a certain "constipation of the creative organs," he said, and it was bad for him to be alone with himself—a fellow with exaggerated demands. There was a limit to the number of pages he could read a day. Living with words could drive a person insane. He needed pauses full of music. Not necessarily consecutive notes threading a single idea throughout a work, but precisely the sporadic bursts of music in an interrupted rehearsal. Under such circumstances he feels exempt from having to organize the chaos in his mind. A rehearsal of this kind does not allow him to become addicted to a single idea. He has to turn his attention constantly to something new. Like someone rummaging through old drawers and finding forgotten letters.

After all this was said, I could not tell him that his presence disturbed us. He gave his word that he would be a "good boy," and in a moment of frankness also promised not to stare at the "Valkyrie." (Later on he changed her name to "Brunhilde." I admire his ability to bestow appropriate nicknames. He calls Friedman "Freudman" . . .) Although Eva does not seem in the least embarrassed to be impaled on the spit of a stare: her own spears are well sharpened, and she hurls them with lightning speed and accuracy.

Egon's presence at our rehearsals gives rise to a hidden tension. I think I understand its source.

A comedy of errors:

Egon imagines that something is developing between Eva and myself. His conscience permits him to loosen this tie. I am married and he is a bachelor. Formally, at least. Accordingly, there is no reason why he should refrain from competing with me for Brunhilde's favors. Each of us has a spear to hurl, a stone to cast, and an obstacle to jump over. He needs some revitalizing rivalry in order not to sink into a deep depression. He has no publisher to fight with here, no critics to curse and abuse. He has no way of knowing that the signs of excessive friendship with which Eva showers me only exist when he is present. Why this should be so—I can only guess. Eva could not but notice the impression she made on Egon ("Palestine has taken a giant stride toward Europe if it holds such a beautiful and elegant woman . . ." he said). For some reason she needs to tease him, and the best way of doing it, without breaking the rules of good manners, is to give him grounds for his suspicions that we are hiding something from him. Why does she do it? Perhaps because she doesn't like witty men. Or perhaps as a kind of protest against his success with women, which offends her aesthetic sense. He is small and skinny and apart from his eyes there is nothing striking about him. Perhaps she is trying to prove that not all women are fascinated by famous names. And perhaps it annoys her that he possesses the kind of Jewish cleverness which is not to her taste. Or perhaps she needs to hurl her spear far and high. The reasons don't really interest me. What concerns me is the end result. I keep on picking up signals and I don't know whether to respond or not. Our silences are being stretched to the breaking point. And the rehearsals of the quartet are no longer what they used to be. There is a tense game afoot. And a secret understanding is coming unconsciously into being between Eva and myself. I can't deny it, an understanding of this nature has something erotic about it. Like music, eroticism is tension stretched to the point where it becomes unendurable.

TEL AVIV, JANUARY 29, 1938

Gnädige Frau Rosendorf,

Madam's letter, which was cold enough to be published in any serious newspaper, afforded great pleasure to the young girl's father. The praises heaped upon her by important musicians deserve to be treated with all due respect. But the fact that none of them suggested she appear in public in "these difficult times" is also worthy of attention. The people you mention, whose influence on musical life in Germany is so great, could have done something more for Anna than make speeches, which costs them nothing. What she needs today, and in my opinion what she also needed a year ago, is to face an audience in order to discover all the spiritual resources latent in her. And if it is so difficult to open the doors of the concert halls to her in Germany, perhaps she should try elsewhere.

And that, my dear Greta, sums up my initial reaction to your so formal letter. I know that one shouldn't react emotionally from a distance, since one often lacks all the necessary information. And I shall say no more on the subject. Letters can not only join people together, but also divide them. Only misunderstanding can result from ironic remarks which are wrongly interpreted at a distance of thousands of kilometers. And by the time one has a chance to correct the bad impression made by a superfluous word it is too late to erase the scars.

I am very worried. What's going on? Why is your letter so reserved? Why did Anna only write three lines? Has someone been putting it into her head that she can cut me out of her biography if only she doesn't write the fourth line? Perhaps these questions too will only cause misunderstanding. But what can I do when everything seems so strange from here, and sometimes absolutely alarming?

I have saved up enough money to pay the traveling expenses for both of you. Unfortunately I do not have an apartment in which to receive you in the manner you deserve, but Frau Becker will be happy to accommodate you in her pension for a really ridiculous fee. There is an excellent piano there too, and it will be possible to practice on it several hours a day.

Here everything is going very well. I am sending you reviews of the quartet published in *The Palestine Post* and the German newspaper. The Hebrew papers, too, carried very good reviews.

I won't write to Anna this time; she is old enough to read this letter. I don't mind if she knows that her father is a little angry. If we don't bring our children up to respect us, they won't grow up to be serious people or learn to educate their own children properly.

Yours with love,

Kurt

Last night I suddenly started crying without any reason. We were playing "Death and the Maiden" and I felt the tears choking me. I apologized and escaped to the toilet. There I burst into terrible weeping. When I came out everyone thought I was ill. (I didn't deny it. I played the role for all it was worth. With tears of gratitude I ate the tasteless rice

Martha prepared for me, as if her concern for my health touched me to the heart . . .)

Something is coming apart inside me. I have to pull myself together.

What precipitated it? Nothing in particular. Everything. The success of the quartet should have afforded me enough inner happiness to protect me against bouts of melancholia of the kind from which I have not suffered in years.

It began the day before yesterday, when it was five o'clock in Germany. Suddenly I saw our little flat as vividly as if in reality. The door opened and someone came in. Greta, sitting on the sofa opposite, smiled welcomingly. The man took another two or three steps and I saw that it was Miller.

Here I must say, in all sincerity, that I have never had any reason to reproach Miller for his behavior. The man is a paragon of virtue. Decent, discreet, humane. When we studied at the conservatory together he was one of the most talented piano students there. Later on he inherited a big business with branches all over the country, and gave up his musical career to take charge of the family affairs. I never saw anything wrong in the fact that he offered, out of friendship for me, to accompany us on the piano in order to prepare each of us for public performances. He is a person whose character makes him the perfect accompanist. He senses you with extraordinary intuition and adapts himself to the most subtle nuances.

As in the cinema—sitting in a dark hall and watching everything happening in front of you without being able to enter the frame and interfere—I saw our drawing room: He comes in and kisses Greta's hand with his usual formality. In his desire to appear as businesslike as possible he sits down at the piano immediately. But Greta, as usual, says: "First of all, coffee. If you don't have coffee we won't allow you to play on our piano." And he smiles. His beautiful smile, gentle and full of consideration, but not lacking in intelligence either. He sits down by the little table, takes a poppyseed cookie—the only thing Greta knows how to bake—and praises it with sincere enthusiasm. Then he drinks his coffee with downcast eyes—he is always charmingly modest, and when he is alone in the apartment with his friend's wife, his manners are like a veritable coat of armor—and announces: "And now to work." They have to take advantage of the girl's absence at her theory lesson—afterward the piano will be busy. Greta smiles, too. A true friend. He knows that time is too precious to waste. There is no need to play society games with him. He has already finished his coffee, and even without friendly small talk he knows that his presence is desired—nay, vital. She rises to her feet, and carrying the tray with the graceful motion of a woman who knows that she looks good from behind as well as before, makes her exit to the kitchen. Perhaps this is the moment when he allows himself to peek with male eyes, but within the boundaries of good taste, at her rounded buttocks and the slender ankles emerging beneath the long skirt of her judiciously selected hostess gown—not too intimate, but not too formal either, a dress worn in honor of a guest who is a close friend (she has two such gowns, one with a Chinese pattern and the other resembling a Bavarian folk costume).

And suddenly, when she returns, as if she has absorbed the look he gave her from behind and no longer has to pretend, she stands in front of him and takes hold of both his hands. And then, without the need for a single word to justify the sudden change between them, he stands up. He can no longer deny the evidence of his eyes, and they embrace with great force, as if all their lives they have been waiting for this moment . . .

But why now?

I've been away for a year already. And I've never imagined such scenes before. Not even once.

I've thought about myself a lot. Would I have the self-control not to poison the good—and useful too, I can't deny—relations between Hella Becker and myself? Was the insane attraction for my landlord's daughter a deep-rooted disease, or a passing phenomenon due to a temporary hunger?

Wouldn't it be better for me to find myself some undemanding woman who would ask for no more than a little consideration and with whom I could have a pleasant, untroublesome relationship, the kind of stopgap love affair from which no one expects too much?

And sometimes I thought about Greta, too. General, undisturbing thoughts. It was a subject we could talk about freely, after all—we're civilized people; we don't expect one another to live in opposition to the laws of nature. We even allowed ourselves to make jokes, in the spirit of the cynical sayings attributed to that incorrigible adulterer Hochbaum: "If there's nothing to eat in the house, go to a restaurant," or: "If your wife doesn't know how to cook, nobody expects you to starve to death." But we both knew that all this was only lip service. Such agreements are hypocrisy. Obviously we have moments of weakness, but we expect mutual respect of each other. There's no point in laboring the issue. My behavior was not always above reproach. To Greta's credit, she did not find it necessary to get her own back. I said to myself that she had the right to avenge herself, although I knew that if she took advantage of that right it would hurt me. I had no trouble in coping with these thoughts.

But I had never seen pictures. And now, all of a sudden.

A casual remark dropped by Egon Loewenthal was apparently to blame for my mood.

It was just the three of us, Bernard Litovsky, Egon, and I. Martha had not yet returned. Eva and Friedman were late. I was tuning my violin and Bernard was chatting with Egon. I overheard their conversation, which was about some scandalous love affair. People I didn't know. They were talking coarsely about adulterous acts, and I had no desire to participate. Bernard likes that style. And Egon has the gift of responding to every man in his own language. To my credit I can state: he has never spoken to me in that vulgar way.

Bernard said about the woman: "She's nothing but a bottle of yogurt."

I could see that Egon relished the expression. If Bernard had said "a cold fish" or "a block of ice," he probably wouldn't even have reacted. But since he had coined a phrase, Egon enjoyed talking to him.

"You're right," he said, "that's exactly what she looks like. Cold and pale and tasteless."

And he laughed. But he immediately added: "Impressions can be very misleading."

"Many men enjoy a false sense of security," he went on. "Since their spouse shows no great interest in sex, it seems to them that there's no danger of her seeking this punishment elsewhere. The poor fools don't realize that this block of ice, preserved in the frozen mold of marriage, melts soon enough in a glass of whiskey. They're in for a big surprise. The same woman who keeps up such a respectable facade in her husband's bed—martyred, never mind respectable!—can behave like a bitch in heat in her lover's bed, where all the rules have been broken anyway . . ."

A moment of revelation. The painful stab of the realization that without knowing it he was talking about me.

Like a sudden illumination. A great darkness.

Today I visited Eva in her room for the first time. Our friendship is growing closer. This makes me very happy, but it also worries me a little.

I've been invited to play in a place where there's no piano. I hesitated although they offered four pounds. I was afraid of playing a Bach partita for solo violin in front of an audience of tired workers. In the end I had an idea: I would repay Eva. I proposed that the two of us play the Saraband with Variations by Handel-Halvorsen. She agreed willingly, but only on condition that we did not share the fee. She was not short of money. I refused. You're insulting my honor, I said. She mocked me: Men keep their honor in their pockets. She suggested rehearsing at her place.

The landlady opened the door—a small, middle-aged woman with a thick braid crowning her head like a tower and a look of grim insult in her big eyes. At first she looked at me as if I were trespassing on private property, but when she noticed the violin she calmed down.

She even brought tea and cookies without asking us if we wanted them.

The woman, whom Eva with mocking affection called Sonichka, thought that my visit was an excellent opportunity to preach a Zionist sermon. Whoever ate her cookies had to listen to her lectures: musicians, rootless people, should be planted in the soil.

Eva evidently enjoyed bringing this little samovar to the boil. And the elderly idealist didn't notice what she was up to. A dialogue of the deaf ensued. The woman said that German Jews might have to pay a heavy price for the "banquet Zionism" they had indulged in all these years. Eva said that the future of the Zionists didn't look any rosier; it was madness to abandon a handful of Jews to millions of Arabs. The woman was horrified: What are you doing here if that's what you think? Eva said calmly: Have you got anywhere else for me? And her landlady declared: There is nowhere else for Jews. The Jews are persecuted everywhere. In America too? asked Eva. If not today, then tomorrow, Sonichka firmly replied. I'm not looking for a place where they don't persecute the Jews, said Eva, but for a place where a Jew can escape from himself.

When we were alone, Eva mocked the enthusiasm of this little woman who knew exactly what was needed: to play well you needed soul and not technique. . . . A nation needed a motherland. . . . A good-looking woman needed to get married at once, so as not to endanger respectable families. . . . And other similar axioms.

In my heart I criticized Eva. These intellectual games were tantamount to emotional cruelty. I myself had no firm convictions one way or the other with regard to the subject of their conversation, but I found her sneering at the woman's seriousness distasteful. However, I did not dare to say so.

After the landlady left us there was a kind of tension in the atmosphere, which found its release in pointless giggles. As if we had been waiting for the moment of her departure in order to burst out laughing. Then we both fell silent at once, as if ashamed of our foolishness. This gave rise to a kind of intimacy, and for the first time we spoke to each other frankly. Not, to be sure, the way I had spoken to Hella Becker. On my first night in the country I had told her everything a man can tell about himself. And within two weeks we were addressing each other with the familiar *du*. My conversation with Eva was about things that you can talk about to anyone. I did not tell her details about my life. And she told me even less. And nevertheless, I have never felt so close to a strange woman in my life.

The hot tea had not been such a good idea. The air was warm and humid and we could not take the instruments in our sweating hands. We went out onto the balcony to cool down in the breeze.

We stood there awhile in silence, as if we had already used up our daily quota of speech. In the yard children were playing next to the garbage bins. A wretched-looking cur ran barking at their heels. On the opposite balcony ugly washing was fluttering in the breeze. A corset that looked like an instrument of torture, and a gigantic pair of grubby underpants. In the apartment behind the balcony a radio was screeching away at full blast.

The outside world, too, did not smile upon us. Even the sea, usually a soothing sight, glared at us from between two rows of white buildings like a blazing sheet of copper.

Suddenly Eva looked at me and spoke in the deep, husky voice of a woman in love.

"Have you ever seen the Steinbach?"

I must have looked at her in astonishment, for she immediately saw the need to elaborate:

"Steinbach on the Attersee."

I had been there. I remembered, too, something I had read somewhere: Mahler had taken a house there next to the lake. When Bruno Walter came to visit him and looked up, entranced, at the mountains, Mahler said to him: "Don't trouble—I've already composed all that."

I couldn't understand the connection. Our eyes were fixed on a bit of yellow sky and a strip of rust-colored sea—what did they have to do with a landscape of snowy mountains and a clear blue lake?

I didn't have to wait long for the explanation.

"I can't do without . . ."

Her face was pale and her lips clamped shut in pain.

"I'm suffocating here," she said after a moment.

After this there was a long, embarrassing silence. I felt that I had to say something but I could find nothing comforting to say. Hesitantly I suggested that we begin playing. There was not much time left, and the work was not an easy one. But she did not move from her place. "Everything here is against me— the climate, the landscape, the people . . . sometimes I feel that I'm suffocating. How long can I live like this?"

I made the most fatuous reply possible under the circumstances: You'll get used to it. Perhaps no better reply exists. And then, in spite of everything, a consoling idea came into my head too: We should be glad that we're not over there, in Germany. She agreed with a nod of her head.

"Perhaps there'll be a war," I added.

"If I didn't have music, I don't know how—"

I didn't let her finish the sentence. I spread my fingers over her long fingers clutching the top of the rail.

The first touch. It's hard to describe the sensation that ran through me. I felt like someone who has performed a deed demanding extraordinary courage. Not the slightest tremor ran through her fingers—neither of response nor rejection. They lay under my hand as if paralyzed.

"Music is a climate of its own," I said, to blur the harsh impression of her words. "It's the motherland of the stateless." I quoted Egon, without mentioning the source. And I added a rider of my own: "Today almost all the greatest musicians in the world are stateless."

"There's nothing for it. We have to play," she said and pulled her fingers from under my hand with a slippery, snakelike movement. The cold of the iron bar on my palm was like a consoling compensation for the coolness of the fingers which had separated us. She went inside and I followed her. "We're wasting precious time." She made an effort to smile. "It may be only a short performance for workers," she said, "but who knows? Huberman may be right. In this crazy country perhaps there may be someone who knows a Schönberg score by heart among the blacksmiths and the shoemakers."

But the moment she raised the viola to her shoulder she asked abruptly: "Are we great?" Before I could understand what she was getting at, she elucidated: "I am not apparently among the great musicians who can survive without a motherland."

I almost blurted out: "Are you fishing for compliments?" But I guessed that it would upset her. She was speaking to me like a friend, and I responded with superficial clichés. I held my tongue. I tuned the violin strings. I played a long A for her to tune hers by. "Perhaps I should start playing on steel strings," she said impatiently when her strings went limp one after the other. "Gut strings are no good in this bloody climate."

But even after the strings were tuned we didn't play. With the viola on her shoulder and the bow in her right hand like a tilted spear, she began talking again: "And maybe there won't be a war. Why should they fight when they get whatever they want without fighting? Hitler's mad, but he's not stupid.

Maybe he thinks like Bismarck: The whole of the Balkans isn't worth the broken bones of a single Pomeranian grenadier."

And then, after concluding the longest political declaration I had ever heard her make in her life, she touched the bow to the strings.

In the second variation I came in late.

"What's the matter with you today?" she asked in concern. "You're not concentrating."

It's the burn of your cold fingers on my palm, I wanted to say to her.

"I received a letter from home," I said. An excuse that had just come into my head. But once said, it immediately stopped being an excuse. I really had received a letter from home, full of obscure hints which I had not succeeded in deciphering. What were the "exams" that Anna had not succeeded in taking? What certificates was Greta unable to bring?

"Has something happened?" she asked without removing the bow from the strings, as a hint that there was no need for a long reply. We had already had tea and talked, and there was no more time to waste. This offended me: when something was troubling her, she was at liberty to take twenty minutes off the rehearsal time, but I had to be content with a telegraphic reply.

"There are hints that I don't understand in it. My wife thinks that someone opens all her letters."

"Show me," she offered. "Women understand other women's hints," and she drew the bow over G and C to hurry me up.

I immediately decided to take up her suggestion and show the letter to Hella Becker. It would be more suitable to expose my wife's troubles in faraway Berlin to a true friend than to a woman with whom I committed adultery in my dreams. My anger, too, I sensed, indicated a dangerous degree of intimacy.

"From letter A allegro. Spiccato perhaps a little more pointed." I assumed the initiative.

She looked at me slyly as if she understood the reason for

my impatience, and wanting to appease me immediately, she assumed a spiccato as pointed as mine. On the spot she entered the spirit of the passage as I understood it, and for a moment I felt like a man coming home after a hard day's work and finding a loving wife who guessed his every wish.

I was not surprised when she began addressing me, unthinking, in the familiar *du*, even though she had not asked my permission. She said to me, before the echo of the final chord in D minor had died away, as if what she had to say were born of that chord: "This may sound strange to you, but there is nothing more important to me today than the quartet."

She spoke without emotion, but decisively, as if she were making some kind of declaration after a lengthy inner debate. From the intent look in her eyes, I understood that her words contained a hint: it's important to you too, the quartet, so we'd better not lose our heads.

She read me like an open book. She sensed the turmoil inside me and felt the need to warn me. If we let ourselves go, we would endanger the quartet. The Rosendorf Quartet would not be the same without Eva.

The barrier being demolished before my eyes had to be reerected.

"It doesn't sound strange to me at all," I replied. "I feel the same as you do," I said, resuming the formal *sie*. "For me too, there is nothing more important than the quartet. The orchestra is for bread and butter and the quartet is for the soul."

"You have a family, too," she said, stating a fact.

Litovsky is obscene as usual. Sometimes I wonder: a man who plays with such balanced feeling, so steeped in a rich musical culture—and yet, on certain subjects, he expresses himself with the crudity of a cart driver.

He's spreading malicious gossip about Eva. Facts, according to him, straight from the horse's mouth.

There's a certain young man, a simple fellow, a construction worker, who sometimes hangs around the place. The fact that he's in love with Eva seems obvious. He sits outside listening to the music, and when we come out he trails behind us for a while without daring to approach. According to Litovsky, somebody told me, he actually had an affair with her. I can't really believe it. A girl who's so careful to keep her distance—what could she possibly find in a fellow like him?

Bernard is attracted to low life. But since he's busy most of the time making music, he finds it in his imagination. And one way of fantasizing fornication with a woman you don't dare speak to is to imagine her in the arms of a passionate lover. All this had an unhealthy effect on me, too.

This morning I found myself stimulated to the point where I lost my self-control. Half unconsciously, my hand reached out, as if of its own accord, to the girl Ruth's head, in a kind of caress which might have been interpreted as an expression of affection and appreciation for a rare musical moment—but she stopped playing and abandoned herself to the caress. Her face was very pale and her eyes blazed. I quickly took my hand away, but the harm was already done. Another barrier had been breached.

When we are removed from our natural environment, moral standards collapse.

In the nineteenth century a girl of her age would have been raising her offspring. But we're in the twentieth century.

The inevitable has happened.

We can't deny our natures. At the beginning I tried to believe that I was only being kind, but the strength of my feelings can no longer be denied. Painfully and greedily I reconstruct every moment of passion, as if it contained some hidden message which I failed to decipher, and salvation depends on remembering every detail in the right sequence.

And there's another sign too: the acute pain it causes me whenever I reflect that the things I once never even dared to imagine, she did with that Russian pauper before me. He's very good-looking, and his stubbornness knows no bounds. He stares at her with eyes which seem to be remembering something, and the thought of it fills me with such terrible pain that I can't take her in my arms without seeing him in front of my eyes.

But I won't ask. And not only out of politeness.

She still hasn't allowed me to look into her soul. She hasn't even told me her life history, which I heard from Egon, who gathered the details crumb by crumb from different sources.

And the dread of waking one morning and finding her gone.

"We must behave as if we've got all our lives in front of us, and as if tomorrow may rob us of our happiness," I said to her.

She looked at me as if I was exaggerating the importance of a relationship which would give her pleasure only to the extent that it did not disturb her peace of mind. She hinted that there was nothing she hated as much as hysteria.

Greta, with the irony which is her substitute for reproach, used to say: "Since you're incapable of superficial relationships, you fall in love with any woman who succeeds in getting you into her bed."

I can no longer doubt that I love this woman, who is incomprehensible to me. People apparently need more than one attachment to the opposite sex. I assuage my conscience with the thought that it detracts nothing from Greta. But I know that this is a lie. Greta behaves as if sex doesn't matter, and seems to think that she should be respected for it. Eva seems not to care if she is respected or not, but the bolder she is the more my respect for her grows. And once I thought that such freedom was a license permissible only between strangers. At the age of thirty-eight, it appears that I am still a boy learning his first lesson in love.

It hurts me to have to hide my love even from her. She prefers temporary affairs. She doesn't want me to "make a big thing of it." Whenever my heart overflows and I let myself go she calls me to order: I have a wife and child and I am responsible for their welfare. As if to say: As soon as things are normal again, and the world recovers from its insanity, you and I won't be able to be more than violin and viola to each other.

The ways of fate are mysterious indeed. I, who have always detested underground operations, and criticized my brother for running after the glamour attached to the life of an underground operator, am now living, because of a simple feeling of love, which seems to me the most natural thing in the world, in an underground within an underground.

We have to hide from our friends the fact that we meet not in order to play duets. And I have to hide how much I love her. I can't even say to her: In the depths of my heart I know that a love which has no future has no present either. In my letters to Berlin there will be empty lines, full of lies.

I fear for the fate of the Rosendorf Quartet.

Second Violin–
Konrad Friedman

FIFTH OF IYAR, 5696

It's four years since I last opened my diary. A long time in the life of a twenty-seven-year-old man. I believed then that I had outgrown such childish nonsense. But now I once more feel the need to write down my thoughts and feelings. A pressing need. Almost obsessive. All kinds of different people keep diaries, among them active, not particularly introspective people, who think that every detail of their lives belongs to history and do not wish to leave their biographers any room for guesswork. Others do so because they imagine they possess literary gifts. In their diaries they practice their writing skills and perhaps note down outlines of stories as well. And some people write diaries in order for others—a girl they love, their parents—to find them and read what they have written and know what hurts them.

I don't fall into any of these categories. What I do isn't history. I'll never have a biographer. Nor do I possess any literary talent. And Dora will never find my diary, because she doesn't even know where I live. And she doesn't have to peek into my diary to know what I feel. If I want her to know what she doesn't yet know, I'll have to pull myself together and write her a letter.

I write in order to sort out my thoughts. Sometimes they come in such a torrent that I feel helpless and confused. Writing is a way of calming myself. It slows me down and forces me to formulate things clearly and convincingly.

The truth is that whenever some change occurred in my life, I took out my diary. At the age of ten, when I decided to convert to Christianity, I wrote in it for six months. Perhaps in the belief that Jesus crept into my room at night and read how much I loved him. I stopped when I began to have doubts. When I decided to be a Jew, I went back to it. The declarations of faith in Judaism I wrote down then were shown by my father to all his friends, with tremendous pride. I was so ashamed that I burned everything. In the Hochschule für die Wissenchaft des Judentums, I jotted down notes for articles which were never written. At the age of sixteen, when I decided to become a Zionist, I wrote down a personal "creed" to test myself by in the years to come. In Eretz Israel I could return to those pages and congratulate myself. In Ben-Shemen I kept a diary for nearly six months. My charges had a greater influence on me than I had on them. In their world keeping a diary was the kind of sentimentality that suited a music teacher but not a cowhand. The kinds of things that engaged my passions, too, needed a talent greater than mine to be put into words. It was easier to quote Rilke. He wrote what I felt more beautifully, but also more indirectly and truthfully. Without hysteria.

This time I feel the need for some kind of reckoning. I have been in the orchestra for a few months now and the time has come to ask myself where I stand.

I won't deny that my present mood plays a certain part too. The room where I live is sad and empty. Apart from the violin, music stand, and a few books, it contains nothing but a bed and a table. Not even a chair. And all you can see from the window is garbage bins, a fence, and the wall of the house next door. Nobody comes to visit me. I haven't got a single friend here. The members of the orchestra aren't my friends. We live in different worlds. They are baffled by the things I say. If I told them all my thoughts they would probably think that I was insane or putting on an act. Perhaps it's a good thing that I have to stop now and hurry to the orchestra. The buses are infrequent here. A regular daily schedule that you are obliged to keep is sometimes a lifeline to people like me. But perhaps I should stop using expressions like "people like me." I myself don't know what kind of person I am.

Before I run off: I'm looking forward to the day when I can keep a diary in Hebrew.

In Hebrew I write slowly. Perhaps I'll write fewer superfluous things.

THE NEXT DAY

Playing the violin was always a sideline as far as I was concerned, even though my teachers advised me to abandon everything else and devote myself to music. I often "used" the violin in order to transfer from one field to another. When I left the Hochschule to study music, nobody objected. If I had told my teachers what I really thought and spoke of the irreconcilable contradiction between nationality and religion in which they were living, they would have been angry with me. This way we parted on good terms. My father, too, would never have been able to understand my disdain for the degree I had obtained only to please him, if I had not told him that music was my whole life. In this way I could hide from him my preparations for immigrating to Eretz Israel, which I knew would hurt him very much.

When I arrived in the country, in 1932, a resolute young man of twenty-two, who had spurned a doctoral degree in order to realize his ideals, I was prepared to bundle up all my possessions—a few books and quite a good violin—and pawn them for a sturdy pair of working boots. I wanted to "sacrifice myself on the altar of national redemption" and burn my violin as firewood. The thought of sacrifice filled my heart with exalted feelings.

The only people I knew here chose a less heroic path for me. They found me work in Ben-Shemen. I was told that it was a boarding school that trained orphaned children to be agricultural workers, and I liked the idea. They hired me to give singing and recorder lessons, but I insisted on working in the cowshed as well. This improved my status with the children, although that was not the reason I went to work there. I really and truly wanted to be a Zionist pioneer. And the more the work in the cowshed bored me, the more I punished myself by taking on the hardest and most unpleasant jobs. Although I liked the company of the big, silent beasts, and even stayed awake at night studying cattle rearing, the physical work in itself gave me no real satisfaction.

I could not give up the violin. This, for some reason, distressed me greatly. As if I had failed to pass some test.

And then I set up the Jerusalem trio with Mrs. Feingold and Mr. Silverman, which kept going until the outbreak of the disturbances. Not a bad trio at all, by local standards, especially if you take into account the fact that I could only devote one day and two nights a week to it. We gave a few concerts too, and we were so pleased with ourselves that we even had the nerve to play for Huberman.

To my great surprise, I discovered that the work in the cowshed had not damaged my technique. My fingers had not grown stiff from the milking and I soon regained my old proficiency. The temporary break had even had a beneficial influence. I had achieved a certain inner clarity and had matured musically. Just as hunger increases the appetite and gives us back our taste for plain food, so the abstinence from music, and the attempt to renounce it, had given me back my taste for its elementary principles. I rediscovered the charms of unpretentious lyricism. I learned to appreciate the value of the silence closing a phrase which had raised a question without answering it. Perhaps recent deeply felt personal experiences had something to do with it, too. Music was once more revealed to me as a human experience embracing a wide range of feelings. The fact that for a while I had questioned the very right of music to exist and had found in the panting, tail-slapping, and excretory salvos of the cows that give us milk moral values more exalted than those in Bach's *Magnificat* forced me to discover in my soul a more serious attachment to the world of the spirit contained in music.

This reconciliation brought me great satisfaction. For a while I was content with this compromise between art and life. Ben-Shemen was a place where I could find happiness. I could devote myself to one thing which I do with reasonable competence, and to another whose importance I recognize. More than that, I did not need. And one day, perhaps, I would have a family too. To my father I wrote: I have found my place. And myself. He replied: "If that is really so, I am happy in your happiness . . ."

When Huberman invited me to join the symphony orchestra I did not give him an immediate reply, which was quite nervy on my part. People were standing in line to take difficult auditions—and I needed time to think about it. At first I told him that I did not consider myself worthy. He smiled. He said that he had heard me in Jerusalem. And then: I'm not offering you the role of concertmaster. Nothing grander than second violin. Do you consider yourself good enough for that?

I suspected that he had chosen me for nonmusical reasons. Apparently he wanted someone familiar with local conditions in the orchestra. He was well aware of the kind of relations liable to develop in a group of people when none of them knew where they were. And my suspicion grew stronger when I told him the real reasons for my doubts and hesitations.

"It's people like you we need," he said with true sympathy, even respect, without a trace of irony.

And then he added: "We all play our part toward realizing the great common goal with our own instruments."

His intention was obvious: our instrument was the violin. Our—a good joke.

In spite of everything, I accepted. For a month I practiced

scales and exercises like a madman to get rid of any signs of rustiness. But after playing in the orchestra for a few weeks, I began to have doubts again. I couldn't really see myself deriving spiritual satisfaction from the life of a professional musician, a man who eats and plays and sleeps, and the only thing that bothers him is that a thirty-second solo didn't come out as well as he could have wished. I couldn't see myself growing old in the orchestra, competing for promotion from stand to stand, accumulating pension rights, and fighting against bringing new musicians to the country before they raised my salary. Even in the days of general exaltation, when Toscanini was presented with the keys to the city of Tel Aviv and a citrus orchard in Ramoth-Hashavim, and had a tree planted in his honor in a Jewish National Fund forest, I remained unmoved. It was all well and good, and the need for an orchestra was acknowledged even by practical men of affairs, but as far as I was concerned, the orchestra was no substitute for the living bond with the land, with labor, with the pioneers. But whom could I say this to?

Dora was in Ben-Shemen and I was in Tel Aviv. And—hand on my heart—hadn't I accepted Huberman's offer because I couldn't bear the situation any longer? We were so close and yet so far.

What is the goal which Huberman and I, to be ironic, serve with our instruments, he with his Stradivarius and I with my god-knows-what?

I think of Zionism. Huberman's goals are more grandiose, but also more insubstantial. I agree that we need the connection with Europe. Without it we would be in danger of Levantinism. That's true enough. I don't believe in the idea of a historic mission for the Jews in Europe. That story is finished.

But I lost my right to preach my ideas to others the moment I agreed to play in the orchestra. Play, violinist—and hold your tongue. I would sound ridiculous talking about pioneering in a tuxedo.

I know all the soothing formulas: if music is the purest form of human consciousness, as Schopenhauer says, then it is essential in the consolidation of a national consciousness, too. Which doesn't help much. What music: Schubert's? Mendelssohn's, because he was a baptized Jew? Or the music that will be created here, with us as the physical foundation on which it will be built?

Perhaps I should not have run away from Dora to a place that is too far from myself. The last sentence came out rather clumsily, but it's very clear to me.

SECOND OF NISSAN, 5697

The day before yesterday Dr. Manfred passed away.

I went to Ben-Shemen to be with Dora in her grief. I won't pretend it took any great heroism to do so, since the roads aren't really dangerous now. There's a certain lull in the disturbances, and there are police escorts for public transport.

But it certainly took courage on my part to go back there and see her.

I left Ben-Shemen suddenly, without saying goodbye to her properly. I was afraid of too emotional a parting. On my part, not hers. And I was afraid of seeing that the parting did not grieve her at all. Perhaps she would even breathe a sigh of relief.

Afterward we didn't correspond. Only once she wrote me a postcard and asked me to send her some music. I sent her what she asked for without a letter. She sent me money, which was insulting in itself, and asked me why I hadn't written a few words. Had she given me any cause to be angry with her? I sent her a letter of apology: I had no reason to be angry with her and I was sorry for behaving so childishly. She understood that there was no point in replying to my letter. If she had asked me to come back, I would have dropped everything and gone to her, and she knew it.

Now I was glad that she did not see my sudden visit as

interference in her affairs. She even respected my need to condole with her, although we did not speak about Dr. Manfred at all. We preferred to say nothing and play. Sonatas for violin and pianoforte gave us the perfect opportunity to be silent together about everything which grieved her and me. Two different things.

This is the place to call a spade a spade.

I went to Ben-Shemen because I had no friends anywhere else. The offer to teach there seemed to me as good as anything else. Once I arrived there, I had a very good reason to stay.

In the cowshed, where every morning the sad-eyed beasts contemplated the tempest of emotion buffeting me from bales of hay to sewage canals with stoic calm, I knew not only the happiness of the righteous, who say little and do much, but also the one, great, true love, which drives a man's soul to frenzy and restores it to tranquility at the same time. Perhaps I would not have experienced the oscillation between hope and despair at such a pitch of emotional intensity if the two things had not been linked together—my pride at the revolution I had carried out in my life and my love for Dora Wolf. Linked? That's not the right word. They were one and the same thing.

Like a somnambulist, demented with love and dread, I went out every night at the third watch to milk the cows, after not having slept enough during the day. The certainty of meeting her at the same time, in the same place, that she would never be late or absent, filled me with such wild joy that all the boring jobs I did in that miserable cowshed, before I learned to milk and was promoted to a higher status, were sacred to me. I always arrived before her, I was strangely wakeful, and for hours before milking time I could not sleep. Impatiently I lay on my bed waiting for the sound of the alarm clock going off in her room, which was situated at the end of the corridor in the building where I lived. I cannot remember any sounds which agitated me more profoundly than the monotonous shriek of that metallic mechanism cleaving the silence of the night. And like it, the echo of her heavy boots on the concrete path leading to the cowshed. The moment her figure appeared in the illuminated doorway, in the khaki clothes which were too big for her, her heavy braid falling down her back and her sleepy eyes smiling at me, I had to take a series of deep breaths in order not to faint. For an entire year I loved her like this, from so close and yet so far, silently, with profound reverence, in secret joy and quiet despair. I did not dare reveal my love to her. I was afraid of being a nuisance. I feared that if she knew how wretched I would be if she turned me down, we wouldn't be able to go on spending so much time together—in the cowshed, the musical appreciation lessons, the staff meetings, and in making music together, which at first had been something to do in our spare time but had developed into public "performances." After my health deteriorated, and the directors of the institution put it down to hard work and restricted me to easy jobs in the garden, the sonatas for violin and pianoforte of the Romantic composers became the only means by which I could express my feelings.

Once I wrote a poem in which I said, in a language that avoided flowery phrases but was still very lofty, that it was the sound of the chains rising from the dark cowshed when the cows shook their heavy heads that unsheathed the sun. There was another line there that compared this noise to the singing of the angels. Dora, who found the poem lying on my table and snatched it up—a breath-stopping moment of frivolity which sent my hopes soaring—read it with an encouraging smile, put it down, and said: "That's the most Zionist poem I've ever read in my life." From her lips this was not a criticism but a generous compliment. Nevertheless my spirits fell. She had not understood that she was reading a love poem.

I was probably the last person to realize that she was in love with Dr. Manfred, an educational consultant from the Jewish Agency, who used to come down from Jerusalem and spend a few days at the youth village. Apparently he was in love with her too, but, loyal to his role as a husband and educator, he did not permit himself to consummate their love, which was obliged to restrict itself to a common enthusiasm for the poetry of Stefan George (I wonder how they avoided discovering the elements in his poetry which were in obvious contradiction to their weltanschauung) and a common circle of friends from their hometown, Würtzburg.

The Jerusalem trio, dismantled because of the disturbances, was my sad revenge. The orchestra was the best solution for the heartbreak which laid me low after my behavior— unpredictable reactions of anger or pity for no evident reason—could no longer hide the love I had managed to conceal for so long.

To conceal? Dora understood my agitation only too well; she only pretended not to see anything. She likes me. And perhaps even more than that. But there is no love in her heart for me. Once she wounded me with an insulting cliché: she felt a special closeness toward me—"like a brother and sister." This amounted, more or less, to a rejection. Dr. Manfred took up all the space reserved in her heart for love.

My condolence visit, which passed in total silence—Dr. Manfred's name was not mentioned once—smacked of more than a little hypocrisy. In my heart I knew that I had come to her, full of an insane joy, to take the place left empty by his departure. Her eagerness to play sonatas with me was a kind of declaration that she did not want me to sacrifice my music for her sake. Not because she thought my talent so exceptional that the world would lose a great violinist if I came to live with her in the village, but because she did not love me enough to accept any sacrifice at all. If I renounced the violin in order to become a pioneer, she would have welcomed me gladly to the pioneering camp. And perhaps, in the course of time, she would even have found that nobody suited her better than I did. But she did not want me to change my life for her sake. Her conscience would not be able to bear the complaints of a pseudopioneer, lamenting his lost talents in order to force her to love him forever.

It was with mixed feelings that I went to play with her. I wanted to talk, never mind about what. I wasn't sure that we would be able to play properly, that the inner tension wouldn't leave its marks on our playing. We hadn't played together for ages, and we no longer had the coordination we had possessed when we played together every day. I was glad when an audience turned up. They forced us to extract the maximum from ourselves. And the fact that so many of them came to listen proves that I did not waste my time at Ben-Shemen. The musical education I had given them had borne fruit. When I wrote and told my father that I was giving singing and recorder lessons, he asked if it wasn't a waste for a violinist like me who had studied under the best teachers— didn't I have anything better to do than teach singing and recorder? I replied that I was doing holy work: boys who grew up without music would have poor and empty lives. He replied with characteristic irony that the words "holy work" should be reserved for more serious matters.

I played emotionally; she, with utter calm. I envied her. She was such a paragon of virtue that she had even renounced pride. In my heart of hearts I wanted to be admired for being ready to give up the violin, while she neglected the piano with perfect equanimity. I felt martyred; she felt exultant. We played a Mozart sonata and then a Beethoven sonata. In the intermission I suddenly saw none other than Kurt Rosendorf sitting among our audience. I was covered with confusion. My hands actually shook. But afterward it turned out that my fears were groundless. Rosendorf is capable of judging the quality of a violinist even at his worst moments. Or perhaps it was precisely my inner emotion that impressed him.

THAT NIGHT, AFTER THE CONCERT

I should have begun here, but my feelings were in such a state of confusion after the bus ride from Ben-Shemen to Tel Aviv with Rosendorf that I couldn't formulate my thoughts. I didn't know how seriously he meant his offer. He spoke with a rather amused expression on his face, like an adult entering into conversation with a child. But after we met in the musicians' room and he asked me if I had considered his proposal, I realized that he was perfectly serious.

He asked me if I would like to play in a quartet that he wanted to set up. Naturally, my first reaction was a polite "I'm greatly honored." But then I couldn't restrain myself and told him that I had not yet made up my mind whether to be a professional musician. Actually, I was delighted that he had approached me. There are at least twenty violinists better than me in the orchestra. And in my gratitude, I shared my doubts with him.

I was absurd. There was a hollow note in what I said. It's obvious, after all, that I've already chosen a musical career. And the moment he stretches out his hand to raise me from mediocrity, I have to begin holding forth about my noble ideals.

I think he was laughing at me. "Well, if you decide before the end of the month, let me know. It won't be too late. I'll keep a place for you."

What idiocy—hinting to Rosendorf that there are more important things in life than music! As if he doesn't know . . . And what, exactly, do I propose that musicians should do? Go and shovel manure as a response to the collapse of Western civilization? Go back to Germany and organize an armed underground? What do we know how to do except make music? He, at least, knows how to do it well. I still have to prove that it's legitimate for me to demand money in exchange for the pleasure I give my listeners.

I did something even more idiotic. I spoke about Dora. I felt an overwhelming need to mention her name. I said that I respected her ability to prefer an educational ideal to music for its own sake. He was not in the least impressed. The loss was not so great, he hinted—she played like a pupil who had been taught to read a score and that was all.

Why did I have to feel hurt? Does the whole world have to fall in love with the woman I love? Isn't it enough that she drives me crazy?

I dreamed that I saw them walking arm in arm and laughing. I've already paired them off in my imagination! Poetic justice. They're both so good-looking, and the same height too, and I'm short and ugly. She deserves something more aesthetic than a monster with a big, frightening head.

THIRD OF AV, 5697

I'm learning to burn my bridges. The quartet helps me to cut off the strong, delicate threads that tie me to Dora.

For a while I found in Rosendorf the reassuring patronage I lacked for so long. I used to have inspiring heart-to-hearts with Dr. Lehman, who took a liking to me, and also with Dr. Manfred—until I discovered that Dora was in love with him. But they were father substitutes, and all I need is an elder brother, whose very existence gives one a sense of security. Rosendorf fits the bill. I am in close, daily contact with him— three rehearsals a week and chance meetings backstage. We hardly say anything to each other, and nevertheless I can sense his affection for me like a kind of comfortable garment protecting me and keeping me warm.

Perhaps it's strange for me to compare him to Dr. Lehman and Dr. Manfred—both extremely articulate people. Rosendorf is a man of few words. Long conversations bore him. Even in discussions about interpretation he contents himself with a hint; he never expounds his views or quotes authorities to back himself up. Heart-to-heart conversations are altogether out of the question. He's shut up in his shell and all that comes out of it is music. He would never behave like Dr.

Lehman, who told me about himself so that I would not be shy to talk about myself.

There's only one man he apparently opens up to. This is the writer Egon Loewenthal, a man I respect and admire. Sometimes I envy him a little and feel angry with Rosendorf, who tells him his secrets because he's a great writer. If Rosendorf was a more open person, he would talk about himself to me too. Even if I've never written a book, I still have something to say.

I see Rosendorf in the light of a spiritual mentor, even though I can't remember him saying a single inspiring sentence to me. Nor can I say that there is any agreement between us about priorities or important issues. Sometimes I sense a certain cynicism in him whose source is unknown to me. In most cases we disagree about politics—in any event, as far as the Jewish question is concerned he astonishes me with his shameful ignorance of the history and sociology of the Jewish people, and even more by his arrogance in taking a stand on issues that demand a minimum of knowledge at least. I suspect that he does not even feel the need to go into these things more deeply, just as he feels no need to study the spiritual sources of Nazism. His skepticism is distasteful to me, and his hostile attitude to Freud, who opened a window into the depths of the human soul, will certainly not bring us any closer. But nevertheless, I feel a wonderful peace of mind in his company, as if it has suddenly become clear to me that all my doubts and conflicts are groundless, and that music is capable of filling our lives with a rich content. One musical phrase can express more than a thousand words.

I admire his natural aristocracy, his seriousness, his generosity, and his humility with regard to great works of music. There's nothing exhibitionistic about his playing, and you never see him pulling suffering faces like our cellist when we play Beethoven's late quartets. By generosity I am referring not only to his willingness to play almost soundlessly when the theme is taken up by the second violin, and other such subtleties of ensemble playing, but also to things which are absolutely prosaic. I cannot but praise the scrupulous equality with which he shares the expenses and the earnings of the quartet which bears his name, because it is only his name which has the power to draw an audience. And that's not all. When he found out that I was saving money to bring my father (who still refuses to come) to the country, he offered me a chance to replace him at a musical evening where he had been invited to play, although he himself needs the money. This ability to part easily with money is a virtue acquired by the third generation of wealthy families. I wonder if his father, who inherited a flourishing paper factory in Frankfurt but remembered the atmosphere of anxiety about money in his parents' home, was as generous. It's only the third generation of affluence, it seems to me, that breeds the natural aristocracy of those who have never lacked for anything in their lives. Rosendorf's extravagance, giving away strings worth a fifth of the salary of a rank-and-file member of the orchestra, comes to him so easily that I suspect he would never be able to put himself in the shoes of a man who has to think twice before spending a penny. He gave Egon Loewenthal an interest-free "loan" which he will never be able to return, while he himself went to live in a house without any privacy so that he can save to bring his wife and daughter here. As soon as he saw that his friend was in trouble—Loewenthal has no steady income, and whenever he quarrels with his woman friend and slams the door behind him, he has nowhere to go—he forgot that his family had lost all their money. That's how he behaves—as if he didn't have a worry in the world, taking it for granted that whatever he needs will fall into his lap, even though the family factory was sold to the Germans for next to nothing, and even that was confiscated when it came out that his elder brother, who managed the business after his father died, is an active Communist.

I know that the admiration I feel for Rosendorf does not yet entitle me to call him my friend. Rosendorf is not a man who bares his soul to others. He is so discreet that he appears to shun overly intimate friendships. "Shun" seems too strong a word—his eyes lack the coldness of those wishing to keep unwelcome guests at arm's length. They signal not rejection, but the wish to be left alone—he is too sensitive, and rubbing shoulders with less fastidious souls causes him suffering.

I don't enjoy any special privileges with him. A fatherly twinkle comes into his eyes when I speak to him, but I can't say that he treats me more intimately than any of the others. Perhaps it's a question of principle, and perhaps it's the generation gap. In all the time we've been playing together I haven't heard him so much as hint at the family problems weighing on his heart. I only visited him at home once—not because I was invited but to give him an urgent message—and he made me welcome, even though he was in the middle of giving a lesson.

When he shared a moral dilemma with me for the first time, I was grateful to him. The girl he gives lessons to is the daughter of his landlords. He teaches her in return for his rent, an arrangement which enables him to save a certain sum. But because of her, he is not free to take a more talented pupil. He has time for no more than five pupils. The moral problem arose when he reached the conclusion that the girl was not particularly gifted. He doesn't dare tell her parents, and blames himself for wasting his time on someone who doesn't deserve it in order to save a bit of money.

I respected him for his scruples. And I respected him even more when I discovered that two of his pupils don't pay him anything at all—one of them because he is a cripple, and the other because his mother is a widow and can't even afford to buy strings.

It seems to me, however, that his conscience should be bothering him on a slightly different score.

I listened to the lesson. The girl is not as talentless as he thinks: she has a very good ear, and if she practices a lot she'll be able to play not badly. Most of the mistakes she made stemmed from a different cause. Rosendorf is so far above such things that he can't see that the girl is simply in love with him. She keeps her arms defensively close to her body, and therefore holds the violin incorrectly. Her right arm is not free to attain the proper fluency in bowing. All her attention is somewhere else: on his soft voice, his delicate touch on her elbows, the wonderful tones he draws from his instrument.

Anyone who has known true love recognizes it wherever it is, even when it is not yet known to the one who feels it. This is the only advantage I can find in the misery of unrequited love—it sharpens our vision and enables us to see into the souls of others.

I wonder if Rosendorf has ever known disappointment. Life—until Hitler appeared on the scene—has treated him well. His gifts were recognized at an early stage, and the best teachers devoted themselves to his education. Nature blessed him with noble, finely expressive features and a spiritual beauty to match the sublime tones he draws from his violin, as if, intoxicated by her own creative powers, she had decided to produce this one paragon of perfection. And she did not forget to grant him wisdom, charity, and mercy, too.

People like him sometimes lack the ability to love. They have nothing but pity in their hearts for creatures less perfect than they are. It's hard for them to feel the self-abnegation that people like me, who are only too well aware of their own weaknesses and limitations, know so well. Constantly surrounded by admirers, they find it difficult to distinguish between love, admiration, and respect. Showered with all the above in abundance, their overburdened arms are liable to lose the most precious gift of all, like a rich man unwilling to accept a present which would have made a poor man very happy, because he no longer has anywhere to put it.

People who have known him since he was a youth don't remember any passionate love affairs. At an early age he married a woman with whom he was compatible from every point of view. She is apparently a woman as gifted and as even-tempered as he is. Like him she knew how to find the golden mean between a musical career and family life. They never allowed the tension created by competition for recognition and prestige to cross their threshold. They have a daughter who inherited both her parents' musical gifts and emotional stability. At the age of twelve she came first in a talent competition for promising young musicians, and a brilliant future is predicted for her. The separation imposed on them by circumstances is accepted by all three as a necessity which must be faced in the right spirit. When a man's wealth and happiness are to be found in his own merits and virtues, his peace of mind cannot be disrupted by an enforced separation from his loved ones. He misses them, of course, but is glad that they are in a place where they can fulfill their ambitions. A soloist who travels from place to place is often away from home too. And Rosendorf, alone in Tel Aviv, behaves with praiseworthy modesty. All the music-loving society ladies, who are trying so hard to lead the kind of life here that was suited to the merry Berlin of the twenties, have been forced to give up their plans to console him in their arms. Eva Staubenfeld, who sometimes likes to show off her cynicism, once said that Rosendorf rejects all the honey held right under his nose simply because he is too much in love with himself to have any room left for feelings for others . . .

I don't like gossip. My interest in Rosendorf's emotional life does not stem from idle curiosity. It is a real need to understand a unique personality, which is sometimes beyond my comprehension. This need springs from my acknowledgment of the necessity of getting to know the members of the quartet as closely as possible. I can't forget the amused look Bernard Litovsky gave me when I once expressed this opinion. "Forget it, my friend," he said. "At your age you should get rid of such illusions. People who play chamber music together don't present each other with the keys to their souls. At most they're prepared to compromise on the tempo, volume, phrasing, and character of the passage they're playing. If they're very professional players, they can unify the technical details too."

There's no doubt that the facts of life confirm Litovsky's words. And if a lot of musicians I've known had given me the key to their souls, I would have found nothing there but a moldy stock of prejudices, superstitions, and banalities. But this does nothing to diminish the intensity of my desire for the kind of spiritual union that applies to every facet of life, at least with Rosendorf. I can't say that the encounter with Litovsky gave rise to the same passionate curiosity. In the course of time I shall no doubt learn a thing or two about him that I don't know now, but for the moment he is one of the people whose masks I am afraid of removing in case I discover nothing behind them. And the same goes for Eva von Staubenfeld, whom I shall never succeed in understanding. Perhaps because I'm not the kind of man she's interested in. I would be afraid to remove her mask too, in case I found something which would make me very sorry—pure, unalloyed egoism. This does not mean that I dislike Litovsky or Fräulein Staubenfeld. I'm very fond of Bernard. His sense of humor is definitely necessary to our quartet. Even the superficiality with which he discusses political subjects no longer annoys me as it used to. He, at least, understands that complete passivity in times like these is inhuman. I can't say I'm fond of Fräulein Staubenfeld. You can be fond of a pet cat, but not a panther. A panther you can either love or hate. I must say that I find the way she looks at me infuriating—as if I were some object that knows how to play the violin and that's all. But I don't despise her or underrate her. I admire her tremendous competence. I myself would never be able to match her ability to return to the right tempo after we've allowed ourselves to slow down a little, as if she had an exact metronome ticking away in her cold heart. And I am full of admiration for the warm, strong, and always pure tones she is able to draw from her instrument. It's a mystery to me how such a self-absorbed person can give so much to others. She arrives at rehearsals with a stiff, neutral expression on her face, the personification of professionalism—I've never seen her sad or happy. Except for that gleam—the gleam of polished glass—which flashes in her eyes at the conclusion of a well-played passage, or the cloudiness which blurs them, like glass touched by dirty fingers, when she is dissatisfied with the results, I've never noticed any particular expression on her face.

I'm keeping a close watch on the peculiar relationship developing between Rosendorf and Eva Staubenfeld. They are powerfully attracted to each other, and very careful to stop halfway. I don't believe it's faithfulness to his wife that makes him behave morally, although I don't reject this possibility out of hand. But we're modern people after all, and no one expects a man in his prime to abstain completely from the satisfaction of his basic needs, unless he's a monk by nature. I've seen Rosendorf look at attractive women in ways that imply that he would be happy to sate his physical hunger as long as it didn't involve baring his soul. Whereas he never looks at Eva Staubenfeld any differently than he looks at me or Litovsky. With one difference: the look he gives us is simple—inquiring or affirming as the case may be—but looking directly at Eva Staubenfeld seems to cost him an effort.

This determination to see Fräulein Staubenfeld exclusively as a violist, while deliberately ignoring her obvious charms, does not necessarily stem from a moral position but rather from musical principles. I see this as evidence of the integrity of an excellent musician who has placed the quartet at the top of his priorities. He is able to control his lust, even though she would yield to him if he wanted her. He seems to be the only man she respects. That the above thought was not far from his mind I conclude from our conversation about the composition of the quartet. I remarked, just for a joke, that there would be a certain symmetry in our quartet: two beautiful people and two ugly ones (an imperfect symmetry: the beautiful ones are beautiful with the same calm, cold, northern beauty, while we ugly ones are ugly in a very different way—my ugliness is sad while Litovsky's is full of aggression). For a moment an enigmatic smile hovered on Rosendorf's lips. As if he were about to retort mockingly: How perceptive of you to notice that Fräulein Staubenfeld isn't ugly—and changed his mind; I might be offended. Afterward he confessed, not completely seriously, that he too had hesitated before inviting Eva Staubenfeld to play in the quartet. When you have an excessively beautiful woman in a quartet, there's a danger that everyone will keep their eyes fixed on her. Then it occurred to him that there might be a certain advantage to the situation. The others would be able to relax and play as if there were no audience—no one would give them a second glance. Playing in a quartet depends on the tension of aiming at a common goal, he said. Anything which distracts attention from the common effort can only be harmful, especially when there's also a risk of emotional involvement. In other words, the violist dressed in Eva Staubenfeld's clothes is more important to us than the woman who takes them off.

Then he added: "But in the end I decided that I couldn't allow extraneous considerations to influence our decision. Staubenfeld (he imitated my way of referring to her without intending to tease) plays so well that she can even afford to be beautiful. I've never heard of anyone being disqualified from performing in public just because they've got a classic body. And certainly not when it comes to playing classical music."

I told him the Hasidic tale about the Messiah's donkey. According to popular tradition he is supposed to come mounted on a donkey, because if he came mounted on a white horse, everyone would look at the horse and not at the Messiah.

Rosendorf laughed heartily and said that the parable was very apt.

I told him that the Messiah would come on the day that the parable was identical to reality.

"I'm learning so much from you," he said, "that soon people will say that I asked you to join the quartet in order to improve my knowledge of Judaism . . ."

I've just read over what I wrote about Rosendorf here, and

it shocks me. Anyone who reads it is liable to think that I've fallen in love with him.

I won't deny that the inclination to fall in love with hand-some men has always existed in me. But I have never tried to consummate it in an obscene way.

TWENTY-THIRD OF HESHVAN, 5698

The quartet has become my second temple. The first one was Ben-Shemen. The room I live in doesn't count. It's only a place to store my few possessions and rest my weary bones. Sooner or later I'll move out, just as I moved out of the first room I rented. I move my things from place to place with no difficulty at all. Each time for a different reason. Last time it was a political argument. My landlord said that the invasion of Abyssinia was justified. Italy was bringing civilization to Africa. ("Of course economic interests are also involved!" he yelled at me. "So what? It's for their own good—those black savages who only climbed down from the trees the day before yesterday . . .") I couldn't go on staying there for another hour. The time before that the reason was economic: they wanted to put the rent up. Another time a baby was born and I realized that I had to leave. I don't mind. In any case home, as far as I'm concerned, is where I can find someone to love. As long as I'm on my own all I need is a roof over my head. I've never been a slave to possessions. My little library—a few classics, a few volumes of contemporary poetry, a few philosophers, and the Hebrew literature I read to improve my knowledge of the language—is all the "fine furniture" I need to give me the satisfaction the sages spoke of. Except for my violin and music collection, of course.

There are no friends who "drop in" to visit. My only visitors are my pupils, who come on the days when the quartet doesn't meet. I devote myself to these pupils to the best of my ability. Teaching for me is not a necessary evil, something

undertaken for financial gain alone, but a mission and a vocation, as people say here. I devote myself to them with all my
heart, and they respond with reserved affection. They find it
difficult to warm to someone who speaks Hebrew with a
foreign accent. They're the first generation born to immigrant
parents and exhibit all the weaknesses typical of their kind.
Their simple lives, without any historical depth, seem to them
the natural state of affairs. Anyone different from them is an
outsider. And anyone born in the Diaspora must have been
somehow distorted by it. It's difficult to argue with young
people so contemptuously confident of their own values, including the false ones among them. And it's not necessary
either. It's only a question of time. The war in which they will
probably take part will teach them something too. (I'm convinced that war is inevitable, and have made a name for myself
here as a pessimistic prophet of doom. Pray God I'm wrong.)

I love my pupils, even the shallow ones, deeply—perhaps
because I am incapable of teaching without a profound emotional commitment to my charges. The teacher and his pupil,
too, are a link in the generational chain. If they don't return
my love, I don't care. I am content if they appreciate my efforts
to transmit not only technical principles but also culture. It's
too early to tell if any of them will become a great violinist. In
any case, the pick of the bunch will end up with Rosendorf. I
won't be offended. I'll hand them over to him gladly. I can give
them the foundations, but Rosendorf can make them into
violinists.

I am not being insincere when I recommend pupils who are
not really talented to continue. I hesitate a little when the
parents can't afford to pay, but I would never tell a boy who
has no chance of becoming a professional violinist to stop
studying just because he won't be able to make a living at it. I
see a hard future ahead for these boys and girls (although
there is a certain relaxation in the tense relations between the
Arabs and the Jews at the moment, blood will still be shed).
Some of the boys will probably join the police force as ghaffirs

(supernumerary constables with special guard duties), or go to man border settlements and abandon the violin for a number of years. But in time they will be grateful to me for giving them the wherewithal to fill their harsh lives with soothing sounds. They'll take out their violins and play at a celebration at some poor settlement, and the sounds they produce will have a cultural significance which cannot be measured in terms of technical accomplishment alone. When cultured amateurs make music for the love of it, they often play as movingly as professionals. As far as I am concerned, I shall always prefer the stammering of lovers to the glib phrases of people who don't mean what they say. I try to instill in my pupils love for music and respect for the awesome responsibility they take upon themselves when inviting listeners to participate in a musical experience. Technical mastery is not irrelevant, but it's not the most important thing.

Besides being my home away from home, the rehearsals of the quartet are also the workshop where I expand my musical horizons. Not my knowledge, which in all modesty I may say often surpasses that of my colleagues. Our discussions about questions of interpretation are an intellectual delight to me at least, although I doubt that all the others enjoy them as much as I do. They, especially Eva von Staubenfeld, are content with brief, practical comments. Sometimes she insults me by the manner in which she interrupts me while I'm in the middle of talking and tries to get Rosendorf to take advantage of his right as the first among equals to decide the issue against me.

My attempts to clarify my position by referring to the broader cultural context, the period, the dominant philosophy, human relations, and the social character of different styles, irritate her. She listens tight-lipped and cold-eyed. As if all these things are irrelevant. As if I'm simply trying to show off my erudition. Sometimes I try her patience and go on at length, to teach her some manners, until the expression in Rosendorf's eyes, although he goes on listening to me with the greatest of interest, signals his dread of a hostile reaction from the lady in question, who is an expert at insulting people without opening her mouth: shrugging her shoulders, staring at her fingernails, or tuning her instrument is enough.

Our arguments about how to play—down to the minutest details: the length of the bow, its position, the amount of hair touching the string, finger pressure, and other such ostensibly technical matters, which give the tone color, warmth, and bite as required—are an important lesson to me in the art of playing my instrument and, at the same time, an opportunity to get a glimpse into the very souls of my colleagues, including the soul of Eva von Staubenfeld. Her taciturnity and reserve do not prevent me from reading the signals she unconsciously transmits. Sometimes I am astonished by her discrimination. Without the least participation of her intellect, she penetrates to the depths. For all the hostility she exudes toward me, I can still appreciate and admire the spiritual riches which run in her very blood. Our true values are those which we do not have to consult on every question that comes up. And true art is an unseen effort.

Our arguments, which Rosendorf prefers for the sake of peace to call consultations, if anyone took the trouble to record them, could serve as an excellent textbook for performers of chamber music. I am already sorry for not having written down the essence of the debates we began at the very first rehearsal, hesitantly at first, and later with great vehemence, each of us in his own style—one with words, another with a persuasive demonstration, and a third by insisting on playing "the way he feels."

When I have the time, I intend to write a book for the use of amateurs at a professional level, and even for professional quartets. Let no one accuse me of immodesty. I am very well aware of the fact that our arguments about questions of musical interpretation are far from providing the basis for a canonical reference book. If it is not written from the outset as an open-ended Talmudic debate, which may often end in a draw, it will not have the right to exist. Who knows better than I that although I often have very firm opinions, they do not and never will constitute Holy Writ: this is how to play a scherzo, this is how to accent the end of a phrase, etc. The very same passage can sometimes be played one way and sometimes another, not only in two different historical periods—because in our time we perceive classicism differently from the way the Romantics did—and not only by two different string quartets—which differ from each other in temperament and character and technical mastery—but even by the same quartet itself in two different performances; one in the morning and the second on the same evening. I know that my last words are a reductio ad absurdum, for the sake of emphasis, of an unconventional point of view. Although every musician knows that different performances really do differ from each other according to circumstances—playing in the heat of a *hamsin* windstorm is not the same as playing in mild weather, and acoustic conditions can wreak havoc with the best of intentions—he believes that he must strive for his chosen version under all conditions. Whereas my book (an egg which has not yet been hatched) will grant legitimacy to these deviations from the straight-and-narrow of a performance ideal determined by rules laid down in advance and allow him to respond to all kinds of moods—his own, his instrument's, his colleagues', the audience's, and even the spirit of the times. Not only that, it will also enrich the anonymous ensemble with helpful advice, gleaned from the experience of a quartet which has performed for all kinds of audiences—keen and critical music lovers, German expatriates who sit with bowed heads, their eyes on their scores, after listening to a recording by the Busch Quartet at home, sleepy factory workers, or high school students waiting impatiently for virtuoso tricks to rouse them from their boredom—and under all kinds of conditions, indoors and out, in school halls, gymnasiums, and cinemas, in quarries and under sweltering tin roofs.

I am also of the opinion that, contrary to accepted wisdom, if a melody passes from one instrument to another, there is no need for all four to play it in the same spirit. There is a special charm, I admit, to reduplicating the melody at different pitches, but I see a quartet as a quintessentially human experience, where even the truth is not the same when it emerges from the mouths of different people. I find a particular fascination in four different interpretations of even the simplest musical statement, such as the fifths with which Haydn opens his quartet.

It was this opinion which gave rise to the suspicion on the part of Litovsky and Fräulein Staubenfeld that my mind is unbalanced. In their opinion—Litovsky said it straight out and Fräulein Staubenfeld applied herself to smearing rosin on her bow with the grim energy with which she is in the habit of showing her disapproval—the above point of view is incompatible with my personality. I am involved in a contradiction which I am unable to resolve. How can a person demand consistency in everything else—politics, morals, philosophy—and then suddenly give anarchy its head? If the one thing is right, its opposite must be wrong. But art is free even when its values are defined with the utmost strictness. It is the safety valve by which we release the irrational emotions that are liable to explode the overheated mechanism of our souls. Operating inside us is an unbalanced system of instinct and reason, in which civilization attempts to introduce order. If we don't allow instinctual freedom an outlet within the safe limits of artistic activity, there will be an explosion. Music is the most arbitrary, abstract, and sublime of all the arts. Born of matter, she frees herself from it with instantaneous ease. Even her strictest laws are arbitrary: rules she lays down for herself without any obligation to keep them, obstacles erected to be jumped over. She makes it easier for us to defend ourselves from the madness lurking in store for whoever discovers the infinity of time. She divides it into units of different lengths. Some are so short that they are over before we even notice their existence. In the bosom of the silence stretching between two ephemeral notes, calm awaits us . . .

Subconsciously, I am quite sure, our Eva too is familiar with the existential dread of entering a forest whose end is beyond your ken. You have to set yourself interim goals; otherwise you will not take a single step for fear of never reaching the other side. . . . Her intellect does not call things by name, but an inner sense tells me that she too knows, as I do, the fear of madness, the pointless pain of existence as such, and she, like me, clings to the notes which lead her on from hour to hour, from moment to moment . . .

THE TWENTY-NINTH OF HESHVAN, 5698

I read what I wrote last week and laugh:

What right do I have to say what Fräulein Staubenfeld feels? And what she dreads and what emotional need music fulfills in her? We haven't exchanged one personal remark. (Apart from the time she once asked me, as an old-timer in the country, if it was true that it was dangerous to drive into the countryside because of the recent increase in hostile actions.)

I've heard a few items of gossip that aren't very illuminating. People say that she's only half-Jewish, on her mother's side, and that on her father's side she's from an upper-class Prussian family. Her real name is von Staubenfeld, but she chose to delete the "von" for reasons best known to herself (and I put it back again when she annoys me by her arrogance). Martha, Litovsky's wife, says that von Staubenfeld is not her father but her husband, from whom she is divorced. She would be happy to wipe out the name and memory of this man, who apparently tried to cut the Jewess out of his own biography, so that she would not harm his chances of advancement to the upper echelons of power in Nazi Germany. Since she could not deny the name written in her papers, she contented herself with removing the tiara from her head and trampling it in the dirt, and without losing any of her pride, descended to the common ranks again.

I find it difficult to believe this story, which probably contains a grain of truth. It's hard to believe that those Junkers, after ruling Germany for generations, can't find a way of purifying their Jewish wives. I find it hard to imagine the man with eyes in his head who would be prepared to give up a woman as striking as Eva Staubenfeld. A king giving up his crown to marry her would make more sense. I tend to think that if she and her husband separated, she was the one who left because he failed to live up to her demands—"von" or not. But it may well be that all these stories are pure fabrication. The persistent silence of our violist simply cries out for some fascinating, romantic tale befitting her splendid figure and secretive face. Martha, who is a little bored because she has not yet found enough customers for her orthopedic exercises, occupies herself with the private affairs of her reserved friend with a passion which oversteps the boundaries of good taste, as if knowing a few facts about the life history of "Lady Enigma"—as Bernard Litovsky calls her—will enhance her status among the local musicians whose biographies are all tediously alike.

My assumption that Fräulein Staubenfeld has more than a passing acquaintance with the dark and insane side of the human condition is not based on factual knowledge—I know even less than the others, who know almost nothing—but on her attraction to modern music, which even Rosendorf sometimes finds hard to digest.

Our repertoire at present includes only classical and Romantic music. We play the quartets of the great German composer and, as a gesture toward the East Europeans in our audience, quartets by Borodin, Dvořák, and Tchaikovsky. The latter are played by Rosendorf with a faintly ironic smile on his lips. He deliberately exaggerates the sentimental nature of the Slavic melodies, which are "easy to approach," as he puts it. As if resigning himself to a certain degree of vulgarity even in the audience for chamber music. At the request of Eva Staubenfeld, we are going to add Ravel and Debussy to our repertoire as well. Not a single really modern quartet. Perhaps we'll play Schönberg's *Verklärte Nacht*, a beautiful Romantic sextet composed before he invented his "method."

To Rosendorf's credit, he does not attempt to excuse his avoidance of contemporary music by the ignorance of the audience. He admits that the fault is his own. Although he is curious about the works being composed by members of his own generation, he is still not sure that he can play them with a spirit of identification. He finds it difficult to play a composition that "doesn't speak to him in his own language." True, he is capable of playing works by Schönberg and Alban Berg, which are written in notation with clear instructions by the composers, but he seems afraid that his playing would be mechanical, pretentious, and false. He would be ready to play such music only when it "touched his soul." Perhaps this is a flaw in his musical personality, in which case he can only regret it. But it is better to admit it than to pretend that he has plumbed the depths of modern music simply in order to keep up with the times.

This shows a degree of intellectual honesty which is not to be sneezed at. Litovsky lacks the humility to admit that he doesn't understand. In his opinion the music in question is nothing but a "fad" perpetrated by mediocrities who feel that they have to "innovate at any price." They can't compose like Brahms, and so they cut themselves off completely from the traditions of their predecessors. In this no-man's-land, where everyone does as he sees fit, nobody can catch them out in their mistakes. "In the olympics of peculiar jumps they hold all the records," he says.

In this matter we are two against two. It's the only issue on which Eva and I are on the same side. This music "speaks to us," in Rosendorf's phrase, in a language we understand.

If Eva had been endowed with intellectual curiosity, her interest could be attributed to a lust for knowledge. Young people everywhere, of our generation or one or two generations older—in a period of rapid change every decade is a generation—hear the pulse of the times. And what about us? Are we deaf? An educated person is not being false to himself when he asks to hear again and again the strange sounds coming from the din kicked up by our demented century. From repeated listening we come to understand that what we have here is not disconnection but the search for new forms of expression to suit our time.

But Eva is not a curious person. Any talk of poetry or painting bores her. Whenever we fall into conversation at the door, she hurries off without waiting for us, even though we all are walking home in the same direction—down Eliezer Ben Yehudah Street. And this stroll together is almost the only opportunity we get to hear Egon Loewenthal's witticisms and to talk about something else apart from music.

This leads me to the conclusion that her affinity with modern music is true and deep. I sensed it for the first time when we were talking about famous violinists. I said that I admired Joseph Szigeti not because he played better than the others—it's provincial to classify artists of this stature as if their achievements could be measured—but because of his contribution to promoting contemporary music. He agreed to record the well-known concertos with a certain company only on condition that they also record Prokofiev's violin concerto.

It was the first time Litovsky had heard Prokofiev's name. But Eva looked at me with affectionate wonder, as one might look at a baby who has succeeded in putting one block on top of the other.

Then it flashed through my mind that the interest a girl with no intellectual curiosity found in the work of modern composers must stem from a spiritual affinity: Eva responded to modern music because it expressed her own feelings in an uncompromising way. She heard in it the urge to destroy accepted forms and to protest against the status quo, and, without being able to put her feelings into words, embraced this music, which expressed the disintegration of values, the fragmentation and disruption of the rhythm of life, and the blurring of the human image.

These hysterical jumps from sphere to sphere, without the melodic continuity our ears are used to and with the total negation of the question-and-answer inherent in classical melodies, find support in apocalyptic prophecies. In these wild rhythms, lacking in any structure or guiding line, I can hear the heartbeat of a time that has gone out of its mind.

Sometimes I contemplate Eva through our two music stands and my heart curdles within me: close and remote denying sister! The two of us alone live the transformation taking place in the music of our times with the same fierce intensity, and she doesn't even know that I'm the only one who understands her. Isolated by the reserve which surrounds her like armor, she does not sense that two steps away from her sits her brother, who can tell her the name of the pain gnawing at her yet ask nothing for himself.

I would be glad for an opportunity to meet her alone. I believe that if we could have a heart-to-heart talk we would become bosom friends. But I don't dare approach such a beautiful woman, whose glassy eyes are like warning signs on an electrified fence.

Sometimes it seems to me that music surrounds her like a high wall. And modern music, in which I find so much pain and despair, is the broken glass embedded in the top of the wall, there to prevent anyone from climbing over it.

I mustn't fall in love with her. It would be folly—folly? Deadly danger!

THE FIFTEENTH OF SHEVAT, 5698

At long last a more detailed letter from my father. He is very pleased to hear that I'm playing in Rosendorf's quartet. He heard him in the previous ensemble, and it gave him "great aesthetic pleasure."

It was the first time he found any merit in Eretz Israel. What an irony! In Berlin I would never have had the chance to play with Rosendorf. He doesn't understand that there are better violinists than me here too, and that Rosendorf took me for reasons that might be just as valid in Berlin (which says more about him than it does about me: personality is no less important to him than technical competence). But perhaps Father is right anyway: my chances in Berlin would have been very remote. I too, apparently, am one of those who should be grateful to Hitler.

It was also the first time that he stopped hinting at the sorrow caused him by his children, none of whom prepared to carry on his life's work—Alfred studied medicine and is now in Boston; Ruth, who studied law and who he hoped would help him, married a physicist and they escaped to Russia; and I, his youngest son, whom he brought up by himself, without a wife, and who should owe him more than the others because of the way he spoiled me and let me study whatever I wanted to, ran away like a thief in the night. It was the worst betrayal of all and the most insulting. To this day I regret the first letters I sent him from Eretz Israel ("What can I do if I'm not interested in manufacturing paper? I only begin to take an interest in paper after letters are printed on it.") Young people are capable of limitless cruelty. How could I have allowed myself to sneer at his life's work! He began the plant from nothing and has every right to be proud of the results. And I, with the unfeeling arrogance so characteristic of the cocksure, overweening young, patronized him. He was the materialist, I the intellectual. . . . If, God forbid, something happens to him because he can't bring himself to abandon the factory, which is dearer to him than his life, I shall never forgive myself for my rudeness.

Today, after failing in my attempts to "make a martyr of myself" (the expression is Dora Wolf's. A beloved woman can be cruel even when she doesn't mean to be. Perhaps because everything wounds . . .) I can understand him better than before. I can appreciate his pride in his material achievements, his reputation as an honest businessman, and the size of the credit he gets from the bank. But in our family, I'm afraid, it wasn't music that destroyed our bourgeois heritage, like with the Buddenbrooks, nor was it the overrefinement of the younger generation, but plain Teutonic rudeness. In Father's eyes it was a miracle that Jews like him were capable of establishing industries and competing with people who had three generations of the Industrial Revolution, capital, connections, status, and professional experience, behind them.

The more I think about it, the more amazed I am at the unfeeling callousness of my reply to him. It scarcely befits one whose daily occupation is the production of feeling in the proper proportions . . .

Last night I went to the movies and saw a newsreel showing a parade of German youth. Familiar faces. Young people I saw in school and in the street. Some of them are good to look at, even in the marching ranks, in spite of thrust-out chests and jutting chins. These youngsters are not necessarily crude or stupid, as people abroad try to make out, which is precisely why they seem so dangerous to me. Youths full of exalted emotions are capable of terrible cruelty. They want to transcend the boundaries of the ego, never mind how.

I compare myself to them and conclude that my callousness toward my father stemmed from the confidence that I had historical justice on my side.

The Nazis believe this too. Callousness frightens me. It can give rise to cruelty. And cruelty is an atrocious thing.

Young people long to transcend their human limits in any way they can. Daring acts. Drugs. Inspiration. A monstrous idea occurs to me: cruelty, too, enables people to touch these limits. Tolstoy, who set out at dawn to watch an execution at La Roquette, wanted to expand his mental horizons. Loewenthal, who usually avoids recounting his personal experiences at Dachau and hardly ever mentions the subject, once blurted out something like this: Young people who take part in interrogations accompanied by torture believe that they are strengthening their character. They want to look their nightmares in the face. They want to see what lies beyond the limits of human suffering. Intellectual curiosity can give rise to perfect evil. Perhaps that's why war appeals to the weak, who are incapable of fulfilling their dark desires without permission from the authorities.

Father's letter also includes an allusion to the partner he took on of his own free will—a childhood friend who joined the Party for reasons of expediency. He believes that he will get the business back when the regime changes hands. What an illusion! He and his foolish friend imagine that they will be able to deceive the Nazis.

THE SECOND OF ADAR, 5698

I play well in our concerts. My control over my right arm, the weaker of the two, improves amazingly. A marvelous steadiness guides my fingers. No exercising could do it. Only the affection reaching out to us from the audience.

I feel an obligation to meet their expectations. I advertised the tickets—I owe them an hour of spiritual uplift. Rosendorf says that it's the chemistry operating in our bodies. The tension, like fear, makes the adrenaline flow in our bloodstreams. The alertness we feel during a concert is like the body's response to danger.

I would rather believe that it is our sense of responsibility which demands that we extract the maximum from ourselves. If the audience believes that we have the power to shoot them like an arrow into another world, then we have to keep our promise.

"You're an incorrigible romantic," says Litovsky. "A concert is an occasion of quite another stamp. You invite people to visit your laboratory. The experiment may fail, too."

Even my stage fright, which obliged me to resign myself to

the fate of being a member of an orchestra, leaves me in the concerts of the quartet.

"The quartet has given me a new personality," I said to Egon Loewenthal. He listened gravely, like a priest afraid that a hasty reaction, couched in secular language, would dispel the magic of the confessional, and afterward, I think, he made a note of it.

The audience likes us. And so do the critics. *The Palestine Post* praised us to the skies. We have brought Europe closer to the Middle East by leaps and bounds, they said. The snob who wrote this review—and may I be forgiven for churlish ingratitude to a well-meaning man—doesn't know that "Europe" no longer exists, and will never rise from her ashes again . . .

The public streams to our concerts wherever we hold them. In Tel Aviv, Jerusalem, and the rural settlements. Tel Aviv suits our convenience. But I prefer Jerusalem—perhaps because of its unique audience who come dressed to the nines, as though they are attending an official ceremony. You can see Jewish Agency functionaries with all the airs and graces of diplomats, army officers in dress uniform, priests in their mysterious robes, and Arab dignitaries in elegant English suits and checked keffiyehs. Litovsky jokes: it's as if they've come to sign an armistice for a single night! The hall too, in a magnificent, high-arched building made of Jerusalem stone, adds a certain lofty dignity to the concert. Partly because of the acoustics, but mainly because it is saturated with the sounds of the past, like a temple of worship. A chamber music concert there is like a prayer for peace among the nations. How beautifully the somber gravity of the late Beethoven quartets blends in there, and how unconvincing Dvořák's "American," op. 96, suddenly sounds to me, its frivolity showing even in the very lyrical second part.

In Jerusalem we are treated with the greatest respect. The High Commissioner himself once paid us a visit backstage. A Jewish Agency official danced attendance on him, behaving as if he were our impresario and making shameless mistakes with our names when he introduced us: he called me Leonard Friedman and jumbled the letters in Eva's name so that it came out Shtaufenberg.

One of the Arab dignitaries, a well-known doctor, invited us to come to Beirut—he had already spoken to the French governor there, and it was all arranged. The man is an old acquaintance of Rosendorf's; they met on board ship. When he discovered that I know a little spoken Arabic—my meager knowledge made a tremendous impression on him—he was so excited that he put his limousine at our disposal and took us for a drive in parts of Jerusalem where Jews don't dare to go, in spite of the relative lull in hostilities.

Success is smiling on us. There is a large audience for our concerts, and from a certain point of view we really are "goodwill ambassadors." Among the musicians too we have gained recognition. The country has never had a chamber music ensemble comparable to ours before. A woman with connections in England is doing her best to organize a trip to London for us. But my truest happiness still comes from our performances in the rural areas.

In the miserable dining hut of a poor kibbutz, or in the village hall of a moshav, where people who are tired to death have gathered to listen to us with bloodshot eyes and burning lids, where a suspenseful silence is sometimes suddenly broken by the lowing of a cow or the barking of a dog, instantly dispelling the magic of the music—there, and only there, do I feel that I am engaged in a sacred task (I haven't forgotten Father's remark). The privilege of bringing these dedicated people moments of beauty and enabling them to contemplate their souls against the background of our music is worth more to me than all the enthusiastic applause of our audiences elsewhere.

In these places I am relieved for a while of the guilt I feel as a failed pioneer who has done more for himself than his people (although Dr. Manfred himself, who coined the last phrase, encouraged me to "bear the burden of my vocation" without guilt, since according to rational principles of the division of labor it would be easier to find me a replacement in the cowshed than in the orchestra, where anyone with "strong roots" fulfills a vital function). As soon as we set out on the journey, which involves a certain amount of danger, I feel the strength welling up in me. My colleagues are not enthusiastic when I arrange for us to play in the country.

"Friedman won't rest until somebody shoots at us," says Rosendorf with an irony that masks plain and simple fear, but he doesn't refuse to go to the remote settlement which has scraped up the money to pay our fee. A symbolic fee, to tell the truth.

Nobody's shot at us yet. The people who invite us usually make all the necessary security arrangements, and they don't invite us when the roads are dangerous. But I would be sorry to rob my friends of their romantic thrills. They can boast of being the only quartet in the world that travels in an armored car with a police escort. Still, Rosendorf would prefer me to show a little less initiative and stop exploiting my connections with musicians in the agricultural settlements to put pressure on their cultural committees to invite us.

To my surprise, I have found an ally in Bernard Litovsky, who although showing little sympathy for the agricultural settlements ("They plant one little sapling and make a fuss throughout the world"), enjoys the trips out of town and the joking camaraderie with the ghaffirs, who try to frighten us in order to impress us with their heroism. In front of a rural audience he permits himself all kinds of grimaces and tricks he would never dare to pull in a concert hall. It seems to me that he gets a special satisfaction out of being away from home and from his little flirtations with pretty girls, even though in town, too, he enjoys all the freedom available to a man married to an educated, independent, and unprejudiced woman.

But he, like Eva—and, to my sorrow, Rosendorf—considers these concerts a gesture of goodwill on our part which brings us no benefits as a professional quartet. These peasants are not our public; they can do nothing for our reputation.

"The quartet is not expanding its audience," said Eva, "when it spends precious hours traveling to play for one or two dozen bored farmers, who don't even have the good manners to cover their mouths when they yawn."

I'm afraid I'll never succeed in convincing them that the "alliance" between ourselves and these "bored farmers" is a value in itself and that in some way, which I would find it hard to explain, it plays an important role in molding the character of the Jewish population of Eretz Israel. These things are beyond their comprehension, which is why they find these excursions ridiculous. What have Schubert and Brahms got to do with the self-awareness of people from Poland and Galicia battling with the Hebrew language? What have Mozart and Beethoven got to do with the self-esteem of semieducated men and women who need all their spiritual resources for the conquest of hard physical labor and for learning the skills essential to their survival here? If we didn't put snobbish thoughts into their heads—i.e., the notion that without chamber music they're missing something—they could devote themselves quite happily to the little homegrown culture they brought with them, without trying to stand on tiptoe to raise themselves to the standards of truly civilized people. Why should they waste their time dozing to the strains of chamber music?

We don't speak of such matters. We don't formulate our thoughts. The attitudes I described above are assumptions on my part, based on casual remarks and spontaneous reactions. When I see the expression on Rosendorf's face shifting from irony to boredom as he listens to someone who has grabbed him by the lapels in order to send his regards to the whole world, and who then forces him to listen to his profound musical remarks, when all he knows about music boils down to Schubert's *Unfinished Symphony* and the "Tarantella" he heard Joseph Schmidt sing on his last visit to the country, I know that I have no chance of persuading him—Rosendorf—that the apparently unimportant chance meeting between himself and this man contains something capable of leaving a mark on the Jewish village, something which will make it different from any other village—in Germany or anywhere else in Europe. Something without which, so my deepest convictions tell me, there is no chance of realizing the dream of being a free people in our land, the land of Zion, in which every village is Jerusalem. But perhaps I am only daydreaming.

I would never make a fool of myself by sharing these thoughts with Eva Staubenfeld, who, I fear, does not even possess the vocabulary necessary to formulate them. It's enough to see the hilarious mood which overtakes her on our rural excursions in order to understand that there is no point in even trying to arouse her respect for these pretentious "peasants," spouting superficial clichés about music in their attempts to ingratiate themselves with us, and often talking pure nonsense. She is so firmly entrenched behind the sense of her own superiority that she doesn't even realize that her behavior sometimes oversteps the boundaries of good taste. On one kibbutz—in Emek Hefer—I saw her, for the first time, trying desperately to amuse a group of music lovers who surrounded her in the intermission—three of them, it turned out later, simply because they were from Königsberg. Her pointless jokes sounded clumsy and graceless, like the attempts of some pampered aristocrat to amuse himself with cart drivers and factory workers in a beer cellar. Later she stunned them with her virtuoso bowing in a Paganini Capriccio. She even let them peek into her blouse and sniggered at their embarrassment. As if in a country village, in the company of benighted peasants, there was no need to maintain the air of gravity and reserve that protected her from the advances of members of her own class. From time to time she'd burst out giggling. Everything was so funny and outlandish: the lavatory, crouching over an open pit; the jam with dead wasps floating in it; the boiling hot aluminum mugs; and the mattress with straw bristles sticking out of it. Like a white woman among savages.

That at least we could say to her credit—she took it all in a sporting spirit: the light that went off in the middle of the concert, the motor that began chugging somewhere, the long, flowery speech in Hebrew, of which she couldn't understand a single word, delivered by the coordinator of the culture committee, who tried so hard to make an impression on her with the handsome figure he cut in his boots and riding breeches. She joked without stopping, as if she had taken a holiday from herself. When some veiled obscenity slipped unconsciously from her lips, the likes of which we had never heard from them before, Rosendorf was flabbergasted. Suddenly she revealed a sharp, sarcastic humor which no other place brought out in her. She suggested playing Beethoven's Grosse Fuge for an encore and gave me a mocking, challenging stare—you can do it, Friedman! It was I, after all, who had suggested playing Beethoven's "Serioso," opus 95, instead of Hugo Wolf's "Italian Serenade"!

"Your lady friends," she once said to me, "really enjoyed the concert tonight. They managed to knit a whole sleeve!" Like a searing brand of shame, I remember my silence then. Denying my beloved Dora I smiled at Eva, happy that she had not forgotten me and left me out of her jokes.

AFTER THE ANSCHLUSS

All the grimmest predictions are coming true. The plebiscite was postponed. Von Schuschnigg resigned in a dramatic broadcast to the nation: "God save Austria." Dr. Seyss-Inquart has been appointed chancellor. The Austrian Jews are worried. Perhaps now at least Léon Blum will have a better chance of coming back to power in France. Perhaps the Western powers will understand now that Hitler can only be stopped by force of arms.

I find it difficult to even write this down. Do I, too, want war? If there really is a war, my father's fate will be sealed.

If only he would come to his senses now. But I'm not at all sure that he doesn't consider the Anschluss historically justified. What right has Austria got to exist? What culture does it possess that isn't German?

The world is changing in front of our eyes, but this afternoon I shall go to Litovsky's house on Hovevei Zion Street as if nothing has happened. We'll play Schubert and Brahms as Joachim, Busch, and Kreisler played them before us and perhaps we won't even lament the fall of Austria. Eva will urge us to begin. Every minute we talk instead of playing is a waste of time. If we don't stop talking she'll pick up her viola and start playing passages until we take the hint.

I was only in Vienna once, on my way to Eretz Israel. I only spent three days there, but I have many memories of the city. My head is full of Mahler now. Father says he's decadent. The attitude of people like my father toward musicians like Mahler smacks of anti-Semitism: a Jew who doesn't know how to behave himself.

THE NINETEENTH OF NISSAN, 5698

Last night I read in the newspaper that Willy Gruenfeld was ambushed and shot. He died from his wounds on the way to the hospital. I wept for a long time.

I haven't got many friends, and although I didn't meet Willy often, I considered him a close friend.

I came across him at one of our first concerts on a kibbutz. We were stuck there for the Sabbath, because of a rumor that there was a mine planted on the road from the kibbutz to the main road. They gave us a classroom with an old piano in it, and we spent Saturday morning rehearsing. We sat on children's chairs and worked on a Brahms quartet. Someone peeped in at the door and asked if he could listen. We agreed and ignored him. He was a thin, ageless man with sad eyes and thinning hair. If he was prepared to listen to an interrupted rehearsal, we had no objections.

For a long time he sat in silence without opening his mouth except to offer us tea, which he brought from the children's kitchen. But when an argument about interpretation broke out between us, he requested permission to say something and surprised us by his erudition. "On this weighty question Brahms expressed his opinion in a letter to Clara Schumann," he said, in a formal, slightly absurd style, "and although his opinion may not be binding, it must be taken into account when it comes to his own work." Afterward he said things that made sense about the tempo, too.

From the expression on Litovsky's face it was evident what he thought: an impudent fellow! But Rosendorf was delighted.

"Do you play too?" he asked.

"A little," he said. "The piano. But lately very little. I work in the orchards, and it's hard work."

"Would you like to play with us?" Litovsky inquired, offering him the chance to make a fool of himself. After giving us advice, no doubt he would like to give us a lesson in how to play chamber music too.

"I'd be delighted," he said, in all innocence.

"But we haven't got any quintet music," teased Litovsky.

"I must have something somewhere," he said, and introduced himself: Willy Sadeh-Yarok (formerly Gruenfeld, I imagined). "But it will take a little time, I'll have to look through the crates."

"We promise to go on rehearsing in the meantime," said Litovsky.

Willy, as naive as a boy, was not stung. "I'll try to be back soon," he promised. I blushed as if Litovsky's rudeness were directed at me, too.

He returned after half an hour with a sheaf of dusty pages— the Brahms Quintet—in his hand, and sat down at the piano.

I was afraid that our little joke was overstepping the bounds of good taste. The Brahms Quintet is a technically difficult work, and I didn't want to see the man breaking his fingers on it.

"Let's try one movement," suggested Rosendorf tactfully, "say the second movement. If we see it's too difficult, we'll leave it."

"In that case, let's try the first," Willy requested and held his scratched fingers over the keyboard, ready to go. His eagerness touched all our hearts.

Even Litovsky stopped sneering. "Perhaps we should start playing slowly. I hardly know the work and there are a lot of black notes," he volunteered, to shift the responsibility for failure onto himself.

"That would be a shame," said Willy. "If we slow the tempo, the movement will lose its vigor and decisiveness."

Out of the corner of my eye I caught the amused look in Eva's cold eyes.

But it didn't last. Willy swept us through the entire movement at an exhilarating pace. Astounded, we looked at each other and at the beaming face of the happy pianist, who was all ready to go on to the second movement as a well-deserved encore.

"But you're an excellent pianist!" Rosendorf could no longer control himself.

"There's no need to exaggerate," said Willy. "When I get worked up, I manage to play somehow, but ever since I stopped practicing my playing has deteriorated."

When we finished playing the whole piece, Willy was transformed by joy. "I never thought I would ever have the chance to play this wonderful work," he said.

He had played it *prima vista*!

Rosendorf was now beside himself. How could someone like this be wasted on hard physical labor? Why, there weren't two others like him in the whole country!

A wonderfully childish smile appeared on Willy's cracked lips.

"Why wasted? I gave up the piano a long time ago in order not to become enslaved. I would rather do something that gives me greater satisfaction."

"You mustn't give up music!" scolded Rosendorf.

And then Willy confessed that he had no intention of giving up music. He simply preferred composing it to performing it.

We accompanied him to a packing shed at the edge of an orange grove, outside the barbed-wire fence surrounding the farmyard, and there he showed us his treasures. A grand piano which had not been tuned for a long time; a wooden music stand with overalls hanging on it; fruit crates filled with scores, books, clothes, and shoes; a bed with a big, friendly shepherd dog lying on it; a contrabass; two clarinets; a child's violin; a hunting rifle; a bust of Beethoven; a metronome; many pairs of socks; a sheepskin; and a pile of stave paper, some of it blank but most of it filled with tiny, scrawled notes.

"You composed this?" asked Eva, and she sat down next to the piano to decipher the scrawl.

Now it was her turn to admire.

"It looks very interesting," she said, "fascinating, even." Her fingers, as if of their own accord, ran up and down on the keys, until they were forced to stop and decipher the score. I envied her: she takes to contemporary music like a fish to water. Progressions which seem to make no sense in conventional terms sound completely natural when she plays them, as if no intellectual effort had been required to transform them from the patterns to which our ears are accustomed.

"Wonder of wonders," said Rosendorf. "It's got melody and harmony. There's something to listen to, and the pauses aren't longer than the music . . ."

"They're only exercises," said Willy regretfully, "improvisations on folk tunes. Experiments. And not very original either. As far as the conception, the guiding idea, even the

method is concerned . . . a bit from Bartók, a bit from Ko-
dály. . . . This piece is nothing to boast about . . . but there are
others, more crystallized, which attempt to draw on our own
sources."

We stood and listened—even Litovsky showed no signs of
impatience—to a long lecture on the sources of inspiration of
the national culture and his own distress at being cut off from
them. He did not see the "exercises," which seemed so successful to us, as his own creation "in the full sense of the
word," since they were based on German folk songs—the
only ones he had absorbed "with his mother's milk" in a small
village near Würzburg. Every year, during the vacation he
received from the kibbutz, he toured the towns and villages of
Eretz Israel and visited the synagogues and mosques, writing
down Yemenite, Bucharan, Spanish, Caucasian, and Arab
tunes. He hoped that if he steeped himself in melodies born in
an Eastern clime, he would be able to "make his music grow"
from "ancient Hebrew" roots. He pursues this project enthusiastically, but a skeptical inner voice tells him that there is
something artificial about a man whose soul is made of Schubert and Brahms but whose passion is for Persian melodies, in
which if he did not hear the voices of the past, he would hear
nothing at all. This music does not pour out of him like
laughter or tears; he imposes it on himself in order to cut
himself off from his "German roots." His natural instincts tell
him that music lacking in spontaneity may be very sophisti-
cated, and even "fascinating," as the lady had been kind
enough to say, but it would never fill the deep need of our
souls to "return to our mother's womb" and "listen to her
heartbeats from within."

It was late when we left the packing shed. Willy could not
apologize enough for making us miss lunch with his "chatter": he so seldom had the chance to share his ideas with a
group of real musicians, he said and blushed. He begged us to
try to understand and not to hold it against him. He lived in a
small community and most of his comrades had already heard

his "speeches." And ideas, as we knew, if they weren't put to the test of a skeptical listener, were doomed to become divorced from reality and just "stew in their own juices."

After the road was opened and we were able to take the bus to Tel Aviv from a neighboring village, we could not get the man who had apologized so profusely for "taking up our time" out of our heads. We competed with each other in singing his praises. How fluently he played, and with a farmer's fingers! ("Unlike that woman who works in the cowshed, manual labor hasn't harmed him at all," said Rosendorf.) And how quick on the uptake! ("The Brahms Quintet at first sight without a single mistake. And the piano isn't the cello," said Litovsky.) And what fascinating music! (Eva repeated the expression, which she seemed to have taken a fancy to.) And what astonishing familiarity with musical literature!

Rosendorf was more excited than any of us:

"How awful to think of a man like him buried in an orange grove, living in such isolation, among people incapable of appreciating his gifts!"

I objected mildly to the expression "buried": the kibbutz he had chosen to live in was a place where he could devote himself to his "hobby" without anyone bothering him.

Rosendorf reacted sharply. For the first time I heard him take a stand, and a very firm one, on a subject that he generally showed no interest in. He hates ideologies. I would never have imagined that he held such firm opinions.

"Persuading a person as naive as him that he'll be betraying his comrades' trust if he doesn't spend his time pruning orange trees is simply spiritual cruelty. First his leaders brainwash him, and then they go off to London themselves to play at politics. . . . This simpleton thinks that the exceptional talents of these leaders exempt them from the duty of working in the orange groves, whereas if he himself devoted his time to music, he would be a parasite. Thank God he agrees to write music in his spare time. In such a fanatical society they would be perfectly capable of persuading him that even that was a waste and that he should be writing patriotic songs for kindergarten children instead."

Unwillingly I was drawn into an argument. I presented my own point of view: the agricultural settlements would not survive if they were composed exclusively of mediocrities. I made a little speech about the idea of the commune. Rosendorf looked at me as if I had taken leave of my senses.

"Look here," he said, addressing me with the familiar *du*, something he would never have done unless he were really angry. "That's all well and good, and I wish them luck, although I doubt they'll succeed in realizing the ideal society they dream about. But no one will ever convince me that it's permissible to take a man like him and suffocate him in a broken-down packing shed . . ."

Then he announced that he would not rest until he had rescued Willy from the kibbutz.

"The sooner the better," said Litovsky, "while his Yemenite roots are still superficial."

I felt very bad after the meeting with Willy, even despondent. Compared with him, I was a mediocre musician shamelessly exploiting my talents.

Rosendorf did not rest, but he did not succeed in rescuing Willy from the packing shed. Or perhaps he did not try so very hard after the enthusiasm of the first few days cooled down. But Willy remained with us. Eva no longer treated "those rustics" like stupid German peasants. Whenever we came to a new place, she would say, in a joke intelligible only to the four of us, "I wonder who the local Willy is," Or, "I think I see a Willy over there, in the second row on the left." Or she would tease the poor fellow in charge of the cultural affairs of the kibbutz and say, "Don't forget to tell Willy to come and talk to us after the concert." And that idiot Litovsky would bellow with laughter when the latter answered in confusion: "But there isn't any Willy here."

God bless his memory.

THE FIFTH OF IYAR, 5698

If I didn't play in the quartet, I wouldn't have had the privilege of getting to know Egon Loewenthal, I wrote to Father, as a hint that I had not left a civilized country to go and live in the desert.

I have always admired Loewenthal's style. His language is clear and transparent. He touches the heart of things with apparent nonchalance. I would read him over and over. I had the feeling that there were prizes hidden in his books for those who knew how to look for them.

The first time he came to Litovsky's house I was as excited as a boy taking an exam. I was amazed to see how much he resembles my father. The short stature, the scant hair, and the eyes looking inward and outward at one and the same time. Even the way he held the cake plate close to his mouth and crushed little pieces with his fork before putting them carefully in his mouth—like a man totally engaged in whatever he happened to be doing at the moment. His round eyeglasses, too, in thin gold frames, which barely covered his big eyes, are like Father's. And perhaps this is why I wasn't surprised when he opened his mouth and the voice that emerged from his fragile throat was my father's voice—high and musical and very soft, as if directed only at those prepared to pay particular attention.

I wrote and told my father that I found a resemblance between him and Egon Loewenthal.

He replied ironically: he was very honored to resemble a great writer. But the latter, on leaving Germany, took German literature with him into exile, whereas he himself would only be able to leave it empty-handed. Happy the man whose pen is his fortune! He can put it in his jacket pocket and go elsewhere. But a man whose one talent is for building a factory from the bottom up has no choice but to stay in the place where his capital is buried.

Even my father's style is a little like Loewenthal's, especially when he employs irony.

Until we began corresponding, I hardly knew my father. I rebelled against him because he "occupied himself with material affairs." After my mother died and I went to study in Berlin, we only met during the holidays. The rare letters we exchanged were also concerned with practical matters: I reported to him on the state of my health and the state of my pocket and he sent me money and good advice on how to save it. There was no room for serious subjects in those modest letters.

It was only after my immigration to Eretz Israel that we became close to each other. His letters thrill me with their fine, clear prose, sparing of words and full of humor. From them I learn of qualities I never knew he possessed and of the broad general knowledge implied by his apt quotations from the best of German culture. Even about music, I have come to realize, he knows far more than I imagined. The observant Jew who sings to himself in a church choir is not only an amateur tenor, whom I can patronize from the heights of my academic education, but a musician with a discrimination and knowledge rare among amateurs. Sometimes I think that my fantasies about abandoning professionalism and joining the amateurs stems from hidden guilty feelings toward my father. I allowed myself to look down on him instead of learning from him. I no longer criticize the attributes he admires—scrupulous honesty, fairness in business, thrift, punctuality, cleanliness and orderliness, impeccable attire, and decency in speech—as conformism and the wish to ingratiate himself with the Gentiles. I wouldn't say now, as I once did, that these virtues, which he has adopted to the point of total identification, are nothing but the bait held out by the upper classes to the bourgeoisie in order to restrain its appetites. In my heart, I've begged his pardon a thousand times for my former contempt.

There is only one subject on which we disagree—uncompromisingly: for him the return to Zion is a religious return to the Zion of the spirit; he sees the Zionist attempt to establish a concrete Jewish entity as the gravest error of our generation. Recently he has begun attending synagogue services again after many years of neglect, and he blames himself for sending me to a Christian school in order to give me an all-around education. I try to persuade him that the Jews have no future anywhere on earth if there isn't one place under the sun which they can call their own. We argue very politely, without harsh words, but we both stick to our guns.

I no longer despise the dreams of the little clerk who aspired to be a factory owner. I blush with shame when I remember what I once said to him: "Your ideals reach no higher than the chimneys of your factory." My rudeness hurt him badly, but he forgave me. My mother couldn't forget it. "You stabbed him in the back," she said. Financial independence was his Promised Land. "If you come by it honestly, you're creating culture," he would say. As a man in control of his own factory he could find scope for all his industriousness and generosity, as well as his innate stubbornness and his passion for the "quality product"—which was a value in itself. And perhaps another typically Jewish wish: to be his own boss and command others in his own style—courteously—with a smile on his lips, with respect for his subordinates.

How heartbreaking that on the verge of fulfillment he was robbed of his dream! And by force. The very "culture" he had hoped to refine by providing a model of a "generous master" repaid him with a slap in the face.

My heart bleeds when I think of his despair. His letters are resigned—like a stoic who has undergone an ordeal in order to learn a lesson from it. Now he can't even afford to visit Eretz Israel. He was too honest to smuggle money out of Germany, and he is not prepared to take "what little I have" from me.

In any case, he doesn't want to come. Perhaps he thinks that Hitler is only the pus from an old wound, which will disappear once the wound heals. It's hard to believe that he still thinks in these terms. Perhaps he's afraid of change or disappointment. My letters are getting more and more aggressive. Perhaps they'll have an effect. He tries to convince me that things aren't really so bad. As long as a man has bread to eat, a shirt on his back, a roof over his head, and one true friend, all is not lost.

I try, without upsetting him, to make him realize that he has to come here in order to save his life. He probably smiles to himself. I'm here and he's there, and I can see better than he?

The argument is endless. It will be won, presumably, by the one who sticks to his guns. I'm more stubborn than he is. I'm his son after all. And perhaps my stubbornness will teach him how attached I am to him.

THE SIXTH OF IYAR, 5698

I look at Loewenthal and see my father. Loewenthal too is both humble and arrogant. The smile on his face, a moment before he opens his mouth to speak, says this: I know that I can charm you with words, and so I shall say less than I intended saying. Only he who refrains from using his influence keeps it. What I don't say, you can guess. The guess is your own creation. You can be grateful to me for making you my partners instead of my blind disciples.

". . . I'll sit at a distance and listen," he said the first time he came.

There was no "distance" in Litovsky's apartment. The minute Loewenthal sat down, his presence was felt. We kept our discussion to a minimum. We played a passage that needed improvement straight through so he wouldn't be bored, and our coffee break took longer than it should have. Rosendorf was already regretting having invited him. I enjoyed every minute. Even Litovsky, who hasn't read a word he's written, was elated. He presided over his little flat like some great patron of an artistic salon. Martha devoted herself to him and

was not satisfied until he had tasted all her cakes. Only Eva
showed no special interest, except if exaggerated indifference
is a sign of attention. Only a great writer could have evoked
such conspicuous indifference; a mediocre writer she simply
would have ignored.

This indifference is not mutual. Loewenthal is fascinated by
her. When I see Eva through a stranger's eyes, I realize how
beautiful she is: her bearing, her body, her face. Every movement seems to imply some greater gesture. And the strange
thing is that her face radiates spiritual beauty, even though she
is hollow inside.

Loewenthal knows how to appreciate beauty. He doesn't
grab, but neither does he try to hide his admiration. Great men
aren't stingy. Loewenthal gives Eva what she deserves without
saying a word just by the way he looks at her. Like someone
gazing at an exquisitely beautiful landscape. And this, apparently, is what finally "broke" her. But all she was capable of
saying to the great writer when the ice was broken was an
announcement that she had once read a book by Thomas
Mann!

I don't dare invite him to my room, even though I really need
a friend like him. Ever since losing contact with Dr. Lehman, I
feel starved for the company of someone I can talk to about
important problems. My only chance to talk to him comes
during our rehearsal breaks, when I occasionally manage to
exchange a few words with him about a book I'm reading or
ask his opinion about some philosophical problem. He is always friendly and responsive, but I can't get rid of the feeling
that his responses are not intended to satisfy my hunger for
intelligent conversation: when he talks to me he raises his voice
unnecessarily in order to attract Eva's attention. But beggars
can't be choosers—I am quite content to enjoy the crumbs that
come my way. And I can't understand how she can coolly reject
the precious gift offered her with such generosity.

Last night I accompanied him home, and it was an intellectual delight. He was amused when I compared certain themes

in Haydn to the Hegelian thesis, antithesis, and synthesis. "Young man," he said to me, "beware. This need to find a common denominator leads to a new barbarism. Apart from which, Haydn died twenty-three years before the birth of the obscure philosopher who did so much harm."

He looked at me with friendly skepticism when I told him that philosophical ideas find their way into music many years before they are expressed in words. But in the end he repeated his opinion, that ideas only gain substance when they find the appropriate garments in which to clothe themselves. "Beware of German metaphysical speculations," he warned me.

Afterward we spoke of current events. Like my father, he thinks that the territorial solution to the Jewish problem is untenable and even dangerous. The Jewish settlement in Eretz Israel, in his opinion, is a transition from one Diaspora to another. But while the Diaspora in civilized countries opened up limitless possibilities for the realization of Jewish talents, the Diaspora in the land of Ishmael meant the danger of cultural deterioration. He was very disappointed in the young people he had met here, especially the native-born, who were preparing themselves to be the Junkers of the Jewish people. As for the sons of the established Jewish colonies, who looked down on the Arabs while at the same time imitating their customs, he felt real loathing for them.

I find it difficult to understand the mischievous spirit which overtakes him without any warning as if he is suddenly tired of being serious. It makes him shoot out puns and pointless sarcasms in all directions. I wonder if this is not a kind of protest against the fate which separated him from friends like Walter Benjamin and Kurt Tucholsky, with whom he could exchange witticisms in the *Berliner Schnauze* he loves so much, and forces him to sharpen his wits on a fellow like me, intent on earnest philosophical discussions, which are not to his taste. If he sees himself as a lion tamer reduced to occupying himself with pet cats, I had rather he didn't speak to me at all.

"My dear young man, you should beware of excessive earnestness," he suddenly said to me. "Not everything that is earnest is serious, you know. We Germans have a dangerous tendency to take ourselves too seriously, which is why we are so gloomy and sometimes cruel, too." Then he quoted Schiller: "Man is completely human only when he is at play." I wonder if he chose this quotation as a deliberate pun on the word "play" in order to make the insulting insinuation that I should concentrate on playing the violin and leave philosophy to my superiors, who are not taken in by "German speculations." "Man, where will we end up if we begin imputing hidden intentions to every innocent tune? My friend Kurt Tucholsky once blamed bad weather conditions for the fact that the German revolution broke out in music rather than elsewhere, I know, but this does not mean that we can find all the sublime and demented ideas of the next generation in the music of their predecessors. Tucholsky himself saw that when the sun came out for a few minutes the streets were flooded with hoodlums. And they made a very different revolution from the one he imagined . . ."

I submit to these sarcasms without protest and also to the confusion into which I am sometimes cast by his ambiguities. In spite of the true enjoyment I derive from music, I am sometimes bored to tears by the company of musicians who can talk only about music, gossip, and salaries. Sometimes I feel as if I am going to suffocate. Even the members of the quartet have this effect on me. Rosendorf is a withdrawn man who is not interested in friendship. He is prepared to share his thoughts only with someone from his own league, like Egon Loewenthal. Eva shrinks from intimacy as from a contagious disease. The very need to open one's heart seems to her a dangerous weakness. And Litovsky, who is sometimes capable of suddenly showing a peculiar interest in political issues, is so superficial that I feel uncomfortable when he begins talking about politics.

Among the members of the orchestra I haven't got a single friend. Many of them treat me as if I were some kind of weird eccentric. They hint that they can't understand what a mediocre violinist like me is doing in the Rosendorf Quartet. There's no lack of ugly talk and spiteful gossip. They say that Rosendorf isn't keen on women, and that he took me because we're two of a kind. What disgusting vulgarity!

But I can't say that I'm succeeding in making friends with Loewenthal. Every now and then he throws me an idea, like an aristocrat satisfying some whim by giving his groom a golden coin. Or perhaps he wants to make me an Eckermann to his Goethe, someone who'll hurry home to write down all his brilliant remarks for posterity.

Come to think of it, that's not a bad idea at all.

THE EIGHTEENTH OF IYAR, 5698

Something strange has happened. Strange and frightening.

But perhaps I'm making mountains out of molehills, and trying to enliven the daily routine with a bit of drama or romance. Or both.

Martha went out to the balcony to water the plants, and when she came back she said: "Look what devotion to chamber music!"

On the stone wall, in a very uncomfortable posture, sat a young man in short trousers and a Russian shirt. There could be no doubt that he was sitting there in order to listen. His eyes, which ignored us completely, were staring intently into the room. He looked like a sturdy proletarian type, a little unkempt, not the kind of person one would usually suspect had a passion for chamber music. We were charmed by the idea that here in Tel Aviv, too, you could come across young men who were prepared to sit in the street in order to listen to music. Especially since the young man in question was a very impressive specimen with strong arms, a broad chest, wiry hair, and muscular legs covered with black curls like tiny beetles. At first I was glad to see him: we were performing a cultural function of the highest importance if we succeeded in attracting members of the working class to our public.

We returned to our instruments. At the coffee break he was still there. He sat on the wall in the pose of Rodin's *Thinker*, and ignored us completely.

And then Martha suggested inviting him in. A nice gesture. Everyone agreed except for Eva.

"Let him sit there until he gets tired."

At that moment we understood that he had come because of her, and that he was making a nuisance of himself by his very presence. A persistent suitor who refused to take no for an answer. Martha's suggestion was forgotten. We drank our coffee in silence and tried to take no notice of him. When Eva left the room our tongues loosened. Since she looked worried in spite of her pretense of indifference, I voiced the suspicion that the man might be dangerous. He appeared to be waiting in order to waylay her when she came out. Rosendorf and Litovsky thought so too. Loewenthal reassured us. He saw a doglike devotion, not at all dangerous, on the man's face, he said, and found something Russian in his behavior. The Russians were capable of tiring the object of their devotion to death in their eagerness to consummate the perfect love.

When we left and the man started following us like a detective, I began to suspect that I was right and not Loewenthal. Especially when we reached Mapu Street, where we usually separate from Eva. There she asked me to accompany her home. For a moment I was glad that she had chosen me rather than one of the others, but it immediately occurred to me that she had done so in order not to annoy him. I'm ugly enough to arouse no jealousy. Unlike Loewenthal, she did not seem to rely on the doglike nature of the love of this admirer, who apparently dogged her footsteps day and night. And the look he gave me when the two of us, Eva and I, set off together and she linked her arm in mine (I nearly stopped breathing when I felt her firm, supple flesh pressing against me) made me think that he was even more dangerous than I suspected. A look of such hatred from a stranger, about whom you know nothing, I had never experienced before, except from Germans when they discovered I was a Jew.

He followed us all the way, sometimes three or four steps behind us, and I had difficulty in overcoming my fear. And when once I couldn't control myself and I turned my head, the contempt I saw in his eyes was unendurable. Why should he despise me so? Because I was afraid of him? Because I dared to aspire to a woman as beautiful as Eva?

What astonished me above all was Eva's behavior. She walked next to me as if we were lovers, chattering incessantly. She spoke about the new recording by Szigeti, about the arms race, about the increase in Arab terrorism, and about some acquaintance of hers who had received a post in the German Foreign Office. I have never heard her talk so much.

Outside her house she lingered longer than necessary to say goodbye, and I saw her looking at him out of the corner of her eye. I suppose she was trying to hint to him, through me, that he didn't have a chance with her.

Suddenly he approached us. I was petrified and made a very poor showing. If he had raised his hand to me, I wouldn't have been able to defend myself. Eva stared at him sharply, and he stopped in his tracks.

At that moment she began to talk about music.

I wonder if he understands German. In any case, he apparently concluded from these last remarks, and from the fact that she did not invite me in, that the only connection between us was music, and turned away. He even sent me a look full of contemptuous pity before making off.

A strange business from beginning to end. The minute he disappeared she went inside without even remembering to say goodbye. I was left standing in the street like an idiot. I can't even begin to understand what's going on.

*   *   *

THE TWENTY-FOURTH OF IYAR, 5698

Eva thinks that allegro ma non troppo means so many beats of the metronome. Giustoso—less than that, and spiritoso—even less. As if Leopold Mozart's *Versuch einer gründlichen Violinschule* was the Holy Writ. This is a mistake. Conventions that were acceptable in the year that Wolfgang Amadeus was born, when a musician was a lackey in a prince's court, are no longer valid today, after half a dozen wars and such drastic changes in the rhythm of life. I don't believe that the same work should always be played at the same tempo for a number of reasons. Acoustics, obviously, make a difference, and so do the audience, the temperature in the hall, which affects the instruments, and even the mood of the musicians.

I suppose we shall never agree. The most we can hope for is mutual respect. I, for my part, can appreciate her worth. As a musician—not a person. I can't understand how a woman who saw hoodlums take over the street can go on accepting at face value the conventions of a complacent culture which came to an end at the close of the nineteenth century. My theory teacher was the same. That good old man, who saw himself as the keeper of the flame of pure German tradition, imagined that preserving the exact traditional measurements of tempo and volume was in itself a guarantee of the survival of a civilization.

But after he was set upon by S.S. in the street on his way to the concert hall and heard his heart beating more than a hundred times a minute, he understood that what was moderato in Haydn's day was no longer so in the days of Hitler.

Eva speaks of "firm discipline," of technical "mastery," of the "authority to command" of the first violin, and other such expressions which are not to my taste.

What Rosendorf's opinion is I don't know. He refuses to

discuss "basic principles." Sometimes he supports me but usually he backs Eva. The politics of human relations are not foreign to his nature, although he engages in them with so much charm and good humor that it's impossible to be angry with him. There are problems and tensions stemming from things that have nothing to do with the quartet. And hyper-sensitivities, too, like Litovsky's to criticism. He is prepared to admit mistakes in tempo, in interpretation, in timing, in almost anything, but never that he played a wrong note. If there is a false note in a chord—someone else must be to blame.

But for the fact that he is such a superb cellist, I would say that Litovsky is the weak link in our quartet. Even in music he glides over the surface of contradictory views without even realizing that they are incompatible. How can such a superficial person be such an excellent musician?

"Nature slipped up where human beings are concerned," says Loewenthal. "Sometimes you are amazed to see the kind of people guilty of the most inferior scribbles. Fine, upstanding people, sensitive souls who would sacrifice their lives for the sake of their truths, fill the Pantheon of Graphomania, while appalling scoundrels, mean-spirited egomaniacs, revolting caricatures of unadulterated wickedness write the most sublime lines of poetry with diamond nibs."

A quartet is a human society in miniature, he once said. All human relations are contained in it. The entire range of emotions from attraction to repulsion, competition to mutual support. A fascinating subject.

A quartet is also an economic institution. The common struggle for survival requires its own compromises and frequent armistices. To Rosendorf's credit, it must be said that he directs the quartet like someone picking his way between broken glass and takes great care not to hurt our feelings.

Loewenthal is surprised at Rosendorf for having brought a woman into the quartet. Wasn't what went on between four men aspiring to both perfection and greatness enough for him? A woman could only complicate the issue. Love, of whatever kind, would make music pale into insignificance beside the major concern secretly engaging all the attention of the protagonists. A woman in a quartet was like a strange insect casting a busy anthill into disarray. You never knew where the next sting would land.

I smiled. Eva is the most stable personality in our quartet. And love affairs are quite out of the question.

THE THIRD OF SIVAN, 5698

We are all very discreet. We never talk to each other except about practical matters. Too much self-exposure can destroy a musical ensemble. A quartet is a group held together with delicate glue. High temperatures dissolve it. About Rosendorf I know next to nothing. I know something about Litovsky, because he likes quoting examples from his personal biography. And I've learned some things from Martha, too. We were alone in the house and had a long chat. She told me details about their family life which Litovsky would probably prefer me not to know. Why they have no children. Why Litovsky is discontented. Private, intimate things. I felt a great need in her to open her heart to someone. We've become friends. She's an intelligent, warmhearted woman, but she's not happy. Partly because that's her nature, and partly because Litovsky is incapable of understanding a woman who isn't happy for no particular reason.

But although we generally avoid gossiping about each other, sometimes we can't restrain ourselves, and we talk about Eva. Not coarsely, of course, and without a hint of spite or slander. You might say that we exchange views—with growing curiosity the more we know her—in the same way that we would discuss a difficult piece of music. Like the way we talked about a new work by Bartók which we couldn't

understand the first time we heard it. There's something embarrassing about this kind of bafflement. You feel that there's
something there, but you don't know what it is.

Rosendorf hates gossip on principle. Litovsky, on the other
hand, isn't averse to holding forth in the style of a man successful with women. But he too knows next to nothing, which
is more or less what we all know: she comes from a respectable family; her mother's Jewish, and she suffered at the hands
of the German in-laws, who were first proud of her and who
later tried to repudiate her for the usual reasons. Some people
say that in the beginning she talked like all the people in her
circle, saying that Hitler was a necessary evil in a time of crisis
for the Fatherland and even condemning the Jews for relating
to national questions exclusively in terms of their own profit
or loss. And it was only after she was affected personally that
she remembered that she was a Jewess herself, a fact she was
far from delighted by. I can't say whether all this is true or the
fabrication of evil tongues. I did not know her in those days
myself, and I suspect everyone who claims to have heard this
or that remark from her lips then of empty boasting. As far as I
know her, she has neither the desire nor perhaps even the
necessary capacity for abstract thought to discuss questions of
this kind and take a stand on them. Indifference is her most
resolute stand, and she maintains it fanatically.

The fact that Litovsky knows no more than I do is a credit
to Martha. She's Eva's only friend, and if there's anyone who
knows anything, it's she. Her silence is a testimony to true
friendship. In our conversation, too, Martha spoke only about
herself, her husband, and the other members of the family
who had remained in Germany, without letting a single indiscreet remark about Eva fall from her lips.

In view of the above, I was astonished when Litovsky
hinted, in the presence of Rosendorf, that he knew Eva to be a
lesbian. Although he made this statement quite casually, like a
broad-minded man who couldn't see anything wrong with it,
Rosendorf was so offended by what he considered an un-

forgivable transgression against good taste that he hasn't spoken to Litovsky since.

THE FOURTH OF SIVAN, 5698

Litovsky is an irresponsible gossip. Perhaps she rejected his advances and he's taking his revenge. Not that I'm shocked by the revelation. I knew lesbians in Germany who were perfectly sound people from every other point of view. What shocks me is that he found it necessary to say it. How could he fail to see that he was casting aspersions, if you can call it an aspersion, on his wife as well? For Martha is Eva's only friend, and the relationship between them is more like a secret alliance than a simple friendship.

They met each other in Berlin, so Martha told me, but they didn't become friends then. It was only in Tel Aviv that they became close. There's something strange about the way they look at each other, something veiled and secretive about their eyes.

But perhaps I'm wrong. Perhaps the friendship between them is that of two women who confide in each other about two different types of loneliness. The kind of friendship that grows up between people who feel misunderstood by their environment. Or between people who respect each other and despise others.

THE THIRD OF TAMMUZ, 5698

Last night's events moved me to the depths of my being. With trembling fingers I sit down to try to introduce a little order into the turmoil in my soul. I can't forget her face in the lamplight, the moment she clasped me with both her hands, the kiss . . . the dazzling light shining from her eyes.

For nine months I never saw Dora. I thought that I had

uprooted her from my heart. For a while we corresponded. Then we stopped. Dora sensed, before I did, the insincerity in this kind of exchange. You write about everything under the sun in order to cover up what's really important. You speak of the suffering of humanity in order to hide your private pain. World affairs are too important to serve as a pretext for wooing.

She knows that I love her and is not prepared to let me go to "the ends of the earth" for her, as long as she is incapable of returning my love in full. If I came to the place where she lives of my own free will, perhaps she would gradually learn to love me, but she would not want me to "sacrifice myself" for her sake. You don't join a commune in order to find a woman there.

A few months ago she joined a group of pioneers in one of the tower-and-stockade settlements in the Jezreel Valley. It was not Zionist socialism alone that led her there. She had fallen in love again, with a man who had been in charge of the Zionist training farm in Germany and had come to join his former trainees in Eretz Israel. But fate was again cruel to her. Her friend was killed when his truck went over a mine. I wrote her a condolence letter and received a very impersonal reply. I wrote again and expressed my disappointment in an indirect way. She was too wise to reply.

Until last night I believed that I had uprooted her from my heart.

When we were invited to play at her kibbutz, we were in a quandary. We didn't like to refuse, but we were afraid of a renewed outbreak of hostilities in the valley. It was suggested that we take the bus to Afula and go from there in a police van with the ghaffirs. They told us that Huberman had not been afraid to visit kibbutz Ein Harod. The roads were not dangerous, they said; the British army was in control. In the daytime people traveled about without fear. The fact that the marauders operated mainly at night in their attempts to sabotage the oil pipeline in the lower Galilee showed that they did not have the capacity to operate during the day. The settlement was well fortified and closely guarded, they wrote.

I was grateful to Litovsky when he said we should agree to go. His manly body hides a romantic, boyish soul, yearning for heroic gestures. Eva supported him. Maybe there was another Willy there, who deserved to have us play for him. I couldn't hide my happiness.

Rosendorf agreed to go after Hilda Moses told him that she had a friend who traveled the roads of the north by himself.

The journey there passed off without any trouble. We enjoyed every minute of it. It was a lovely day: the sky was clear, and the heat was quite bearable. In the distance the tiny settlement looked like a pointed, broad-brimmed Mexican sombrero. The drive along the dirt road in the middle of the tall, ripe grain in the company of the ghaffirs was an experience in itself. They were a band of high-spirited youths whose schooldays were not far behind them. They tried as hard as they could to impress Eva with the terrible dangers of the journey, from which, of course, they would save her. I envied them. They were so happy in the useful task they had undertaken to perform. I often envy simple, healthy people whose natural instincts tell them what has to be done, and who don't bother their heads with existential questions. I remembered myself at their age: a bundle of nerves, a bleeding heart, a walking question without an answer. I was glad to see that a new generation was growing up here, simple and uncomplicated, unworried and content with their lot. Strong Jews unburdened with inherited Jewish suffering.

We received a moving welcome at the gates of the fortified yard. I remembered Goethe's words: "You're not really alive except when you enjoy the glad welcoming looks of others." They greeted us as if we were reinforcements who had arrived in the nick of time. Music suddenly gained an extra human value.

Needless to say, the most excited person next to the barbed-wire fence was me. Although I had prepared myself for the moment of my meeting with Dora, and I was determined to behave with the proper restraint, befitting the circumstances and the presence of strangers, I nearly fainted when I saw her standing in the kitchen door, wiping her hands on the apron she had just untied from her waist. Her face seemed younger than when I had seen her last; she was thinner and seemed taller. She was wearing clothes of a nondescript color—khaki faded in the wash—and her bare, sunburned legs looked very long in the short trousers which were too small for her. Unlike me, she did not try to hide her joy in the meeting. The beaming smile on her pretty face made the falsity of the grave expression I had assumed even more glaring. She approached me with perfect simplicity and shook my hand, to the astonishment of Eva, who made no effort to hide her surprise at coming across a beautiful woman who managed to look elegant even in rags, and who spoke good German, in a place like this. (My stock must have risen in her eyes when she saw that we were old friends, and even more so when Dora asked me to come and help her in the kitchen after we had stored our instruments in the room they had prepared for us.)

I was happy as a child when Dora invited me to go for a walk with her (after we had bathed in cold water in the ramshackle tin shower in the yard). Obviously, we had to keep within sight of the guard on the watchtower, but it was enough for me that she was happy to be in my company and that she felt the need to tell me about her life in the commune and how full and rich in content it was. She even spoke frankly, for the first time, about Dr. Manfred and about her boyfriend, with whom she had lived without getting married, since neither of them believed in religious ceremonies, and all my hopes sprang wildly to life again because she had never spoken to me so intimately about her love affairs before.

We walked around the settlement for nearly an hour, sometimes along narrow paths, and during all that time we never touched each other once, not even by accident. And it is precisely this caution which makes me feel that the physical awareness was there between us all the time, even though we ignored it (this is the only way I can understand the kiss, which apparently came like a bolt from the blue).

At the concert she sat in the first row and it seemed to me that she never took her eyes off me. I haven't played so well for years, especially "Death and the Maiden." Altogether it was a good concert in spite of the conditions: the wind lashed at the tent flaps, a dog barked without stopping, the guards changed in the middle, and we were accompanied by the monotonous noise of a generator which was not always in harmony with our key. The ringing of the bell, too, sounded to us at first like one of the disturbances to which we had to resign ourselves in a place like this. Until we realized . . .

From that moment on everything happened with terrific speed. To our credit it should be said that we didn't stop playing in the middle of the movement—the Scherzo of "Death and the Maiden"—even when we understood that something serious had happened because several men left the hall at a run—quietly, though, so as not to cause a disturbance. (From their behavior we understood that we were expected to go on playing.) And immediately afterward we heard the sound of an engine outside, and people shouting, "Hurry up!" "Wet the sacks!" and "Where's the key to the arms cache?" By the time we finished playing the Scherzo we saw the horizon reddening through the window. I can't remember ever having played the last movement at such a clip. This made a great impression on the vestiges of our audience—a few girls and a boy with his leg in a cast, and two other men standing in the doorway, waiting for someone, who applauded enthusiastically before hurrying outside too, leaving us alone with the head of the cultural committee and two girls who had apparently prepared the refreshments that I did not have time to taste. As soon as I had put my violin away in its case and asked Eva to keep an eye on it, I went out into the yard, partly in the hope of meeting Dora, who had left with the first wave, and partly because I was so excited by the whole affair. In all my years in the country I had never been so close to the scene of action. I had time to think that there was something ugly in this enthusiasm of mine—the results of working people's labor were going up in smoke and I was busy accumulating exciting experiences and deriving a strange aesthetic enjoyment from the speed and efficiency of the kibbutz members, who had organized themselves with astonishing rapidity and were operating with enviable purposefulness. Like an experienced army, some of them were checking the guns while others loaded a truck with beaters and damp sacks, and someone else harnessed a horse to a cart with a water tank on it. Before I had time to be angry with myself for behaving like an observer instead of a participant, I too was on the truck, in my white shirt and best trousers, looking strange and out of place, like some sort of Pierre Bezuhov, a tourist on the battlefield. All this happened before I had succeeded in locating Dora, and the next thing I knew we were outside the gate. It was only then that the others noticed me, giving rise to respect but also to cheap jokes at the expense of the "fiddler," but I forgave them because they meant no harm, and within a few minutes we were in the fields, a long line of men facing a wall of flames leaping higher with every gust of wind. We worked for what seemed like hours, until we were ready to drop, each of us, as it were, choosing a flame of his own and waging a private war against it. The sack in my hands had already disintegrated into sooty threads, but still I went on beating my flame, which kept on leaping up again, with a fierce joy inappropriate to the circumstances, and little sparks flew around me; one of them got into my eye and hurt a lot, and my white shirt, the symbol of my surrender to bourgeois values, gradually took on local color—black stain after black stain. . . . Then we heard shots, and one of the ghaffirs was hit, and someone yelled to lie on the ground and move away from the flames, which had died down in the meantime (one whole field was burned to cinders). When I hurried to take shelter behind the railway embankment, someone else was there before me, bending over the wounded ghaffir. I saw to my amazement that the tall stranger, coolly using the wounded man's gun to return the fire of the dark figures clearly visible beyond the flames that were alternately springing up and dying down, was none other than Bernard Litovsky. He had managed to change his clothes before joining the second team of fire fighters, which was both better organized and more efficient than ours . . .

The way Litovsky, who had served in the German army, conducted himself was universally admired, and after they had gotten over their excitement about the ghaffir's wound (which turned out to be very superficial), everybody began praising him to the skies, and I immediately took back everything I had against him.

At first I felt a little jealous because they were all so busy talking about him that they forgot to mention me, and the way I had rushed to join the first contingent, but this absurd dejection vanished as soon as we got back to the kibbutz yard, where I found a surprise waiting for me that changed my feelings from one extreme to the other.

In front of everybody, to the extent that they could see in the darkness, Dora came up to me with a smile that affectionately embraced my grotesque appearance, and said in the warmest, most tremulous voice I had ever heard from her—exactly like the voice in which she used to speak to Dr. Manfred—that she had been very worried when I suddenly disappeared. And without any warning, she suddenly clasped my arms in both her hands and planted a long kiss on my cheek, and then another!

At the age of fourteen, when I first discovered Bach, his music affected me greatly. It aroused a deep feeling in me that I can only call religious. At that time I was already thinking in

terms of "illumination," "divine revelation," and "the elevation of the soul." And I thought that nothing would ever shake
my soul to the depths like that music. Until now, when Dora's
kiss shook me so profoundly that I felt on the verge of collapse. If I hadn't leaned on her, joyfully and helplessly, I would
have fallen down. She thrust me gently away. It would soon be
dawn and my friends were waiting for me. The armored car
which was to take us to Afula had already entered the yard. In
the light of the projector circling on the watchtower I read the
promise on her face. When we parted, she said she would
write and tell me how the wounded lad was getting on (I didn't
even know his name), and I took the fact that she felt she
needed an excuse to renew the correspondence between us as
an encouraging sign. Embarrassment is a feeling that may
hold out the promise of love. In the days when she was in
complete control of herself I had no place in her heart.

This is how I understood the kiss and the embarrassment
that followed: if I could share the monotony of her daily life,
without burning fields, perhaps she would be able to love me.

When we got onto the bus in Afula, Eva said: "It seems that
Friedman is more of a Don Juan than we imagined . . ." But
her words did not fill me with pride. The only words I could
think of were Dora's, which said hardly anything but contained a great message:

I had been called back to the starting line. My love had
passed the ordeal by fire in the burning fields of the kibbutz
and emerged like tempered steel.

Now it only remains for me to hope that love can be not
only a great conflagration, like the love I feel for Dora, but
also something that grows as gently as the grass in the fields,
the first seeds of which sprouted in her soul last night.

I shall cherish the blue shirt the girl in charge of the kibbutz
commissary gave me—to make me look like a "human being." And one day I'll go there to deliver it in person, clean and
ironed.

SUNDAY, NOVEMBER 13, 1938

My dear father,

I read the news from Berlin in this morning's paper with grave concern. I don't want to say too much. My heart is not with the young man in Paris who wanted to save his people's honor and did grave harm instead, but I think we have to read the writing on the wall. The people who burned down synagogues didn't do it out of religious fanaticism. They wanted us to understand: anyone prepared to desecrate the Holy of Holies won't take pity on people.

I hope that some good will come of it at least, and you will wake up from your illusions. The Third Reich is not an accident of history, as you fondly imagine. It will be with us for a thousand years, at least.

I beg you, get up and leave while you can. Don't worry about being a burden on me. Now that I have been promoted to principal second violin I am earning twenty pounds sterling a month (you can work out how much it comes to in marks yourself; I don't know the rate of exchange). The quartet brings in something too, not much but something. If I take six or seven pupils, I can make twenty-six pounds sterling a month, which is not bad at all, considering the living standards in the country. I have a little saved up, too. We won't be able to live in the style you're accustomed to, but we won't starve.

Please, Father. Don't hesitate. Things are going to get worse in Germany. I'm begging you. I worry about you day and night. If anything happens to you, I'll never forgive myself for abandoning you to your fate when you needed me. I'll be the happiest man in the world if you come to live with me. I'll rent a flat big enough for the two of us, and I'm sure that a man like you will have no trouble finding work quickly.

Your loving son,

Konrad

P.S. I might take a Hebrew name (first name, not family name). I thought about Nimrod, but it sounds a bit too pretentious. If you would prefer me to call myself Menahem, after your father, I'll be glad to, although it too contains a promise of consolation I doubt I am capable of fulfilling.

Viola—
Eva Staubenfeld

In the days when I was suffering from a mysterious inflammation in my right wrist and couldn't bow without pain, and no drugs, massage, electricity, or physiotherapy helped, I was forced to give up the idea of a career as a soloist. The pains got worse whenever I had to stand on a stage by myself, opposite thousands of eyes fixed on my body, and they subsided only when I could hide in an orchestra behind a music stand and conductor. I was advised to consult the specialists who were then in fashion.

Dr. Blecher, an outstanding disciple of the Vienna school—then at the height of its fame—offered his services without charge. The subject of professional blocks, especially in art, interested him personally, and he was therefore prepared to take me on without being paid for his trouble.

I saw him eyeing my breasts—I exposed them as much as I could on purpose—with the restless look I know so well, and I told him to go to hell in the politest way possible, giving hypocrisy a slap in the face.

"You always pay more for what you get as a present," I said.

He wasn't offended. What else had he done over seven or ten years but learn how to submit to all the insults crazy people like me hurl at saints like him, who've ruined their health in the attics of Vienna so that they can save us from the devils stoking the hellfires in our souls?

"You must obtain treatment, my dear Fräulein. You shouldn't neglect it. It will get worse later."

You can't ridicule this type either. They're immune to the sneers of people who deserve only compassion. They have a way—all their own—of driving us up the wall and coming out on top. They gaze at us with a pious, holier-than-thou expression, and forgive us for the rudeness erupting like pus from an open wound, like priests who know that God is always on their side, and never on the side of the lost souls they are trying to bring back to the fold.

They use a special jargon, too, which exempts them from having to measure up to the layman's sense of truth: "The Fräulein is too hard on herself; there's no pity in her heart, not even for herself; she's incapable of giving of herself, or receiving either . . ." As if this reserve of yours, which they see as a symptom of something neatly pigeonholed under a technical term and professional classification, is a transparent trick, resorted to by a sick mind to guard its disgraceful secrets from them. But they don't give up easily. Patience is a tool of the trade—it's what people pay them for, after all, that long-suffering smile that fills their coffers with cash. And the more obstinately you conceal the truth, the more you pay through the nose. As far as they are concerned, my "hostility"—skepticism, apparently, is permitted only to the mentally healthy (a health, by the way, which they themselves seem to have renounced of their own free will, as the Orthodox renounce independence of mind)—is only one more symptom of my illness.

If he were a woman, I think to myself, a good-looking woman who is resentfully desired, because even though she is unprotected she reserves the right to give herself only to whomever she herself desires, he would learn a thing or two about the male sex. Even the books he reads, which are full of filth of every kind, don't know everything. Perhaps because they were written by men and the fundamental hypocrisy that's second nature to them "represses" from consciousness all the obscene lusts they can't find self-righteous interpretations for.

Why should I bare my soul to him? I stared straight into his eyes and found no difficulty in discerning their general drift, which was not, apparently, subject to the dictates of reason. They were staring straight into the delta of my blouse, which afforded a broad enough expanse of gleaming udder to leave little to the imagination, despite the interference of a cheeky strip of lace.

He's not stupid. He realized immediately that he had been caught red-handed. He began rapidly regurgitating the contents of a pseudointellectual article—which I had also read—in order to satisfy my curiosity before I decided whether I should satisfy his. Talking helps us to understand, he said. He wasn't going to interrogate me, God forbid, but help me to free myself of a heavy burden that had been weighing on my soul since the days of my early childhood. I myself, at my own pace, would dig into that buried treasure in order to vomit up the grain of poison I swallowed all those years ago as a helpless and innocent child.

I wondered how an intelligent man like him, who had the skill to cut out an inflamed appendix if he wanted to, chose to engage in such charlatanism. What made him think that in one hour a week, over a limited period of time—even a long one—he would succeed in finding out more about me than I have myself after peering into that bloody pit for twenty-nine years? If you don't know yourself after nearly thirty years, you might as well go to church to be saved by the priests. And if you do, you don't need experts. If only he hadn't offered to treat me free of charge. I might have been able to believe he possessed enough stupid honesty or mental limitations to stop him from going overboard when a momentary doubt about the validity of the theories governing his behavior threatened to jeopardize his career. But after he volunteered to dig into me for nothing—first my soul and then (he must have promised himself "subconsciously," since he would never dare to confront himself consciously) my body—I couldn't understand how he could still expect me to believe that his controlled observations would help me to find my way through the sewer into which I was cast by a moment of unrestrained lust. I won't pretend that it smells of roses down there.

I know more than I want to know already. If any outside help is required, it's only to block up a few windows that afford too good a view. I know all the vermin scrambling around in my soul. I don't need to throw them any bloody bait from the illuminated parts above.

It's all so obvious and ugly. I don't even want to call things by their name.

There's no need to classify the rubbish before you throw it out.

Dr. Blecher was forty and I was only twenty-two, but I knew more about life than he did. He patronized me with the conceit of a dullard who got good marks at the university and whose friends think him clever, and I laughed at him. True contact between us was a lost cause.

A good-looking woman, unfortunately, is forced to know things that her ugly, long-suffering sister has no conception of. The latter knows only the stupidity of fools and the cruelty of cads; the former also knows the foolishness of the wise and the baseness of the noble.

I don't need any favors, thank you. I have instruments of my own, I said to him.

Which, for example? he said.

I asked him if he had ever tried music as therapy.

I was in for a surprise: Dr. Blecher played the flute. A little smile of triumph appeared on his lips, which were dry with lust. He was prepared to treat me with my own "instruments." Music could serve as therapy, too, he agreed. He was not dogmatic. The main thing was to get results. But since we couldn't find any works for flute and viola, he was unwillingly obliged to allow a violinist from the Philharmonic to join our therapy sessions. It was a comedy of errors. She couldn't understand why I had invited her to play with a block of wood like Dr. Blecher. He was clumsy and plodding, and he played false notes. If he was my lover, she said, I should play on his flute rather than letting him torture Beethoven. After the second session she refused to play with him. The two of us could find someone better. She turned up at the third session with the principal flute of the Philharmonic and Dr. Blecher sat admiringly on the sidelines. The idiot didn't understand that I was making fun of him. What did he think—that a person who couldn't play in tune and whose tone was hollow and colorless and who used the sole of his shoe as a metronome could "use music" as therapy? Maybe for himself. Not for me.

After showing him how small and insignificant he was, I agreed to try his method, too. I went to his clinic and lay down on the couch. I could say whatever came into my head. The rude rejection he had suffered at the hands of two women who played better than he put our relations on a firm footing: I could hurt him and he couldn't hurt me. When I lie on his couch, I'm the one who's sitting, and he, on his chair, is the one who's lying down.

In this situation I've even permitted him to speak of my suffering, and it gave him the greatest pleasure, even though I didn't "suffer" in the sense that he meant. I didn't tell him about the experiences I'd been through, but not because they'd been repressed into my subconscious, as he imagined. They were right there on the surface, like a kind of technical skill I had already acquired and had no further need to practice. I learned this from my violin teacher: to make your hand more flexible you have to play the difficult passages with your fist, and only afterward relax your grip.

In the end I got sick and tired of listening to his perverted ramblings about suffering and misery and took him by surprise by asking him if he wanted to go to bed with me. He had the nerve to be insulted but quickly recovered his professional expression and said that my frankness showed that the treatment was helping. I said that a little honesty wouldn't hurt him either. And then he admitted that he would like to go to bed with me, but his professional ethics would not allow him to. His lips trembled, and he himself understood that the treatment had come to an end. I'm too hard for a delicate creature like him. The idiot had fallen in love and lost an interesting case. Not to mention a sure source of income. Because I would have paid him if he had really helped me. But a woman who has no need to talk about herself is a hopeless case.

I'm better at treating my psyche than Dr. Blecher. I don't need him or any of his kind. In the analysis I perform on myself there are no loopholes or lies.

In fact, I never really stop it except when I'm asleep. And even then I have dreams that demand to be deciphered. But they're too confused and I'm not sure that it's worth the trouble.

All I have to do is look out of the window—and I'll see myself, exposed and naked. But if I look out of the window, I'll stop playing the viola. Always the same picture: laundry in the wind, as if there's an endless pile of dirty linen pursuing the wretched housewife opposite, and whenever she's not quarreling with her husband, or shouting at her children, or cooking, or beating the carpets, or polishing the furniture, she's busy with the laundry that she hates from the bottom of her heart. She hates her life, the weather, the children running wild in the yard, and me because I play when she's trying to sleep. There's always a pair of coarse female underpants hanging on the line, not quite clean—if she can't get rid of those ugly stains at the bottom, she should buy another pair and not wave the flag of the hopeless struggle against the uglier aspects of womanhood. Weighing down the line next to them is a gigantic corset which looks like a medieval instrument of torture—a woman who requires one of those would do better to give up the battle. The corset rubs up against a fat man's underpants, one of the vulgar men who play cards on the balcony and whose poker faces hide the furtive looks they steal in the direction of my window, in case I should do them all a favor and get undressed—maybe one day I'll do just that, and upset the show of cozy family life they put on for the benefit of their guests. Only the little children's undershirts, which look like dolls', dripping water, do something to improve the repulsive view . . .

And the radio never stops blaring at full volume!

"Laundry on a line, the banners of the hopeless battle for order and cleanliness," said Egon Loewenthal, standing on my balcony and peering into the opposite windows—only six meters away—with the curiosity of a writer who imagines that one peep into an empty room will enable him to understand its occupants. How happy he'd be if they put on a show for him so that he could add it to the private collection of memories from which he pulls out the scenes he needs for his writing. "The white flags of surrender of the exhausted housewife who once dreamed of writing poetry and going on the stage . . ."

I should never invite him home. He's perfectly polite and tries to give the impression that his subtle advances are no more than an occasion for phrasemongering. (He's got Hilda Moses, who worships him as if all that writing really meant something, waiting in his bed.) But subtle hints can be cruder than imploring puppy eyes, like the pair that God, in a moment of wickedness that overcame all other considerations, stuck in the face of that idiot in the Russian shirt who follows me around as if a single invitation were a subscription ticket for the entire season. Loewenthal's innuendos can be extremely unpleasant; they're so subtle and discreet that if I respond he'll have every right to accuse me of rape. In the street he's a charming escort, like a lively, amusing animal cavorting around you without ever bumping into you, but the moment he sees four walls his eyes begin to squawk. And I don't want to quarrel with Comrade Sonichka either. It's enough that I annoy her by my very existence: an un-Jewish Jewess, belonging and not belonging.

"Being Jewish is a moral obligation," she says in her bad German, and jumps out of her skin when I say that being Jewish is an accident of birth, that Gentiles hate the Jews precisely because they try to make people believe that they have a moral obligation toward anyone who had a drop of blood sucked out of his penis on the eighth day.

Lately she's despaired of me, but she still hasn't despaired of marrying me off to "a nice boy." She examines every man who comes into the house suspiciously. If he's "serious," she serves him tea and cake. If not—like Loewenthal, whose act she's quite incapable of comprehending—she listens behind the door convinced of her moral right to do so, like a soldier doing reprehensible things in a noble cause: a husband worth his salt will rid me of the peculiar ideas that loneliness and disappointment put into my head. To this day I think she regrets the rich cake she wasted on Rosendorf. She thought him a bachelor and decided he was the ideal match for me. When she found out that he had a wife in Germany, she suddenly discovered false notes in his playing, too. A woman of high principles and solid virtues who believes in whatever has all its feet planted squarely on the ground: houses, chairs, the family, honesty, loyalty, and national pride. She doesn't trust artists, who permit themselves to stray from the straight and narrow. Women like me frighten her. We have neither right opinions nor true feelings. What do I need with music? She can't understand. ("With her it's all surface veneer," I once overheard her say to her friend, a Russian Jewess with a bun on top of her head and the no-nonsense look of a prosecuting attorney in her eye, when I didn't have the patience to listen to her outpourings about the happy life she led with her carpenter, who earned his bread by the honest sweat of his brow and brought up his children to be decent people. "There's no feeling in her heart at all. And she plays without any soul—nothing but technique and outward show . . .")

But basically she's a kindhearted woman. Once I gave her a

free ticket—to a regular concert, not one for workers. She suffered all evening, she told me. She couldn't stand the unreality of the people and the elegant women who came to show off their new dresses. She suffered from the smell, too. Like a drugstore where a bottle of perfume had been broken, she said. She only likes the smell of the sweat of working people, she says, and I believe her.

When I close my eyes I can forget the view from the window. Then I can see the view from the window of the summer house we had on the banks of the Attersee when I was a happy young girl in a happy world.

Rosendorf thought I was talking about Mahler.

He's afraid there's going to be a war. I don't know if he's concerned for his family, or afraid that the postwar world will no longer be what it was before. Music is the motherland of the stateless, he says. I suppose he heard this from Loewenthal. This is the only consolation of those who are not sure if they are really great enough not to need a motherland. If Loewenthal was Thomas Mann, he would be in America. If Rosendorf was Szigeti, he'd have a quartet in London. If I was a great violist, as that flatterer Litovsky said I was, I would be in the Zurich Orchestra.

In Palestine there's no room for the stateless, only for the state-hungry, says Loewenthal.

Only I dare to say: we are all going to degenerate here. In spite of Huberman's patronage and the limited enthusiasm of Toscanini, who treats us like some Italian Renaissance prince, this country will never have a serious orchestra by European standards. The best musicians will leave; the mediocre will remain. The only thing that can save us is war.

And there will be a war. Although I told Rosendorf there wouldn't be, because he's so sensitive and the least little thing upsets his balance, in my heart of hearts I know that war will indeed break out. Not because of Hitler—evidently a manipulator of genius, who knows how to go to the brink and take advantage of the stupidity and cowardice of the leaders of the Western democracies—but because as long as it's up to men, it's inevitable.

It's men who make wars—not Nazis or Bolsheviks or capitalists with vested economic interests (the theory propounded by Konrad Friedman, a soft man with something pure and feminine and slightly twisted in his character, which involves him in inner contradictions and makes him demand consistency of himself as a supreme male value) but men who conduct wars with savage cruelty and go to die in them with the enthusiasm of fools.

Inside every man there is a child who was never given the opportunity to act out his cruelty. When I see them in their rigid, gaudy uniforms, marching in procession to the strains of crude, boring music, keeping step in time to a monotonous rhythm, puffed up like peacocks, chests out and chins up, submitting to barbaric rules of duty and discipline and loving every minute of it, running after rank and prestige, ready to give their lives for the sake of a medal, I am filled with horror and dread. They won't rest until they have destroyed the civilization that was built up over centuries of restraint. They'll never give up the right to dominate, to demonstrate their strength, to fight for superiority of any kind. Nazism is simply the exaggerated German form adopted by the hurt male pride defeated in the last war. Until they gather for their victory parades and march into the capital cities of a Europe that hates them, they'll never be satisfied.

Even Litovsky, who was forced to flee Germany because of his Jewishness—what's he proud of? Of being an officer in the German army and winning some medal there? And he despises Friedman for having evaded military service—how grotesque!

"Some of the finest human qualities are displayed on the battlefield," he said to us once, and he never forgave me for bursting out laughing. Martha told me that he was hurt to the quick. But I never meant to insult him. My laughter stemmed from despair. I was sorry for Martha, whose only child is two years older than she is.

We women pay the price for this appalling male backwardness. Men are a thousand years behind women, whose sense of responsibility and feelings of compassion are part of their bloodstream.

I have no pity in my heart for these flawed models of the human species, who take advantage of their physical strength in order to dominate women—creatures superior to them in every respect—and turn them into their property. Sometimes I wonder at their indignation when someone stronger than they are takes advantage of his strength in order to dominate them. They themselves would never hesitate to use their strength to subdue a woman.

It's enough to see how they promise us to themselves as a prize they deserve for their achievements—glory on the battlefield, success on the stock exchange, family lineage, literary awards, victory in the boxing ring, or some scientific discovery. Even the most refined members of the sex sometimes look us over with the appraising eyes of a merchant assessing the value of a piece of goods and asking himself how much he should invest in it.

And then I have no choice but to pull down the blinds and switch on the electric light. In a locked room, facing a bare wall with my eyes closed, I can wipe men out of my mind and play a Bach partita as if nothing existed but this—this music, this moment . . .

Sometimes I dream that the men from the opposite balcony approach me and touch me with fat, dirty fingers. I wake up in disgust and discover that what woke me up is the saxophone of the downstairs neighbor who practices wedding music from early in the morning, schmaltz that makes me want to vomit.

Dr. Blecher's right—I'm antisocial, cold, disdainful, a man-hater, complicated, full of inner rage, and God knows what else. So what? How would it have helped me if I had told him ugly details about my life? I can imagine the kinds of ideas that would have come into his head if I told him that I'm capable of going to bed with two different men on the same day, and I can't see anything wrong with it. Each of them would get something different and neither of them would lose by it. I would do it without any shame if only I didn't know how corrupt and ready to take advantage of weakness men are. But if someone really aroused me, I wouldn't hesitate. I don't owe anyone a thing. I'd do it, just as I'd submit to other experiences, because I need to understand myself, to probe myself to the depths, to know how far I'm prepared to go and what kind of monster lives in the labyrinth whose end I have not yet reached. The only thing I'm prepared to do without is drugs. They affect my mastery of my instrument. Sex does something for me that no chemical substance can do. I've tried them, but they never did anything special for me. Like a long swoon, without the sense of time passing. I don't want to give up the sense of time.

Dr. Blecher would never believe me if I told him that I'm capable of wholehearted love. And here, too, a number of people simultaneously. That's how I love Rosendorf, with a warm, pleasant love that never bores me or gets on my nerves. He's a wonderful man who gives me the feeling that the world of music would lose something important if I didn't exist. True, my love for him is more like the love of a mother or a sister than the love of a woman, but sometimes I feel a strong desire to touch his penis, completely unexpectedly, and see his pure blue gaze turn gray. I won't do it, because he worries so much about the quartet. He's afraid that it will be damaged if the professional framework is disrupted. I'm a little afraid, too, of disappointment. It's easy to please the lechers, hard to satisfy serious people who expect some sort of transcendence from love. I doubt if he could stir me as profoundly with his prick as he does when he plays the second theme of the third movement of

Beethoven's Opus 132, with his eyes closed and his lids trembling, as if he has been touched by the hand of God.

Am I capable of going to bed with Litovsky too? Maybe. He's a real man. In bed he's probably entertaining and uninhibited. But I can't trust him. A man of such infantile ambitions would see a gesture of goodwill on my part as a victory over me. This idiocy would deprive me of any enjoyment. Fools make me dry up. And a dry fuck is a very doubtful pleasure. I like Friedman too. But I wouldn't go to bed with him. He'd be liable to die of sorrow when he discovered that he wasn't giving me any pleasure. The one I'll go to bed with in the end will be Loewenthal. The only thing stopping me is that it would cause Hilda Moses, who pretends to be a liberated woman, unbearable pain. I'm curious to know if it's any different with a really clever man. But my laziness is sometimes greater than my curiosity.

I'd have to be crazy to tell all this to Dr. Blecher, or anyone else. The secrets we keep to ourselves are the last place where we can find a refuge from ugliness. What help could I possibly get from a man whose theories would all come out in my mouth if I sucked him? . . .

Chamber music is my therapy.

It fits in well with the recommendation to improve my communication with my fellows. "You should expand your mutual relations with your colleagues . . . cooperate with others. . . . It's the only way to break out of the vicious circle of your withdrawal . . ." Interaction—that was the key word. And I heard in it all Dr. Blecher's yearning for the mutual relations he wished to consummate in my body.

I know of no other form of "interaction" which demands mutual attention of the kind demanded by chamber music. The cooperation of a chamber ensemble applies to subtle nuances of feeling which nonmusicians don't even know exist. The most minute fluctuations of mood are signaled from one person to another in the mute and secret language of the body: a quick nod of the head, a movement of the arm, or a slight flutter of the eyelids—if you fail to respond to such signals at once, chamber music is not your field.

I came to it at a relatively late age, in a kind of disappointment with myself. At the age of ten I was a child prodigy and all the world wished me well. At the age of fourteen I discovered that I stood on the stage like a circus performer astonishing the audience with her tricks, incapable of expressing any emotion between laughter and tears. When I played Bach's partitas, they sounded shallow and boring. I played the Brahms Violin Concerto like a series of acrobatic feats. I wasn't playing musical works but strings of fascinating exercises for the violin interrupted by sentimental intermezzos. I didn't have the inner resources to sustain the continuity of a musical composition, whose essence consists of maintaining the right balance between tension and relaxation. At the age of seventeen, at the height of my fame, and at a moment of poetic justice (my father, who up to then had participated in my education by means of his bank account, came to ask my mother's permission to acknowledge me and grant me the full extent of his protection), when everyone was predicting a brilliant future for me, I abandoned the violin for the viola— an instrument which fascinated me by its warm and "erotic," as Litovsky says, tone. Within a year I had mastered the entire repertoire I found in the music shops.

Thus I discovered chamber music, which freed me from the tremendous emotional strain of playing the viola concertos, and at the same time saved me from the tedium of an orchestra, where people don't have to take personal responsibility for the quality of the music and develop herd characteristics. Chamber music strikes the right balance between personal responsibility and teamwork, and for someone like me, who needs a little break from time to time after a bout of espressivo has drained the marrow from my bones, it's a good place to calm the restlessness seething under the frozen exterior the good God saw fit to give me ("After the age of forty a person is

responsible for his own face," said Dr. Blecher, quoting someone else, but I'm only twenty-nine, and I don't feel in the least
guilty about my misleading appearance). The Baroque composers must have been thinking of me when they wrote their
music, in much of which the main role of the second violin and
the viola is to maintain tempo regularity and bring the first
violin back to the right tempo after certain ritardandi have
slowed things down too much.

And lo and behold, my first chance to play in a quartet
worthy of the name, a first-rate quartet of the kind I longed to
play in while I was still in Berlin, only came in this accursed
country, to which I was exiled owing to political circumstances that had nothing to do with me, and because of a race
to which I never saw myself as belonging.

One always runs into the obstacle of the egocentric first
violin. In Berlin I was a candidate for two different chamber
ensembles, and in both cases I was turned down at the last
minute. No reasons were given. Such decisions are completely
arbitrary. After all, you can't go and complain because a
better musician won. But both times I sensed an ambivalence
stemming from male chauvinism. The first violin was afraid
that he might have to behave chivalrously and compromise his
artistic principles because I was a woman. They would both
have been very happy to accommodate me elsewhere, as long
as they could keep their quartets exclusively male. One of
them, whose external appearance was not designed to attract
the spotlights, might also have feared that I would distract the
attention of the audience from the music. ("Hearing a
woman's voice is indecent"—says Friedman, quoting the Jewish sources. They too, like the Christians, hold that the flesh
must be subdued to elevate the spirit.)

Even Rosendorf said that he had "hesitated" before inviting
me to join. "You're too beautiful," he said. He said it humor-
ously and without affectation, as if confiding in me, in a
moment of weakness, an irrelevant consideration.

"You're not so ugly yourself," I said to him. "At least half the audience will direct their opera glasses at you."

(We even resemble each other a little. Like brother and sister. We're both tall, thin, fair-haired, and blue-eyed. If their theories of race were true, Dr. Goebbels would be playing trios with Konrad and Bernard, and Rosendorf would be posing for the Nazi propaganda posters as a perfect model of the pure Aryan type.)

It soon transpired, however, that he was afraid not of having to share the limelight with me but of "emotional complications."

I promised him "emotional neutrality" as far as the quartet was concerned. I didn't have to put it into words: when I sit opposite a music stand I'm a sexless creature. If my playing expresses any kind of femininity at all, it's a hidden, elusive quality. I can play with a virile attack which few men I know can match on any instrument whatsoever. In any event, in relation to the other three people performing a string quartet with me, I am nothing but a viola, joining and separating from each of the other instruments at the composer's bidding. I don't have to impose strict discipline on myself to be safe from dangerous liaisons. My limited but concentrated experience of life is a sufficient guarantee against vain romantic illusions. The treacherous element in the male character is only too familiar to me.

Perhaps this is the curse of beauty: it forces you to become acquainted with the dark side of men who, as far as other, even quite attractive, women are concerned, never stop conducting themselves like polite, civilized human beings.

I didn't have to make much of an effort to keep my promise.

One of the key words in the therapeutic vocabulary is "balance." You have to achieve a degree of inner balance, Dr. Blecher used to say.

Why? Who says that I have to be "balanced"? What rack do

I have to lie on in order to balance myself? Why not rather seek balance in terms of our relations with others?

Our quartet is "balanced" from every point of view. Two with a natural tendency to break bounds—the first violin and the cello—and two with a restrained rhythmic sense—the second violin and the viola. Two with a "declamatory" tone—if one can define in words the penetrative power of an intense, forceful tone—the second violin and the cello—and two with an introspective tone, singing to itself and giving rise in the listener to the feeling that he has overheard an intimate conversation by mistake—the first violin and the viola. Two whose love of Baroque and Romantic music makes them superb interpreters of the classical repertoire—the first violin and the cello—and two with a fine ear for the nuances and subtleties of contemporary music—the second violin and the viola.

It wouldn't be going too far to say that we are also two men and two women. And I'm not referring to the theories of the young Jewish genius who committed suicide. The feminine element in Rosendorf's character is neither a weakness nor a perversion. On the contrary, it even gives him a certain advantage.

Rosendorf's playing is among the most beautiful I have ever heard. The sweet tone he draws from his violin, reminiscent of Jascha Heifetz, puts him in the first rank of contemporary musicians. It's only an accident that he hasn't won the fame he deserves. Perhaps because he devoted himself to his quartet, and perhaps because a certain sensitivity with regard to his Jewishness made him keep a low profile instead of elbowing his way to the top. He's thirty-eight years old. Maybe he's already missed the boat. A man of his age has little chance of making an impression on the musical milieu, which likes to discover young geniuses. In an out-of-the-way place like this—despite the headlines Huberman and Toscanini are making in the world, mainly for themselves—there's no chance of his making a name for himself. The fate of really great violinists is decided in Europe and America.

I should be glad of the chain of events which brought him here, but I can't help regretting a great talent being wasted in a small place. I wouldn't be able to play with a violinist of his caliber anywhere else in the world. I weep for him with a happy heart.

This man of delicate sensibilities is more German than any German I know. He's refined to the point of fragility. The feminine element in his character finds perfect expression in the gentle works of Schubert, Schumann, and Mendelssohn, and also in a few works by Brahms in which the composer lost control of himself.

Femininity doesn't weaken the attraction to women. A feminine man woos them with a melancholy, heartrending expression. He simply begs them to take the initiative into their own hands. The response is well-nigh guaranteed. I suspect that he too, like the heroes of the Romantic period he expresses so well, harbors the same ambivalence, if not outright hypocrisy, toward women that one finds in the average healthy stud: abject worship of a woman of superior social class, side by side with a passionate desire to wallow in the mud with the defenseless servant girl dependent on his good graces. The same modest ambivalence that gave a number of the composers of that century the disease that drove them insane. Music did not suffer from their disease; it gained works of exquisite beauty. Who cares that it was only their own miserable fate they were lamenting there and not the sufferings of humanity? By the way, I don't believe that Rosendorf would risk going to a whore. He wouldn't know where to find one and would be ashamed to ask. But I don't think he would need her services in the first place. I'm prepared to bet that there are plenty of women, cultured young ladies with artistic aspirations, who would succeed in getting him into bed if they were given the chance. He would screw them with a shy smile of guilty surrender, without taking the least responsibility for the results, if only they put out their hands and touched him where a man is powerless, on that

pathetic worm which for some reason—what an irony!—
symbolizes manhood and virility. He himself, I imagine, in
obedience to strict moral standards and loyalty to the nobler
part of his personality, would never take the first step, which
would deprive him of the right to be the victim of circumstances. To be on the safe side, he always seeks the company of
women like me, or Frau Becker, or Martha, or Hilda Moses—
women with whom there can be no risk of any kind of emotional involvement. Each one for a different reason: me—
because the quartet means more to him than a passing affair,
which, according to his stereotyped view of women, would be
very hard to end; Hella Becker—because she's done him so
many favors and bound him to her with ties of gratitude
without thinking of the consequences, i.e., that he couldn't so
much as touch her now without being denounced by his conscience for selling his body for material benefits; and Hilda
Moses—because she's a strong woman with both feet on the
ground, the kind of woman he admires from the bottom of his
heart and is therefore incapable of loving, but also because
she's the property of a friend whom he also admires and
respects. The natural instincts of property owners tell them to
beware of touching other people's property if they don't want
to be robbed in return. By the way, Rosendorf's wife, too, is
apparently a woman who knows her own mind, the kind of
woman whose protection he always seeks. She's a woman
after my own heart, even though I don't know her. She did
him a big favor when she relieved him of the need to take the
bold decision which separated them from each other for an
unspecified period of time, an arrangement that reduces the
points of friction between two artists competing for position. I
will never marry a musician.

Rosendorf speaks about his wife with reverence, but not
with love. On her slender shoulders (I saw a picture in my
mind's eye: a mezzo-soprano apparently drawing her strength
from pure willpower rather than the inflated sounding box of
most of the famous opera singers, whose bodily dimensions

make a mockery of the love scenes on stage . . .) she had taken responsibility for the musical future of three members of the same family, each more gifted than the next.

He would never have been able to suggest such a cruel, simple solution. Only a woman passionately convinced that her daughter was a female Artur Rubinstein would be prepared to deprive herself of love in order to realize a long-term plan. Poor Kurt is already suffering from the separation from his family—even if only because of urgent carnal needs. But perhaps I'm doing him an injustice, and he's simply missing his daughter. He often stares into space, as if pondering the correct tempo to choose, but the truth is that he's far away, in Berlin or somewhere else. Brahms carries him there particularly quickly. When he gets a letter from home—which has been happening less and less frequently recently—he's preoccupied with it for hours on end, busy interpreting what's written and what's not. Greta behaves as if the German censor has nothing better to do than read her letters, which are full of "secret" information about her financial situation and newspaper clippings about herself and her daughter.

So much for the women in the quartet. Kurt and I. You could hardly call Friedman, the second violin, a particularly masculine type. He's one of those eternal vacillators who can never make up their minds who they are and what they want to be, but his playing is extremely masculine, if the word can be used to describe his powerful, often irrelevant bowing and the sharp, very exact spicatti testifying to perfect control of an extremely strong right hand. On second thought, I take back my definition of masculine. Most of the men I've known were in love with their own vacillations. They interpreted their own indecisiveness as a deliberate stretching out of a pleasant interim state, like deliberately delaying ejaculation by distracting their thoughts from screwing. (Von Staubenfeld, the uncle and his son. Two perverts . . .) I respect Friedman's masculinity because he doesn't ask himself what he wants to be but what he wants to do. In choosing between the two great loves of his life, music and politics (such insanity is very rarely found among women), he is torn to pieces. He doesn't deign to discuss with me the weighty questions oppressing his soul because he considers me a rootless, egocentric, narrow-minded creature who has nothing in her head but music—and even that only on the technical level, without a deep understanding of its human value. I can only smile at the way he's pigeonholed me, simply because I haven't got the patience to listen to his nattering at rehearsals. He drives me up the wall with long lectures, which are supposed to prove why a sforzando, which I play with an up-bow just as well as he does with a down-bow, has to be done the way he does it. And I can't stand the way he shows off his encyclopedic knowledge, especially whenever Loewenthal's around. I'm prepared to admit that there's a connection between music and weltanschauung, but I can't understand why we have to look for it in every single bar. Not every modulation is a challenge to the powers that be. It often has a simpler function—to relieve boredom. But Friedman's never happy unless he succeeds in turning every change in the structure of the piece into a conspiracy against absolutism.

There's one thing I can say to Friedman's credit—his anger brings his positive sides to light: loyalty to his values and a steadfast, disinterested stand on principle. These are the moments when I like him best, even though his anger is often directed against me. He can't bring himself to be angry with Rosendorf. His attitude toward Kurt goes beyond friendship (lately they've begun calling each other *du*) and is more like a love affair, in which Friedman plays the part of the man tirelessly courting his beloved, and Rosendorf the part of the woman who permits herself to be loved. Among the weaknesses of this man, for whom I feel an affection I try not to show—in addition to his childish confidence in his own originality (although all he manages to produce is stuff the Zionist leaders already ground out at the beginning of the century)—I count his stage fright, which is so bad that I've even considered telling Rosendorf that we should ask him to give up his place in the quartet in favor of a violinist who doesn't lose his wits every time he sees an audience in front of him.

Sometimes I can't resist imitating him, he's such a scream. Even before he steps onto the stage, the warning lights go on in his eyes. He launches an energetic attack on last-minute technicalities and manages to put the danger signals out, but they soon go on again, like the electric bulbs on an advertising sign. Then he looks down anxiously at his clothes, frowning when his eyes light on his fly, a place which invites catastrophe (once he forgot to button it up and it gaped when he sat down). When he sees that all is in order down there, he stretches his neck, sticks out his chest, clears his throat, and hugging Rosendorf's back and lengthening his stride to shorten the via dolorosa from the wings to his chair, he throws himself, as if jumping into icy water, at a crouch onto the lighted stage. At that moment he becomes as panic-stricken as a rabbit caught in the headlights of a car, and from then on he proceeds like a sleepwalker in a nightmare, swaying unsteadily from side to side until he collapses onto his chair. The next moments are devoted to a maddening organization of his immediate surroundings: he moves his chair backward and forward, examines the backrest, as if he were actually planning to lean against it during the course of the concert, pushes the music stand about, puts on his glasses, tunes his strings unnecessarily, clears his throat again as if about to make a speech, and only then notices that we are waiting for a sign that we can begin. . . . If we begin—God forbid—with one of the Haydn or Mozart quartets, or even the Rasoumoffsky no. 1, which opens with sharply pointed eighths in the second violin and viola, all three first lines will be occupational therapy. The inner struggle going on in the heart of the poor second violin—forcing his trembling hand by a sheer effort of the will to tap out these even eighths with a regularity worthy of a line in the *Iliad*—is a titanic battle that makes us all hold our breath.

But the minute he overcomes his terror he plays so well that we forgive him for his moments of panic. He is the only one of us who always, always plays better and more correctly at a public performance than at the most successful rehearsal. His response to the audience is so great that all his warmheartedness and love of humanity go out to them in a manner which cannot but move the listener.

His endearing ugliness attracts the attention of women who know how to appreciate perfect devotion. I suppose he would think I was making fun of him if I told him this. I often see some female eye in the audience fixed on him in wonder at the touching enthusiasm he invests in playing long accompaniment lines as if the responsibility for the whole piece were his.

Everything about him seems out of place and somehow twisted, but nevertheless, the overall effect is one of wholeness and clarity. The big head, the protruding eyes, the hooked nose, the beetling brows, the ears sticking out at right angles to the skull, and the negroid lips, which he sucks in like a pink doughnut when playing fortissimo, and piano too, as if tasting the sweetness of some forbidden fruit which he would not dare enjoy in daily life. Privately I call him "the hunchback of Notre Dame," although he sits as straight as a ramrod, because whenever he plays on the G string he raises his right shoulder (to ensure the lightness of his arm) as if threatening to smash the violin to pieces if it should let him down.

I can't imagine a woman in his arms, except as a gesture of goodwill. But I'm not representative. There must be women who respond to that kind of emotional intensity and like to see a man swooning with love, worshiping their sour-smelling bodies as if they had the gateway to eternity between their legs. I wouldn't mind betting that these are the loves of Konrad Friedman. And until he finds a woman of this sort, he probably suffers from wild fantasies and masturbates in secret. And if we take his religious education, even though he rebelled against it, into account, he must hate himself like hell when he does it.

Whenever he opens his mouth to say something, in such deadly earnest, I see before me an intelligent child of eight who at the age of eighteen turned into a perfect ass. When he should have laid bold hands on a girl's breast, he thought that it was his duty to recruit her first into the service of all the lofty ideas running around in his head.

For a while I played with the idea of opening the door myself into the dark room where he keeps his lusts locked up. I would like to see the spectacle of a martyred saint wallowing in what he calls filth. But I changed my mind. I promised Rosendorf that I wouldn't do anything to give rise to erotic tensions in the quartet. And Friedman, I'm sure, is precisely the man to be thrown off balance by an intimate event. Besides, going to bed with me would probably spoil his chances of ever enjoying sex with another woman. As that man von Staubenfeld, who asked me to call him Father, said on one of those loathsome meetings, his phony paternal love saturated with dark lusts and a slimy sense of sin: "A beggar who has slept on silk sheets will no longer be satisfied with a straw mattress."

Dr. Blecher used to say that all this preoccupation with erotic fantasies that I had no intention of putting into practice was a kind of self-deception. It was easier for me to admit to them than to face the truth. There are apparently grave matters stuck somewhere in my subconscious, like sinful souvenirs, which I am trying to obliterate.

Nothing is obliterated. But I feel no need to reconstruct the facts and certainly not to examine my feelings toward them at this late stage. I have only one feeling in my heart—profound loathing. And if I was once inhibited by a certain shame, today I am able to say it to myself with perfect composure: I hate them, all of them, everyone who was related to me in any way—my biological father, whom I hardly knew; his brother, the old goat; my cousin-husband, Herr von Staubenfeld; the handsome fool, his brother; the filthy lecher—each and every one of them, including His Highness, the head of the clan, who brought me into being with a drop of his sperm and wanted to wreak some foul, secret lust on me. From the moral point of view I was a creature of sin and consequently belonged to the world of rottenness. A lump of flesh you needed when you felt the desire to take a quick trip to those forbidden haunts. A filthy crew, my family. Each and every one. (I exempt my mother from the list—a pitiful creature who was all set to exploit her beautiful daughter for her own ends but who was forced to return me to my father the moment he discovered he had some use of his own for me. I can't hate her, but I can't help despising her.)

Actually, I'm quite content to be a person without any connections. I don't owe anyone anything. I can choose a new family for myself. All that survives of the old one is the lesson they taught me about human beings. Like the etudes I threw away after I finished the conservatory. I no longer needed them. I already knew how to play.

I have no problems in getting any man I want into my bed. If I looked at Litovsky for more than three seconds he'd have an erection. Loewenthal would be ready to betray his noblest ideas with me. The British officer who escorted us to Jerusalem, and who hasn't missed a concert since, would be prepared to spread the Union Jack underneath me as a sheet (no need—I'd prefer it as a cover). But I am apparently looking for the one man who wouldn't go to bed with me under any circumstances at all, as Dr. Blecher said in one of his rare moments of real insight.

When I feel the urge, I have no compunctions about picking someone up on the street. The trouble is, they won't leave me alone afterward. God only knows what made that idiot in the Russian shirt pour his heart out to Litovsky and go into all the gory details about what happened in that shack on the beach during those three days when I went mad and forgot to take the necessary steps to preserve my anonymity. Did he want to present his case to a tribunal of my colleagues? What do I owe him? What makes these backward creatures with male genitals between their legs think that we women can't get out of bed feeling as free as they do? If we feel like it, we'll open our legs again; if we don't—we won't. Intercourse doesn't give them any rights over us, any more than settling money on us entitles them to regard us as their property.

"A woman's right to her body is exclusive and absolute," I said to Martha, who was so sorry about the whole affair.

"Maybe you're right," she said, "but the only victims of this enlightened point of view are the women themselves."

Martha, who knows that "every man dreams of getting his hands on a really corrupt woman for once and discarding her after" and can speak as plainly as one who accepts human frailties and sees no point in getting indignant about them, nevertheless finds it difficult to understand how a woman, just like a man, might suddenly want to test her own destructive powers and "pick up" some good-looking boy ready to "curse God and man," as Egon Loewenthal says, just to get his head between her legs and experience dumb carnal love, with no past or future, and no sense of sin, with her. Martha can "understand" that it might be possible, and that according to the dictates of natural justice there is no reason why the right to give way to human weakness should be reserved for men alone—but she wouldn't like to see her only woman friend torn to pieces in the arena which very few women, and then only those possessing unlimited material resources, have dared to enter through the lions' gate rather than that of the victims.

It was my mistake. Tel Aviv isn't Berlin or Frankfurt. It's impossible to be anonymous here. It was pure idiocy to pick him up outside the concert hall with my viola in my hand. But he was standing there as beautiful as a Roman statue, and his eyes were blazing with such passionate desire that I couldn't resist the temptation to be God Almighty, who acts with utter arbitrariness and is worshiped nevertheless, and make the impossible possible.

Three days of paganism. But the little fool, who tried to show off his knowledge of German—he knew about a hundred words, but I didn't need a single one—believed that the things we did to each other, shamelessly, anonymously, bound us together for all eternity. He interpreted the groans of lust, which I allowed myself to utter out loud, as pledges and vows. This is probably why he was so astounded when at the end of the three days' leave from the orchestra I gave him to understand that my interest in him had been fully satisfied, and that not only did I not intend seeing him again, but that I would also succeed in wiping him from my memory, and it would cost me no great effort to do so.

This he apparently found intolerable. And so he decided to entrust the memory to others as well, for otherwise he might begin to think that the whole thing had taken place inside his head.

"Man is an animal who makes promises to himself," said Nietzsche, and I was the promise made to himself by a weak man who could not bear the thought that a woman, who for three days had submitted to his will like a slave, was stronger than he. He was absolutely baffled. What had he done wrong? he asked himself. How could I ignore him? It was incomprehensible. Even criminals have the right to a fair trial. And here there weren't even any charges (Loewenthal once mentioned some Czech who wrote about something similar, but I can't recall his name).

What could I tell him? That I was hungry and felt like getting stuck into some spicy dish, and he just happened to be there, a piece of meat calculated to satisfy my appetite? It would only insult him even more. As long as I keep quiet, he can console himself by imagining that I've got a guilty conscience. The trouble is that the simpleton seems to want to atone for his sins and offer me absolution by proposing marriage! That's all I need. I have no intention of marrying for love. If I ever agree to put my hands in chains, they'll be chains of gold. Since he failed to break my silence, he broke his own.

In a moment of weakness he was tempted to believe that the demonic gleam in Litovsky's eyes was a spark of sympathy—and he loosened his tongue.

If only it had ended there—with one of them pouring his heart out and the other satisfying his curiosity—the quartet need not have been involved. My colleagues aren't so narrow-minded as to be shocked by a wild and short-lived love affair. But that chatterbox Litovsky was so excited by the idea of discovering my secrets that he not only rushed off to tell the story, but added his own interpretations too, as if drawing a moral lesson from the facts was the only way to justify his gossip. As if it was only his wish to contribute to the investigation of human behavior that obliged him to poke his nose into other people's intimate affairs.

The reactions of my colleagues surprised me. Before I found out what had happened I sensed a certain change in the atmosphere. At first I only noticed the infuriating way Litovsky was looking at me. I couldn't understand why he was suddenly grinning as if he had caught me red-handed. As if I had ever pretended to be sexless. The way men look at a woman with a bad reputation. After that they begin making obscene remarks and hinting that they want a piece of the sale too, with a reduction for damaged goods. Day after day I could sense the confidential information spreading and compare the reactions of the others—a strange combination of astonishment, self-righteous disapproval, ugly curiosity, and hidden lusts.

I suppose I should be grateful to Litovsky for not letting it go beyond the circle of the quartet (and Egon Loewenthal). In this way he was able to relieve himself of the burden of the secret lying like a heavy stone on his heart, without seeming like an irresponsible gossip. The quartet is a family which forgives its members their weaknesses. A glue which holds us so fast together that no little moral weakness can separate us. We wouldn't dismantle the only home we have in a foreign country even if it came out that Rosendorf had sex with minors and Friedman went to bed with men.

Rosendorf took it badly. (Friedman implored Litovsky not to tell him, but he insisted that it was his duty.) In the morning, at the orchestra rehearsal, I saw the pain in his eyes and the question fluttering at the tips of his lashes. The quartet rehearsal in the afternoon was a mess. Weak men are worse than children when unacknowledged anger forces them into impulsive, irrelevant reactions. Every trifling disagreement developed into full-scale, total war. I felt as sorry for Rosendorf as a parent for a child who complains of imaginary pains because of anger at some deprivation.

I no longer had any doubt that he was secretly in love with me, a love which he forced himself to deny. Such a love is not necessarily a source of pain. As long as it doesn't go beyond a vague sentiment directed at a person from whom we expect no more than that he exist and smile at us—it can be very pleasant, especially when it isn't serious. It can give us quiet, painless happiness. But the moment it becomes serious all the miseries of unrequited love immediately appear—the dark lusts, the wounded pride, and the deceitful atmosphere surrounding the encounters of people who deny the sexual attraction between them and approach each other with grotesque cunning.

Rosendorf hasn't actually made a pass at me. He would never be so vulgar. But now there is a gleam of lust in his eyes. If I open my legs for everyone, why shouldn't he jump in too? I imagine that even his lecherous thoughts are couched in decent language, and that the things he does to me in his imagination are done gently and with a reasonable degree of respect and gratitude. Still, it annoys me to think that he only allowed himself to desire me after the conversation with Litovsky. As if now that it's come out that I'm a loose woman, and not too picky, he too can enjoy what's there for the taking.

There's no point in being angry. After all, nothing has happened—only a dirty gleam in his eye. And there's no point in saying: Keep your disgusting looks to yourself. He wouldn't understand what I was talking about.

I've got no one to blame but myself. Martha's right. A woman is always the victim of excessive liberty. Are we really forbidden what they are permitted? Maybe. Our conspiracy has to be deeper and darker.

I regret the respectful atmosphere, which is no longer what it used to be. The politeness is still there, but now it is more of a ritual than a simple expression of esteem.

Men will never grow up.

Even Egon. To his credit, the above gleam never came into his eye. He welcomed the sensational news. He has not changed his style of wooing—with the sad pride of a man who has nothing to offer but his soul. The only difference between the Before and After is in a new frankness. Something along the lines of: Welcome to the exclusive club of the free spirits. There are a lot of men in it and only a few women. His eyes said: I'm delighted to know how much we resemble each other. We both defy the conventions of bourgeois society, not only in theory but in practice. The last veil of hypocrisy has come down between us, and we stand before each other naked. We know that morality is only an instrument for the imposition of a civilization founded on the subjugation of natural instincts, and prefer to order our lives according to the pleasure principle.

My relations with Egon have not changed. Only been clarified, as it were. But there's been a real change in Hilda Moses. She's become more friendly. Partly because she admires my behavior and partly because she now feels a need to keep a close watch on me. My daring—to take a man who attracts me into my bed and then discard him like a squeezed lemon— arouses her imagination. She herself would never dare. But for safety's sake she'll keep me as close to her as she can from now on, so that Egon won't have to go looking for me somewhere else.

The only one who acknowledges a woman's rights over her own body as a self-evident truth is Friedman, whose experience of sex, if any, is less than that of the others. He's the only one who wasn't shocked and never sent me any lecherous looks. He goes on treating me with the same respectful reserve as before, and he has not stopped seeing me as an equal opponent in the framework of the quartet. We always disagree. But if at first he used to wear me out with his endless explanations and interpretations, now I welcome them. The debates over interpretation were a kind of battle for his status in the quartet. In this battle there were equal rules for men and women. He would argue with me passionately, forgetting all about the obligations of odious male chivalry and hurling insults at me like some embittered critic pouncing on a flawed composition. And I was grateful to him for it.

I was struck by the fact that the man who showed the most maturity in a really important matter was also the most sexually innocent of the lot of them. He was revealed to me in a new light, and I found myself beginning to like him, even though a few months earlier I had tried to persuade Rosendorf, who cherishes an incomprehensible admiration mingled with mocking affection for him, that we should replace him with a more stable violinist who did not suffer from stage fright. Once in a while I give way to a fit of sentimental gratitude that impels me into reckless acts of generosity. In one such moment of enthusiasm for a grand goodwill gesture, I was ready to present Friedman with a modest testimonial by way of my pudenda. If I had been sure that the battle would be a protracted one, I might have gone ahead. But I'm afraid that he would surrender immediately. And in fact, he sensed that something was afoot and begged for mercy. He suddenly felt the need to tell me about his love for a girl he met in the youth village where he taught music before joining the orchestra. He spoke about her with such childish adoration that I could only envy a woman who was the object of so pure a love. From what he said I understood that he had never touched her and that she apparently did not return his love—on the contrary, she was in love with a married man and was faithful to him, even though he was faithful to an incurably ill wife. Nevertheless, he felt as committed to her as if he were married to her. That's what he's like, he explained to me: a one-woman man with no room in his heart for frivolity or shallow emotions.

I envied him for being so devoted to his principles and listened to him singing her praises with a hint of skepticism: a wonderful woman, a paragon of virtue who had renounced real musical accomplishments (Rosendorf, who once heard her play, was not impressed) in order to realize her Zionist ideals—something which he, Friedman, would like to do but could not, partly because of an unforgivable weakness of character and partly because of the quartet, which is for him, as for me, his true home.

I fear for the future of the quartet. Kurt shows signs of great strain. Martha thinks that events in Germany are disturbing his equilibrium. They affect us all, but he is more sensitive than the rest of us, and with him the effects are physical, too. He's pale, has no appetite, and is often absentminded. Hilda says that he must have suddenly realized that the "arrangement" between him and his wife is self-deception. He'll never see his family again unless he goes back to Germany. People in the know advise him not to contemplate such folly. Once he gets back in, he'll never get out again. His wife demands that he find work in America, even as a second violinist. She refuses to come to Palestine. She's convinced that over here their daughter will be buried forever.

If Kurt leaves, we'll never find a replacement of his stature (we tried to call ourselves the Palestine Quartet, like the Palestine Symphony Orchestra, but the name never caught on. Everyone goes on calling us the Rosendorf Quartet). For me it would be a great loss. I have no strong attachments here except to the quartet. My homeland is the place where I can play chamber music at this level. (Sentences like this infuriate Friedman, but I'm not prepared to say that I've fallen in love with the view of the Jerusalem hills simply in order to please him. I hate almost everything my eye falls on here.)

I'm considering whether to attach Rosendorf to me in a different way, too. I wouldn't hesitate if only I could be sure that it would make him happy. But sometimes I think that it would only undermine his confidence. He might fall head over heels in love with me and be terribly upset when he finds out that as far as I was concerned, it was only a gesture of good-will.

But maybe now that he's discovered the true state of my morals, he'll be prepared to enter into an adulterous liaison without any illusions or fear of emotional involvement. Sometimes I ask myself how he satisfies the sexual hunger written all over his face. He certainly doesn't go to bed with Hella Becker. And I can't believe that a man of his fastidiousness would go to a whore. Nor has he got the guts to pick up some little fan from time to time. Masturbation saves time, but it can't take the place of the real thing.

People in the know say that the situation in Germany will soon clear up, and then perhaps we'll all be able to return (except for Friedman, who'll probably insist on staying). Only Loewenthal refuses to believe that people are coming to their senses there, for the simple reason that an enlightened country can't endure the rule of the street for long. He doesn't believe that the bureaucracy will overcome the Party hoodlums. He doesn't think that the transfer of Jewish affairs from that maniac Goebbels to the bureaucratic trio of Göring-Himmler-Heydrich is evidence of any change. According to him, the Nazis won't be satisfied with confiscating the property of the rich Jews, but will try to expel all the Jews from Germany, including hard-working, productive people who bring real benefits to the German economy. He says we should rid ourselves of illusions. In the coming decade none of us will be able to go home. Even though the Germans are coming around to the idea of transferring Jewish property abroad, in the form of goods to be bought by the Western powers, this doesn't mean that life there is returning to normal.

If the situation improves in Germany, Kurt will be able to dedicate himself to the quartet without having to worry all the time about things that he can't do anything about. If there's no change for the better, I'll go back to my original idea.

In the meantime, I can't offer Kurt anything but the advice I offer myself—to find the purpose of life in music itself. Not as a refuge from daily cares, but as a way of life in its own right. Making music is liberating hard labor. It gives time meaning. Playing scales and bow exercises is the wilderness of ennui on the way to the Promised Land. The boredom of exercising can be borne with patience when you know that every minute brings you closer to the goal.

If I wasn't a musician, I'm sure I would go mad. The moments of elation are so few, and the hours of treading on one spot so long.

In hours like these I can understand women who long to bear children. Their lives pass in vain labor—they clean and others dirty, they cook and others guzzle, their fine dreams are torn to bits one after the other, and the pleasures of the flesh lose their flavor—but in the moments of their darkest despair they can console themselves with the thought that something is growing out of all this misery.

But then I remember my mother. And I take it back. A crushed flower, she used to look at me with that painful look I shall never forget, and her beautiful eyes, in the frame of her tortured face, would wish me a better life than hers. It would tear my heart to shreds, and all I wished for was a life without false glamour.

The poor woman taught me to love my father in the hope that he would love me. And how she abased herself to him to secure me a proper education and social position. With a feeling of unbearable humiliation, I remember how she dressed me up, in clothes too daring for a girl of my age, and presented me, with a gleam of triumph in her eyes, to the family which had spewed her out, as a kind of proof that heredity is stronger than environment. A miserable triumph. At that moment I was sorry that my successes at the conservatory had made the required impression and I had been found worthy to return to the bosom of the family, alone. Without my mother.

Alone. Without my daughter.

I say daughter, although there was no way of knowing the sex of the lump of flesh they removed from my belly. A moment of weakness. I should have brought it up, the little creature that had grown inside me for two or three months. My hatred for its father should not have blinded me.

Sometimes, when we're playing a Haydn quartet, I'm there, in the magnificent house where nothing had changed for two hundred years. Cinderella invited to the Prince's ball. How easily I betrayed my mother with my father! A poor child devouring with her eyes the chandeliers, the crystal vases, the Chinese jars, the stuffed deer, the dresses, the drinks, the gold jewelry, and the false manners. And how hastily they sent me to my fate the minute the Jewish connection threatened their privileges! If I had had a Communist lover, I would probably have become one of them.

Dr. Blecher is wrong. I have repressed nothing from my consciousness. I remember everything. Like the pieces I learned in the conservatory. I know them by heart. But I no longer play them. I only have to play a scale or two, and I'm in shape. And in the same way, I only have to remember a thing or two to be able to confront my thoughts with my feelings. I'm a woman whose values have been warped by life, but I've learned to live with it.

When I play my instrument, I'm a completely different person. I'm capable of being childlike and happy. I love all kinds of music. I'm not consistent in my preferences. Sometimes I think like Goethe, that music doesn't require innovations, because the more familiar we are with it the more profoundly it affects us, and sometimes I think that a world which lives at a crazy pace like ours can no longer be satisfied with tempi which came into being in more hopeful times. When I listen to Bach, I think, like some of his blind disciples, that the world would lack nothing if it contained only the music of Bach. And then I play Mozart and Beethoven, and I'm sure that my life would be a poor, wretched thing if I had never known their works. Schubert can bring tears to my eyes, and Brahms exalts my spirit. But Shönberg too speaks to me in a language I understand. I could mention a hundred names here.

But as a musician I am flawed. I don't know how to express myself. Almost always everything comes out a little less than what I feel. Perhaps you really do have to know how to love in order to give your all in music. Perhaps Friedman was right when he described me so harshly. I'm a true German: complicated, sentimental, and cruel. If only he knew that I was also barren . . .

If Kurt leaves us, I shall go to England. For the time being, this is only a vague plan; perhaps I'll apply to some orchestra or other, but I don't believe they would take me on the basis of recommendations alone. I'm not known well enough. If some English conductor comes here, I'll ask him to hear me play. Another possibility: a concert tour of the Rosendorf Quartet in Europe. There seems some chance of this. But the talk of war reduces it from day to day (Loewenthal says that there won't be a war: the West is weak and divided. The Soviet Union has liquidated its entire military leadership. Hitler is the only statesman today who knows what he wants.)

If I have to, I'll marry the Englishman.

I'm not ashamed to say so. Most of the women in the world marry in order to improve their position, but only a few are prepared to admit it.

What holds me back is the fact that I tried it once and failed. But Edmond Grantly is not Fritz von Staubenfeld. He is neither false nor coarse. His manners are genuine. And his chivalry, although as courtly as that of the von Staubenfelds, is not cold and haughty like theirs. And he, apparently, loves me with all his heart.

Sometimes I am astonished—such delicacy of feeling in a soldier (he's a lieutenant colonel, or something of the kind, serving in Intelligence—actually heading it). He would never say anything that might be considered importunate, as if saying what he felt would be tantamount to exerting a pressure incompatible with good manners. Even his compliments are cautious, in case I might doubt their sincerity. He's never complimented me on my appearance, and the only thing he ever said about my playing was that it blended well with the overall tone of the quartet, which, according to him, is one of the best he's heard in recent years (he's spent a lot of time traveling in Europe over the past few years and knows almost all the important quartets). And nevertheless it's unmistakable: he's head over heels in love. He's proud of himself for not giving way to the need to pour out his heart. He's waiting for a sign. As long as he doesn't get it, he won't embarrass me with demonstrations of affection.

He's an amateur musician with enormous knowledge. One of his friends is the composer William Walton, whose Viola Concerto he brought me for a present, together with a charming note full of humor.

I'll have to work hard to master this complex material. I won't have any technical problems with the difficult passages, but I'll need the help of someone capable of understanding such a work in depth.

I can imagine the goose pimples breaking out on Sonichka's flesh when she sees the pink-faced Edmond Grantly going in and out of my room. The sight of me and the *goy* bending over Walton's music, our shoulders touching, will fan her patriotic feelings to fever pitch. She won't take such a betrayal of national principles lying down. She'll look daggers at me. But I'm afraid that without him I won't be able to get to the bottom of a work which, as he says, is so very English.

I want to perform the piece with the orchestra. Negotiations are taking place now between the musicians' committee (which includes Litovsky) and the management. The management is interested in giving the senior musicians solos instead of raising their salaries, but in Litovsky's opinion the committee isn't powerful enough to get them to include a work not selected by a conductor in the repertoire. He himself isn't enthusiastic about the idea of the orchestra playing a work by a contemporary British composer.

"Why not?"

"Because Britain is denying the Balfour Declaration."

I couldn't believe my ears. "What on earth has that got to do with music?!"

"Everything's connected," he replied grimly, as if I were some chit of a girl who understood nothing.

Every hour he spends on the beach with the Tel Aviv hoodlums brings out one more layer of chauvinism. Two years were enough for him to shed the skin of culture he brought with him from Germany. He's already forgotten that only a short while ago he was enthusiastically defending liberal opinions.

Later he was ashamed of talking like a bigot and saw fit to reinforce his position with an additional argument. "The local audiences aren't ready for contemporary music yet. They have to be prepared gradually."

That's not true either. There's a large public of ex-Europeans here who want the orchestra to play contemporary music. Walton may not be known here yet—I didn't know him myself until I met Edmond—but last year there was a letter to the newspaper signed by a hundred and twenty subscribers from Haifa demanding that we play one symphony by Mahler and one by Bruckner every season. (They bought subscriptions for a pound and imagine that these give them the right to plan our programs . . .) And the list of composers they demanded we play included names like Reger, Alban Berg, and Hindemith.

Edmond proposed marriage to me in the most indirect way imaginable. In the normal course of events, he casually informed me, his term of service in the Middle East would be up in September 1939, in just over a year's time. I have until then to "examine my feelings." He didn't actually say so, of course, but it was obvious what he was getting at when he suddenly started talking about the political situation—a subject we've never once discussed in all the time we've known each other. After the annexation of Austria, he said, more and more people were demanding that Germany be stopped by force of arms. Meaning that if war broke out his plans would be subject to change.

In other words, I have time to make up my mind—either until September 1939 or until war breaks out. Either way I have plenty of time to think about it.

To think about it. The expression is apt. My feelings aren't the question. I'm not in love with him—that's obvious. But he is certainly a man with whom I could live under the same roof—on condition that it be big enough for us to lose each other from time to time, like the family estate he's due to inherit in the forseeable future. This is not a question of greed, as people might suppose (I can just imagine how Friedman would criticize me if he could read my thoughts), or a provincial longing for the glamorous lives led by the aristocracy, whose darker side I know only too well; I simply need enough space to keep a reasonable distance between myself and the man I live with. I would never be able to stand the sticky closeness of a man following me around like a shadow. I need room to breathe, as much of it as possible. If I succeed in making a career for myself as a soloist—Edmond believes that I'll be discovered in England—I'll be free only when I get on the train taking me somewhere else.

Poor Edmond. He had to go and fall in love with someone

like me. But I won't be able to say yes or no to him until the future of the Rosendorf Quartet is clear.

The charm of absolute integrity illuminates the handsome face of this man, whose courtship, too, seems to be the result of long-term strategy. Every period of time has its own goal to conquer. For him the war and I are inseparably bound together. The irony of fate: once more I shall have to plan my life according to the vicissitudes of events in Europe. These politics, which don't interest me in the least, pursue me everywhere. While Edmond, an utterly political animal, is obliged to plan his life according to the chances of survival of the Rosendorf Quartet.

The few Englishmen I know are charming people, full of reserved dignity, natural courtesy, and subtle humor. Such people arouse my curiosity and sometimes also a desire to test their authenticity. Up to now I have not yet had a chance to discover if this fair-tempered man, this perfect gentleman, maintains his characteristic calm in moments of crisis. A strange creature: Tchaikovsky brings tears to his eyes, but he received the news of the death of his father, whom he loved and admired, with a "stiff upper lip," so as not to display his grief in public.

Sometimes I'm sorry I wasn't born in England. If I, like the great artists, had been given the privilege of choosing a motherland, I should have chosen England. But a woman can use her charms to change her motherland. How shocked Sonichka would be by this thought.

If only we didn't have to get married, I would be happier. I should prefer a "gentleman's agreement." Children are out of the question anyway. I would go to England tomorrow if I could be sure of finding another Rosendorf Quartet where I could play the part of the viola.

I'm really an Englishwoman who was born by mistake to a Jewish mother in Germany.

*   *   *

To understand how it happened, you have to understand the circumstances.

It wasn't planned. It happened spontaneously, even though I knew that it was going to happen before Kurt realized what was going on. We had a free evening on a weekday, when a concert in Jerusalem was canceled. First he came to my room and we played duets for violin and viola—Bach, both volumes, one after the other, Mozart, Handel—until we got tired of it, maybe because of the frivolity of breezing through all this music—like glancing around an art exhibition—without any intention of preparing anything for public performance. Then we talked for a while about the situation in Germany and about our colleagues: Friedman and his intermittent moodiness, Litovsky who had been behaving strangely lately, as if playing in the quartet was no longer his first priority (Kurt is convinced that the champagne he drank in Beirut at the French governor's residence, after playing the solo in the Saint-Saëns Concerto, has gone to his head, but I think it's something else, although I don't know what), and about Sonichka, who immediately finds a pretext for coming into my room whenever the silence seems suspect to her. And she did, indeed, surprise us with a Viennese strudel together with the eternal, obligatory tea and took the opportunity to sit down and practice her Yiddish on us, after which Kurt invented an urgent appointment and I accompanied him, to buy cigarettes, so that I would not have to pay for the tea and strudel by myself.

We set out together, joking a little about the good woman and our own nastiness, when Kurt suddenly said with true regret that there was something reprehensible about our attitude toward Sonichka, as if the fact that she had been born in Russia was enough to deprive her of the right to be treated with respect, and somehow, without noticing, we passed the kiosk at the end of the street, and the second one, on the beachfront, was closed. I felt a sudden urge to see the stormy waves which we could hear crashing onto the shore, and poor

Kurt, who can't bear a few grains of sand in his shoes, was obliged to trail along behind me, because it was unthinkable to let me go down alone to the deserted beach, where God knows what types hang around at night. It was a magnificent sight, the wall of foam crashing at our feet in wave after wave, like a Bach fugue breaking forth from the depths of a giant organ, a theme pursuing itself with slight variations and holding us spellbound. And the moon, too, cast its own spell over the scene, which was both frightening and calming at once.

I don't know how long we stood there silently facing the sea, absorbing the salty smell into our lungs and ignoring the stench rising from the leather-curing plant next to the Moslem cemetery. Who knows how long we would have gone on standing there if two suspicious-looking characters hadn't walked past, reminding Kurt of the fact that some important Zionist leader had been murdered there a few years before. He didn't like admitting his fear, but after the two men had passed us and we saw that they were fishermen come to drag their boats higher up on shore for fear of the storm, he hinted that we had better leave. No one in his right mind wandered around the beach at night with a woman who looked like me and a precious Guadagnini under his arm. Although at first I wanted to test his courage and pretended not to understand his hints, after a few minutes I felt sorry for him and said, "All right, but you'll have to give me something good to drink because a stormy sea makes me thirsty." Full of happy relief, he began hurrying up the hill, but the cafe on the corner was closed, and when we reached the boulevard, he sat down on a bench to shake the sand out of his shoes, and I sat next to him and held his violin and said that I didn't mean tea or coffee but something stronger. To which he replied that he had a bottle of French cognac in his room, as if I didn't know he had received it as a gift from Hella Becker. I heard the hesitation in his voice. Was it improper to invite a woman to his room at night?

"Isn't it a little late?"

"Late for what?" I asked.

And when I stood up to go, he seemed to hang back a little in embarrassment, which only strengthened my desire to put his scruples to a real test, although I was not yet sure exactly how.

The thing which finally made up my mind for me was the savage shrieking coming from the Youth Movement clubhouse, which we passed on our way to the workers' quarter. Through the wide-open door we could see about thirty or forty youths. They were sitting on the floor or on benches lining the walls and competing to see who could yell the loudest. Such strange, full-throated roars I had only heard before in the wine cellars of Hamburg, before the drunken singing gave way to cursing. What infuriated me above all was that their screeching was supposed to be Schubert! I felt a terrible loneliness.

I felt as if we were exposed on a raft which had come loose from its moorings and was floating out to sea, buffeted on stormy waves, while the lights in the windows of the little houses resembled the lights of the receding shore. What have we got in common with these people sitting on their porches and playing cards for pennies? I thought, people who were petty and mean even in their gambling. These were the people who sent their children to the Youth Movement, in the belief that a new Jewish race was growing up here. All we had in common with them was some meaningless sign on our identity cards, which was more like a mark of Cain than a statement of fact. We were crowded here together like a pack of Jews standing on the seashore on the Day of Atonement to cast their sins into the water. But in reality we belonged to two different nations, as different as nations can be from each other. They were at home here and we were in exile, without any sense of belonging at all. Although Kurt claims that he is becoming more "acclimatized" every day, and has already learned to curse people out in Arabic (a bus driver who didn't stop at the station), I don't believe a word of it.

Kurt was the one who felt the need to talk first. After a long silence almost anything sounds right. To my surprise he continued my own train of thought and said that whenever he looked at the sea, he seemed to see a coast on the horizon. And the coast was the coast of Germany. It made him feel restless. And I, for whom restlessness is a normal state, said that it was the same with me, although on the coast that he saw he had a wife and daughter, whereas I did not want to even think about the one von Staubenfeld who called himself my father and the other von Staubenfeld, with the fat, greasy, gold-ringed fingers, to whom I was still married under German law, although they had crossed my name out of their family Bible. And then I added that a stormy sea affected me like strong drink.

No decision was actually taken, as I said before, because what happened might just as well not have happened too. At that moment Kurt made his first mistake when he said, "Then perhaps you shouldn't add alcohol as well"—a wisecrack which was like an invitation to sin, the kind of wisecrack men throw around when they want to hint that they would be only too happy to be at your side when you're not responsible for your actions. Although it was actually only a harmless joke, without any seductive intent, I replied in the same coin: "Tonight I don't care if I get completely drunk"—a hint which immediately made anything possible, but at the same time left a loophole open for retreat.

At that moment I saw in his eyes the reluctance or fear which beforehand I had only heard in his voice. I was rather taken aback, since at this stage I had no way of knowing what he was so afraid of. I imagined that the source of his reluctance was moral, if anyone knows what that means. Perhaps the last thing connecting him to his family is his self-imposed abstinence, not such a difficult task when the permanent candidate is Hella Becker (that black widow spinning her web around him with tireless persistence).

But precisely because of this reluctance, which annoyed me—I'm almost ten years younger than he is and it's grotesque for him to behave as if I'm dragging him into sin—I decided to be cheeky and say that I hoped I was invited to take part in polishing off the expensive French cognac, even though I was actually the one who had issued the invitation and he himself had not yet confirmed it—or perhaps he intended bringing the bottle outside or letting it down in a basket from the balcony. He didn't even smile. He had the nerve to glance at his watch again, although it was only half-past eight, a perfectly reasonable hour to bring a visitor, even a female one, back to your room, even if there is a clause in your contract forbidding you to put people up for the night. After that he mumbled, "Of course," in a tone which made it quite clear to me how happy he would be if I said goodbye there and then. But his lack of enthusiasm is what made me resolve to go to his room with him whether he liked it or not: the desire to tear the veil from those beautiful, melancholy eyes of his had become irresistible.

When we arrived at the house, he behaved strangely too: he left me at the gate and walked to the end of the fence as if to check whether he hadn't left his light on by mistake, and when he came back it occurred to me that the relief on his face was due to the darkness in all the other rooms. On the stairs he still showed signs of apprehension, stealing up softly and hesi-tantly as if listening for voices from the apartment where he lived. It was only when he opened the door and the dark flat received us in silence that he seemed completely reassured. He immediately switched on all the lights, as if to announce to the world at large that we had no evil intentions, a demonstration which only brought him closer to the act he feared so much. At that moment I finally made up my mind that I would not leave the apartment until I had liberated this good, naive man from all his childish fears and false morality. I would do it very patiently and gently, like removing cactus thorns from a fin-gertip with a pair of tweezers.

He poured the fine cognac into two yogurt jars—the only glasses in his room—and then raised his own to the light, as if to conclude the ceremony as quickly as possible: perhaps I would be satisfied and leave before his landlords returned. It was impossible not to sense his tension. *"A votre santé,"* he said and poured the lot down his throat at once, like a Prussian peasant taking his schnapps, while I proceeded with deliberate slowness—first warming the cold yogurt jar between my hands, and only then taking the tiniest sip, which I rolled around my palate for ages, and even raising the jar to my nose for a connoisseur sniff, while he looked on with an impatience that increased in obverse proportion to the tempo of my movements. I realized that his conflicts had ceased to be of a purely moral nature—if such a thing exists—and were now taking place on a lower level, over which he did not have full control. He poured himself another drink—chivalrously offering me one too, although my glass was still almost full— and his reason for doing so was obvious: he wanted to throw himself into the adventure he now knew was inevitable, like a vessel with no will of its own. By the slight tremor in his hand, usually so steady, I could guess that there was now no need for pretense. It was time for plain speaking, which would no longer come as a surprise.

I laid my hand, still a little warm from rubbing the glass, on his, which was very cold, and said in a voice slightly husky from the alcohol ("When you're drunk you can get a monk into bed just by the sexiness of your voice," the permanently randy von Staubenfeld would say): "With the light on or off?"

I specially chose this formula to make him go to the trouble of putting out all the lights he had lit, and since I knew the answer in advance, I could say "I knew it" even before he managed to get the words out of his panic-stricken mouth. Naturally he wanted the lights off. His voice sounded so miserable and so funny, like the strangled sound of an oboe with a split reed, that it was hard not to smile, but I restrained myself in case he interpreted my smile as one of triumph. I didn't want him to think that I had planned it all in advance and he had fallen into my trap. Instead, I tried to play the

game the way he wanted it; we had only meant to have a drink
together in order to celebrate our common loneliness, which
gave us the strength to carry on in a country where the youngsters didn't know how to sing and the adults didn't know how
to live, and the thing we had feared and resisted simply happened of its own accord, so that nobody was to blame.

He didn't dare embrace me, let alone kiss me, before putting
out all the lights in his room and the rest of the house. His face
was pale and intent, his blue eyes darkening to gray, as in the
moment before a concert when he felt the full burden of the
responsibility he bore. It was clear to me that he would not
retreat now, even if a sudden attack of conscience interfered.
And the moment he took me in his arms he stopped being
afraid and let things happen in their natural rhythm. He
helped me to get undressed like a gentleman, carefully avoid-
ing unnecessary contact, and only when we were both completely naked (I was surprised to see how thin he was and how
independent the huge projection in his loins) he began to feel
my body, as if he were worshiping each part of it separately
and not moving on until he had given it its due, like a man
with a highly developed aesthetic sense who knows that every
detail in a work of art has its proper size and weight, and also
its own necessary duration, which may not be diminished by a
single second, and that you cannot interfere with the natural
sequence without spoiling the structure of the whole.

The darkness was not as dense as it appeared at first. There
was a nearly full moon, and the lights were on in all the
neighboring balconies, and in the dim light filtering through
the curtain I could see the tortured expression on his face, the
expression of a martyr succumbing to something stronger
than he was—that mysterious force which rouses the organ of
shame and draws it shamelessly toward the source of pleasure
opening up before it. He was stunned when I told him that he
could do whatever he liked, even though I didn't mean anything peculiar (you can never know what a man will understand by this sentence), only that he could enter me without

taking any precautions. "Come in already, come in," I said in the formal third person, not a very successful joke in the circumstances; "you deserve not to suffer any longer." He was offended and asked why he "deserved" it.

"Because you're a good man."

"Is that enough?"

"You want to know if I go to bed with all the good men I know?"

He apologized. That wasn't what he meant. Instead of encouraging him, however, my words appeared to have had the opposite effect.

When he was inside me, with a slow movement that alternately intensified and weakened, I thought of the solo for the first viola in Schönberg's *Verklärte Nacht*, but I didn't say anything for fear of insulting him by my lack of concentration on what we were doing. I was also afraid that he might give it a false romantic interpretation. This was a meeting of two hungry people, not a night of exaltation.

At that moment there were footsteps on the stairs. I couldn't understand why he was so alarmed. Had he intended getting it over before they came back from the early show and putting on the lights the minute we were dressed and decent?

In any case, the sounds behind the door, so very close, induced a sudden, embarrassing limpness. He withdrew and collapsed on my belly, all shriveled up. And only after the footsteps receded from the door and the radio began playing the evening concert from the Voice of Jerusalem did he slowly recover his strength, not without my help, and succeed in finishing the job—joylessly, halfheartedly, and with justified feelings of guilt toward me.

He was so despondent when he lay beside me, exhausted, listening tensely to what was happening behind the door, that I felt the need to comfort him and keep my disappointment to myself, although, needless to say, the gates of heaven had not exactly opened for me. There's not much chance of a woman obtaining satisfaction from such a hasty meal, but what I

succeeded in saying, with the brusque sense of humor that
sometimes runs away with me before I can stop it—something
along the lines of "Not too bad for the first time around"—
only made things worse. I could hear his dejection in the
darkness even before he opened his mouth and said in a
trembling voice, the poor little boy: "Was it really so terrible?" And when I didn't reply at once, for fear of making
things even worse, but only smiled to myself, and my sensitive
lover noticed even this quiet smile in the darkness, he added:
"Didn't you enjoy it even a tiny bit?" And I couldn't help
laughing again, softly. I swear—how can a woman help being
amused by the need of a man to hear that the way he fucked
her was the most exciting event in her life? After all, I could
hardly pretend that this frightened fumble had roused all the
devils in me! I must say that I was a little hurt that instead of
respecting my honesty he interpreted my behavior as cold and
patronizing, and even my response—"I'm very glad that it
finally happened"—sounded to him like evading the issue,
whereas it was actually the plain and simple truth. I really was
pleased that I had succeeded in bringing down the barrier
between us and could now come to know this shy and sensitive man in the way that only the body is capable of knowing
another. And I already knew him well enough to restrain
myself from saying what was on the tip of my tongue: that
precisely because he had failed to do himself credit, never
mind the reason, precisely because he was so sad and pitiful, I
loved him in his weakness with a glad and tender love such as I
had never known before, like the love one feels for a helpless
baby afraid of some imaginary danger.

I couldn't say anything like this to him, of course, without
hurting him even more. Even a man as gentle and enlightened,
as civilized to the fingertips as Kurt finds it hard to renounce
the childish male pride that demands success at any price, a
pride which is fatally wounded by pity. And so I pulled him

toward me and cradled him between my breasts in the hope
that he would feel what words could not express—the pleasant warmth, not sexual but extremely sensual nevertheless,
which he aroused in me, like the big baby he seemed to me at
that moment, and sang to him sotto voce, almost soundlessly,
the Brahms "Cradle Song," a musical riddle which he apparently solved immediately, since he quickly said that he had
better not fall asleep.

He had to stay awake in order to carry out his plan: to
escort me home as soon as everyone in the house fell asleep. I
wouldn't have minded waking up before dawn and getting out
of there after the newspaper deliveries and before the milk-
men, at the hour when people are most soundly asleep. But he
was afraid that Sonichka might call the police if I didn't come
home before morning and seemed surprised that I wasn't in
the least disturbed by the fact that she knew whom I had gone
out with. How typical of him to be afraid of his own shadow, I
said to myself, but I put it down to his credit that it was my
honor he was worried about and not his own, and reassured
him: by the time my pious landlady noticed my absence I
would be safely tucked in bed, sleeping the sleep of the just.

After that we fooled around a little longer. He was astonished by the things I was prepared to do, and probably
couldn't make up his mind whether to put it down to generosity or depravity. And I'm sure he thought about the boy
Litovsky had told him about too, and the things we had done
together, and lamented the fact that he was not the sole bene-
ficiary of such uninhibited delights. But as soon as I got up he
insisted on kissing me on the mouth, apparently in a kind of
symbolic act designed to demonstrate that my vulgar acts had
not demeaned me in his eyes and that he loved and respected
me as much as before, when we were united in the bonds of
conventional bourgeois respectability, head to head, and the
male on top. If I had intended to degrade myself in order to
ensure that he would not, God forbid, fall in love with me but
would receive my favors in the spirit they were given, a free

gift to a friend and no more, I had failed in my designs. Even though I had behaved like a whore, he didn't forget for a moment that I was a lady who deserved his respect and whom he was even permitted to love.

There is one part of a man that doesn't know how to lie, and accordingly I had no need of gallant gestures in order to sense—or rather, to know—that after the initial excitement and surprise (his wife never resorts to such tricks, I'm sure) further stimulation wouldn't work any miracles. The only thing capable of arousing him anew would be a return to the moment before, to the hidden invitation in that first sentence, which had made it all possible: "The sea makes me drunk." What wouldn't he have given to turn the clock back to the magic of anticipation and the suspense of uncertainty!

"Sleep, my baby, sleep," I sang in a whisper.

And he slept. A restless sleep at first, interrupted by every little sound in the other rooms, and then, with the quiet, tranquil breathing of a child permitted to sleep in his mommy's bed.

Before daybreak, when I was awakened by the clock ticking ceaselessly in my head, I wanted to slip away quietly without waking him up, but I couldn't restrain the impulse to give him one more kiss on his smooth, boyish body, whose touching thinness stirred feelings in me that I didn't know existed. He jumped up in alarm although my lips had scarcely brushed his skin and was immediately as wide awake as a soldier aroused by a bugle call. Partly because he wanted to accompany me, and partly, no doubt, because he was embarrassed by the sudden impudence of his private parts, he pulled on his trousers with quick, clumsy movements that made the naughty thing wave about like a flag. Incredible though it may sound, he actually blushed when he saw me looking in that direction. I persuaded him that there was no point in his coming with me: I would steal out like a cat and nobody would notice, I promised. Because that's what he was afraid of, I knew—one of the members of the household waking up and asking who was there. At first he insisted, in a voice that tried to be firm but came out crushed. Then he realized that if I left alone, even if I woke them up by making a careless noise, he would be able to produce some plausible excuse. But if he went out and came back again, he would have to invent a more complicated story—he could hardly tell them that he had gone outside to record the warbling of the birds—and all his efforts to maintain a respectable facade, compatible with the middle-class standards that slowly but surely impose themselves here even on someone as broad-minded as he is, would be wasted. As for walking through the empty streets at dawn, Tel Aviv at night is like a friendly village where anyone who wakes up before half-past five in the morning greets anyone else he meets in the street. If the need arose, I could always tell them that I was delivering the milk, I said to him as I pushed my full but empty breasts into my bra, and he smiled sadly—his humanity doesn't desert him even when he's tense and nervous.

And in order to stop him looking at me with that sad look, as if he were mourning me and himself and the paradise of strangeness we had lost that night, I evaded his farewell embrace and even resumed the formal mode of address. He was amazed. I had been and would always be an enigma to him. I couldn't say what I wanted to: do me a favor and spare me the sorrowful partings; in another few hours we'll meet again, as close and as remote as we always were, tied to one another by a bond stronger than the temporary connection of our sexual organs. There was no chance at all that he would understand what I was talking about. Men are so securely entrenched inside themselves. . . .

The first time he asked if he should take precautions. When I replied with an irony he didn't understand: "No, I want children," he was stunned. And he was even more shocked when he realized that I'd been joking. "I'm empty inside and I'll never have children." He didn't dare interrogate me about how it had happened; although I seemed to him a vulgar woman, capable of speaking about intimate matters without batting an eye, this vulgarity did not suit the image in his imagination.

In any event, on the first evening he only gave me a look of sympathy and forgave me for my bluntness and my need to shock. In the final analysis, I myself was the victim of my own nasty joke. What I refrained from saying was that I had no need of a child of his. He himself fills that role to perfection— a charming child who falls asleep on my shoulder with a touching sigh of happiness. I want to hug him with true maternal love after he emerges from me soft and wet and pathetic and full of concern. Sincere concern that he might not have been good enough to me, that he might not be able to compare to his predecessors, about whom he never stops thinking, although he denies it, and that I might decide to abandon him and go back to them because he has disappointed me.

After the first time he was more relaxed. Once he had no more need to fear making me pregnant, he behaved more freely and even hinted shamelessly that he was interested in pleasures that may previously have seemed to him depraved (his wife is probably afraid of damaging her vocal cords), and once or twice I even really enjoyed the act itself, which was as uninhibited as I could have wished—the root of my pain is the source of his joy. All kinds of fears have an immediate effect on him; any momentary weakness induces anxiety and casts him into a deep depression, from which I have my work cut out extracting him. A man like him needed a liberated woman like me in order to discover, for the first time, what a woman's body holds in store. And it didn't take long before I began to sense the danger signals. When a sensitive man like Kurt becomes addicted to something, it's very hard for him to abstain from it.

As far as I'm concerned, I don't mind having a temporary love affair with no future. It even suits me, as long as life itself is so unsettled and nobody knows what will happen tomorrow. I won't pretend to be so calculating as to say that it suits my purposes because as long as the love affair lasts, there's no danger of the quartet breaking up. . . . But Kurt isn't the kind of person who's capable of casual intimate relationships. He's the kind of man who falls in love with the woman he goes to bed with. His conscience would never permit him to do it simply in order to satisfy a passing hunger. He needs to believe that only an overwhelming, irresistible passion is capable of sweeping him into the bed of a woman who isn't his wife. If only he would spare me his doubts and ridiculous feelings of guilt—but he considers them proof of his love for me: it is stronger than his moral inhibitions, to which I am expected to relate with the proper earnestness. But I never asked him to justify our behavior to God and man. Once he made me so angry that I said that there was no guarantee that his wife in Berlin wasn't busy doing exactly the same thing that we were—nature will have its way, and music, which arouses our passions, cannot satisfy them. He replied solemnly that what his wife did was her business, and his own moral purity was his. And if I refrained from laughing out loud, it was only because I sensed how important it was to him for me to believe that only a great love could have overcome his moral scruples about betraying his marriage vows.

In the beginning, I tried to hint to him that I did not see the relationship between us as anything more than an intermezzo between two stages of life, but I soon understood that he too, like his predecessors, was incapable of appreciating the aesthetic beauty inherent in the decisive, existential act of taking matters into your own hands and concluding something bound to end sooner or later anyway, and clearheadedly choosing the perfect time for doing so, one moment before the inevitable decline. I missed this moment, when one day he suddenly burst into tears and then lay for a long time sobbing on my bosom and confiding his secrets to me—about the women who pursued him and his successful attempts to evade them, and about those who succeeded in subduing his pride and subjugating him to ugly relations of give-and-take, and also, something he regretted as soon as the words were out of his mouth, about his attraction to unripe fruit he was forbidden to touch. At that moment I understood the fear which had suddenly seized hold of him that first night, when we heard the little girl's voice behind the door. He hoped that I would reciprocate with confessions of my own—about the men I had loved and the men who had hurt me—in a kind of infantile, emotional promise that he, with his love, would mend what his predecessors had damaged. My silence disappointed him, but with exemplary chivalry he kept on talking nevertheless and continued to confide to me every nuance of emotion that stirred in his breast, every fleeting reflection, every budding thought, even the slightest shifts of feeling, as if he wanted to commit his total personality to my treacherous memory, where—and only where—he would be himself, whole, innocent of falsity and pretense, painfully honest but utterly free.

Last night I had a strange conversation with Loewenthal. He began talking about Kurt and suddenly took me by surprise and asked me if there were intimate relations between us. I denied it vehemently, but he didn't believe me, although I succeeded in looking him straight in the eye without blushing.

I wondered why he wanted to know. If he assumed that the true answer was affirmative—what did he conclude from it? That the door was open, or that it was locked? In any case, when he saw that I wasn't cooperating, he left me alone. And perhaps he didn't come to any definite conclusion, since he failed to take the opportunity to say something clever, as if he had made up his mind to leave things as they were for the time being until the situation became clearer, to both him and me.

I was glad to talk about Kurt to him, like a young girl happy at the chance to speak about her lover. This need to talk surprised me. I don't usually feel the need to share my emotions with others. My secrets don't oppress me and I'm not looking for a kindred soul to unburden myself to. But this time I felt the need to report on the change in my life, without calling it by its name. I won't try to define it to myself either. If I went to heaven and were asked by my Maker whether I love Kurt Rosendorf, I wouldn't be able to give an unequivocal answer. I would only be able to say this: that it's a long time since I was in a state I permitted myself to call happiness, even though it involves not a little suffering. It is very hard for me to see the suffering of the man lying in my arms who is fearing so for the future.

Every conversation with Egon, even a slightly embarrassing one, is a fascinating lesson. I've learned a lot from him about the world situation and various people, and something about myself, too. When I look into his eyes, I find myself there, naked and unadorned.

"Rosendorf," said Egon, "is the typical example of an artist who derives his inspiration from the renunciation of fulfillment—one who is in love with the split second before the note comes into being, and seems to suffer from the necessity of taking the step to the next note, which cancels out its predecessor and demands all the attention for itself. And from this point of view he's a true artist, because art is the eternal yearning for the moment before fulfillment."

On the basis of his attitude toward art, Loewenthal speculated about his attraction to the unripe and the immature. As an example he mentioned his friendship with Friedman, who was immature from every conceivable point of view, and the love for little girls, which could never be consummated.

For a moment I couldn't believe my ears. I didn't know if it was an ugly innuendo or simply a general observation about the nature of an artist in love with the moment before consummation. In any case, I thought about myself. What was the unripe and unfinished thing he had found in me? What was the thing that was always on the point of arriving and never arrived? And the only thing I could think of was my barrenness, which promised me that I would remain a girl until the moment when I suddenly withered. But when I'm with Kurt, I'm a fulfilled woman. The thing I feel when the agitated baby emerging from his loins quivers inside me is a strong, deep maternal feeling, which is the maturest and most complete thing that a woman can feel in the depths of her being. . . .

Kurt, it seems, has fallen in love with me, just as I feared. And from now on his despairing love will make us both miserable. For I too am struggling inside the net of gold and silk which I wove with my own hands. If I don't put an end to it soon, if I'm not as cruel to myself as to him, I'll never be able to break off this liaison, which fills the long intervals between one meeting and the next with expectation—from the moment we part from each other until the night when he takes the nipples of my dry breasts in his mouth, and awakens the tremor I thought I would never feel again.

Strangely enough, whenever he begins the rhythmic movement inside my body, I hear the same passage in my mind: the viola solo from Schönberg's *Verklärte Nacht,* with the glissando recalling a muffled cry, which even I, who detest schmaltz, permit myself to play in a schmaltzy way—the same motif which came into my mind the moment he penetrated me for the first time, as if I, too, am trying to take us back every time to the sweetness of the moment before. I ask myself why this line in particular? Because of the melody, reminiscent of a rising and falling rhythmic movement? Or perhaps—as Dr. Blecher would surely interpret it—because of a subconscious wish for purity and a childish aspiration to surrender pride and dignity and produce a perfect love from my damaged body? A love like the one in this Romantic work, where the beloved tells her lover that she bears the child of another in her womb, and he takes it upon himself to be a merciful father to the sins of others . . .

I want to break it off and I can't. In my heart I welcome these cursed times, when everything is temporary and there's no knowing what tomorrow will bring and any attempt to plan for the future is absurd. In my heart of hearts I know that

I'll never have the strength to tell this good, loving man that we should play the last chord and conclude the marvelous work of art we have been composing with our perfect bodies fortissimo, instead of letting something so wonderful and beautiful disintegrate between our fingers.

I won't have the strength to do it because I know that he will be mortally wounded. And I have no intention of losing the part of the viola in the Rosendorf Quartet.

Cello–
Bernard Litovsky

I feel the need to write things down. Writing helps to clarify the mind. It also provides documentation. If something happens, there'll be a record of how it happened and why. If the treatment that Martha's undergoing succeeds and we have children some day, they'll be able to find out from these notes about the man who was their father.

In our family it is customary to record the family chronicles in a fat volume. At the beginning a detailed description of every event, however insignificant, and later only major events—births, Bar Mitzvahs, marriages, serious illnesses, and deaths. In the last generation even that stopped. The negligence of the members of my generation put an end to the recorded history of an illustrious family, which arrived in Germany from Poland at the beginning of the seventeenth century. I am the last offshoot of our branch.

It's hard to know where to begin. It would be too pretentious to begin with the first stirrings of Jewish feelings—they did not move me to make any changes in my life. But for Hitler, I would be sitting today in some German orchestra, striving and scheming to achieve the status of soloist. I still have aspirations in that direction, but in the meantime, changes of the utmost importance have taken place in my life. I don't know where they'll lead me yet, but one thing is clear: my life today bears no resemblance to what it was a few months ago, even though from the outside nothing seems to have changed. I go on playing in the orchestra, in the quartet, giving concerts, performing occasionally at musical evenings, and teaching a few pupils. I hardly have a minute to spare.

There's one thing I must mention here: none of those closest to me, neither Martha nor the members of the quartet, knows anything about my other life.

There are some things that I shall have to refer to obliquely. You can never know whose hands these papers will fall into. Unnecessary words can only do damage.

Since there's no knowing exactly where the starting point occurred, perhaps I should begin with here and now. The rest will become clear of its own accord.

I could begin with any of the quartet's rehearsals. A detailed description of the relations between us, including our endless arguments about musical and other questions, together with an attempt to chart the esteem in which we hold each other, to one or another degree of sincerity, and the way this, too, affects the relationships within a group of people who are obliged to work closely together whether they like it or not— all this should provide us with a key to understanding the inner tension which is created and released among us. And none of us is the most flexible person in the world, to put it mildly. From this tension it should be possible to deduce our deep need both to be very open with each other and to keep our secrets fanatically to ourselves, and in this way to understand a number of puzzling facts about our behavior to each other. But lacking, as I do, the analytical talents necessary for this kind of description, I shall have to content myself with a simpler account of the sequence of events.

I could also begin as follows: if we hadn't had an argument one day about the precise meaning of three piano markings in Schubert's Quartettsatz, and if, behind this theoretical argument, there hadn't been an attempt to accuse me of hogging the limelight at the expense of my colleagues, and if Friedman hadn't annoyed me with his pedantry and I hadn't imitated his voice—I'm very good at mimicking the voices of people and animals—and if Eva Staubenfeld hadn't accused me of vulgarity, an accusation which wouldn't usually have infuriated me to such an extent, but which coming from her made my blood boil, because I happen to know something about her which puts me in the shade as far as vulgarity is concerned—and if Rosendorf hadn't taken her side, and if I hadn't felt a need to warn him against her, knowing how dangerous it would be for a man as sensitive as he is to fall in love with a vulgar woman like her—then maybe I wouldn't have told him, with the purest motives in the world, simply in order to help him—even though the results were the opposite—the shocking things I had heard from the young Russian who came to listen to the rehearsals of the quartet. When I was a child we used to play a game: if this—then that. Any answer could be the right one.

In any case there's no knowing how things would have turned out in the end.

Perhaps it really would be best to begin with my strange meeting with the Russian. Chance is an extraordinary thing. In some indirect way that meeting not only affected what happened to us in the quartet, but also provided me with the end of the thread into the labyrinth in which I am trapped today.

It was simple curiosity, not any desire to establish a Lonely Hearts' Club or to expose the secrets of Fräulein von Staubenfeld, which prompted me to approach the young man sitting on the wall opposite our house like Rodin's *Thinker*, staring at our living room, an ordinary room in an ordinary Tel Aviv flat, two rooms and hall with all modern conveniences and an open porch, as if it was the Holy of Holies. I guessed that it wasn't a love of music alone that transfixed him to number 27a Hovevei Zion Street. I saw the humble, doglike way he looked at the lady, who took care to leave the house with a male escort and walked past him without so much as a glance in his direction—and I imagined that I would hear the usual sad story of unrequited love from this loverboy obstinately dogging the footsteps of his disdainful beloved. I had no idea that I was in for anything so spicy.

Simple curiosity—and also the childish passion which has never left me since the silly, happy days when I devoured the trashiest detective stories and dreamed of a future as an explorer or a spy catcher cracking codes and solving mysteries—only to find myself in the end deciphering musical scores. Eccentrics, cranks, people obsessed by idées fixes, and even ordinary nonconformists have always captured my imagination, and this young man definitely appeared to belong to the above category. A Dostoevskian type, a romantic clinging to his one great love and refusing to acknowledge the facts of life, who looked like a sad-eyed athlete. I didn't know if we had a common language. Perhaps he only spoke Russian and Hebrew, in which case conversation would be difficult, if not impossible. But I was determined to break the conspiracy of silence we had woven around him anyway. I felt in my bones that something interesting would emerge from an attempt to find out more about him. Often, when I bent over her music stand to see if there was a mistake in her part or mine, I would sense his presence across the street. It was as if his jealousy were so violent that when the smell of her hair and armpits rose in my nostrils, it jumped right out of his body and interposed itself between us. I thought it would be poetic justice if I invited him in after the rehearsal and let him breathe the smell of the coffee she had drunk and listen to the voice of a man who was lucky enough to be able to talk to her whenever he felt like it.

Martha wasn't in that afternoon, and as soon as the other three left the house, I stole out after them. Before he had time to slip off the wall, I accosted him with all six feet of Bernard Litovsky, with the obvious intention of getting into conversation with him. I was standing so close to him that he had no alternative but to react.

At first he didn't recognize me. He had never seen me standing up, and apparently he hadn't realized that I was so tall. He was taken completely by surprise, because I let myself out of the kitchen door and approached him from the rear. But for my beard, he would never have identified me. The confusion that overcame him when he realized who was standing in front of him proved more clearly than a thousand character witnesses that there wasn't a drop of violence in his hefty body. On the assumption that I had come to rebuke him for spying on my house he explained—at first in Hebrew, but when he saw that my understanding of the language was limited, in German, which as I learned later he had studied in Prague—that he had no intention of disturbing us, he was simply a lover of chamber music, and he hoped that we didn't mind him sitting and listening from a distance. We were not yet on the kind of terms that would have permitted me to tell him to cut the crap about chamber music, but my eyes apparently said it for me and forced him onto the defensive, which made my invitation to come inside and have a cup of coffee even more of a surprise. By the time he recovered it was too late to refuse.

He trailed after me unwillingly, and he was happy to hear that we would be alone in the house. Female company apparently makes him uncomfortable. Once we were inside, we introduced ourselves politely. The Hebrew name he had adopted amused me—a free and rather bombastic translation of a German name which had ended up in Russia—but good manners prevented me from smiling. When we arrived at the living room door, however, I could have laughed out loud and he wouldn't even have noticed; he was so spellbound by the presence—in absentia—of the woman he loved! He stepped inside like a cat, as if someone were liable to stop him from entering. Like a music student trying to gate-crash a concert without buying a ticket. And then he breathed in the smell of coffee and cigarette smoke hanging in the air as if it were incense in a cathedral. For a while he stood contemplating the table with the dirty coffee cups on it as if he had been granted a vision of the Holy Ghost. He must have been trying to guess which of the chairs had had the honor of holding her glorious buttocks. This wasn't difficult, since there was only one cup with lipstick marks on it, and then he reverently lowered his own bum onto the chair in question. And if he hadn't been embarrassed by my presence, he would probably have lifted the cup which had touched her lips to his, and drunk its bitter dregs. He didn't embark on the confession which was on the tip of his tongue, apparently waiting for the right moment in order to burst out, until we had chatted for a while about this and that, and discovered a degree of agreement between us on certain important subjects, such as physical culture, the Soviet Union, and fascism. Only then—after I turned the conversation to the opposite sex, and warned him, in order to help wean him away from a hopeless love, that Eva Staubenfeld's only interest in men lay in dominating them—did the dam burst.

It was an astonishing story. Both in its contents and in the fact that he could tell it to a man he had known for less than an hour. I myself would never have revealed to my closest friend intimate details of the kind which he disclosed to me in an increasingly husky voice, like a lover's whisper, giving rise in me both to curiosity and to a kind of shudder of revulsion at his hopeless attempt to reconstruct the details of their love-making and derive a perverted enjoyment from them. In a vocabulary whose poverty obliged him to resort frequently to the crudest and most obscene expressions, he described in graphic detail all the acts of love, both natural and unnatural, in which he and Eva had indulged during three days and nights, on a weekend of leave from the orchestra, in the dilapidated shack where he lived on the beach in the north of the town, from the moment she had approached him outside the concert hall, where he was standing and devouring her with his eyes, and said to him dryly, as if he were a porter she wanted to hire to carry a piano: "You can come with me, if that's what you want," until the moment when she wiped herself between the legs with a wet towel and got dressed in silence, with an expression of profound boredom, and walked out of his life without explanations. Ever since she had been acting as if she had never seen him before. All his attempts to approach her had been rudely rejected. At first she would at least give him an angry look, which showed some kind of relation, but afterward she had apparently decided to ignore him completely. She walked past him with her eyes high above his head, like a child ignoring a big dog, in the hope that if he didn't look at it, the dog wouldn't see him.

He was well aware, so he said, that he was no match for her; she was a snob who needed luxury, and she would never be prepared to share the life of a construction worker. He wasn't even asking her to come back to him. He was resigned to the fact that it had been a passing episode. All he wanted now was for her to listen to him one more time, so that he could tell her what a profound change had taken place in him since their meeting, which had awakened all the spiritual resources latent in him, and that he loved her with a pure, deep love, which had not been sullied by contact. On the contrary, all the acts which to others might seem dirty were pure and beautiful in his eyes. She did not need to fear him. He was prepared to be her slave to the end of his days. But even this little thing, just to listen once to what he had to say, she refused to grant him. She shot him that pale look of hers, which regretted one thing only—that he hadn't evaporated into thin air, that he hadn't turned to dust that minute she'd had enough of him. She wouldn't even give him the chance to tell her that he was prepared to do even that for her—if the mere fact of his existence upset her peace of mind, he was prepared to make his exit from this world.

"Come, come," I said to him when he produced this last sentence.

I permitted myself a note of skepticism and inquiry. A man prepared to evaporate in order to purify the air breathed by his beloved did not describe her behavior in bed to a stranger.

He was offended: "If you had ever known a love like mine, you wouldn't speak like that . . ."

I tried a logical argument: what did he need another meeting with her for? To tell her what a tremendous impression she'd made on him? It was obvious. He could leave her alone. She had already gotten the message.

But this offended him too. The words had to be said, for until then they would lie like a stone on his heart.

I suggested that he write to her. The smile of an intelligent child spread under his Bedouin mustache. He'd already done that. All his letters had been returned unopened.

What remained with me after he left was his innocence. I shared this impression with Martha. A man can steep himself in lechery and emerge as innocent as a child.

Martha came to the strangest conclusion from my words: in the depths of my heart I too was in love with Eva. Otherwise she couldn't understand what this intimate discussion with a stranger was all about. With profound distaste she described the scene she saw in her imagination: two men in love gossiping about the woman they love, each of them enjoying the suffering she causes the other.

Since she spoke in resignation rather than anger, I didn't bother to refute the allegation. She herself said that she had no fears on Eva's score. She was a woman with a conscience, and she would never hurt her friend. Besides which, she was surrounded by young bachelors, and what would she want with an old broom like me?

She almost goaded me into proving that I was far from an old broom. But I would never take the risk of making advances to a woman like Eva Staubenfeld. I won't be a hypocrite: if I found her in my bed I wouldn't turn her out of it, but falling in love with her would be fatal. She probably fucks the way she plays: absolutely professionally, but without any soul.

All I said was: However much I enjoyed looking at Fräulein Staubenfeld, I could never fall in love with a woman like her—

cold, calculating, conceited, hard, ambitious, and indifferent, and so grand and elegant too, so artificial and remote. She would have to show some human flaw before I could fall in love with her.

Martha immediately jumped to two extreme conclusions:

One, that I had now found the flaw in Eva I had been looking for, and would therefore be able to fall in love with her; and two, that I loved my wife because she was flawed.

You can never be too careful of what you say to a woman. Even in bed.

I shouldn't have told Rosendorf. Certainly not in detail. Friedman was right: "Don't tell him," he begged me. "He'll take it as a personal insult. He wants her himself but refrains from making advances to her out of respect for her feelings— he's a married man!—and she goes and picks up men in the street. Besides, it will hurt him by upsetting a basic assumption: that people capable of playing chamber music perfectly are self-restrained people who can control their passions."

What nonsense! As if someone corrupt to the core can't be a great artist. But Friedman surprised me. I was sure that when it came to things like this he didn't know his ass from his elbow.

Rosendorf, naturally, refused to believe it. The contemptuous way he looked at me—a madman who masturbated with Eva in his imagination! And did I have to tell the whole world about it too?

I was really hurt. What did he mean "the whole world"? The only people I had told were him and Friedman.

"Two too many," he said.

I was pained by the hostile look in his eyes. Against my will I found myself muttering an apology.

"You can take it or leave it," I said. "I'm only passing on information received. And only to the people who have to know."

"Nobody has to know what other people do in the dark," he said in an ironic tone, but I sensed that he was trembling with rage. Obviously, it's more convenient to be angry with me than to believe what I say.

I took the risk of trying to explain why they "had" to know. I said something to the effect that people who play together have to know each other through and through. And he said, with the same offended and hostile expression, that we were indeed gradually learning to know each other. And in the same breath he added, as if this was all he had learned from our conversation, how much it grieved him to hear a "cultured person" like me using "obscene language." Because "obscenity" disgusted him more than any other form of vulgarity.

The irony of fate: I wanted to protect him from "Brunhilde" (what a brilliant nickname! Like the name "Jesus Christ" he gave to Friedman. Loewenthal knows how to hit the nail on the head. Eva really is the queen of the Niebelungs, competing with the men with her bow), and I myself was wounded by the spear I threw.

I learned my lesson: discretion is a two-way shield. It prevents you from betraying others, but also, and more important—as life in the underground teaches us—it prevents you from betraying yourself.

Rosendorf could never reconcile himself to the thought that behind her aristocratic appearance and exemplary sensitivity—Fräulein Staubenfeld shrinks from raised voices and discordant sounds—is a female in heat who picks up strangers in the street. To his credit, he has succeeded in concealing both from her and the others—Friedman, Martha, Hilda, and Egon—that he knows something which might bring a gleam to his eye whenever the subject turns to modesty and restraint and suchlike musical virtues, or justify impatience, if not disgust, when she earnestly defends her demand not to let ourselves be carried away into overemotional or too-passionate playing—which is what happens to the quartet, in her opinion, whenever the word "apassionato" or a similar recommendation appears in the text—and keeps on forgetting that she has already informed us of the fact that onions are even better tearjerkers than Tchaikovsky, and that any drunk knows how to shout from the guts, and that unrestrained passions are cheap and vulgar. ("In the late quartets," she says in the tone of one pronouncing Holy Writ, "Beethoven did not intend expressing extreme emotions, but profound thoughts.")

He has made no attempt to dislodge her from the role she has taken on herself—the policeman of our sense of proportion. His thin lips, sometimes twisted by sorrow or effort, never smile ironically when she lectures us self-confidently about the Golden Mean, or when she curls her lovely, cock-sucking lips whenever he gets carried away and his violin begins to make the scraping noises (that never even reach the fourth row) which show that the musician in him has overcome the professional and make him a true artist and not some technician afraid of his own shadow. He listens to her like a polite little boy when she quotes her great teacher, who sent her into the world with clear instructions about how to play what ("Chamber music is not a religious rite, nor a public breast-beating, and even in the most turbulent passages of the *Grosse Fuge* we have to remember that a chamber music concert is a professional performance, in which a small group of musicians, which unfortunately does not include drums or cymbals, has to keep the attention of a bored audience from flagging . . ."), and his blue eyes rest on her with the devoted attention of a diligent pupil, until you begin to think that it has never even crossed the mind in that handsome head that there might be a contradiction between her demand for clarity and lucidity, dignity and self-control, and the way she lusts after the vulgar pricks of the proletariat (which is not strictly accurate as regards that construction worker, who is neither an ignoramus nor in the least vulgar and even possesses an enormous appetite for learning and knowledge and a natural delicacy, as if he had never been through the boorish mill of the revolution and slept with lice and rats—but she couldn't know any of this because she never let him open his mouth except when she wanted him to stick out his tongue to lick her cunt). On the contrary, it sometimes seems that discovering that she's flesh and blood like the rest of us, and not some caryatid made of Italian marble, so far from making him lose his respect for her, led him to treat her more respectfully than ever, as if she had suddenly been revealed to him in a more interesting light, and he has made up his mind to devote greater attention and deeper study to the subject of Eva von Staubenfeld, as if she were some Mozart quartet, which on a first reading seems perfectly simple, but after you've performed it many times in public you discover that you still haven't plumbed its depths.

From a certain point of view the incident did, nevertheless, disturb the delicate balance which had been maintained in the quartet until then—not, however, in the way that Rosendorf feared, but in another way entirely. If up to then there were situations in which, after an argument over interpretation, he used his position as first violin to impose his authority on the rest of us—the responsibility for the melodic line does, after all, rest mainly with him—we now have two power centers to contend with in the quartet, first violin and viola. And he frequently bends his will to hers. I can't explain his behavior, nor do I want to. It may be the *nostalgie de la boue* of a well-brought-up boy, or the guilty conscience of an honest man when he discovers contradictions between his true desires and what he calls his values. Personally I don't give a damn either way, but I have the right to be angry when a sensitive person like him, who takes offense so easily, doesn't realize what a fool he's making of himself by taking her side even when she's wrong. It's so important to him to suck up to this whore with the airs and graces of a holy virgin that he doesn't scruple to insult me—the only member of the quartet who never tries to upstage the others, although he knows very well that a cellist with less restrained competitive instincts than me has a thousand ways at his disposal of drowning out the first violin. A man like him should know how to appreciate someone with a big, powerful instrument who curbs his natural inclination to get the maximum out of it. If there was anything vulgar about me, I could play our duets so that next to my cello his violin would sound like a plaintive bleat. But enough. There's no point in dwelling on it. It was a mistake, I admit it, but no more than that. One veil was removed from Fräulein Staubenfeld's face, but there are enough left to cover up a lot. And there's apparently a lot that needs covering up.

I don't pretend that now that I know what she's capable of when she's shut up in a room with a stud who can satisfy her vast appetite, I know her inside out and there isn't a single dark corner of her soul that I haven't looked into. I can't say that I understand her or that I can read her like a book, to use an expression of Martha's—a shrewd, clever woman who nevertheless cherishes the fond illusion that people she knows are incapable of doing anything to surprise her (which is why it's so easy to hide things from her). I proceed from the assumption that Fräulein Staubenfeld has secrets which will never be revealed, not even after I've played the entire repertoire of chamber music with her. I don't think that the above-mentioned contradiction between the striving for clarity of expression and the panting after crude lusts is a real contradiction which cannot be resolved in terms of human feelings. I'm well aware of the fact that human beings are complicated creatures; I'm no saint myself, and I haven't always refrained from going to bed with girls who were profoundly moved by my playing, and played on my instrument in return. And I can't say that I was in love with all of them either, so I'm in no position to judge Eva Staubenfeld or call her to order. It's her hypocrisy that infuriates me, not her low moral standards. And also her mental cruelty, if that's the right definition of her behavior to the Russian lad. A woman can do whatever she likes with her body, I don't deny that, but torturing a man who's done her no harm, and apparently did her a power of good in those three days which she wiped off the calendar, shows a profound hatred of the entire male sex. Anyone who's seen, even from a distance, how he worships her and devours her with his famished eyes, cannot but sense that she isn't simply burning her bridges by ignoring him, but taking a mean revenge on a man who saw her in all her nakedness and heard her moans of passion, as if it's his fault that she picked on him to unload the burden of her long-unsatisfied lusts.

I was shocked by his picturesque description of their first meeting after she suddenly left his shack and took off without even bothering to reply to his question about when they would meet again: she walked past him as if she didn't know him from Adam, and when he tried to accost her and talk to her, she gave him a look full of such venomous contempt that he almost fainted from shock. I asked myself what could cause an educated woman like her, who had studied music and dance and art, to behave so viciously toward a man who by her own fault had fallen so desperately in love with her. On no account could he understand—who could have?—what had suddenly changed in him or in her, after she had writhed beneath him and crouched on top of him and opened the gates of paradise to him, and all he asked was for her to say a few words to him, even something as meaningless and noncommittal as that's life, or that's human nature, one day we love and the next we hate, or something along those lines—anything to stop him torturing himself with doubts that something he had said or done had made her reject him so suddenly, and make it possible for him to apologize for the terrible thing he had done or said—but she refused to throw him even this crumb and chose instead to torture him with her insulting silence.

At first I attributed her behavior to a certain type of arrogance. Fräulein von Staubenfeld, we must not forget, spent a not inconsiderable part of her life among people who chose their sexual partners from the population of servant girls and laundresses without feeling the least moral obligation toward these social and educational inferiors (at the bottom of the ladder were the defenseless daughters of the immigrants from Eastern Europe, who were simply thrown out of the house if they didn't have the sense to take precautions and got themselves into trouble; and on the rung beneath them, the Jewesses).

Martha and I have often discussed this aspect of Eva's character: the aristocratic arrogance and the rest. Martha tried to excuse her hostility to men by the traumatic experiences of her youth. According to Martha, the von Staubenfeld family, one of the oldest and most influential in Prussia, treated her and her late mother with incredible viciousness, leaving scars which later gave birth to a compulsive need to revenge herself on the people who damaged her and everyone who represents them in one way or another.

This kind of fashionable interpretation strikes me as a not very serious attempt to dress trite cleverness up in pseudo-scientific terms. Anyone can bandy these theories about and one interpretation is as good as the next. You can always find evidence of emotional deprivation, as they call it, to justify villainy if you want to. If you poked about in the soul of the Viennese house painter presently occupying the office of the chancellor of the Reich, you could probably find plausible explanations for everything, including his megalomania, his wickedness, and his hatred of the Jews.

But the life history of our Brunhilde could just as well have led to a completely different conclusion: namely, that if the humiliations she suffered in her youth because of her social status and Jewish origins didn't teach her that solidarity with the persecuted is the only proper answer to such phenomena, it shows that her soul is as black as pitch in spite of the fairness of her face. Precisely because of the way she herself was made to suffer as a young girl, she should have realized that she had no right to hurt the feelings of an uneducated Jewish lad from Eastern Europe, even if God saw fit to punish him by sticking a penis under his empty stomach. Is it his fault if he possesses a strong, shapely, classical body, developed by hard labor and a medicine ball to the perfect masculine proportions that she loves to degrade? Why did she have to choose him to represent the male sex in general and serve her as the wooden doll into which she hammers her nails in order to hurt us all?

Exactly what they did to her she did to someone weaker than herself. I have no doubt about it. And if that's not despicable, what is? No one born into this class, even without the benefit of marriage vows and formal rights, is free of the instinctive need to humiliate anyone available for humiliation, as if they can only show their superiority by trampling on somebody else. It will take another hundred years to get it into their heads, and the heads of the rabble who doff their caps to these stuffed shirts born with a silver spoon in their mouth, that birth does not give a man any divine rights: at the most it's a matter of luck which enables some people to start life on the right foot.

Any man who passes within her field of vision can feel the hostility from her passing glance. Except Rosendorf, who gets special treatment from her. Perhaps because he's not man enough to attract the hatred aimed at us all—he's slender as a candle in danger of going out if you raise your voice, and sensitive as a woman (even in the way he plays the violin there's something ingratiating, a kind of shrinking from sharp edges), and there's something sad and soft in his eyes, as if the only emotion with which he is intimately acquainted is the emotion one feels when seeing a kitten left out in the rain . . . Because of his femininity he enjoys the friendship between women who admire one another, like the close alliance existing between our three women—Eva, Martha, and Hilda Moses—who give every man who intrudes upon their sessions the feeling that while they may be resigned to his presence they would never include him in anything of real importance (the way my father, the only Jewish officer, felt in the officers' mess of his regiment, which was full of anti-Semites).

None of this is intended, God forbid, to cast aspersions on Rosendorf's masculinity—women are attracted to him in spite of his fragile and delicate appearance. Hella Becker, for example, who runs a German-style pension with a high hand and who is the kind of strong, masterful woman you find in old Jewish families accustomed to giving orders to servants for two hundred years. She pursues Rosendorf with the pertinacity of a collector of objets d'art, determined to outbid all rivals for the Chinese vase on which she has set her heart. Even Hilda Moses, who is beginning to get tired of pretending to be so liberal-minded that the great writer's unwillingness to marry her doesn't bother her at all. The day she decides to teach him a lesson and make him afraid of losing her, she'll probably choose Rosendorf for the job, the only man who makes her feel both intelligent and desirable, even though the only reason he treats her with such respect is his childish admiration of Egon Loewenthal. Even little girls fall in love with him, perhaps because of the shy, boyish smile that appears on his face when he doesn't understand what people are saying to him. In any case, Eva likes Rosendorf a lot, and they seem to have reached an agreement that the friendship between them will never exceed the limits of feminine solidarity. They've invented a new kind of love without sex, without pain, and without expectations, and anyone seeing them from a distance when they're playing, smiling at each other with boundless pleasantness—the kind of intimate smile that strangers are permitted to see—might well think them brother and sister.

Nevertheless, his reaction to my story was not in the least

like that of a brother hearing about his sister's escapades, but more like the pain of a betrayed lover. (Friedman surprised me by the acuteness of his perception. I would never have believed a virgin like him, of all people, capable of intuitively grasping the complicated relationship between those two. I put it down to his credit. And to myself I noted: a man can be a great chatterbox without being a fool.)

Friedman is one of those who should take Eva's hostility toward him as a compliment. In other words, she sees him as one of us, a real man who deserves to be hated. She groups him with us, enemies to be punished, and not with Rosendorf, who has been allocated a place of honor in the no-man's-land between the sexes. I understand that his obstinacy, his loyalty to his beliefs, his willingness to fight for his principles, which are sometimes rather confused, the way he stands his ground on political and other questions—all these things make her place Friedman squarely in the enemy camp. In any case, he is as well aware as I am of the tremendous tension in the quartet, a tension we succeed in hiding, like a feuding family during the visit of some important guest. We're like two enemy camps during a cease-fire—Friedman and I in the male camp, Rosendorf and Eva in the other.

The difference between me and Friedman is this: while I am capable of enjoying this tension only as an observer when I am not directly involved in the fighting, he enjoys precisely those moments when he himself is the source of the tension. Tense situations are the climate in which he flourishes. The dialectic in which he believes with a fanaticism equal to that of the ultra-Orthodox Jews (my grandfather was one of them and I know what I'm talking about) teaches him that everything of value results from the clash between two hostile tendencies. Conflict sharpens his childish mind, which has never overcome the schoolboy need to prove to his teachers how well he has learned his lessons. Even his playing improves when he succeeds in convincing himself that there is some dialectical contradiction or other between his right hand and his left.

Sometimes I get tired of tuning the strings of my ego in order to adjust myself to this odd group of people who are constantly at war with each other. The sharpest words used by the combatants are "schmaltz" or "vulgar," but anyone familiar with us knows that they are far more wounding than "idiot" or "sonofabitch" could ever be. As far as I myself am concerned, I would prefer defeat to the burden of an unresolved conflict dragging on for years. Sometimes we're like a bunch of madmen locked up together in a cell, and they won't let us out until we've learned to produce a pure, true tone. The funny thing is that from the outside we look like an extremely well-knit group. Eva never forgets to remind us at the orchestra rehearsals when our next rehearsal is, as if she needs to make everybody jealous of her for having a quartet. To be someone of whom others are jealous is apparently a pleasure not to be sneezed at by a woman who requires a steady supply of stimulation. But she doesn't need to try so hard. All she needs to do is raise those two dead volcanoes of hers—prettier ones I've never seen in my life—and all the women in sight will immediately retire from the competition. However, when you combine us, the result is both harmony and sharp contradiction. Rosendorf and I respect each other, but are also wary of each other. We're the best members of the quartet from the professional point of view—there's no need for false modesty—but also more dangerous to it than the others. Neither of us has given up the hope of taking his rightful place one day as a soloist with an international reputation. Today we prefer the quartet to individual "moonlighting" on the local scene, even if it would bring in a bit more money, but if the clouds clear up in Europe, I wouldn't bet against either Rosendorf or myself trying for a second chance. Even though we may have missed the boat by now. The world loves child prodigies, and both of us are pushing forty. Before we have

time to turn around, we'll be old men. Rosendorf was offended when I hinted that he was only marking time in the
quartet. If Hitler disappears tomorrow, the Rosendorf Quartet will disappear with him.

Eretz Israel isn't a bad place in which to wait for the right
opportunity. Although I myself am not too pleased with the
orchestra—the differences in the standard of the musicians is
too great—it's made a name for itself in a relatively short time.
Conductors of the first rank are prepared to come. True, some
of them do it as a protest against Mussolini and Hitler, but
there's nothing wrong with that. They're here and that's the
main thing. They notice the best of us even sitting in the orchestra; and if you're lucky enough to play a solo under their baton,
there's a good chance they'll invite you abroad too.

To tell the truth, if Eva made bolder use of her feminine
attributes, she too would be in the running for a career as a
soloist. From this point of view, I can only agree that her
behavior is exemplary. She judges herself with a cold eye and
recognizes limitations that others can't even see. Whenever
she's offered a solo, she prefers to play a work for two instruments, like Mozart's Sinfonia Concertante, in order to lean on
a better performer than herself. She knows herself very well
and realizes that she needs someone enthusiastic to infect her
with his own enthusiasm. In Friedman's opinion, her limitations stem from the fact that she doesn't like the thousand-
headed monster sitting in the dark concert hall. If you can't
give yourself to the love of the anonymous people coughing in
the intermissions, you're not a real soloist.

As far as her playing in the quartet is concerned, I have no
complaints. I wouldn't say that she is cold or lacking in bril-
liance. She blends in well and occasionally obtains marvelous
tones from her instrument. But this is only because she is
swept along with us. If we were to leave her on her own, she
would play like a good pupil and that's all. It's as if there's
something inside her holding her back. Perhaps the fear of exposure. To tell the truth, I had hoped that her adventure on the

beach would open her up a bit, especially now that we all know about it—she can't play the holy virgin with us any-more—but this didn't happen. She pursed her lips as usual, as if she's never opened her mouth except to put food in it, and sat down on her chair like a convent girl passing through a crowd with her arms folded lest anyone, God forbid, touch her breasts, and went on playing in her precise, measured way. Anyone would think that she had never let her hair down in her life and was incapable of producing a single scratch, even in a moment of real happiness.

(That reminds me of the way she laughs at jokes—very rarely, only when it's really funny—with the pursed lips of a child refusing to open her mouth for the dentist, and a look of suffering in her eyes, as if she's being forced to do something against her will, like someone who had hoped for a bargain but was obliged to pay the full price in the end.)

Friedman and Eva, too, are allies and enemies at one and the same time. As far as loyalty to the quartet is concerned, they have a certain advantage over Rosendorf and me. For both of them the quartet is home, and the orchestra a place of work. Home in the sense of family. Friedman was left alone in the world after his father committed suicide, and Eva cut off all connections with her large family. For both of them the quar-tet is the place where they reach their full potential. Without it they would drown in the depths of the orchestra, and conse-quently they cherish it like the apple of their eye (they know that we could easily find replacements for them, too). But this doesn't stop them from quarreling incessantly over trivialities and risking the alienation of Rosendorf and myself.

Interestingly enough, on questions of technique Eva and I often find ourselves on the same side. It makes Rosendorf really mad (although he hides it) that we always disagree with him and Friedman about the nature of Mozart spiccati, which they make too pointed for our taste and more suited to the period of the great virtuosos of the nineteenth century. He sees this alliance of the basses against the violins as a rebellion against his leadership. I suspect he's a little jealous of Eva's taking my side against him. But he can always count on the loyalty of Friedman, who tries to copy the first violin.

Wonder of wonders, there are hidden points of contact between me and Friedman too. I respect his untiring attempts to understand technical details. He refuses to be satisfied with metaphors such as "a softer tone" or "a dim color" or "with feeling" and so forth, but tries to arrive at a more accurate description of what should be done—how much bow, where on the string, how much hair, what kind of vibrato, etc. In this matter I'm behind him all the way. What gets on my nerves about him is the way he never stops trying to fit every line into an all-embracing system, seeing every chord as an expression of the important idea in the air when the composer, who lacked any formal education, sat down at the piano to compose his ration for the day—half a quartet or a madrigal and a half. A violinist like him will never make a soloist, if only because of his stage fright (for the first few minutes of every performance he sits on the stage as if he's been caught with his pants down and is trying desperately to find the right posture to hide his private parts . . .). I sometimes find myself going too far in ridiculing this man, who goes out to do battle for his musical principles with banners flying and surrenders at the sound of the first shot, but I can't help being amused by his determination to pronounce his opinion on everything under the sun.

Another thing we've got in common is our attitude to politics. I don't know if we're close to each other in our opinions—my own, which are few and clear, I keep to myself—but we agree that these things are of crucial importance. With all due respect to music, we would never say, like our first violin and viola, that we're not interested in anything else. I'm not crazy about the expression "relevance to real life" that Friedman uses all the time, but since I don't know a better one I have no alternative but to quote him: Rosendorf thinks that he's a moral man because he doesn't steal other people's property or touch their wives, but these days that's not enough. From the minute Hitler came to power, a nonpolitical man is an immoral man. One day we'll be punished for not reading the writing on the wall, says Friedman, for not raising our voices against the Teutonic madness, for not joining the Zionist movement in time, for not putting our instruments away and learning to do something useful with our hands.

In some miraculous way Friedman manages to be both an ardent Communist and a messianic Zionist at once. Inner contradictions are evidently the natural state in which he produces his most brilliant ideas. He's capable of saying in one breath that music is the most sublime of arts, and that chamber music is an aristocratic entertainment which the bourgeoisie elevated to the status of a holy rite; that the quietest sound is the purest of sounds, and that music sounds no sweeter to his ears than the noise made by a machine producing something for the benefit of mankind.

In any case, when I talk about "relevance to real life," I don't mean only political involvement. In my opinion "real life" includes physical culture too, which as far as Friedman is concerned is a total waste of time. I'm prepared to waste a lot of time and energy in order to feel that I'm alive. The effort I invest in music isn't enough for me. Besides, playing the cello makes my spine curve. It's the way I have to sit and hold my arms that does it. And in order to look like a human being, I have to activate the right muscles and not let them degenerate.

Actually, if I wasn't a Jew, I'm not sure I would have chosen music as a career. I was good at math and also at sports. With a little effort I could have reached the top. But I couldn't make up my mind, and in the meantime I lost a good few years. At an early age I learned from my parents that if I didn't want to be like them I would have to excel at something. And quickly. My dream then was to be a German cavalry officer and the national obstacle race champion, but at the age of sixteen it became clear both to me and to my parents that the shortest way to the goal we had set ourselves, i.e., to climb somehow into the ranks of the Jewish elite, was via music. The conclusion was eight hours a day at the cello—it's a miracle that I didn't get sick and tired of it in a few weeks—and within eighteen months I won a youth competition. The continuation wasn't as easy as the beginning. The determination of a Jewish child, who had grown up in the meantime and married— a woman from an established German-Jewish family, naturally—to persevere in the marathon race to the top involved a process of self-destruction which continued for fifteen years and made me miss the chance to start a family in my single-minded dedication to the needs of my career. I didn't even notice how the devoted, loving woman at my side was deteriorating from year to year, and from abortion to abortion—for nothing could be allowed to hinder our mobility as we moved from town to town in my pursuit of my goal: first cellist in the Berlin Philharmonic. And when I finally got there, the ignorant rabble voted for the madman from Vienna and put an end both to my musical career and to my and Martha's chance of having a family. In the meantime, Martha contracted rheumatic fever and was forced to abandon the piano, and all that was left to her of music was the little drum on which she beats time in the eurythmics lessons, which are a great innovation here. But I didn't set out to talk about Martha. She's a woman with a rare ability to accept life as it is, without blaming anyone, not even me. I, too, follow her example and instead of cursing my fate I try to make the best of things and wait patiently for the day when a musician of international stature will be able to leave this tiny country for a European concert tour—airplanes, which are less of a rarity than they used to be, can make the trip from here to Europe in seven or eight hours—on the assumption that if the threat of war is removed this will not be an impossible dream.

In the meantime, I have returned to my two old loves, mathematics and sport, the first as a hobby, to which I devote myself in my spare time, and the second as daily obligation I fulfill every morning. Real life, which Friedman likes talking about so much, to me means the sense of power coiled like a spring in the body of a man who gets up early every morning, summer and winter, to go down to the sea and feels the fierce vitality of the blood coursing through his veins. After my morning run, exercise with the medicine ball, and swim in the stormy sea, after flying low along the beach (and on Saturdays, along the deserted Eliezer Ben Yehuda Street) on my powerful, noisy motorbike, I feel like a new man. Most of the fellows I meet on the beach are construction workers and carpenters, and a few of them are happy-go-lucky loafers existing on God knows what. Friedman would probably envy me for my contacts with the "people" he longs to be part of but can't. I can imagine how they would laugh at his pedantic way of speaking and physical clumsiness.

I'm proud of being able to feel one of them, even though some of them seem to do nothing but wrestle each other and show off their strength all day. They're quick and sharp and good friends in a pinch as well, and they don't lack honesty and modesty either, in spite of their showing off and interminable contests of strength. They accept me as one of them because I can meet them on their own ground and not because they've seen my name on the notice boards. Some of them have never heard a concert in their lives. They respect me because I'm strong and quick on my feet and know how to enjoy winning and don't make a fuss when I lose, and also because I treat them like equals and don't patronize them or behave as if I'm slumming. They know how to distinguish between someone who really needs the friendship of simple, healthy people who don't regard the human body as a crude instrument full of ugly lusts and savage appetites, and those who come to rub shoulders with the "common man" to salve their consciences or wallow in the dirt.

I won't deny that I derive enormous pleasure from the cultivation of my body, which I don't have to be ashamed of even without all this exercise, and not only because I'm improving the instrument within which I live, but also because athletics gives our movements the grace and ease that come only after you've learned to hide the effort involved in acquiring them. In physical activity, just as in music, a fluent performance is one in which there is no trace of the sweat and strain invested in achieving it. I need only say that when I come back from the beach, bathed in sweat and with sand between my toes, I feel as if my soul has been purged of all its poisons.

But I never dreamed that these workouts on the beach would completely transform my life.

I owe the meeting first of all to Eva's lovesick swain. I might have met the beach boys in other circumstances, but it was my acquaintance with him—one of the most prominent figures in this unconventional band—that paved my way into the inner circle.

At first I didn't realize that I was standing before a turning point in my life. Although I threw myself into their games, which could have been dangerous, when they discovered that I earned my living as a cellist, they respected me for not guarding my fingers—as recklessly as if I were risking my life in some sacred cause, I attached no real importance to them. Danger can be an exciting stimulant to a person whose greatest occupational hazard is snapping a string in the middle of a concert. I like tests of courage, taking risks, swimming in stormy seas, navigating fragile craft between sharp rocks in a strong current, keeping my balance on rooftop balustrades no wider than the breadth of my foot. If there was a circus worthy of the name here I would offer them my services just for the heck of it.

This side of my character is a closed book to my friends in the quartet. Not because I try to hide it. If any of them were capable of appreciating the beauty in the sheer intoxication of physical strength, I might have shown them a trick or two. But

Rosendorf is totally absorbed in his music, and Friedman is the kind of person who thinks any energy that doesn't produce electricity is wasted, and as for Eva—her hostility would only increase toward a man who regards his masculinity not only as a biological fact but also as an ideal, and she would no doubt despise my efforts to improve my physical fitness as empty boasting. Even Loewenthal, a bookworm who worships beauty, despises sport. The glory of the Jew lies in his spiritual strength, he says. And a lot of other nonsense along those lines. If he knew the part played by physical training in overcoming pain, he would change his mind. I would have expected him to know how to appreciate gratuitous acts, which strengthen the character. It's mind that overcomes matter in these games, not the opposite. But you can't make a person like Loewenthal change his opinion. He made up his mind about sports years ago: something for stupid Americans and Germans who have to compensate themselves on the sports field for their defeats in war.

Martha sometimes makes fun of my "body worship" to other people. At first I didn't care. It's no secret, after all. But because of her prattle my colleagues have begun making jokes about my "paganism," and their jokes disguise a certain resentment at the low company I keep. In Rosendorf's eyes it amounts to a betrayal of music. Music should be enough to satisfy the hunger for a life full of content, and if it doesn't satisfy me then my attitude to it must be superficial. Lately he's been discovering signs of this in my playing. He doesn't say so in so many words, but I can sense that he's disappointed in me. He was shocked when he found out that one evening I took part in a jam session with Shpigelman, who plays the saxophone, and a mediocre pianist, in a seafront cafe. He thought it degrading. It's true that I did it partly to teach Rosendorf a lesson for being such a snob, but I did it mainly because Shpigelman fascinates me. Playing with him was one way of finding out more about him.

Today, knowing what I know, the need to keep my meetings with Shpigelman secret has become a serious matter. Even the jazz band, with hindsight, is revealed as a cover story fabricated by Shpigelman to explain the connection between us.

I was astonished by Loewenthal, who also saw fit to denounce jazz in no uncertain terms. He of all people, an enthusiastic advocate of anything new, should have understood that jazz is not a symptom of the decadence of Western civilization, but the fresh, vital roots of a different culture. Marxism can confuse even clever people. What has jazz got to do with American imperialism? If I was any good at improvising, I wouldn't have any scruples about returning to that cafe. But my head's full of European music and none of my improvisations can take off from the musical forms with which I'm familiar. To be a good jazz musician, I'd have to forget everything I know. It's true that Shpigelman paid me compliments, but they too were directed toward one goal only: to ensnare me in his net. I'm not angry with him. I enjoy struggling there.

Shpigelman is a friend of the Russian's. Both of them were members of a construction workers' team that wandered around the country from job to job until they settled in Tel Aviv. He's a short man with coarse features and sharp, deepset little monkey eyes. And like a monkey's, they fix you with a suspicious, almost hostile stare, as if he's afraid that if he takes them off you for a minute you'll kick him in the balls. For a while I thought mistakenly that he was one of the Russian's crowd. Since the Russian spoke and he was silent, I assumed that he agreed with him about everything, that he was one of those disillusioned Communists who wants to hold the rope at both ends, but finds it increasingly difficult to be both a Communist and a Zionist.

As a rule I tried to avoid getting involved in political discussions. I don't know enough about local issues, and I've got nothing new to say about the regime in Germany. My romance with proletarian views came to an end while I was still in Germany. A few of my Communist friends tried to get me to join an artists' cell. And while I sincerely admired the works of Brecht and Weill, the attempts of my friends to apply Marxist doctrines to music left me cold. Their ideas were so vulgar that I began to suspect that in other spheres, too, they had nothing to offer but a clenched fist.

In Eretz Israel I certainly didn't seek them out. Things here are too complicated, and there's a lot to learn before you can begin to find your feet. Friedman has succeeded in converting me to Zionism, and for the time being that's enough for me. As far as I'm concerned, being a Zionist is a revolution of a hundred and eighty degrees. I don't know how to march in more than one direction at once. I've begun to study the subject. Like Friedman, I believe in action, not phrasemongering. For Friedman what has to be done is obvious: to set up as many settlements as possible. But he himself sits in the orchestra and plays in the quartet and teaches children to play the violin. Whenever we go to play in some agricultural settlement he comes back with the feeling that he's betrayed his vocation. He finds it difficult to console himself with the marginal role allocated us by Huberman—to turn this Levantine country into a branch of Europe—and he would like to take an active part in settling the land. In his place I wouldn't have talked so much about things I had no intention of doing. If all I can do is play the cello, I said to myself, then I'll play the cello and shut up. I'll try to play as well as I can—in the orchestra, the quartet, solo, whatever comes my way—and I won't give myself any medals for doing it.

At this stage Shpigelman came into my life. I felt comfortable in his company, both because he isn't a big talker and because he was the only one of my new friends who had any connection to music. He's got the courage to like what he likes and never tries to ingratiate himself with me, like the Russian, by running down all the autodidacts who compose sentimental patriotic songs here for schoolchildren. Both of us listened

without comment to the arguments between the leftists about
who was more left-wing than the other. These people are
ready to tear each other to pieces over a political slogan. The
closer they are to each other, the greater their mutual hostility.

These arguments would take place in the shade of the kiosk
on the beach and continue in the evening in a cafe where some
of the fellows met to play chess. I never went there, of course,
but the morning sessions alone left me cold. For some of them
all this talk about the class struggle was nothing but a transparent excuse to explain why they'd left the "labor brigade"
or the kibbutz and why they weren't putting into practice
what they preached. I respected Shpigelman's silence. For one
reason or another he had landed in Tel Aviv—a young, single
man who could get up in the morning and go wherever he
wanted to—and he didn't try to excuse it by some disagreement or other that he supposedly had with the labor movement. He hardly ever opened his mouth, and when he did it
was only to ask for clarification. From time to time I would see
him sitting in the dairy cafe not far from my house, writing in
a little notebook. One day I went in to say hello and for some
reason he seemed embarrassed to see me.

"What are you writing?" I asked him.

"An outline."

"An outline of what?"

He smiled. "One day we'll have to decide what really has to
be done."

I thought he was making some private joke and forgot
about it until sometime later, when the true meaning of this
enigmatic sentence was revealed to me.

When I had already become involved, although I still didn't
realize how deeply, I understood that Shpigelman's silence
was less innocent than it seemed. It was the method by which,
after lengthy observation, he recruited people who appeared
reliable and discreet into his group. Like a wolf isolating the
sheep which have strayed from the flock, he hunted down two

or three members of our crowd and recruited them into the ranks of his organization.

I wasn't on his list at all. He assumed that the step from the orchestra to the underground would be too difficult to take. At first he was drawn to me because I wasn't a snob. Once he even said so to me. All the serious musicians he knew looked down on him even before they heard him, just because he played the saxophone, and at weddings, too. The decision to recruit me into the organization was taken after the quartet was invited to dine with the High Commissioner.

I'm not in the habit of discussing the musical side of my life with my beach companions, but after our dinner with the High Commissioner was written up in the papers I couldn't avoid answering a few curious questions. I described the pomp and circumstance of dinner at Government House to them, making fun of its absurdity. Shpigelman's eyes gleamed. He disappointed me by his provincialism. Huberman made no impression on him because he was a Polish Jew, but the names of the wines on the High Commissioner's table made him go weak at the knees, like some country bumpkin who had listened wide-eyed to tales of counts and princes as a child but had never set eyes on anyone more important than the head of the local fire brigade.

In this too I was mistaken. It wasn't the wines and the footmen that interested him, but the security arrangements. He wanted to know all the smallest details. I wasn't much use to him, however, since I have a poor visual memory for everything but notes and figures. Unless I make up my mind to remember something I see, I quickly forget it.

After the interrogation about the security arrangements at Government House, various eccentricities in his behavior began to make sense to me. And then we had our first talk about the political situation. A very worrying situation.

Even people like Rosendorf and Eva, who live here as if they were on a desert island, are worried about what's happening in the country. They're not disturbed by the conflict between the Jews and the Arabs. They rely on Great Britain to control these gangs of hot-tempered hoodlums—which is how they see the armed Arab revolt—and restore law and order. They ride around the country in armored cars with the stupid courage of people who haven't got a clue about military matters. The minute they see a British policeman with a gun in his hands they feel secure. When we played in a kibbutz where the fields were set on fire, I saw no signs of fear in their eyes. The ghaffirs wore uniforms and hats with badges, and that was enough for them to feel that they were under the protection of the armed forces, which were stronger than any unorganized rabble.

But the moment the confrontation between the Jews and the British began, they started showing the first signs of political awareness. They began criticizing the leaders of the Jewish community, who were provoking a great power. We even had a little quarrel, which Rosendorf quickly covered up. I said to Eva, more or less, that she didn't know her ass from her elbow if she was capable of defending the British position on the land question. There was an argument. The first political argument in the quartet. Eva said that if the Jews had a choice between Palestine and America, they would all go to America, and therefore it was wrong to endanger the small minority living here under British protection in order to promise to those who had no intention of coming here land in which they weren't in the least interested. Even Friedman was shocked by her attitude and said that even he, who was usually moderate and peace-loving, thought that this time the British government had gone too far, and that there might be no alternative but to take extreme measures. Rosendorf was obliged to intervene: surely we weren't going to quarrel because of the White Paper! And of course we stopped. We went back to doing the only thing we know how to do well, and left the great questions of the day to others.

To get back to Shpigelman. From his questions I guessed

that someone was dreaming up some kind of terrorist action. I told him that I hoped the leaders of the Yishuv, the Jewish community, weren't contemplating doing anything silly. Government House was well guarded, and the place was swarming with police.

After this there was no point in pretending any longer. Shpigelman, alarmed by his own frankness, adopted a threatening expression and hinted that if I told anyone about our talk his life would be in danger. I told him not to worry, I wasn't the kind of person to endanger a friend just to make an impression of being in the know. He seemed reassured, but after this I noticed that he was keeping an eye on me. Once he waited for me after a concert and rode all the way to the bus terminus with me just to tell me not to mention our talk to the Russian.

I was astonished. I thought that the two of them were inseparable, but in my eagerness to impress him as a man who knew how to keep his mouth shut and never asked superfluous questions, I pretended not to find anything odd in his request. And thus I went on laboring under a misapprehension for quite a while longer. If I had known then how dangerous it was to make friends with Shpigelman, I might have been deterred.

In the first weeks of the war, when everyone was arguing about the Molotov-Ribbentrop pact, I still believed that Shpigelman, like the Russian, was a member of the Haganah— something which you didn't talk about except in private. In my naiveté I supposed that Shpigelman's request to keep the connection between us a secret from the Russian was intended to prevent the latter—who for some reason I imagined was higher up in the organization than Shpigelman—from vetoing my recruitment into the Haganah. In my heart of hearts I couldn't blame him for his doubts—a public performer with an appearance as conspicuous as mine was hardly ideal material for an underground organization—but I was glad that

Shpigelman, who seemed to me more intelligent and more levelheaded than his friend (I couldn't imagine him madly and hopelessly in love), found me worthy nevertheless. There must be things that someone like me can do too. When I'm on leave from the orchestra I can give weapons instruction. Besides the fact that I'd be good at it, and would enjoy it too, it would be a smart move from the security point of view—the British would never suspect a man who had dinner with the High Commissioner of being a member of the Haganah. I assumed that the Russian saw himself in some sense as my sponsor, and would feel responsible if something happened to me. There was something rather proprietary and protective in his attitude toward me—as if he, the intellectual of the group, was the only one capable of appreciating what a loss to the world it would be if a cellist like me were, God forbid, to break his fingers.

In any case, I was perfectly willing to keep it a secret from the Russian, in order to make sure that he didn't place any obstacles in the way of my recruitment into the Haganah. I decided that my place was there; I had no desire to be a cultural asset whose fingers had to be kept in cotton wool (if I had managed to keep them from harm in the German army, I would manage in the army of the Jewish people, too), and for a while I tried to avoid the Russian so as to prevent him from putting a spoke in Shpigelman's plans.

And so I remained in ignorance of certain vital facts until it was too late.

When the Russian found out, he was furious.

A few words about the Russian. He's a man of firm principles and strong character. His intellectual confusion stems from gaps in his education. He had hardly any formal education at all, except for the year he studied agriculture in Czechoslovakia. Like most self-educated people, he often jumped on vehicles traveling in opposite directions. But once he picked something up he kept a firm hold of it, as if his mind closed around scraps of knowledge like a clenched fist.

He has a strong sense of music and great sensitivity. Once he wept when I played Fauré's "Elegy" to him at his request. This was on the same day that he had gotten into a fight with some Arabs and beat them up. During the course of time I came to believe that when he was sitting on the wall outside my house, ostensibly in order to gaze at his beloved, he was actually cultivating the single-minded dedication to an obsession, which he regards as proof of a strong character. Love of chamber music was not just a pretext; he really and truly loves it. He acquires musical knowledge with the persistence of a tourist in a foreign land laboriously learning to speak the local language. Once I heard him humming complicated passages from Beethoven's Quartet Opus 135 and jumping from one octave to another without hitting a single false note.

At first his taste in music was limited to the second half of the nineteenth century. Romantic music is capable of moving him profoundly, and Schubert—to the point of tears. Recently, however, he has begun to come out with all kinds of original opinions, which could be instructive in predicting the reactions of an audience open to new departures. I use him, without mentioning his name, in arguments with my friends about the repertoire. The Ravel Quartet, for example, made him think of something Mediterranean, full of light and sunshine. I persuaded the others to put it back in the repertoire, in spite of its failure with our usual audience, who come to concerts to be moved, to think about themselves, and to applaud enthusiastically when something well known is played. He seems to possess the intellectual curiosity typical of those young musicians who listen to Stravinsky, Berg, Hindemith, and Toch with the alert attention of someone trying to solve a riddle.

Lately he's given up sitting on the wall and contents himself with talking about her whenever he can attract my attention. I'm his sounding board. He tries to explain her inhuman, unnatural behavior and excuse it by the cruel spirit of the times. Thus he manages somehow to connect it with his disillusionment with the Soviet Union and his grief at the defeat of the Republicans in Spain and the blacks in Africa. The fact that she's German plays a role too. Perhaps all this makes it easier for him to bear the agonies of unrequited love. His suffering becomes part of some larger doom, and takes on a dignity and majesty which makes it possible for him to enjoy it as he would a sad piece of music. A life full of splendid tragedy is better, after all, than ordinary boredom and depression.

He, Shpigelman, and I were playing a secret, three-handed game with me right in the middle. At the same time as I was keeping Shpigelman's secret from the Russian, I was keeping the Russian's secret from Shpigelman. I felt like a master conspirator holding the ends of all the threads. It was only later that I realized the risks I had been taking.

I thought that I knew everything they were each trying to hide from the other. But I was mistaken about one thing, and the mistake was a serious one. I thought that they were both members of the Haganah, and that it was only security precautions which prevented the subject from ever being discussed between the three of us—like in the Communist party in Germany, where the cells are kept strictly apart. Shpigelman's hints were a little clearer than the Russian's, but the latter also dropped enough hints for me to understand that he was going off to take part in an officer's course. In this he was no doubt breaking the rules of the underground, but he couldn't resist the need to impress me with the fact that he was a responsible citizen, not just a loafer with nothing better to do than mope over a hopeless love affair.

I was drawn to the affairs of the underground with an attraction which was not without reservations but which was still not cautious enough. I saw them as a game tailored to meet the needs of wild young men, afraid of waking up one day to find that they had grown old without doing anything worthwhile. They had no homes or families or proper professions, and their underground activities filled their lives with some sort of content. They lent a special significance to the idle expectation of some great event. Everything here looks so mean and small, but they long to believe that it's only the rough sketch for an imposing monument. Jews are always ready to imagine that the messianic era is just around the corner.

I'm not criticizing them or scoffing at them. I myself enjoyed the game-within-a-game that we played together, Shpigelman, the Russian, and I. In this comedy of errors we were both the actors and the audience.

I began to suspect that I might be the clown when Shpigelman's hints started becoming as heavy as the strings of a contrabass. The struggle against the British had to take on the character of a war for national liberation, he declared with the burning eyes of a martyr, as if he himself had already drawn his sword and charged into the fray, but the hesitating masses were allowing him to fall on the battlefield alone.

It gave me quite a shock. But I didn't take what he said too seriously. Hilda Moses, who knows what's going on, had given me to understand that the Haganah was a semiofficial organization, that the British knew of its existence, and that almost all the young men in the settlements were members. I assumed that Shpigelman was talking about a political struggle and perhaps a few protest actions like demonstrations, hunger strikes, and so on.

But then he went on to speak of actual violence.

For a while I let him circle me on tiptoe, as if an unwary step might wake the sleeping British lion, who had nothing better to do than listen to Shpigelman denouncing the British Empire in biblical language, but in the end, I said that Great Britain was too great for him to take on single-handed.

Shpigelman was wounded to the quick.

"We can cause them tremendous damage if we know how to act in the right way," he said in a passionate whisper.

"You and me?" I asked.

"Each of us in his own way."

I was stunned when I discovered the role which had been allocated to me.

He imagined that we were in and out of Government House every other day, and wanted me to smuggle dynamite into the place in my cello case—no more and no less.

Luckily for me we had no forthcoming concerts in Jerusalem, and no invitations from the High Commissioner either. One gesture was apparently quite enough as far as he was concerned. But the mere fact that I was a party to so desperate a secret meant there was no going back for me.

Shpigelman, who suddenly turned into a sinister character from a different opera, hinted that if I talked he would take a very grave view of the matter. He didn't even have to show me the butt of the revolver in the shoulder holster under his jacket for me to understand just how dangerous he was. He didn't even bother to swear me in. It was obvious that I was already in up to my neck, without any need for theatrical initiation ceremonies, and any indiscretion on my part would be considered treachery.

One thing was made clear again, this time emphatically: if anything came to the ears of the Russian, it would be tantamount to handing them over to the British.

"Isn't that going a bit too far?"

"You can't trust them," said Shpigelman vehemently. "They're nothing but imperialist lackeys."

Very late in the day, therefore, I realized that even this happy-go-lucky band of beach boys, so naively and touchingly cultivating, as if for their own enjoyment, the image of the "new Jew" who knew how to hit back at his attackers, were no less passionately involved in politics than the rest of the country.

The Russian, as I later learned, knew everything a Haganah man needed to know about his friend Shpigelman, who had left the Haganah to join the extreme, militant organization of the Stern Gang. From a certain point of view, you could even say that he was shadowing Shpigelman. He kept an ostensibly friendly eye on him, sniffing around to make sure that he wasn't recruiting converts to his dissident cause. His unofficial role was to bring straying sheep back to the fold. Anyone infected by Shpigelman's prophetic pathos was brought back into line by the Russian. Most of the lads were warned in time: Shpigelman was suspected of membership in a dissident organization that refused to accept the authority of the consensus, and any attempt at subversion on his part had to be reported immediately.

The Russian did not see fit to warn me, however. In the first place I was not a member of the Haganah. And in the second, he knew that prophetic language had no effect on me. My Hebrew was poor, and nearly all the words in it seemed bombastic to me. Shpigelman spoke to me in a broken German, which was actually Yiddish reinforced with words from half a dozen other languages, and I was incapable of appreciating his eloquence. His words sounded to me like empty slogans copied from the Communist jargon into the Zionist one. If I listened to him at all, it was only because he aroused my curiosity. Here comes another fanatic, I said to myself, with the light of divine madness burning in his eyes. From the first I felt that the rhetorical questions he posed were leading questions, intended to drum the articles of the faith into my thick skull. But I pretended not to understand what he was getting at and forced him, as part of the game, to surmount yet another obstacle: the stupidity of a dull-witted German Jew.

The Russian, who was not oblivious to the growing intimacy between me and Shpigelman, assumed that the initiative had come from me. He was aware of my weakness for eccentrics and imagined that I was courting Shpigelman in order to enrich my collection. I didn't seem to him the kind of person to be carried away by extreme ideas. He thought that he knew me well: a cynic, a non-Zionist, someone who preferred hanging around with a bunch of loafers to studying the burning issues of the times, someone who might risk his neck for the hell of it, but would never sacrifice himself for a lofty cause—a man like me would be of no use to Shpigelman's organization, which needed fanatics with Zionist ideals burning in their blood. He refrained from warning me for another reason, too: he wanted to keep me out of one area of his life at least. After pouring out his heart to me, he was embarrassed at the thought that there was someone who knew everything there was to know about him. One secret he was determined to keep to himself. He hinted that he had a rich, interesting life which he couldn't tell me about, and he enjoyed the idea of having an advantage over me, which made us equals.

Shpigelman was cleverer than the Russian. He chose me for the very reason that the Russian thought would make him reject me. No one, including the British, would believe someone like me—a member of the orchestra and a string quartet, a halfhearted Zionist with no deeply rooted political convictions—capable of being swept off his feet by extreme ideas. But not only true believers join underground organizations. Their ranks are full of adventurers pretending to hold convictions they don't really feel. And they are often the boldest fighters of all. Direct action is the only way they can commit themselves to an idea whose feasibility they frequently doubt. They need action, and the rest is secondary. People like this don't require proof of the feasibility of expelling Great Britain from the Middle East. They don't give a damn if all the activities of the terrorist organizations put together amount to no more than a mosquito bite as far as the British are concerned. They want to be the mosquito that bites, not the solid citizen waiting patiently for the policy decisions of his elected institutions.

Shpigelman had good reason to assume that I was one of the above. But he failed to take into account my German sobriety, and the accumulated experience of someone who had already been burned by an extreme ideology that promised neat solutions to all the problems of the world. However, I too failed to take something into account: behind Shpigelman's pleasant manner was a powerful personality, which would not hesitate to exploit me ruthlessly for its purposes. His conscience would permit him to let the Jewish people lose one cellist. We can afford it, he would say to himself. We've got plenty more of his kind. Better to risk him than a front-line fighter. I have no doubt that he'd be sorry if something happened to me. But he doesn't spare himself, so why should he spare me? Especially since I'm not serious, the kind of person who only joins the underground to fill some emptiness in his soul.

When he warned me, with an authority and forcefulness that took me completely by surprise, that from now on any blabbering to the British lackeys would be tantamount to treason, I knew he wasn't bluffing. People like him don't make idle threats. And you can't go and prove to some kangaroo court of theirs that you're innocent. Punishing traitors has a powerful educational effect on new recruits. Shpigelman would take that into account, too, if there was any doubt of a miscarriage of justice. He had a legion of smart lawyers in his soul, ready and willing to offer their services to a great cause for nothing.

The day Shpigelman warned me to keep away from the British officer—Eva's new friend—I was horrified. How the hell did he know that I'd spoken to Grantly at the mayor's reception? We had only exchanged a few words standing up (he asked Eva to introduce me to him and told me that he was a close friend of William Walton's) and I was already being reprimanded for it. I wondered if he was following me around himself or if he had representatives everywhere. I told myself I was making mountains out of molehills, but I couldn't settle down to my normal way of life.

"What's the matter with you?" Martha asked me. "You've been so tense lately."

I wasn't really worried, but at the same time I couldn't dismiss it from my mind. And I didn't have anyone I could talk to about it either. I didn't want to frighten Martha. I couldn't consult the Russian because he'd just left to fight in Spain. My

friends in the quartet wouldn't be able to advise me. And
Loewenthal was the last person I would confide in. You could
never tell how he might put you into his books. And besides,
he hung around with people who might talk out of turn.

In the end I decided on Hilda Moses.

She's a serious person, intelligent and discreet. The type of
woman, usually rather plain and clumsy, who lets men exploit
her devotion and kindheartedness. They always love more
than they're loved, and their loyalty to those who ask them to
keep a secret knows no bounds. Perhaps I shouldn't say "the
type of woman." But if there is such a type, she belongs to it.
She may be a little boring, partly because Loewenthal amuses
their guests enough for both of them, but even this is all to the
good. Since she feels no need to be interesting, she won't go
around offering her friends tidbits about how that cellist,
Litovsky, got himself into trouble.

She listened attentively, without revealing what she
thought. Afterward she said something about Shpigelman:
she understood him but she didn't justify him. In the end she
reassured me: he wasn't as dangerous as I seemed to think; his
organization was small and weak, and they wouldn't harm a
Jew. After all, what they needed above all was a sympathetic
population into which they could disappear.

Before we parted she promised me to take care of it in a way
which would hurt neither me nor Shpigelman.

I didn't dare ask her how. I trusted her. I don't know why.
Instinct, I suppose. My faith in quiet, kindhearted women
knows no bounds.

In the meantime, the great plan was shelved and I breathed a
sigh of relief. I had needlessly canceled a concert in Jerusalem
on the grounds of ill health, a lie which made Martha suspect
that I was hiding some fatal disease from her.

But my relief didn't last long. Eva's Englishman, Edmond
Grantly, invited the quartet to play in an officers' club in the

south of the country, and Shpigelman somehow heard of it. I was scolded for keeping it to myself and ordered to make sketches of the means of access to the club. In a combination of idiocy and frivolity—I persuaded myself that the whole thing was nothing but an exercise to make an impression on a new recruit—I remembered as many details as possible and put them down on paper when I came home. Just to be on the safe side, I wrote my comments in Hebrew, with my left hand. Afterward I decided this had been a mistake—my spelling mistakes were enough to give me away. I was praised for my work, and discovered that I really am an idiot. The compliments went to my head and gave me butterflies in the stomach.

I was astonished when Shpigelman ordered me to make friends with Grantly.

"It will be useful when the time comes," he hinted heavily—an arch-conspirator brilliantly planning ahead.

There was nothing easier. The British officer was only too eager for our company. A man who had received an excellent musical education, he never missed a single one of the quartet's concerts.

I don't know exactly what he does. In any case, it's something to do with Intelligence. He's also friendly with one of the leaders of the Jewish Yishuv and with a Jewish Intelligence officer stationed in Egypt. I received all this information from Shpigelman, although the point of knowing it was not at all clear to me. One thing I knew for sure—his interest in us was not purely musical. Eva had dazzled him, and he was courting her as single-mindedly as Shpigelman in the pursuit of his own goals. For a while he tried to ingratiate himself with her by showing sympathy for Jewish aspirations, but once he understood that the Zionist cause left her cold, he resorted to his astonishing musical memory, which seemed to have the desired effect.

I wonder when he'll learn—the hard way—that her demonstrative, public friendship is no guarantee of love or loyalty. How can this affable Englishman understand the twisted mind of the half-Jewess, who is using him to spite all those who demand that she recognize her Jewishness as a duty toward her people? Even Rosendorf feels uncomfortable about overfriendly relations with the representatives of the Mandatory government. She doesn't love him, of that I have no doubt. Despite his masculine role, he's actually quite effeminate, all fresh and soft and tender—like a delicate young girl wearing a Hindenburg mustache. In short trousers his pink legs look scrawny, like a chicken's. But this woman would be prepared to make love to a piece of cheese if she thought it would hurt somebody.

Who knows better than I do that she's incapable of loving anyone but herself. And she only loves herself out of spite.

God help whomever she chooses. He'll be a famished man—hungry when he enters her and hungry when he comes out.

I don't know if I'll ever know what happened and how. In any case, the end was swift and dramatic, with everything rushing toward the inevitable conclusion. At first I only sensed that something was up, without knowing exactly what. Two of the boys from the beach were arrested, and Shpigelman disappeared. I was left without contacts or information. I decided to carry on as usual, as if nothing had happened. But I couldn't hide the fact that something was wrong. Everyone interpreted it in their own way. Martha thinks that the love for Eva, which I had succeeded in suppressing, has finally broken out. And nothing will make her change her mind. She'll never forgo a chance to forgive me for sins I haven't committed. Rosendorf is sure that I was upset by the cool, critical reception of my performance of the Schumann Cello Concerto, and his attempts to console me are truly touching. Nothing could be further from my mind at the moment than an irritating com-

ment by some music critic. Friedman thinks, with some justice, that I'm worried by the situation in Europe. The only
one who hasn't noticed anything is Eva, who's apparently to
blame for everything. I could hardly tell her I was worried by
her relationship with her British officer, or ask her to be
careful with what she said . . . He must have questioned her
about me, and she probably talked her head off without realizing what she was doing. After he asked me casually one day,
when he came to fetch her, if I knew someone called Isaiah
Zlotnicker, otherwise known as Zelig Shpigelman, I was sure
that his job had nothing to do with Military Intelligence. I
kept cool, putting on a poker face and asking him to spell the
names for me, but I felt as if the noose were tightening around
my neck. And then two strangers came to the flat when I
wasn't there and questioned Martha about our relations with
Grantly. I reassured her by saying that they must be Haganah
men, putting out feelers to see if they could exploit our connection with him, but I was badly shaken. And after Shpigelman was shot by detectives who broke into the room where he
was hiding, I even considered escaping from the country. For
two weeks I was sick with fear, and I never left the house, even
for orchestra rehearsals. When nothing happened, I hurried
around to Hilda Moses, the only person I could talk to freely.
She assured me that it wasn't the Haganah who had betrayed
Shpigelman to the British—but she couldn't say for certain
that it wasn't some mistake of mine that had led them to him.
She suggested that I should lie low in one of the kibbutzim for
a while, but on second thought she herself rejected the idea.
My disappearance from the orchestra platform would attract
attention and serve as a proof to Shpigelman's friends that I
was involved in the affair. She promised me that she would
consult the right people and give me their answer.

Until then I'm living in a state of suspended animation.
With superhuman efforts I play my part in the orchestra and
the quartet, but my mind is somewhere else entirely. When the
audience applauds, I hear shots. Whenever I see someone

coming toward me in the street, I imagine him pulling out a revolver. Shpigelman's friends will condemn me without even putting me on trial. I told Grantly that I didn't know anyone of that name, but I could see from his face that he didn't believe me. It was pure insanity on my part to go to the meeting place in order to warn Shpigelman. They could easily have followed me. Why is Hilda Moses taking so long? I have to meet someone in authority so that I can swear to him that I never told Grantly anything.

I curse the day that I met Eva Staubenfeld. How happy we could all have been if only Rosendorf had chosen some nondescript violist instead of insisting on this woman, who brings bad luck to everyone who crosses her path.

Another moral of my story: a battlefield is no place for a tourist. Unless he wants a stray bullet in his back.

String Quartet–
Egon Loewenthal

TEL AVIV, FEBRUARY 1937

I would prefer calling these notes "The Diary of an Exile," but what is legitimate in Paris is not legitimate in Tel Aviv. In Montparnasse, this title would be a simple statement of fact. In A.D. Gordon Street, the irony is too profound to be employed purely and simply for pleasure. The grim, determined people with whom I break my bitter bread in Eretz Israel would see it as a provocation. Black humor is not something to which their minds are attuned.

Ideologues in general find humor difficult to digest. Totalitarian systems regard it as subversive. Heavy sarcasm against enemies and potential enemies is all they permit. Humor directed against oneself is a luxury only enlightened liberals can afford.

I have already paid a heavy price for my sense of humor. The Nazis, turning a blind eye to better-known writers who expressed their disapproval in more respectable terms, found it necessary to wreak their vengeance first of all on me, even though my esoteric writing had no influence on the masses. It was Greek to them. My subtle humor never penetrated the ranks of the proletariat. The appreciation of my enigmatic barbs was confined to only a small group of aficionados. Nevertheless, I was found worthy of being sent to a concentration camp.

Herr Goebbels's consultants read and failed to understand. But they sensed the black humor behind it. And that was enough to gain me promotion on their blacklist.

Far be it from me to compare the humorless insanity of the German nationalists with the stern seriousness of the saviors of the Jewish people. But my writing, which sticks out its tongue at anyone who sets himself up as a saint, will find enemies in their camp, too. And why should I provoke my benefactors? They have provided me with a safe refuge and given meaning to my life—is the only way I can repay them by making a rude gesture in their direction?

The question of meaning requires clarification. They see me as a man who has been uprooted and given a chance of putting down roots in a new place. I won't argue with them. I'm honored to belong to the Chosen People returning to the Promised Land. But in the matter of roots they're mistaken.

I am a German writer who thinks in German, writes in German, and loves and hates in German. It gives me pleasure just to look at the letters of the word "German" on the page. And it looks back at me sternly, like a stepmother who might agree to love me on condition that I not break any grammatical rules.

My Zionist friends wouldn't understand the pain in my discarded title; they would say I had lost all sense of decency, that I was prepared to sell my own mother for the sake of an apt phrase.

People who are content with a vocabulary of three hundred words, which they inflate with the help of pathos, would find it difficult to understand why we writers have no motherland but our mother tongue.

(Correction: except for very famous writers. The world is their motherland. They could live at the North Pole and publishers would send messengers to collect their manuscripts there. Their books are translated into seventy languages before the ink's dry on the page. If I was one of them, I would be living now in Paris. I tried to stay there, but I didn't get a visa.

Famous writers gave me recommendations, but in the French Interior Ministry and the American Consulate nobody had heard of Egon Loewenthal. An unknown writer is like a bad poet. He might as well be dead, as the Chinese proverb says. When the officials stared at me with their cold eyes, I felt like a premature baby born before he had learned to breathe. If they didn't connect me to an oxygen tank immediately, I would die. I slunk away with my head bowed and my tail between my legs. At that moment I hated the French like a true German: a nation of snobs who had invented great liberties and small meannesses! Who decided, in this city which spoke of fraternity, how many émigré German writers to let in? How would it harm them to take in one more German writer, who wrote for a journal nobody read?)

Being connected to the biblical oxygen tank saved me from thoughts of suicide. Why should I make things easier for my murderers? To tell the truth, at first I didn't know what to do. Going back to Germany was out of the question. Switzerland, too, was in no hurry to open its doors to a black humorist with nothing to sell on the black market. I didn't even think of Palestine. But a lucky friend of mine, a Zionist and not a bad poet, whose family in America sent him a ticket there, gave me his ticket to the Promised Land.

"At least you've got someone you can talk to there," he said. "My family in America knows less about German poetry than I do about rodeos."

I got on the ship and sailed to the land of my fathers, but the air I need is steeped in the breath of German-speakers. I found a few of them in a certain Tel Aviv street, and in a village where they rear chickens to the sounds of Bach. But they can't provide the intellectual milieu for a German writer.

Someone once said to me: "The only fortune the Jews smuggled out of Germany is German literature." But here in Palestine it's a worthless currency.

I am teaching myself to appreciate my hosts. Paris threw me out. Tel Aviv welcomed me with open arms, even though I'm not Thomas Mann or even Lion Feuchtwanger. I'm simply someone who agreed to be Egon Loewenthal and accept his lot in life, to quote Schönberg.

But it isn't easy to take the forgiving looks of people who think that the only thing stopping you from falling on your knees and kissing the earth is your pride. Prouder men than you have kneeled here.

THE NEXT DAY

A diary is a form of communication with an unknown reader. Every diary is secretly intended for the eyes of others: it is a letter to anyone who will be prepared to love you even after you tell the truth. In a diary you don't have to worry about digressions: you can let anarchy run riot. You don't have to worry about structure and plot: you can put down only what is urgent and authentic and demands to be expressed. A diary is the gateway to the soul: only the truth gains entry there.

The trivia of daily life, too. For the things that happen around us take on their full meaning only after we have organized them in our minds to tell our friends about them, like music that fills with warmth when somebody is listening. Our friends? Not necessarily. Because if we address ourselves to someone we know, we're liable to omit some unimportant detail in case he wrinkles up his nose and wonders why we thought it worth mentioning at all. But it's precisely the unimportant things, of which we took no notice at the time, which will come to claim their due on Judgment Day.

Tel Aviv is a suburb of a nonexistent city. It's not even thirty years old and some of its buildings already give off a smell of old age. Most of the houses are plastered white, as if to celebrate their separation from Jaffa—a dark, swarming, dirty Mediterranean town, out of bounds to us for security reasons. "The first Hebrew city," as everyone calls it here, has known very little peace and quiet in its short life. It has already seen its sons going into exile, during the war between the English and the Turks, and fighting among themselves as well. And despite the determination to be a happy Jewish town, there's a tinge of bitterness in the air. There's fierce rivalry between a number of Zionist factions, each more extreme than the other, and nevertheless there's something not unpleasant about the place. The poverty's discreet and the wealth unostentatious. The houses of the middle classes are as modest as the houses of the poor. A few people of means have built themselves the homes they dreamed of in northern climes. For the workers they build apartment houses in the Bauhaus style, like the ones built by the Werksbund in the Weissenhofsiedlung in Stuttgart (they remind me so poignantly of working-class neighborhoods at home that I am surprised when I draw closer and hear a babble of foreign tongues—Yiddish, Russian, Polish, and Hebrew—instead of German).

A European is bound to be a little taken aback by the provincial pride typical of everyone here, from great to small. They can hear the wings of History beating in the most insignificant events: every building is a neighborhood, every neighborhood a town, every clump of trees a forest. An intersection where it's a rare event to see a car pass is a square. On the steel skeleton of a new building the engineers pose for photographs with the foremen, the workers, and anyone who held a spade or threw a shovelful of cement onto the foundation stone. They don't build houses here—they build a Homeland. They don't write books—they build a Culture. Schools aren't a place where you learn grammar and arithmetic but the place where the "soul of the nation is forged." The need for rhetoric is well-nigh hysterical. Every clay figure wants to be a monument, and work songs are the Psalms of tomorrow; every pen-pusher who can speak five or six languages but insists on writing Hebrew, which he doesn't know properly (correcting other people's grammar mistakes is a national sport here), is sure that he's writing another chapter of the Bible.

Sometimes I envy the Zionists their convictions. And if I occasionally suspect them of deluding themselves in order to gain entry to the Kingdom of Heaven—I have to admit that it works. Every day, with increasing astonishment and anxiety, I meet people who really and truly believe that their every action is heralding the dawn of redemption. A dozen and a half pathetic communal farms, which can't even produce a loaf of bread without public assistance, constitute a Settlement Movement; a little factory that makes stockings (called after a town in Poland) constitutes Jewish Industry; a Jew from Salonika who established a bank is the local Rothschild; a few hundred young boys learning to dismantle a revolver in secret are the skeleton of the Jewish army. No wonder some of them really and truly believe that they can defy the British Empire. Some of them even believe that fascism and Zionism can be allies: the Zionists will help the fascists rid Europe of its Jews and in exchange the fascists will help them expel the British from the Suez Canal. . . . What lunacy!

Sometimes I ask myself: can't they really see how hopeless it all is? A handful of Jews will never be able to set up an independent state, not even in the land of their fathers. A small minority will come; the rest will prefer to live wherever else they are granted equal rights. Who would agree to exchange European culture for provincial improvisations in a dead language? And the Arab national movement won't allow a foreign body on its soil either. Only British protection will make it possible for some sort of Jewish National Home to exist—a home which will never be more than a temporary refuge. The persecuted will find shelter here, but they'll leave again the minute more enticing opportunities beckon from across the ocean. Jews have never known and will never know how to live by the sword. The attempt to produce a younger generation of narrow-minded fanatics who will agree to serve as cannon fodder for the messianic madness of their fathers is doomed to failure. When they become parents in their own right, they'll rebel. In the meantime, the Arabs, who don't lack madmen of their own, will grow stronger, and in the end the tender buds of Jewish hope will be wiped off the face of the earth.

I don't believe that intelligent people can't see this. But they prefer to delude themselves with daydreams and believe in miracles. How many more catastrophes do they need in order to realize that miracles were granted to our forefathers but not to us? History knows no mercy. Like God, she extracts payment for the sins of the fathers unto the third and fourth generations. A slight historical error swells to huge dimensions. Like this ingathering of the exiles on the jaws of a volcano. Like the revival of the Hebrew language, which will cut off an entire generation of Jews from the European languages that gave birth to the concepts of modern science, modern literature, and political thought.

From my window, which faces east, I can see the hills of Judea and Samaria. A wall of blue above which on a clear day you can see the antennas of the Voice of Jerusalem next to Ramallah—the air is so pure here. Jerusalem itself, the city of mystery, I haven't yet seen. The road there passes through dozens of Arab villages, and Arab guerrillas often attack Jewish vehicles passing through their territory. The convoys to Jerusalem are accompanied by army and police escorts, but it's still dangerous, and I'm not prepared to risk my life in order to satisfy my curiosity. I can wait for better days. In the citrus season, in autumn, so they say, the hostilities will be interrupted. The Arabs will want to market the Jaffa oranges, which are the main exports of this poor country.

Perhaps I'm being spared a disappointment, and the Holy City will turn out to be one more squalid town whose poverty-stricken inhabitants pick stones off the mountainsides and sell them to gullible pilgrims as relics from Solomon's Temple.

I have no option but to stay here, in the "first Hebrew city," as uninspiring as it is ambitious. I go from cafe to cafe, none of which bears the least resemblance to the Romanische Cafe, known to the Berlin bohemia as the Cafe Megalomania. In the absence of friends, I console myself with coffee with whipped cream, which is not at all bad. For the price of a cup of coffee I can read a goodly number of magazines from all over the world. When I find an article I need for my work, I furtively cut it out. In the early afternoon the cafes are deserted. Everyone here has adopted the Mediterranean siesta as a regular daily habit.

There are a couple of artists' cafes here too, but the patrons yell at each other in Russian or Hebrew. Most of them have never even heard of me. And the few who have read one or two lines of my prose aren't bursting with curiosity to know how I feel here. They are too serious to take any interest in a Berlin satirist writing in an off-putting language. Berlin's role in history is over. It has become a center of hoodlumism, whereas this is a center of international culture. Apart from the fact that showing too much interest in an émigré writer with fraying cuffs is dangerous—who knows, he might need a small loan to pay for his coffee.

3/17/37

The most important cultural enterprise in the country is the recently established symphony orchestra. One of the reasons for this is the universal language that it speaks (an irony which the Zionist culture lover prefers to ignore). The stuff produced in Hebrew doesn't come up to European standards. Or perhaps the stylistic nuances don't come through in translation. In any case, I read a few stories translated by Dr. Shalom, and I wasn't impressed.

The orchestra was founded with the express purpose on the part of its founder, the Polish violinist Bronislaw Huberman, of "strengthening the ties between Eretz Israel and Europe," so that we wouldn't be doomed to live here in a "cultural exile." So he said, and he knew what he was talking about.

Rosendorf gave me tickets and I went to hear them. Not bad at all. But the excitement here is really provincial. Over the orchestra, over every pronouncement by Huberman, over Toscanini's theatrical gestures. The farmers of Ramoth-Hashavim have given him an orange grove—a gift which he probably has no idea what to do with. On a women's training farm his wife was presented with two week-old chickens—presumably to prevent her from starving on the plane to Rome. Or perhaps they wanted to hint that it was nobler for a woman to earn her living from farming than from being kept by her husband. . . . The maestro reciprocates their love. In Jerusalem, before dining with the High Commissioner, he listened to a lecture on Hebrew literature. A highly significant symbolic gesture. And Huberman declared that Toscanini "has entered the history of a land full of mystery"—whatever that means.

The orchestra is an important humanitarian project, but according to Rosendorf it saved only seventy-two out of five hundred applicants. So a sense of proportion is in order.

"There's nothing more European in the world than the Jews," said Huberman, who believes in the historic mission of the Jews in Europe. Did he bring the Jewish musicians here to mark time? Or perhaps he realizes that only music is capable of maintaining the tie with Europe. "It would be a tragedy," he hinted to the Zionists, "if the Jewish people were now to cut off their connections with Europe, to the development of whose culture they contributed so much."

4/12/37

It's been a long time since I visited my diary. I do so now in order to announce that nothing has happened. Except that spring has arrived. But it too is only a premature summer.

From my window, which faces Jerusalem, a hot wind assails me and shrivels my willpower. How perverse of me to sit down to write today of all days, when my head is heavy and my hands are damp with perspiration. With a heavy heart I shall lament the winter, which died a sudden death.

I already have one local friend here—the sea. When twilight falls I stroll along its shores to introduce some order into my thoughts. A mirror that reflects my moods.

The beaches are suddenly full of people, exposing their white limbs to the blazing sun. With the complacency of summer vacationers, they play and cultivate their youthful bodies, oblivious to the Jaffa mosque rising menacingly in the south like the watchtower of a concentration camp.

The young boys throw themselves between the legs of the camels carrying sand for mixing concrete on their backs. Spectacular leaps—as if they are practicing for their heroic deaths. I thought of the young men of Catalonia running in front of the stampeding bulls before the fight. Now they are fleeing from the low-flying planes.

When it's calm, the sea is as blue and clear as an inverted summer sky; when it's angry, it's green and gray and purple, and the foam on its lips spews up a terrible fury from the depths. And then there's a haze in the west, like a wall closing off Europe. The haze rises above the horizon like the mountains of a distant land. At moments like these I am full of longing for Germany. Lines of German poetry buzz in my head, and in my heart is only a deep pain.

I return to my room full of inspiration and I can't write a word. I feel like a stowaway discovered at sea and cast off on a desert island.

With trembling hands I write a few lines in my diary, in the only language that sings in my soul. But I can only write about myself. I'll never be able to write about this country, which gives me shelter. For I shall never put down roots here.

This certainty encloses me like a fetal sac and returns me to the womb which cast me out before my time.

I shall never make my home in a place where I can't publish my books. I sit on the Tel Aviv beach and write a letter to the Germany of tomorrow. Listen, Germany, listen! Somewhere on the Mediterranean shores a man sits weeping for your fate, a man who burned his fingers smuggling a glowing ember from the smashed altar to keep it alive until the glorious temple of the eternal Germany is rebuilt.

I won't exaggerate my importance—greater German writers than I are living now in Switzerland, in Paris, in Los Angeles, in New York, and other places in the world. Perhaps they can guard the burning embers better than I can, but I don't know if any of them is paying a higher price for this love of the ideal Germany which no longer exists except in our books.

Last night I went to see a German-language movie. The enraged audience roared and screamed at the sound of the German words, which were like balm to my soul. Last week someone set fire to a newspaper kiosk because they sold a German magazine there. I had an article in it myself: on the miseries of German writers in exile.

The feeling of transience affects everything. Even relations with the other sex. You don't have to be my enemy to say that I have no right to go on exploiting the woman whose bed and food I share forever. I think so too—but I can't be false to myself.

H. is an intelligent and endlessly patient woman. I don't believe her when she says that she agrees with me that this is no time to get married and have children. She's pretending that she prefers putting it off until the situation in Europe clears up. But how long can she wait? She's thirty-two years old, and nobody knows what the future will bring. The poor girl, who grew up in bohemian Berlin in its finest and craziest years, can't permit herself to deviate from the bon ton of the Romanische Cafe. But it's impossible for a person playing some sort of secret role in a national movement to be faithful to the anarchic creed of those addicted to the drug of art. She is denying her natural feelings when she claims that the institution of marriage is no longer valid. Principles to which my allegiance is halfhearted at best, she proclaims from the rooftops. How touching is this need to defend me against those who accuse me of being a parasite, prepared to eat her food but not to marry her!

I am not deceived by her devotion to anarchist ideals. Her true feelings reveal themselves in her moods. Without any warning, like the eruption of a distant earthquake, her grief for the world being destroyed before our eyes bursts forth. These sad lies break my heart. Who knows better than I do how easily I could comfort her for this weltschmerz? But if I ignore her cry for help, it is not out of cruelty.

I really and truly am incapable of getting married and having children. This may be a deep flaw in my character, or a passing sickness. In any case, here in this place and now at this time, I simply cannot see myself as a father devoted to his children. When I try to imagine myself holding a baby in my arms the picture blurs and fades in an instant.

What kind of a future would my children have here? How many years would they live before they were killed? I'm not so selfish as to bring children into the world as a means of enriching my life. If I can't promise them any kind of future, it would be better for them not to be born.

Another cause for concern: could I provide a European environment for them within the four walls of an apartment containing an enclave of pure German culture? I suspect not. They would grow up in these sunny streets, where children run wild all day long until late at night. I wouldn't be able to protect their tender souls from the shallowness, the arrogance, and the bloodthirstiness which are typical of the younger generation here. And what language would they speak? Would they learn German, a language which has been banned here with bell, book, and candle? Or would they perhaps be doomed for the rest of their lives to speak an artificial language, to which a few new words are added every day, without the growing pains of a culture which is built up gradually, layer by layer?

Would they ever be able to read the books written by the father who made so many jokes about his suffering, in order to discover where they came from before deciding where they wanted to go?

I have no illusions. I will never be able to lay even one brick in the temple of culture of Eretz Israel. My skepticism is the last thing they want here. The messianic Zionists from Eastern Europe would stone a man for thinking that the Jewish genius is in grave danger from the Palestinian adventure. Everything that sharpened the senses of the archetypal Jew in his struggle for survival, his efforts to carve out a good place for himself in European culture, is in danger of going down the drain here, where the younger generation is being brought up on a new, secular orthodoxy, without the values of a universal religion or the traditions of European humanism. Isolated from Europe, the taste of the Jewish Yishuv is liable to degenerate into a nauseating Levantine kitsch.

Like an invalid, I sit down at the desk which does not belong to me, or the cafe table, and scribble a few lines. I lack the peace of mind necessary to compose an essay, let alone a novel, which demands the concentration of all one's spiritual resources. I can't close my window on the world and shut myself up inside the four walls of my own creation. The house is in ruins and the zeitgeist blows in and sweeps the notes from the tabletop. It seems I shall have to postpone my plans until I know where I am, and what I'm doing there. All I'm capable of writing in the meantime are the jottings of a shattered soul, an outline for a novel which may never be written. In the bitterness of my despair I even considered writing a biblical story, intrigues at the court of King Solomon. But for this, too, I could summon up neither the necessary patience nor the humor—the court jester's entrance ticket to the royal palace.

My diary is a kind of box into which from time to time I throw the tail end of an idea or the fragment of a thought—the broken bits of colored glass of an occasional bon mot, the string ends of unconnected associations, tangled balls of useless analogies, fables in search of a moral, philosophic junk, rusty nails of wit, dry twigs from the Tree of Knowledge—like the survivor of a shipwreck cast up on a desert island, collecting everything he can lay his hands on to build himself a raft.

My friend Walter Benjamin thinks that all writers are hoarders by nature (the lucky dog knows French and has no need to seek refuge in a language he doesn't understand). I can't imagine a more unsuitable instinct for a Jew of our times—unless he doesn't mind leaving his collection to his persecutors when they force him to flee for his life. But I have to admit that for me even jotting down ideas on bits of paper stems from a passionate hoarding instinct. Even the most nonsensical thought may not be thrown away. Who knows? Perhaps it will come in handy one day.

A writer is the only person on earth who isn't wasting his time when he listens attentively to the drivel of an imbecile—he's learning how the mind works when it's got a screw loose. An insignificant incident which wants to be remembered should take place in front of a writer. That way it will have a chance of being documented. Sensible people should beware of making friends with writers. Everything is stored away in their memories, waiting for the right opportunity. A writer's mind is like the ragbag of a careful housewife who never throws a garment away in case it may come back into fashion one day. His chest is full of obsolete sayings, portentous phrases that have lost their credibility, comic situations which have died tragic deaths, and false prophecies waiting for their moment of truth.

I part easily from material possessions. Without undue regret I sold all my family heirlooms to my mean neighbors for next to nothing—heavy furniture saturated with the memories of three generations, antique crystal, souvenirs, portraits of my ancestors, posing full of dignity and self-importance, and even medals (two of the twenty-five thousand Iron Crosses awarded to Jews during the First World War hung over our fireplace, in memory of my two patriotic uncles).

I only mourned the books I was forced to leave behind. Ten thousand books, both old and new, filled the family library—from wall to wall and floor to ceiling—in our old house. An irreplaceable loss. I shall never see its like again.

There was no need for the Nazis to examine my nose or my penis to know that I was Jewish. It would have been enough to see how eagerly I pick up a new book, or how reverently I stick together a torn page in a volume of erotica published three hundred years ago.

And now I live in a house with only two hundred books in it. Half of which are in Hebrew.

The only decent library I know of here belongs to a German Jew who lives in a suburb of Jerusalem. In other words, I would have to drive for two hours in an armor-plated car with an armed escort in order to look at a book which I could have found on the shelf in my parents' house in Friedrichstrasse with my eyes shut.

I read the first pages without pleasure. To my regret, I find them redolent of a self-pity which I detest. The attempt to give them an air of historical documentation was not successful. They are guilty of exaggeration and ingratitude.

It's stupid to ignore my good fortune in landing in H.'s house. And her characterization is inadequate, too. Something extraordinary happened to her on her way from the Fatherland to the Promised Land. As a student in Berlin she embraced her exile gladly, intent on exchanging the fleshpots of her parents' home for the spiritual values she hoped to find in the Romanische Cafe. And there of all places, in the company of a few monsters of egoism and a few common cads, who exploited her wealth and generosity, she lost all traces of selfishness and found the ideal of selfless service to a revolutionary cause.

This part of the story is still a secret. All I know is that she was active in the Zionist movement in a way that demanded exceptional courage. Which is apparently why she no sooner arrived in Palestine then she was entrusted with some hush-hush job whose exact nature is not at all clear to me. She goes in and out of the homes of high-up Mandatory officials, but what she does there I don't know. She tells me nothing, and I don't ask any questions. This suits us both. When we part, she won't have to worry about my talking out of turn.

H., who once wanted to live in a commune, is now content with a commune for two, where one is in charge of earning the money and the other of spending it. She demands nothing of me but to be allowed to love me. What more could I ask? What gives me the right to describe my life here, free of the need to work for a living or the humiliation of running after publishers, as imprisonment in a jail where the jailers can't understand my language? I demean myself by exposing these imaginary wounds. When I remember the days of my poverty in Paris ("There are more German writers here in one arrondissement than there are French writers in the whole of France") I know how grateful I should be for my good fortune. Here I am a free man. Sometimes I feel profoundly at peace, like a man lying on his back in a forest, halfway between sleep and wakefulness. And I don't lack for love and appreciation either.

I count my blessings not only out of a sense of duty, but in order to sharpen the description of the pain of being uprooted from the German language. These bitter pages were written by a man who lacks neither food nor love, but lives as free as a bird on the boughs of a bountiful tree. A bird whose tongue has been cut out.

We writers lack the gift for dealing with happiness. Between the leaves of a book there is room only for withered flowers. Our moments of serenity are deadly dull. Satiety too is not our theme, except when it turns to nausea. When our castaways succeed in building rafts and sailing back to civilization, they forget to mention the fresh spring water they drank and the bananas that satisfied their hunger.

5/1/37

Last night I had a bright idea: instead of collecting crumbs at random—organizing the material as the draft of a novel about a string quartet.

An idea born in a moment of weakness. A counsel of despair. If I can't sharpen my pen into a sword to fight the Nazis, at least I can devote my meager resources to the elevation of beauty. I shall focus my microscope on the mutual relations between people who only know how to play pure, beautiful notes. In the eyes of my Communist friends this decision amounts to an evasion of responsibility. I shall no doubt be accused of "escapism."

Although I break out in a rash when people talk to me about the "function of art," I can't ignore the fact that at certain moments one has to stand up and face the storm. More than one hunger is satisfied by the need to publish. The striving for perfection nourishes the childish desire to repair what others have destroyed. The passion for order is a temptation to organize the disorganized world, where the laws of probability are broken every day. Literature is the sweet illusion of a perfectly ordered world between two cardboard covers. There is a proper degree of modesty in a writer's acknowledging his inability to spoil Hitler's appetite. But putting a string quartet under a magnifying glass in 1937, when the Nazi beast is devouring Europe, is undeniably tantamount to deserting the battlefield. On the Day of Judgment I shall be sent to the penal colony of History for the crime of desertion. I shall be sentenced to oblivion. You don't have to subscribe to Marxism, like Brecht or Walter Benjamin, to recognize the force of their argument here. Of all the subjects in the world, they'll say, this idiot chose to dissect the relationships between a group of musicians playing, in our crazy century, the happy works of a hundred years ago! It would be hard to imagine a place more remote from the reality of our times than this room, where four fiddlers are getting ready to perform their version of something that has already been played countless times before.

But in the end I came to the conclusion that the choice was right.

A string quartet is a microcosm. It reflects the quintessential experience of human society as a whole. Within its closed circle, a strained fraternity, in which all human passions are held in check, comes into being, as in every community whose cohesion is a vital and necessary condition for the performance of its role.

Art cannot report on reality like a newsreel. Nor does it possess the power to falsify it. At most it can offer us distillations of human perspectives and human relationships.

I shall take the risk of being denounced by the generation which knew not the nationalist madness. In time they will learn that abandoning the effort to crush Nazi Germany by dint of a diligent pen contained within it the seeds of a Futurist manifesto: the words which prostituted themselves and went whoring with soldiers are no longer capable of becoming pregnant and giving birth. The only role left to them is that of music.

I found grounds for optimism in this: a way of washing words clean from the filth of the lies, purifying them in a ritual bath, so that they can be used to express ideas again. Perhaps. After the good men beat the bad men and wash the blood off their hands.

In an excess of enthusiasm I sat down at my desk to write.

Like a Catholic nun who has chosen to love God, I began to weave a delicate lace such as the German language, overladen with ideas, has never known before. And with a sense of vocation: for these words, murdered by Herr Goebbels, I am sewing silken shrouds.

To tell the truth, the idea occurred to me some time ago, when I met Rosendorf and he told me that he was thinking of putting together a string quartet. But then it was just another idea, one of half a dozen constantly running around in my head and competing for my attention. I did not imagine then that I had found the balm for my wounds.

Like every redemptive idea it seemed too simple to be feasible.

The outline for the novel

The question of the form will be resolved later. The content is clear: disjointed lives in search of harmony. Four different characters dedicated to the creation of a unity outside time and space. The yearning to attain transcendence by means of abstraction.

For further consideration: how much daily life to put into the background? How much musical terminology, which won't mean a thing to a reader with no training in music? The framework will examine the mutual relationships between real characters. Any changes necessary to maintain the rhythm and credibility of the action can be introduced in the final stages.

The characters

1. Kurt Rosendorf. First violin, born in 1900, in Berlin. Tall, blond, blue-eyed, morbidly sensitive, a pure Aryan type, more German than the Germans.
2. Konrad Friedman, second violin, born in 1911, Würzburg. Medium-sized, a clever monkey with Paganini's head but without his virtuosity. Very Jewish. Sharp-witted. A Talmudist. He could be a Communist propagandist, believes

that if everyone killed one fly a day we could free the world of flies.

3. Eva Staubenfeld, viola, born 1909 (?), Königsberg. A female Rosendorf, without his morbid sensitivity. A meeting place of contradictions: her eyes give off warmth and her lips—venom. Very reserved. But when she plays—a yielding sensuality, as if she's undergone a personality change.

4. Bernard Litovsky, cello, born 1898, Schleswig-Holstein. An athlete amusing himself with the cello. Plays with dangerous opinions like a self-confident snake trainer. Behind the apparent superficiality there's a cunning which is difficult to gauge. Married. No children.

For further consideration: How many of the other characters need to be three-dimensional? Greta, Rosendorf's wife, and their daughter, Anna, are both in Berlin, a distant presence; Hella Becker, in love with Rosendorf; Martha, Litovsky's wife, a woman with the life gone out of her, very intelligent, Eva's friend; Hilda Moses; the narrator; and others.

Technique

For a while I played with the idea of writing the novel simultaneously—a kind of mosaic with a sentence devoted to each character, creating a logical sequence with every fourth sentence before and after it. I abandoned this idea very quickly. This kind of technique, like the stream of consciousness, burdens the poor reader's mind with riddles demanding solutions instead of letting him concentrate on the really important questions. You would have had to read my novel with some kind of special decoding card, with slits for the relevant lines. Tricks like these can safely be left to our friends, the Futurists. It's enough for me to puzzle my reader with implications beyond his grasp and answers to questions he never knew existed.

Information about music to be kept to a minimum. Only

facts which have more general implications. There's no point in introducing terminology familiar only to professionals.

Limitations

The main drawback in writing about music is the frequent need for adjectives and adverbs. I envy music its ability to pass from mood to mood without having to justify a sudden access of optimism, for example. Its "proofs" are "mathematical": certain combinations result in certain effects and that's that— whereas words become entangled in ambiguities and choke in the webs they spin themselves. But literature isn't music, and a writer who uses collage today is simply being a slave to fashion.

Life itself is a collage. The aim of art is to show the connections between disconnected things: experiences, objects, tenses, words, pictures, sounds, dreams. The role of a mosaic is to create the impression of the integration of the parts, and not of the disintegration of the whole.

Conclusion

With all the revulsion from the Sisyphean effort of transferring reality to paper, I have no alternative but to tie myself to people, facts, time, and the logical syntax of a deciphered dream.

I won't escape into madness, which is the last refuge of the honest German. Many artists have chosen it as a way of declaring to History that they no longer intend to interfere with her course. I shall go my own way: logical syntax will return Germany to the sanity which is difficult to maintain in a northern climate. The myth and the dream serve the interests of the mediocre talents working for the Nazi regime. My protest will be my subject: music.

Kurt Tucholsky said: "Due to bad weather conditions, the German revolution broke out in music." Where myth is more powerful than human feeling, ritual executions can be performed to the accompaniment of the sublime music of Bach. Only words can protect human beings.

5 / 2 / 3 7

I made Rosendorf's acquaintance on the voyage here. Before that I'd seen him in Berlin, at a distance of twenty-five rows. I liked his playing, not only because of the quality of the sound, but also because of a certain degree of restraint which I found pleasing in those days of mass hysteria. He did not try to draw attention to the part of the first violin. And although he is capable of expressing extreme emotions, he did not exaggerate in the direction of theatrical gestures.

I wanted to tell him how I felt at the time, but I hung back. I don't know enough about music. After the concert, in the "green room," I saw an expression of distaste for his vociferous admirers on his face. He offered them his long hand with a kind of anxiety, as if afraid they might press it too hard. Distress signals went on in his eyes when his arm was enthusiastically pumped up and down. I decided to leave. One more anonymous admirer would make no difference to him.

When I saw his Modiglianian figure on the deck, I recognized him immediately. His appearance is absolutely distinctive; everything about him is elongated and upward-striving. Natural aristocracy has no need of airs and graces, I said to myself. Even the clumsiest movement, like dragging a heavy deck chair, has an aura of grace about it.

Absentmindedly he stood on the deck, as if he had put his violin down for a moment to concentrate. When he bent down to pick up a newspaper that had slipped out of his hands, I remembered how I had admired even his stylish bow to the audience—without excessive gratitude, like a man who humbles himself only before art. He walked on the deck like an actor in a silent movie, utterly indifferent to noises, smells, and the overtures of bored passengers who seemed to think that traveling together in a floating box made us boon companions.

I did not approach him. I myself am wary of deck chair

friendships. Friends made on board ship allow themselves liberties they would never dream of on land and take up all your time with their idle chatter. I said to myself then: a romantic character from a sentimental novel. Not for me.

Someone introduced us to each other. He had read *Ancient Glory* and wanted to meet me.

I was glad to meet a violinist who reads books. He was glad to meet a music-loving writer. We had a very short conversation indeed—I about music, he about literature. If he had spoken about new books (and if I had announced that I worshiped Bach) our friendship would probably have ended there and then. But he spoke about Pohl's book about Mozart, and I told him that I made an effort to understand Schönberg, out of intellectual curiosity, even though I rarely enjoyed him, and consequently we became friends immediately. I feel a special affection for people who read old books and don't feel obliged to keep constantly up to date.

An unthreatening friendship developed. Sensitive people never cling; they need no more than a flicker of an eyelid to understand that the conversation has come to an end. Which is just the way I like it. My time is too precious to waste.

We spent short periods of time together frequently. We found ourselves in agreement on questions of taste. We put a stop to intimate conversations in time to prevent them from degenerating into self-pity. Both of us were traveling toward the unknown, and both of us were going downhill, professionally speaking. I saw him as my mirror image.

Both of us wear the bloodstained Jewish hair shirt in the same way—with shame and pain and without pretending that it is the uniform of the Chosen People. Both of us bear the mark of Abel on our brow.

Certain sensibilities unite us too: we both shrink from emotional outpourings and prefer concise, accurate formulations. My readers might be surprised if I were to add: both of us shrink from rudeness.

True, I have sinned in this regard in the past. In the written, never the spoken, word. I have written acrimonious articles and obscene skits. But these were weapons in a political struggle. Face to face, even with the most benighted opponent, I refrain from wounding sarcasms. I would never take pride in shaming my fellows.

Nature will have her joke, or perhaps she wanted to teach us some lesson: it's hard to imagine twin souls in two more different bodies. Rosendorf is northern, I am southern. Rosendorf is very handsome, which is something no one would ever call me. He is a pure Aryan vessel into which the profound, wise sadness of the Jew has been poured. I am short, squat, short-armed, thick-fingered, black-haired and -eyed, hooknosed, and restless. A classical Jewish type, with all the silly, irritable pedantry of a German.

The question is if I too have a place in this novel—a writer who was in Dachau. Perhaps as a metaphor. A man like Rosendorf, who ran away from pain and abandoned his wife and child, worries about how he would have reacted to physical degradation. But Rosendorf refrains from asking, even though he is consumed by curiosity. He often brings up the subject of his revulsion from violence. He hopes that I will be tempted to talk about Dachau. Once he even hinted that the fact that I don't tell him about that period in my life shows that I'm not sure of his friendship.

6/2/37

When Hitler came to power, all the frogs in the overheated swamp of the artistic milieu woke up. They croaked with a peculiar glee: all our dire prophesies have come true! A doubtful pleasure—to say "I told you so!" Only a few of them realized that the time had come to roll up their sleeves. The majority believed that now that the true face of the Third Reich had been revealed, the forces of progress would be joined by the bourgeoisie concerned for their own civil liberties. Only the Jews among us read the writing on the wall: the world will not be redeemed as long as one Jewish child is crying in it.

I don't know when I will find the strength to document what I went through behind the barbed-wire fence. It will take a lot of time for the necessary distance to be created. All I remember is this—in a consciousness increasingly dazed I said to myself: whatever remains in my memory after a decade or two will be vital; the details I forget will be redundant.

In moments of unendurable degradation, the mind escapes into unconsciousness. The jerking of the needle recording the twitching of the soul is registered somewhere in the depths of the unconscious mind. When the time is ripe a clear chart will rise to the surface. In the meantime, a rough outline is enough.

At first I was pleasantly surprised. They didn't start hitting me right away. They let me stand at ease until they had finished writing down all my personal particulars, and then a polite, smiling officer came up to me and removed my glasses. After that I couldn't see a thing. I heard the crunch of the lenses being ground under the heel of his boot and I was sent out of the room. For a week they let me stumble into things until I learned by heart my daily route—from punishment to punishment. Then the humiliation began.

I thought to myself, with private irony, that the richly idiomatic German I used in my replies to their idiotic questions was a kind of retaliation. They wanted to hurt a Jew, and I offered them a German writer.

One of them understood and hit me on the mouth. As if to make it clear: their obscenities were more German than the literary language on my lips. I was being beaten to shut me up, not to make me talk.

When I polish a German phrase to shine like a diamond, I am taking my revenge on them. Anyone who wants to know what Germany was in the fourth decade of the twentieth century will have to consult Jewish writers.

A rehearsal of the Rosendorf quartet:

A few days after I arrived in Tel Aviv, after several days of a delightful vacation on Mount Carmel as the guest of the local Goethe Society, I met Rosendorf in the street. We stood there chatting enthusiastically for a long time, as if taking up a conversation that had been interrupted in the middle. Friendships flare up easily between refugees in foreign lands, trying to hide their anxieties from each other. Both of us pretended that we were settling down nicely.

I wasn't sure that we could be real friends because of the difference in our incomes—he with his steady salary and me with pocket money. I could never be friends with a man who earns more than I do, unless he was the soul of tact. Rich people revolt me.

Rosendorf, as it turned out, was not only the soul of tact, but very hard up himself (the silly fellow sends money to Germany to pay for his daughter's music lessons). In spite of this, however, he always paid for the coffee we drank together. I'll never forget his apologetic smile when he did so. As if to remind me that he was not to blame for the unfairness of a world in which the performer earned more than the creator. Absentmindedly he would reach for his wallet and quickly snatch the common bill, which it was his duty to pay.

He also saved me the ticket money for the orchestra concerts, the fragile thread connecting me to Europe. On the days of the concerts I ached with hunger for music—music, which lives in eternal yearning for a past one-tenth of a second long. Music is the warm bath in which I soak my aching limbs. For hours I would listen to records scratched with use in the empty apartment from which H. was absent most of the hours of the day. I did not despise even the sentimental music rising from the cafes on the beachfront, where I wandered aimlessly, as long as I could be in a space full of music. So I was obviously glad to go to the quartet rehearsals, even though I knew that I would not hear entire movements played straight through there, but an endless series of arguments over every detail.

From the first meeting I was entranced by the tight aesthetic structure of the ensemble. A string quartet seems to me a perfect expression of the economy of means. And the players—like monks, unsparing of themselves in the strict adherence to the rules of their rites. For hours on end I listened to their arguments and found nothing in the so-called laws whose rules they accused each other of breaking but the longing for order and discipline. By their obedience to the rule, they, like the monks, will gain immortality.

At first I wanted to write an essay about music as a religious experience. I found a historical irony here, a kind of servants' revolution: Music, which began by serving Religion, ended by usurping her mistress's throne; the anonymous organist expelled the priest from the cathedral, and the music of Bach took the place of the Holy Ghost. But after coming to know the characters more closely, I returned to my original idea of writing a novel, in the hope that it would be able to convey more faithfully the tension between freedom and submission in the lives of those who have entered a strict framework and accepted its rules.

I tried to rid myself of the prejudices of a writer who envies musicians. The truth is, the instrumentalist has only a very restricted leeway—to determine the tempo and dynamics—and this, too, only where the composer has not given absolutely specific indications, and to the extent that his colleagues let him. Sometimes it seems that the musician is nothing but a bird standing on a telegraph wire and absorbing the meaningless hum through its little claws. But it was easy for me to free myself of the patronizing attitude of the composer toward the performer—what do they know of the triumphant joy of sitting in the evening opposite a page of polished prose? For what was my life until I attached myself to them and made them into a draft for my novel? In the morning I waited for supper and at night I tossed and turned on my bed trying to make the sun rise quicker. My life was spent in anticipation of the unexpected—a message from abroad, a declaration of love from some unknown admirer, or even the reassuring results of a urine test. In the rare moments I could spare from my preoccupation with myself, I envied the tranquility of those who had their sights fixed on distant goals, such as the redemption of the Jewish people or socialism in our lifetime, and could go to bed happy at night: the least of their acts during the day, apart from the dreary necessity of earning a living, had brought them closer to their goal.

I have learned quite a lot; even my language has been enriched by musical metaphors. Sometimes I regretted not being a painter. I wanted to draw an exact picture of the sight before my eyes: four figures in a common effort of response; although they are so different, they try to play like one person. Even the way they play shows how different they are. Rosendorf plays with melancholy despair, and Friedman—with rage; Staubenfeld with hostile submission, and Litovsky—like a lover seeking the erogenous zones on the body of his beloved.

Before long they began to regard me as a kind of house critic, by whose reactions they gauged the achievements of the quartet. I never missed a single one of their concerts in Tel Aviv. I observed the transformation brought about by public exposure—the excitement aroused by the presence of an audience, even one incapable of judging the quality of the performance. I studied their individual behavior—Rosendorf oblivious to his surroundings, showing no sign of effort, Friedman moving his body energetically in the attempt to demonstrate the hidden intentions of the music to the layman, Staubenfeld concentrating reverently on the music alone, keeping completely still so as not to draw attention to extraneous details, and Litovsky full of joy at the opportunity of making love to his audience, with his head shaking and his eyes closed, like a child hiding behind his eyelids, dying to be found.

After a few rehearsals I discovered a story within a story within a story. The draft will include everything. You can never tell what will add color to the final version of the novel.

The rehearsals usually take place at Litovsky's house. After the rehearsal we all walk home. Friedman goes south, Rosendorf and I west, and Staubenfeld north.

One day she asked me to accompany her home. The request was neutral, without a trace of coquetry, but the heart is a well-known fool. I was sure that I had been asked to play a minor role in somebody else's story.

On the wall of the house across the street sat a muscular, curly-haired youth in short trousers and an embroidered shirt, with a martyred expression on his face. Although Staubenfeld ignored him completely, I took in the situation at a glance. My foolish hopes flew out of my head as quickly as they had entered it.

We walked a long way without the slightest attempt at conversation on her part. A silence which succeeded in embarrassing me.

I never lose my head in the company of pretty women, whose prattle might hold a trap for fools. I always let them run on until they trip themselves up on their own loquacity. From time to time I utter an interrogative grunt and continue undisturbed to think my idle thoughts. A little cruelty is necessary to protect ourselves from pests. If social life is a sentence to which we are obliged to submit, we owe it to ourselves, at least, to serve our term with as much intelligence as we can muster. But Staubenfeld beat me at my own game. After the silence mentioned above, she suddenly asked me a direct question about Brecht and I was forced to answer. How many words I wasted in vain in the attempt to explain a few simple ideas! I wanted to talk about music but she kept changing the subject. In the end the conversation degenerated into a discussion of the weather. Here, too, I did not shine. She said one sentence: How strange it is to live in a country without a spring—and taught me the secret of economy.

Suddenly she glanced quickly behind her shoulder and then said that there was no need for me to accompany her all the way home. I too looked back, and saw that her stubborn lover had abandoned her. My role, that of the Beast protecting Beauty from the handsome young man, was over.

Staubenfeld's lover will have no place in my novel. Piffling romantic episodes of that order can safely be left to the clichés of trashy romances for chambermaids. My interest lies in the string quartet as an entity outside time and place. Human relations in a closed sounding box. Even if I fail to create the distilled, concentrated essence which the quartet symbolizes, the attempt will help me at least to collect my scattered thoughts. And thoughts threaded onto a single string have a chance of turning into a necklace.

10/2/37

I abandoned the draft because I began to have doubts: aren't I burdening my novel with a role too heavy for its shoulders? Can a story about music really be a protest?

My attraction to chamber music, which began in Berlin, stemmed from my objections to the use of music to inflame the masses. I hated the trumpet calls arousing fierce passions in the hypnotized mob, and the drumbeats to which organized hoodlumism marched in the streets. Even symphony music began to frighten me, as if the conductor's control of a collective functioning contained some kind of threat to reason. I escaped to chamber music like someone fleeing from the city crowds and din. Just as I wearied of prose packed with reality and preferred the allusiveness of poetry, so I preferred the passionate whisper of chamber music, beckoning the magical to emerge from a dream, to symphonic music stewing in myths. I felt a deep need for an intimate encounter devoted to deciphering a modest experience. But this is a long way from a political protest. I have to beware of losing my sense of proportion.

I can only say this: events in Germany have turned me into a chamber man. I want to compose prose without a plot, to write a novel without a dominant character, to live in a world without heroes. The story of four German Jews exiled to Palestine in 1936 with musical instruments in their hands is the only thing I can think about today.

I don't know yet if I'll be able to write it.

10/11/37

After a concert: Bach, Mozart, Mussorgsky.

Music can't escape from time. You can hear the pulse of the times and the spirit of the period in it. Except for Bach. When people play Bach I am in non-time and non-space. Musicians in black bow ties from nowhere transmit from generation to generation music which is timeless.

Baroque music bears me on a magic carpet of sounds to a very specific place indeed. A palace, a high ceiling, crystal chandeliers, women with bare bosoms afraid of their own instincts, dark lusts in the eyes of men afraid of hellfire, a prince noisily gnawing a pheasant wing while the child prodigy who plays the piano is presented to him. I am one of them, and my stiff collar is choking me. There is a phony sweetness in the air.

I looked at the members of the quartet. Is it possible to know a man by the way he plays a musical instrument? I asked myself. It is. Even by the way he stirs his tea.

I asked Rosendorf. He smiled. Of course it's possible. You can sense the changes taking place in his personality, too. Once he had a Prussian Junker as a second violin. The only sounds he knew were forte and fortissimo. They had to get rid of him, in spite of the social advantages he brought them.

By the way, we have begun to address each other in the familiar mode. But when I ask him about the other members of the quartet, he shuts up like a clam. He suspects me of "collecting material." He feels an aristocratic revulsion from poking his nose into other people's affairs. About Staubenfeld he refuses to say a word. Is there a liaison in the offing there? The only one he's prepared to talk about is Friedman, as if Friedman were some kind of phenomenon. One may examine him from a certain distance and admire his exotic plumes.

The relationship between character and style of playing is far more complex. Like the relationship between taste and ideology. A man may be unfaithful to his opinions with his taste, and vice versa. Not only that, but you sometimes find people with the same views whose tastes are poles apart. And the opposite. Take Rosendorf and Staubenfeld: two different points of view, but in matters of taste two hearts which beat as one. From the way they look at each other when they're playing you can see the flame of mutual understanding flaring between them. Even if they're not in love yet—I wonder how long they'll be able to withstand the compelling power of this unity of taste.

They really are as alike as brother and sister. When they're playing, their movements are calm and full of self-confidence, but when they're not, their fingers have a slight nervous tremor, like a hunger to realize the music stored up inside them.

Goebbels could photograph them as two perfect examples of pure Aryanism. He himself, by the way, looks like a rat of Semitic descent.

Rosendorf lets his hair down with Hilda. He evidently feels the need to talk about intimate matters occasionally. He doesn't trust me. Women are better listeners than men. He hinted to her that he's faithful to his wife in Germany. I don't believe him. All it means is that he wants to impress Hilda with his decency.

Everybody wants to impress Hilda with their decency. It gets on my nerves. After all, she herself does things which aren't exactly honest. She makes friends with government officials in order to get their secrets out of them. But a person whose character bears the stamp of truth can apparently dabble in lies without being infected.

Hilda says that Rosendorf is immune to falling in love because he loves women in general. The truth is that he's in love with himself—a man so full of love.

Friedman really is a phenomenon. A dyed-in-the-wool intellectual. His mind is a laboratory for processing all the information available to an educated man, just as his body is a laboratory for research into vegetarianism. He's too serious. Every idea that passes the test of his intellectual scrutiny is immediately turned into a code of behavior. In a country like Palestine, where philosophers build roads, this is a dangerous attitude for a violinist. He's liable to feel like a parasite for not contributing to the development of the country.

He's younger than Staubenfeld but he looks older. Staubenfeld is apparently twenty-nine. She's one of those women who don't change at all between twenty and fifty and who will suddenly decide one day to start acting like an old woman.

Friedman is the most serious person in the group. The others aren't exactly frivolous, and Staubenfeld can be glum, but with him it's a vocation. In the earnestness with which he regards the obligations incumbent upon his theoretical conclusions he reminds me of a monk, horrified by the least sign of frivolity and mortifying himself because he has discovered traces of lust in his heart. He only laughs at jokes with a sociopolitical point. Even laughter has an educational mission with him.

I find an element of naiveté in him which is liable to turn into cruelty. Sensitive souls with radical opinions are capable of taking drastic measures to defend their ideas. Friedman's belief in Zionism and the unique local brand of socialism, which will be born from scratch, without having to destroy the old capitalist world, is nothing but a modern version of the vision of the End of Days. It is a belief in the coming of the Messiah which has taken off its skullcap and put on khaki. Not prayers and supplications will bring Him closer, but correct actions. Friedman hears the footsteps of the Messiah in the clanking of the turning tractor wheels. In the Soviet Union, God is electricity; here—agriculture. True, Friedman does not actually worship his God with the sweat of his brow—he only talks—but many true believers do no more. For people like him, belief is an existential need. When they discover doubts in the labyrinths of their souls, they banish them with whips.

May God preserve us from the perfectionists who force themselves to live in harmony with the world. In their opinion, every disharmony leads to a yet more perfect harmony. They were born determinists and will die with a question mark on their lips. They don't believe that there are accidents in the world. Anything we can't account for, in their opinion, fits into a comprehensive plan beyond our understanding.

Friedman believes that there has to be a connection between a musician's weltanschauung and his style of playing. A superficial attitude toward the issues of the times will lead to playing without depth. Staubenfeld upsets all his theories. Nothing interests her apart from the battle of the sexes, and she plays as if she's read all the books in the world. He has a problem: the facts don't behave according to plan. There's no order in the world. Fools play like angels and clever men play false notes. Staubenfeld, who thinks that history is a record of the war between the sexes and lacks his knowledge of the innovative ideas which are going to change the face of music in our century, plays Hindeminth, Stravinsky, Berg, and Toch better than he does. Baffled and moved, Friedman listened to a child prodigy from a working-class suburb of Haifa playing Mozart as if he had sat at the same table as Esterhazy. How could you play Mozart if you couldn't tell the difference between Salzburg and Hamburg? How could anyone who had not read Michael Kolhaas understand Beethoven's late quartets? Was it really enough just to read the notes and markings on the score?

In every Friedman the longing for a settled life in the shade of an enlightened Church exists side by side with the wild impulse to wander from country to country without striking roots anywhere. There is nothing easier than tempting him to spread out his treasures before you. One philosophical "hmm" is enough to set him off on an exhaustive exposition of the current state of his ideas on everything under the sun. Recently he has come to a definite conclusion: there is no understanding German music outside the historic context. German music has always served as a means of expression for the enlightened ideas of its time. Since its abstract form protected it from censorship, it was able to express revolutionary ideas more forcefully than literature and poetry. It preceded philosophy in predicting the future. It foretold the decline of the West. Firsthand experience of the Teutonic beast gave you a far deeper appreciation of Mozart and Schubert than someone who simply heard a melody and enjoyed it. From what depths of hatred, cruelty, stupidity, and insanity this striving for refinement, for brotherhood and freedom of expression, had emerged!

It's impossible not to like Friedman, although he can be very tiring. When he talks to you he pushes his face right up to yours, as if you need to know exactly what he had for breakfast. He pronounces lofty ideas sotto voce, like a conspirator who has found you worthy of hearing a secret or two. In this he's a true German. Even when he's alone, he's a member of some secret society preaching purity and chastity and wholewheat bread. If you listen carefully, he'll initiate you into the secret signs of the society. And from then on, when he plays something in the special key of the sect, you'll know that he's transmitting a secret signal meant for your ears alone.

Rosendorf endures his long speeches patiently. The others are less tolerant. Staubenfeld raises her eyes to heaven in despair. Litovsky throws in cynical remarks: all this business of music belongs to the pure pleasure department of the corrupt classes. Friedman passionately defends the idea of the social mission of music. It's all very diverting and adds a bit of spice to the quartet rehearsals.

How Friedman got into the orchestra is something of a mystery to me. Better musicians than he were rejected. Perhaps Huberman had extraneous considerations. Putting someone like Friedman into an orchestra, which is in danger of degenerating into a purely professional body, is like introducing a secret agent for humanism. Yesterday he said to me: "In all music, even the gayest, there's a certain sadness. Every note leaves the world in sorrow and laments its predecessor, which was cut off in its prime." I asked him if he'd give me permission to use this. With a shy smile he confessed that he had once had ambitions to write himself, but he had given them up. He wouldn't write in German, on principle, and his Hebrew would never be good enough. Poetry, he said, one could only write in one's mother tongue.

I can't help liking him. The most sensitive artists are the ones who question art's raison d'être. Ordinary technicians are not distressed by doubts, and moral problems don't make them lose any sleep. They are the ones with sharp elbows and the ability to sell themselves. Unfortunately in this matter, too, there is no justice—the technicians are sometimes better artists than their more sensitive colleagues.

A second violin who doesn't dream of a good place in the first violins is a valuable asset to an orchestra. And a dedicated musician like Friedman, who plays half a page of eighths, mezzo piano, with as much enthusiasm as if the responsibility for the entire performance rested on his shoulders, is more important to a quartet than a superior technician for whom technique, in the words of Huberman, is a "servant tyrannizing her mistress."

Friedman is also an amateur philosopher. I wonder if he's capable of writing anything coherent. A confused soul can stray forever in a forest of contradictory ideas. The richness of his vocabulary doesn't do him any good. There's a vast treasure trove of words and ideas stored away in his brain, but if he sat down to organize them in sentences and paragraphs the result would probably be chaos. A creative writer goes from the forest to the trees. First he has a picture in his mind and only afterward he fits in the words. Anyone who starts with the words will end up writing a dictionary.

Friedman plays with the idea that he hasn't yet decided to be a musician. As if his doubts can save him from the disgrace of making a living from his feelings and wipe the mark of Cain from his brow. There's something deceitful about it too. He sins and repents at his pleasure. Like an adulterer enjoying both his fornication and his guilty conscience. Gobbling sweets and crying over the starving children in Asia. If he wasn't so naive, I'd be revolted. I hate saints. Party machines are full of them. They are the pure-intentioned servants of tyranny. People have come across them in the Cheka too, I hear. Pity for the world and cruelty to people. But Friedman is a sensitive soul; I'm sure he'd shrink from cruelty.

A YEAR IN PALESTINE

Encouraging news from Germany. A well-known lawyer, a recent arrival from Germany, tells of a reshuffle in the Nazi Party. The moderate group behind Göring, Himmler, and Heydrich have gained the upper hand over the radicals. High-up army officers have been fired, and Jewish affairs have been taken out of Goebbels's hands. In the Foreign Office they realize the harm done to Germany by extreme actions. Hilda sees this as a positive phenomenon. The trio are interested in property and will encourage emigration. Goebbels, fighting the influence of the Jewish spirit on German culture, would never be satisfied with your money. He wants your life.

My relations have not been harmed. Most of them are the offspring of mixed marriages, and their wealth is modest. After I left, the black sheep of the family, they were left alone. Their situation is far from brilliant, but they don't complain. Their letters are getting more and more obscure, like the letters Rosendorf gets from his wife. She seems to want to break off connections with him in order to improve their daughter's situation.

Last night Rosendorf gave a Bach recital. He swept me back to Germany before Hitler. Bach expresses a different Germany from the one which grew out of Lutheran theology. He gave the church its due, but he doesn't belong to the tribal tradition. I find no distinction in him between culture—which rests on the primordial forces in the collective unconscious—and civilization, the instruments and institutions which create human society. Bach expresses a primeval Germany, but one which is at the same time progressive. He draws his inspiration from the organized structure which he himself created—rational music which leaves plenty of lebensraum for the instincts.

Bach the musician is beyond my comprehension. As if there were no connection between this celestial creature and Bach the man, the nondescript figure of a provincial merchant with a crude sense of humor. In a letter to his family he complained about the weather: the clear sky and mild winter are bad for his career—the old men are taking their time about dying.

(Research into the private lives of great men teaches us nothing. But neither can research into the work itself teach us how to create. Only the mediocre can be imitated. The highest music does not find a form for familiar experiences—it gives expression to the inexpressible. It threads nameless feelings onto the string of time. Feelings which can be named have no need of music—they search for words.)

THE NEXT DAY

Non-German music sounds to me like an artificial combination of sounds. German music flows of its own accord. Every sound is born out of the one before and inherits it when it dies. You meet them like old acquaintances whose names you have forgotten. Like a familiar face in the street. You raise your hand to your hat—but what the hell is the fellow's name?

I had an uncle who came from Poland. Music was far from his mind. But in order to earn a German visiting card he forced himself to listen to German music. Listening to Beethoven's late quartets was the sentence he served for his Jewish materialism. The initiation ceremony into the exclusive club of the cultured was to keep his eyes open for forty minutes, which, for him, lasted as long as eternity.

When I listen to German music, I hear German words. I hear the angry stammer of Beethoven rebelling against the sanctification of a status quo that awards prizes to the submissive. I hear him grinding his teeth at the sight of the procession of liveried courtiers and courtesans in fancy dress on their way from the music room to the tea room, expressions of bored amusement on their faces—their response to his attempts to shock them.

I am trying to learn English again, but I shall never feel at home in Anglo-Saxon culture. I am incorrigibly German. Even the way I walk, according to Hilda, is subject to the rules of German grammar. Where one step would suffice, I take two.

A writer without a language is like a eunuch in a harem. The most he can do is smile at life. But he doesn't feel like it. What need does he have of a ticket to Utopia? They don't talk his language there.

I bathe in a sea of sounds like a man floating on his back in calm water with the rumble of distant thunder in his ears. Concentrating on the technical details of music is a barrier against remoteness. Measurable facts fill your soul with joy and sorrow.

The suffering of our predecessors is measured by our need for regular doses of hope and despair. A hundred years before I was born, a lackey in a princely court, with no more knowledge than would fit into the head of a contemporary twelve-year-old, knew the right dose of pain and pleasure, reflection and joie de vivre, pity and rage, to fill my soul with boundless happiness. How did they, who knew so little, succeed in transmitting to future generations the magic recipe of reconciliation to life in the form of the sonata—in the Allegro, which is all measured joy, and the Largo, which gives itself over to melancholy thoughts, and the Scherzo, a laughing mask, and the Vivace, which rejuvenates by means of the vitality of the frontier districts: thème russe, polonaise, à l'hongroise, à la turque, where ignorant peasants celebrated the cycle of nature at a time when it was even crueler than human beings?

There is no doubt that there is a connection between character and sense of rhythm. Any attempt to nail it down in words, however, would be absurd.

I find a clear connection between Rosendorf's pianissimo—a sound as ethereal as a dreaming baby's breath—and his ability to detach himself from the here and now and devote himself to the music as if it were not a form of entertainment but an act of redemption, or at the very least a dangerous surgical operation. And the same goes for Staubenfeld's strict metronomic regularity and hatred of "schmaltz" and her reserved attitude toward people. The steady rhythm protects her privacy, as it were. Perhaps she's afraid that fluctuations of tempo might betray a lack of restraint in her feelings.

But my book will not deal with the diagnosis and definition of these relationships. It will set the facts side by side and invite the reader to draw his own conclusions. If I were a painter, I would probably put patches of color on the canvas without drawing sharp outlines around them.

By the way, the composers who wrote precise metronome

markings on their scores—a quarter note equals so many beats to the minute—lacked a sense of history. The rhythm of life changes from one generation to the next. Only in the eighteenth century was it still possible to believe that what was, would be. Everything happened then at the speed of dictation. Clothing was heavy, change slow, and thoughts promenaded as lazily as the householders of south Tel Aviv on Saturday afternoons in their striped pajamas. The thoughts of a man listening to a single news bulletin today run from Nanking to Berlin with the speed of light.

12/31/37

Another year over. According to the calculations of an optimistic friend, in 1938 Hitler will be no more than a history lesson. I'm afraid that we're only at the beginning of the lesson. The bell has only just rung.

A conversation with Staubenfeld. A woman who is more afraid of friends than of enemies. Every pun puts her on her guard, as if it contained some kind of attempt to intrude on her privacy. I'll have to beware of making jokes whose point she can't understand if I want to be counted among her friends. Do I want to? Making love to a humorless woman is like taking part in a ritual ceremony.

Staubenfeld has sentenced herself to life imprisonment in an olive-tinted marble statue. For what crime? She won't even make friends with her jailers. Perhaps she's afraid that if she laughs out loud all the devils locked up inside her will break out.

Music armors her against life. It's like the coat of mail worn by her ancestors when they went into battle. Her endless practicing protects her privacy. You'll never find her in the beachfront cafes among the writers, painters, actors, and poets. Artists should be capable of wasting time, their most precious possession.

Staubenfeld lives in a closed circle: the orchestra, the quartet, Martha, and a few pupils to whom she is devoted in her own strict way. It's hard to believe that a woman like her wastes her nights on sleep. But she apparently keeps her favors for herself. She doesn't object to being worshiped from a distance, although she would prefer to be admired for her music rather than her breasts. But anyone who tried to come close to her would be burned by the frost. Her character won't let her enjoy the degree of freedom available to a woman blessed by nature with a body as splendid as hers. Perhaps it's the arrogance of a girl spoiled by her own beauty. Or perhaps it's plain stinginess. Her experience of love has taught her that it's a simple transaction of give-and-take. You can't receive without giving. And the pretty little girl jealously guarding all her dolls never learned to give.

Hilda explains her behavior in terms of her life history. I wonder if we know enough about it to come to conclusions. The story of her life is so melodramatic that it has no place in literature. The woman who plays the viola in my novel will have to be content with a less spectacular biography.

Staubenfeld was born in a romantic novelette, and there she spent her childhood and youth. A tear-jerking tale of forbidden love between a riotous nobleman and a chorus girl from the lower classes. The fact that the mother was Jewish is an unnecessary complication in a story which has an unhappy ending in any case. In the beginning it was of no importance at all. Even if she'd been a Christian, her father would never have married her mother.

Gossip has it that the father was prepared to acknowledge his responsibility, but his overbearing family took over and made sure that good order was maintained. Since the girl refused to get rid of the baby and was not prepared to remove herself from the scene either, they sent her to another town against her will. As befitting decent people, they promised her a decent living.

Neither Jewish nor proletarian indignation was aroused in

the mother's breast. The chorus girl, intent on bettering herself before it was too late, converted to Christianity, married a country teacher, and put her daughter in a convent. When the girl was discovered to have a gift for music, she was brought to Königsberg. The father, from a safe distance, began to take an interest in her education. Later on, after the mother died, he gave her his name and protection. But the return of the beautiful girl to her father's home was far from a fairy tale. One of her uncles fell madly in love with her and tried to rape her, and the only way to avoid a scandal was to transfer her to the Berlin branch of the family. There, too, her presence disturbed the domestic harmony. A cousin, ten years older than she, a career diplomat about to be transferred to Washington, fell in love with her, broke off his engagement to a well-connected girl, refused the American posting, and asked her to marry him. This time the family did not succeed in interfering, and for a short period Eva von Staubenfeld was doubly entitled to boast of her ancient name and lineage. For a brief while she enjoyed a settled family life and established herself as a promising musician in the Berlin Philharmonic.

The racial laws put an end to it. If it had not been for her coldness, perhaps von Staubenfeld might have given up his career in the Foreign Office and devoted himself to his blemished family, but the love he found in the arms of this disdainful woman was apparently inadequate to compensate him for the ruin of his career. This time, with the active assistance of the political establishment, the family managed to finally rid itself of the Jewess.

She was not victimized. She went on playing in the Philharmonic even after the other Jews were fired. But one day she suddenly left Berlin and went to Frankfurt and from there to Palestine—and here she apparently decided that from now on any cooperation with the male sex would be on her own terms exclusively. A decision which she has held to with a resolve that does her credit in view of the ever-increasing number of candidates for her favors.

I would be sinning against the truth if I failed to add the name of the writer of these lines to the list. This fellow, whose cunning suffers from an overdose of honesty, courts her in his own way. He advises her to read books in order to enhance her general knowledge and warns her against the narrow-mindedness which deprives music, too, of depth. In the hope that if she reads books, one of his, too, will presumably come into her hands. If he can't compete with his body, perhaps he will have a chance in the contest of minds. More than one woman, tired to death of good-looking men, has sought comfort in the arms of a sad-eyed monkey. This monkey, who has no illusions about playing the role of the lover in the legitimate theater, is free of false modesty. His ugliness is not a strong enough force to repel women. Many members of the sex have a perverse tendency to fall in love with weak men. He has the patience to wait and see. In any case, he has nothing better to do. Proof that his intentions are not academic lies in the fact that recently he has been trying to earn an honorable living. He has started writing articles for a provincial paper and giving all the money he earns to the woman who has been keeping him up to now. He can't boast of his faithfulness to her, but he's not a scoundrel nevertheless. It's true that he hasn't touched another woman since he landed on these shores, but unfaithfulness need not necessarily be expressed in deeds. And from the moment that he began to think of another woman, he has been trying valiantly to earn his own bread.

His wooing takes on more than one form. Sometimes it derives its inspiration from an old-fashioned opera: courtly manners, graceful gestures, flowery language, ironic exaggeration, and obsequious bows. Sometimes it borrows the language of a student who has emptied his balls in a whorehouse to free them to pay court to a spoiled darling with a private income—a language full of double entendres and poetic obscenities. And sometimes it adopts a rough, proletarian frankness: Tell me, my girl, who gave you the right to grab all the good looks for yourself? But Staubenfeld is not impressed. She smiles pleasantly and he should be grateful that she doesn't laugh in his face.

In my novel she has no place. I would never put a girl I tried to go to bed with in one of my books.

3/14/38

Vienna's final hour. The Vienna of Kraus, Mahler, Schnitzler, Freud, and Herzl is no more. Her frivolity did not save her from the seriousness of others, just as the sensitivity of the victim does not do away with the cruelty of his persecutors.

In the era of the radio bad news reaches its destination immediately. But perhaps precisely owing to this speed, the essential facts are still shrouded in obscurity. Now it's the turn of Czechoslovakia, after looking up to Germany all her life long. The Allies won't save her.

There are times when even the most personal diary fills up with facts from the newspapers. Even their clichés take over our style. What use is clean language to us when old men are being forced to sweep the sidewalks with their beards . . .

The quartet's meeting was devoted to Vienna. As a gesture of solidarity they played only music composed in Vienna. They talked a lot too, reminiscing and mentioning the names of friends still living there. The atmosphere was full of gloom: like people in a hospital talking about illnesses and acquaintances who have passed away. Staubenfeld recovered first: it would do Vienna no good if the quartet was not ready for its concert next week in the Jascha Heifetz Hall.

"The only thing we can do for Vienna is to play more beautifully and more correctly than the Germans," said Friedman.

A childish, if touching, idea. But I myself am trying to do the same thing with the German language.

3/19/38

Even though the hostilities have not yet ceased here either, I sometimes feel as if we're living in a kind of damnable placidity, as if Vienna hasn't fallen, as if there is no threat of war.

In our own lives insignificant events take place. Litovsky was invited to play on the radio. Rosendorf received a letter from home. Martha had an ulcer attack, Hilda received a promotion, Friedman read a book which excited him.

Only in Staubenfeld's life great things have happened: a viola string snapped in the middle of the concert, and her stubborn swain left for Spain.

In the intermission I met her outside the hall. She was moving among the crowd and smoking a cigarette as haughtily as a battleship in a fleet of merchant vessels. When she saw me she said nonchalantly: "At last I can go outside for a breath of fresh air."

And then she told me that the young man who had made such a nuisance of himself the previous year had gone to fight in Spain, to save the Republic.

She said it with a contempt that made my blood boil. I suspected her of deriving a spiteful satisfaction from the fact that his disappointed love had driven him to risk his life in a lost cause.

I remembered a little contretemps I had once had in Berlin with Bernadette (nobody knew her last name), one of the prominent figures in local bohemian circles.

In her day she was the sun around which the lesser stars revolved. All of them suffered an eclipse when a larger planet came between them. I remembered her as a witty girl with the charm of reckless youth in her face. As a poetess she did not capture my imagination. She attracted her peers like flypaper—they flew to her and never learned their lesson.

She had the gift of packaging cliché-ridden images in glamorous wrappings. Every change in the literary climate found her ready. She knew how to worship Stefan George and Bertolt Brecht at one and the same time, like Heine's cantor who prayed in the synagogue and sang the Masses in the cathedral. She had only one advantage over other poets: she could pay for her drinks in even the craziest days of the inflation.

At first she kept her appearances in the "Cafe Megalomania" to a minimum, like a precious object whose rarity makes it more expensive. But after a young poet had committed suicide on her account (one of those who smiled at her on the sidewalk because they couldn't afford the price of a cup of coffee), she began to come every day—wearing a black dress, to demonstrate her mourning in public, like a mute monument to grief. Not many people saw through the dignified sorrow to the shameless pride burning in her fine black eyes, the pride of a poet who had won an important literary prize.

Unable to endure the performance of this tragedy queen and the insolence of the black dress, shamelessly flaunting the twin sources of the poor fool's despair, I told her that if we were Red Indians she would no doubt be wearing the scalps of her victims around her neck.

"Not yours," she replied, "because the dandruff would dirty my dress."

If I didn't tell Staubenfeld what I thought of her it wasn't because I was afraid of a similar retort, but because I've grown up since then and keep my witticisms for the paper where I can trim off my excesses. A writer is a man who knows that puns, neologisms, epigrams, crushing retorts, and so forth are obstacles one has to overcome on the way to the clear sentence, stating its contents with felicitous leanness, without a hump or paunch. With my tongue I beware of sentences that can't be rubbed out. Every superfluous word consigns two necessary ones to oblivion.

With Staubenfeld there's no need for plain speaking. From the tone of your cough she can tell what you think of her, like the sensitive instrument that reveals your high blood pressure even when you're feeling fine.

She gave me a mind-reading look with a question mark at the end of it, as if to say: It wasn't I who sent him to Spain, you know, and I can hardly be blamed for what happens to him there.

"Why don't you say what you think?" she said, with a steely glint in her eye.

"If you insist . . . In my opinion you might have treated him more gently."

"Are you trying to teach me how to behave?"

"God forbid."

"In that case please mind your own business."

Then she smiled. "Don't be offended. I saw from the way you looked at me that you blamed me, and I was annoyed. He didn't go to Spain because of me. A romantic soul will always find a woman to make him unhappy and a war he can come back from covered in glory."

The things that were on the tip of my tongue to say to her when I accompanied her backstage remained unsaid. The last thing I wanted was to make a fool of myself and earn her undying contempt. I felt profoundly dissatisfied with myself. Against my better judgment, I was joining the ranks of those romantic souls who are irresistibly drawn to the suffering of unrequited love.

I spoke to Friedman and Litovsky about the Russian boy. Friedman said that the Jews had a special talent for fighting in other people's wars. Litovsky said that he only wished he could go and fight there himself. Rosendorf, with whom I traveled home on the bus, was surprised to hear that the war in Spain was still going on.

"I don't read the papers," he apologized. "They're too depressing. Letters are quite enough for me."

9/6/38

Over here the autumn is greener than the summer. A sudden isolated downpour washes the leaves and they glisten with a springlike verdancy. The faces of the people, too, seem brighter, happy at the prospect of the end of the heat, although the summer sometimes returns in full force, and the sun beats down mercilessly on bare heads. Perhaps the cruel light will let us be for a while.

Last night I emerged from the street where Staubenfeld lives—she allowed me to accompany her to her front door but did not invite me in—and as I was walking, sunk in thought, past a stinking leather factory, somebody suddenly shone a torch in my face. I could barely make out the shapes behind the torch. All I could see for certain was that they weren't in police uniforms, and I was scared stiff. A few years ago Chaim Arlosoroff was murdered not far from this very spot. They shone a torch in his face and shot him. I can't imagine how anyone could possibly benefit from my death here, but fear isn't affected by logical arguments. There were two of them. They wanted to know what I was doing in this deserted part of the street. I didn't dare tell them that it was none of their business. I said that I had been visiting a woman friend. My accent was enough for them to lose their grimness. Their voices, which had been authoritative and threatening, suddenly became amused and relaxed. They were tall, young, and strong, and once they had taken a good look at me, the idea that my nocturnal wanderings bore a romantic character seemed to them supremely ridiculous. I felt like someone brought up before a kangaroo court and judged: a pathetic creature.

This morning I met a prose editor from a Hebrew publishing house, which is about to bring out a translation of *Ancient Glory*. An embarrassing meeting. The editor, an author in his own right, knows my work inside out, and I have not the faintest idea of what he himself writes—all his work is written in this outlandish language which I can't succeed in mastering (my English and French have improved here beyond recognition) and in which I can barely buy vegetables in the market.

I did not enjoy this goodwill gesture toward a victim of fate, but an author cannot afford to stand on his high horse with an editor who is prepared to devote his precious time to others and who wants praise for his generosity as well as the translation and editing fees, which in any case are more than the author earns. He hinted that translating my tortuous style into Hebrew demanded linguistic acrobatics unprecedented in the Hebrew language. I understood that I would be obliged to give up part of my royalties to compensate him for his efforts. I could console myself with the thought, he told me, that now that the fruit of my spirit had returned to its Hebrew roots, it would suck its sap straight from the eternal wellsprings of the holy tongue. I did not disillusion him. Why rob the peace of mind of a man whose self-esteem depends on the superiority of a dead language, which all the flogging in the world will not revive? Hebrew writers are even worse off than we are. They are doomed to eternal destitution in the arms of an embittered wife; we have a chance of resurrection after bourgeois common sense prevails over messianic madness. Even though words themselves are being ruthlessly tortured there, outside the territory which has fallen to the dominion of the wicked the pure German language continues to live its independent life.

Once he understood from my reactions that I had no great expectations from the royalties due to me from the Hebrew edition, we were free to talk about literature from a more disinterested point of view. The usual stuff. Provincialism and universalism. What constitutes Jewish literature—literature written by Jews, or literature in which the characters are concerned with specifically Jewish questions? Or perhaps all literature that identifies with the oppressed can be called Jewish literature? I didn't ask him if there was any point in writing literature that would not become part of Western culture, or logic in gushing over something as ephemeral as the folklore of the Jewish Yishuv in Palestine, or sense in putting one's pen at the service of any political movement— Zionist or proletarian—or whether there was any chance that Hebrew would ever become the language of the Jewish intellectuals who played so vital a role in European, and American, culture. I limited myself to expressing a cautious skepticism regarding the Zionist movement's ability to persuade those Jews who were not actually on their way to Palestine to learn a language they did not need to earn their daily bread. At the back of my mind was something Huberman had once said to Friedman, three years before the establishment of the orchestra. Huberman said that unless they adhered to European values, the Jewish minority in Palestine was liable to slide into Levantinism in the confines of a messianic ghetto, which would be no less dangerous than the ghettos of Eastern Europe.

My interlocutor read between the lines and guessed what I had left unsaid. The artificial revival of the Hebrew language on ideological grounds leads to an inevitable superficiality: only the mother tongue, in which the first meetings with mother and father, with fear and joy, were experienced, can produce profound literature. And in the ideological debate between Hebrew and Yiddish, in their competition for the souls of the educated East European Jew, I was on the side of Yiddish, not Hebrew, even though I am not particularly enamored of this mongrel language without a proper grammar. I am on the side of Yiddish because it exists and there is no need to create it in the meetings of the National Language Committee, which invents a new word every day to enable the native Jewish population to switch on the electricity and listen to the radio.

When he realized that I had no intention of changing

my language in the middle of my life, he asked me what, in that case, made me a Jew? A question I have asked myself on countless occasions, but one which I would have regarded as too intimate to ask someone I had only met fifteen minutes before. The answers I gave myself were none of his business.

I am a Jew because I was born a Jew and my self-respect won't allow me to run away from my fate. I am a Jew because I want to live in a world where God exists even if He doesn't exist in heaven. I am a Jew because I can't deny my feelings even when they contradict my beliefs.

The rudeness of his question provoked me into paradox, and I said that a Jew was someone who put a high value on choice. When our nation was young, she believed that she had been chosen above all other nations. Now that she was grown up—the right to choose was greater than the right to be chosen.

He rose to my bait and asked me sarcastically if that included the right to stop being a Jew.

"Of course."

And then, with undisguised resentment, he asked me if I had chosen Eretz Israel, or if someone else had chosen it for me. Without making any attempt to spare his feelings, I replied that while others may have chosen this particular via dolorosa, for me the question of leaving the Jewish people was purely academic, since a Jew was never allowed to forget where he came from or asked where he wanted to go. He insisted on knowing what I would have chosen if the question had not been purely academic.

"A writer is not free to choose. His language is his motherland."

I made a very bad impression on him. He seemed to be regretting the months he had wasted in bringing an ingrate like me back to the fold. He had stretched out a fraternal hand to pull me into the pure waters of the Hebrew spring, but I preferred to wallow in the German swamp.

11/16/38

After Kristallnacht they removed a Wagner overture from the Palestine Symphony Orchestra's concert program. There was a vociferous argument in the quartet.

Rosendorf said: "An infantile reaction. Music is music, and the political opinions of the composer are irrelevant. You can find anti-Semitic remarks in Mendelssohn's letters, too. Are they going to ban him?"

Friedman and Litovsky found themselves, to their displeasure, in the same camp. If certain music was offensive to people's feelings, it shouldn't be played—never mind if the feelings were based on an erroneous conception of the relation between music and life. Martha supported Rosendorf. She had apparently quarreled with her husband about something else and felt the need to disagree with him. Staubenfeld was indifferent. She doesn't like Wagner. He is a professional tearjerker and gets on her nerves. He employs too many means to say simple things.

An interesting aspect of her character was disclosed here. I took her side without thinking, although I could sense that nobody believed in my sincerity. But the truth is that I really was sincere, and Staubenfeld had only given a banal expression to my own vague feelings. Something sinister grows from the music of this furious man who aspires to the Romantic crown. The passionate emotions it arouses with regard to the glories of a fictitious past are nothing but an attempt to divert the national pride of the German people from Immanuel Kant and Johann Sebastian Bach to the savages who drew their swords when a verbal retort would have sufficed. From this point of view it really is allied to the violent instincts which are taking the place of rational political debate in Germany today. I suspect that the Jews annoyed Wagner by the mere fact of their existence, because of their skeptical attitude toward genius. With all our admiration for outstanding talent, we lack the tendency to idolize genius. Wagner, who idolized himself, suffered from the persecution mania endemic to geniuses. Anyone who refused to recognize his divinity was guilty of blasphemy and had to be crucified. But it was unreasonable of him to blame the Jews. If he hadn't stuffed his operas with Teutonic monsters, the Jews would have fallen over themselves to join the Wagnerian movement. It had taken them over a hundred years to accustom themselves to the Christian symbols pervading German music, including those which were far from sympathetic toward the Jews—and now they were being asked to bow down to the heroic spontaneity of barbarians who carried their honor on the tips of their spears!

Wagner succeeded in making me quarrel with Friedman for the first time. Like many Zionists, he sees everything, even something as insignificant as the ban on Wagner, as proof of the rightness of the Zionist cause. I permitted myself to voice a certain skepticism with regard to this kind of national pride. And this led me to the subject of Herzl and the theatrical tricks to which he resorted in order to capture the imagination of the East European delegates to the Zionist Congress. I spoke rather harshly. Herzl, who was a brilliant feuilletonist but a mediocre playwright, was perversely attracted to the theater. He collected a few dozen Jews in a Swiss hall, made them dress up in tuxedos, and believed that he was putting the conscience of the world on trial before History. Three years after the Balfour Declaration it transpired that the return to Zion was the beginning of a hundred years' war.

Friedman was flabbergasted. The twentieth century, he assured me, would be remembered in history as the century in which the Jewish revolution took place: one of its hands holding a hoe and the other a Hebrew dictionary.

I could have kissed him on both cheeks. What childlike naiveté!

I am coming to the conclusion that naiveté is not a state of pristine innocence, but a way of defending an irreconcilable inner contradiction. It is the ability to ignore the facts and hide behind wishful thinking. Such naiveté can breed great cruelty.

12/12/38

Lately I have felt longings for the piano. Once upon a time I played quite well. But after years of neglect I've forgotten everything I knew. Hilda has acquired an old piano and I've decided to recover my loss. A faint hope. But soon I shall be able to play "Anna Magdelena" without stopping, and easy pieces by Schubert and Schumann. Hilda wants to prepare a surprise for our friends: she'll sing Schubert lieder and I'll accompany her on the piano. Rosendorf is encouraging me. Even if I can't become a pianist, I shall be able to fill my head with music and banish some of the thoughts that make me sad.

Secretly I suspect that playing the piano is a way of trying to come closer to Staubenfeld. Perhaps one day I might be able to accompany her on the piano and tell her in music what I don't dare tell her in words. Dreams of Spain! A Hebrew expression which I heard from Friedman the other day, and which is particularly apt to my present mood. For recently I find myself thinking frequently of the poor lad who went to Spain. As if I had undertaken to take his place, the other day I suddenly found myself lurking about in Staubenfeld's street. Things are getting out of control. I'm beginning to behave like a character in a novel I'll never write. Only a complete fool, an incorrigible romantic, would allow his heart to stray after a woman who will never be his. As if the quota of fools must be filled— one has gone to Spain and I have stepped into his shoes.

When Staubenfeld heard that I had begun to play the

piano, she sniggered and said, "And tomorrow I'll begin to write," as if it were inconceivable that anyone could do both. When I was informed of her comment, I found it both conceited and in poor taste. And I was secretly furious with her: what did she think, that making music for the love of it could be compared to graphomania? When I recovered from my rage I interpreted it as a touching attempt on the part of a man in love to find a flaw in the beloved in order to lighten the burden of his love.

If anyone had told me in my youth that at the age of forty I would be behaving like an adolescent and trying to pick holes in a girl who did not return my love, I would have burst my sides laughing. Today I know that love is always adolescent. By the way, I'm not at all sure that if Staubenfeld actually did decide to write something she wouldn't produce spare, polished prose without a redundant word. She would probably write the way she speaks. Clear, precise sentences, economical and challenging in their directness.

I'm sure I must have made a fool of myself when I sat down to improvise on a tune from *The Magic Flute* at Martha's birthday party—we were playing charades and this was my "punishment" for guessing wrong—but Staubenfeld didn't laugh at all. She looked at me in amazement, as if I were a child prodigy, and said that if I practiced regularly and seriously we would be able to play Schubert's Arpeggione in about a year's time.

This too is one of the signs of puppy love: the acrobatic leaps from despair to hope.

With one casual sentence she bestowed value and meaning on the coming year. When a man is looking forward to something, his days don't go by in vain. And if he can bring the date of his bliss forward with his own hands, there is a point and purpose to everything he does. Every line of the Arpeggione that I conquered with my fingers would be a giant step forward on the way to the Promised Land.

12/25/38

Another year draws to a close. Politically everything is in a terrible mess; in my own life things are growing clearer. I am a man who is prepared to renounce his past. When a man begins to live in his memories, it amounts to a declaration that the present is the end of the line. If I blot out my memory, the future may agree to give me a nice surprise.

Humor protects me from pain, hate, and self-pity. I would be prepared to renounce revenge too, if only I could go back one day to a place where the birds sing in German.

All evening I listened to Bach. Religion sought to subdue the flesh in order to elevate the soul, and thus, according to Heine, gave birth to sin and hypocrisy. But in its attempts to enlist music in the service of religious feeling, it restored sensual joy to the flesh. In Zen Buddhism music is the sacred text. They sought to subdue the flesh by the negation of thought, but in music, too, there is a stream of ideas. When we speak to God in sounds, we are seeking divine approval of our carnal desires.

Goethe believed that music did not need innovations—the more familiar it is, the more profoundly it affects us. He was wrong. We do not choose to listen to the music we love, we love the music to which listening has accustomed us. If we were to listen to Schönberg from our infancy, it would become as much a part of our world as the sounds of the language we speak.

There is no music sweeter to my ear than the sound of the German language.

The same sensitivity which sharpens our artistic sense is also that which blunts it when we try to skip the work and go straight to the feeling. In music, true feeling begins only after the work is done.

On days when I am excessively sensitive, I know that my

creativity is at a low ebb. In the past, I used to take the anti-Semitism of the red-necked Bavarians as a compliment. I couldn't understand my friends, who were wounded to the quick by every anti-Semitic remark, when they never stopped making anti-Semitic jokes themselves.

An unpleasant argument with my translator. He considers my German too "low," and believes that it lies in the power of the language of the Prophets to elevate it. I told him that I was afraid elevated language would murder my intentions. His fanatical devotion to Hebrew is pathological. He defends its honor as if speaking any other language on the soil of the Holy Land endangers its position. He is a member of the Language Protection League and heckles loudly and furiously if anyone dares to address a public meeting in Yiddish. But for his innate respectability he would probably go around setting fire to kiosks that sell German-language newspapers.

He behaves as if he has taken over the rights to my book. I used ready-made linguistic materials; he created his from scratch. He really seems to believe that every neologism he invents is laying the foundations for a new culture here. The strange thing is that for all his solemnity in defending the honor of the Hebrew language, the words he invents are mainly slang and obscenities, in which this ritual language is so poor. He listens to the children and writes down their mistakes. Any miserable little shoot of local folklore is cherished and cultivated here until it rots from overwatering. I wonder what kind of writers will grow up among these boys and girls, who know only one language, one that lacks popular idioms and useful words.

He sees me as a devil's advocate, an agent provocateur of the forces of darkness. Although he hasn't come out with it in so many words, he has thrown out hints that I suffer from a warped personality, a soul distorted by the Diaspora; I hate Jews, myself included. In his opinion, any Jew who writes about the shortcomings of his people without pulling his punches is fawning on the *goyim*. The usual charge against anyone who refuses to turn a blind eye to Jewish faults. I stand accused: a Jew without roots or robust folk wisdom. Not to mention my illiteracy when it comes to political affairs.

I depress him profoundly. It's easier to straighten a dog's tail, in the words of the Arab proverb, than the back of a Diaspora Jew like me, who bent to kiss the hand that beat him. What more has to happen in that cursed Germany, so beloved of the Jews, for them to understand that they have no part or parcel in Goethe or Bach?

We speak to each other only about niceties of style, whose Hebrew equivalents are beyond my understanding. Once he took me with him from the quiet German ghetto in the north of Eliezer Ben Yehudah Street to the noisy cafe frequented by the Tel Aviv bohemians. But I didn't get into conversation with anyone there. All I got when I opened my mouth and said something in German were angry looks. I was able, however, to follow the literary debate, since every second so-called Hebrew word is foreign.

I sensed a certain optimism, which was in need of constant refueling in case, God forbid, it cooled down. They apparently believe in the cultural message borne on the wings of this movement of national revival. Such naiveté may well be capable of producing something. I was glad that I couldn't participate. I could only have poured a drop of poison into their wine. If they are happy believing what they believe, who am I to rob them of their peace of mind? I suspect that my inability to learn Hebrew stems from a deeper source: something inside me rebels against the hasty adaptation of an ancient language to practical ends. Maybe I'll know how to read a newspaper one day. The Jewish heritage, insofar as I need it to broaden my mind, will come to me in German translation. If the Jews have a message for the world, it will reach its destination on the wings of languages universally understood. I wonder if in the twenty-first century the Hebrew language will have any more disciples than it has today.

1/15/39

When I read the composer's indications at the beginning of a movement or the Italian words written under the staves— allegro moderato, molto espressivo, ritardando, and so on—I remember Erich. Since I don't know who will remember him when this generation dies out, I shall commemorate him here.

Erich was a Communist poet whose poetry betrayed his political convictions. It was meant to serve the revolution, but when it emerged into the light of day it was content, with all due modesty, to serve an individual mood. He was angry with me for not going far enough. A moderate socialist is a Communist's sworn enemy. But we had something in common: we both deliberately and provocatively emphasized our Jewishness. He was very offended when his comrades in the Party advised him to play down his Jewishness. You're a talented propagandist, they told him, but the moment the real proletariat discovers that you're a Jew your most eloquent words will lose their persuasive power. I stressed the part played by Jews in German literature in order to expose the true face of the phony liberals. In Dachau the barriers fell. There, where human communication is limited to the essential minimum, we discovered the riches of a language without words. We were able to carry on long conversations based entirely on the names of literary characters. We threw each other lines of German poetry as code words. We emasculated the language in a touching attempt to avenge ourselves on our jailers. One day we had a conversation about music. Look, he said to me, over the past three hundred years Germany has been responsible for almost all the major developments in music, but it was the Italians who succeeded in introducing their language into it; and it was the German Jews who made manful attempts to naturalize German words in it.

The very act of classifying people into Jews and non-Jews serves the anti-Semites, but not even the cosmopolitans among us are immune from it. Even from music, an international language from every point of view, the Jewish nose pokes out. There are people who listen to a record and are prepared to risk guessing which of two violinists is of the Mosaic persuasion, although nothing could be more different than the playing of Huberman and Heifetz, for example. Staubenfeld says about Rosendorf that he doesn't play like a Jewish violinist. A compliment which she was hard put to explain. Is a Jew one who plays too plaintively, or one who has a compulsive need to excel? One whose fingers are greasy or one whose emotions are exaggerated? I wonder if she would have turned up her nose at my writing, if her demands on literature were as severe as her demands on music? Would she have discovered in my prose, too, a Jewish compulsion to exaggerated virtuosity with words?

The wish to be a citizen of the universe, whose sole allegiance is to the human race, and whose only passport his natural curiosity, is an illusion which neither our enemies nor our friends will allow us to cherish. Both demand that we present a clear identity card. Not that I'm comparing the Nazi system of classification to the moral pressure exerted on me by my well-wishers in the provincial town where, due to force of circumstances, I now live. The former branded my passport and deprived me of my rights. The latter want to increase my rights in the Kingdom of Heaven on condition that I agree to wear the Jewish straitjacket. I feel like bursting with suppressed rage every time I see the benevolent, patronizing smile with which they send me to hell with their blessings whenever I express my opinion on the validity of the Zionist idea as applied to the Jewish people as a whole. They are prepared to let me learn the hard way, like a wise father allowing his son to sow his wild oats until experience teaches him the error of his ways. A Zionist version of the Talmudic saying: Israel, even when it sins, remains Israel. You don't have to be a Zionist for their fantasies to become your fate. If you don't want to freeze to death, come in out of the cold.

Staubenfeld put her finger on the common ground between us. Both of us want the world to be our oyster, she as a musician and I as a writer. Neither of us will succeed. I, because my Jewishness is a hereditary disease. She—because she is not talented enough to expand her lebensraum. Both of us want to be what we are, but others force us to represent abstract categories. I am a writer in exile, and as such I am expected to be resentful and embittered. She is half-German, and therefore people will find Prussian elements in everything she does. Even in the quartet she sometimes finds herself the target of a united front. Her sensitivity to the metronomic pulse and vehement objections to slackening the tempo at the end of a phrase are interpreted as signs of a Germanic harshness—the inflexibility typical of a descendant of Junkers.

Encouraging signs of a lively humor have begun to make their appearance lately. Encouraging, because the fortress of a humorless woman is surrounded on all sides—either everything collapses at once or everything is so well guarded that there is no crack through which a wandering troubadour can slip. Her humor can be interpreted as a sign of favor; it is a hidden treasure which she shows only to close friends.

Her humor reaches its height when she talks about her landlady, a fanatical Zionist who never misses the chance to bring a straying lamb back to the fold. She gives her long lectures on the importance of the agricultural settlements and the Labor Federation. Since these lectures are dished out together with nourishing suppers, Staubenfeld submits meekly to the tedium of the conversion process.

Her descriptions of this Russian woman were so amusing and picturesque that I expressed a wish to meet her. But Staubenfeld, who is more cunning than I would have imagined, refused to take the hint. Her eyes said it more plainly than words: she wouldn't invite me to her room again until I stopped looking at her with the eyes of a lovesick calf. But I doubt if I'm capable of resuming the easy charm of my manner toward her before I became aware of my feelings.

1/29/39

Litovsky is furious with Staubenfeld for "fraternizing with the enemy." According to him, she's letting the Englishman fall madly in love with her, with the kind of desperation of which only those who need all their resources to keep a stiff upper lip are capable, because she wants him to make her greatest dream come true: to go and live in the British Isles, in a northern climate, behind a screen of fog to protect her privacy, and play in an inhibited English quartet; and thus to get rid, once and for all, of the Jewishness which, as far as she is concerned, was never more than a biological accident for which she does not deserve to be punished so severely.

He'll never say anything to her face, because he doesn't want to make trouble in the quartet. But behind her back he positively boils with rage. The frivolous Litovsky is one of those animals who take on the colors of their environment. The patriotic flame is quicker to leap up in him than in Friedman, whose convictions are sincere. It offends him deeply that of all her suitors it's the pink-kneed Englishman she allows to carry her viola case to the army car waiting outside the concert hall with an armed soldier on guard. Lately he has avoided talking to her in rehearsals except when absolutely necessary. If only she had carried on the affair in secret, he might have forgiven her. But Staubenfeld likes being provocative. As soon as she saw the reproachful looks of her colleagues, she began inviting the Englishman backstage. Lately, to his credit, after the demonstrations against the government, he's stopped coming in uniform. But perhaps it's because he's afraid of being attacked.

I won't say anything, of course. She has the right to get to

England riding on the back of a British officer's love. Every human being has the right to live wherever he's happy. I certainly won't attack her for betraying the "motherland." If I, a racially pure, declared Jew, want to run away from the Promised Land, how can I demand that she, a half-Jewess, attach herself to the Jewish people? What I do find painfully upsetting, however, is the cold, unfeeling calculation of her behavior. There's no reason why I should fight his battles for him, but can't he see for himself that she doesn't love him?

Her cynicism should make it easier for me to get over her. Any man with a shred of sense in his head would run for his life from a woman like her. But instead I do everything in my power to come closer to her.

I almost lost control and said things I would have regretted when she asked me, of all people, for English textbooks. I think she did it on purpose to hurt me. Perhaps she believes that my sickness is curable by shock treatment, like exorcizing madness from the brain by measured bolts of electricity.

3/16/39, BEFORE DAWN

Czechoslovakia has fallen to the Nazis. The war in Spain is coming to an end. And I reflect on music as a metaphor of the human condition. Freedom within the bounds of given limits. Everything is written, and the extent of choice lies between piano and sotto voce. A fortissimo cannot exceed the limits of what the string can endure. Emotion cannot go beyond what good taste permits. Humor cannot be sharper than the spiccato.

In the field of human history, freedom is even more limited. You were born to a Jewish mother. Into the middle class. Your aristocratic gestures are grotesque. You have no kingdom to give up for a horse. Your generosity is worthless. In solitary confinement you can hit the wall once with your right fist and once with your left. Everything is foreseen and the freedom of your choice is limited to struggling at the end of the rope. Freedom is the recognition of social necessity. A great gospel. Opium for the starving intelligentsia. A banquet at which the disciples of Socrates can sit down to sup with Talmudists and Hegelians. Even the Marxists are prepared to drink a toast to it. And the Zionists, too, have cut themselves a slice of this holy bread. You are not what you are, but what your times have made of you. In the divine score everything is written: how the oboe will wail, what the first violin will say to the second, when the viola will sob, when the ram's horn will sound its blast, how far the Jew will wander, what exile he will call his motherland, in what language he will sing his despair.

On the island where I was cast ashore there are many beautiful birds, but I can't understand their language.

Staubenfeld's British friend thinks that we Germans suffer from a persecution complex. We believe that Hitler wants to conquer the world. He thinks otherwise. Hitler isn't insane. He is succeeding in obtaining his ends by peaceful means. He has no need of war. He knows very well that London isn't about to dig trenches for the sake of some foreign country. So: there won't be a war.

But I know in my bones that there will be.

In Hebrew literary circles there is a strange complacency. They argue about the usual subjects: about committed literature, about modernity, and about the right of a poet to be obscure. But in practice every one of them is enlisted in the service of the national cause. Most of them come from Russia, and I, like Rilke in his time, can only take the Russians in small doses. They are too excitable for my taste.

One of them told me that if war breaks out it will be the end of Jewish culture, and all that will survive is what is written in Hebrew. A strange man—he knows seven languages fluently yet insists on writing in Hebrew. In his opinion, anyone who says "art for art's sake" drives it out of the world. He judges writers by their attitude toward the Jewish question. We argued passionately. If we clear our bookshelves of all those who didn't like us, we won't have much left, I said. Anyone who's witnessed book burnings must reject with disgust any attempt to ban literature on extraneous grounds. The opinions of writers shouldn't make any difference to us. Only their works exist. Balzac was a scoundrel, Tolstoy an old lecher and a bad actor, Palestrina a gold digger, Gesualdo a murderer, and Dostoevsky a madman. Art is created from the flawed, not the whole. From wrong, not right. From pain, not happiness.

He said that according to my logic, war should produce great works of art, whereas experience proved that when the cannons thundered the muses were not silent, but jabbered nonsense.

5/22/39

A blazing spring. Not a single cloud in the sky. A heat haze rising from the sea, whose depths are Prussian blue.

The quartet are on leave. Litovsky is in the hospital after taking part in some demonstration. Patriotism is the last refuge of a frustrated musician. Europe and America are barred to him and only the gates of heaven are left. He runs with the pack in order to provide an outlet for the male instincts which playing the cello can't appease. The storm troops are full of fellows like him, who need hearty male company in order to fill some emptiness in their souls.

Staubenfeld jokes: how clever of him not to raise his hand to protect his head; his hand is more use to him than his head. The more the British lose their sense of humor, the sharper hers becomes.

The excursions of artists into the dangerous battlefield of social ideas, and back into their lairs to lick the wounds which leave no scars on their souls, give rise to pity mingled with revulsion. But Litovsky's superficiality protects him from recognizing the irony of his situation. Rosendorf criticizes him severely in the name of the neutrality of art, which I don't believe in either. Who knows—the skull of the young man smashed by a policeman's truncheon in yesterday's demonstration may have held the solution to the squaring of the circle.

Friedman, who also participated in the demonstration, but not in the front lines, thinks that an artist incapable of giving his life for a just cause in a fateful time isn't a true artist. According to this theory, an egoist can't be a great musician. Reality proves the opposite. The selfishness of Rosendorf, who wouldn't risk a finger to ensure the rights of the Jewish people to Palestine, doesn't prevent him from giving himself wholeheartedly to an anonymous listener, for whom he feels no fellow feeling at all. This dedication has nothing to do with noble sentiments or lofty principles. The moment he sits down opposite his music stand with his violin under his chin he is engaged in a dialogue with the world. The nervous tremor of his vibrato is the enthusiastic stammer of a man in possession of some truth which he can't wait to pass on. What is it that he is so eager to convey to others? Is it some human essence which cannot be expressed except in music? Even Rosendorf, I suspect, would shrink from a further abstraction of the most abstract of all things. He would be content with a simple definition: his message is the color of a sound and the nuance of a feeling. What was conceived in pastels may not be executed in oils. Where the composer has written "allegro" there is no room for mournful notes. To someone unfamiliar with the technique of making music, this may sound even more abstract, but to the musician absorbed in solving a technical problem—where on the string to place the bow and how much hair to bring into direct contact with it in order to obtain a particular timbre—nothing could be clearer or make more concrete sense. Players forgive composers their declarations about the revolutionary mission of music—in the struggle for civil liberties, for example—and judge their music by its ability to arrest attention. True, certain operas, even by composers without much imagination, may have played a marginal role in social or national struggles. But this was due to the words rather than the music, which played the ignoble role of lending persuasive power to a libretto unable to stand on its own. Chamber music has no words. Only Beethoven and Haydn sometimes sighed on the margins of their scores in words. All music wants to say is music.

5/23/39

And nevertheless, when we listen to music, our heads are filled with thoughts and not only with sounds. All kinds of different thoughts. And the same thoughts don't come back when we hear the same piece again. In other words, what music offers you is a mood. The rest you have to fill in yourself. And the living contact between the performer and his audience does not give birth to an electric spark which makes them partners in a single endeavor. On the contrary, watching the musicians is liable to distract the audience from the music. How many of the men sitting in the hall are making love to Staubenfeld in their imaginations, instead of immersing themselves in the mood which the music is supposed to be creating?

Last night I put myself to the test of sustained attention to the music while following the printed score. I chose Beethoven's Rasoumoffsky no. 1, a work I know well. I didn't raise my eyes to peep at Staubenfeld's breasts even once. But already in the first movement, resolved to follow the progress of the melody as it passed from instrument to instrument, the development of the theme, and the anticipated surprises of clever modulations from key to key, I found my imagination incessantly straying. The innocent drumbeats of the second violin and the viola reminded me of a parade in Berlin, clear-eyed, callous youth raising their arms to hail the Leader, and for a moment I even felt the familiar cramps in my stomach when I was asked to show my identity card and knew that this time I would not escape. With difficulty I banished these scenes from my mind—what did they have to do with the glorious sounds produced by a composer who pursued justice and apparently loved Schiller more than he loved Goethe? When I tried to concentrate on Beethoven, I succeeded in detaching myself from the here and now and focusing my attention on other extramusical matters, such as his deafness—in the year the quartet was composed, 1802, it had not yet reached the point where he had to use his imagination to hear it—or the architectural structure of the work, which became very concrete at the sight of the staves—a thought which for a few moments took me away from the music itself to thoughts of its affinities to other arts, how much closer it was to architecture than any other art, a castle in the air built in time not space, erecting temples with windows open to the world and tension-saturated spaces, into which every generation introduced their own anxieties. I kept thinking that all these speculations, so useful to the music critic, were distracting my attention from the experience being conjured up for me from the depths of the past by the dedicated efforts of four friendly people, whom I was learning to know very well, but trying very hard at this moment to forget—if only I had the strength to distract my thoughts from this woman, my love for whom was painfully sharpening my senses, as easily as they were distracted from the music—and then I remembered Beethoven again, Beethoven the love-starved child, who grew in years but not in height, and whose great mane of hair hid a beet-red, pockmarked face which drove its owner to despair. I went on thinking of him, and of myself, alternately, during the second movement, Allegro vivace e sempre scherzando, a lighthearted, jocular movement, but studded nevertheless with melodies too weary to laugh, a movement which gives musicologists grounds to connect his republican views with the stormy temperament that refused to submit to the conventions which bound Mozart and Haydn—who would miss a chance to enlist the genius on his side? Even the French tried to make out that he was really a Belgian during the First World

War—and from here, by a shortcut, to the boy Egon Loewenthal, seventeen years and two months old, adventurous and afraid, who set out with firm resolve and quaking knees to volunteer for the imperial army during the worst days of the year 1917, in order to come back, like his uncle, with an Iron Cross, for the glory of the family and the honor of the Jewish race, which was ready to lay down its life on the altar of its belief in the justice of the German cause. He came back with no belief in anything, neither in himself nor in any abstract idea seeking to emerge from literature into real life, where shrapnel flew shrieking furiously through the air, and an astounded boy, his brains spewing from his skull, fell flat on his face in the mire, and back to Beethoven, with the soothing sounds, in a hushed, unhurried piano, announcing the third movement, Adagio molto e mesto, so mysterious, enabling us to immerse ourselves thoughtlessly in the music, as if these conservative harmonies were the damp compresses on the feverish body—three months in shock, in a hospital behind the lines—music heavier than words, tired of ideas and loftier than pity, beyond sympathy, affirming the purifying power of the yearning for the peace of resignation, a hymn of thanksgiving to the suffering which gives birth to those immortal works of art on which all the superlatives in the world have been lavished, a Titan struggling with the gods, said Wagner, divine, said Tchaikovsky, whose God was an old composer creating his symphonies directly from nature. And straight after that, impelled by a cruel realism, my imagination returned to the wretched composer, the tame lion of the pampered daughters of aristocrats, who relieved the boredom of their lives by fantasies of love affairs they had no intention of realizing, and who were the unworthy objects of his immortal love. How embarrassing, in the middle of this divine music, to let my imagination run riot: all these sublime, immortal sufferings were born in a filthy cradle, when the pockmarked man, his cloak hiding his face, loomed into the squalid alleys of love, and there, on filthy sheets, stinking of the sweat and sperm of strangers, experienced for the first time in his life the sufferings of mortal love, which squeezed the white pus from his loins and sowed the seeds of disaster in his body, infecting one part after the other, from the guilty organ to the guiltless ear. Afterward I saw him in my imagination hiding in his attic, rubbing mercury into his eternally polluted skin, a form of treatment which got rid of the external symptoms but did more harm than good—I heard it all here, in the titanic struggle between the violin and the cello, the ignoble pain, the fear and the hypocrisy, the Christian sense of sin, and the defiance of fate—"My work is done," he declared on his deathbed, a piece of hypocrisy which did nothing to relieve the earthly pain but something to mar the unearthly suffering. . . . Can it be possible that some of these glorious lines would never have been written if the doctors of his generation had known the cure for syphilis? Only at the end of the movement was I able to recapture the state of vegetable thoughtlessness, and my mind emptied of ideas and filled with music, entities of sound fighting for a limited and strictly divided piece of time, joining in temporary alliances, separating in argument, and joining forces again in a common cause, as in a fugue, with increasing density, Communists, Jews, Social Democrats, lunatics, gypsies, priests, and embezzlers, degraded into one body by the concentration camp, tapping on the walls to communicate— but behold, out of the mists beyond the barbed wire, a rural, Bavarian serenity, green meadows from horizon to horizon, red-tiled roofs peeping through quiet foliage, a church spire and low peasant huts, and a ray of sunlight pierces the clouds, like a distant trumpet call of Mahler, heralding the approaching clearing of the skies. Over there freedom, ordinary little lives, without anxiety, Salzburg, bitter beer to sweeten the afternoon nap, and your heart fills with envy at the happy boredom of these stupid peasants enjoying their *schmaltz-musik*. . . . And suddenly, *de profundis*, a smothered, embarrassed cough, and you lift your eyes from the score, a priest rebuking a blasphemer—what happened? What's all the fuss about? Something human touched something human; one distress touched another, Beethoven's tortured conscience and the bronchitis of this anonymous lady, the mistress of some latter-day Titan, a milliner or construction worker. . . . And the majestic figure of the old Hindenburg surfaces in my memory, his dry, disdainful cough breaking the perfect stillness of Beethoven's *Generalpause*, without any feeling of guilt, confident of his rights to this moment of silence, without having to compete with the drums and trumpets, and everyone listened reverentially, even the conductor, with his back to the royal box, waited patiently, as if he had read the privileges of the ruling classes in the score, until the old man had cleared his throat of the idea which had stuck there. . . . And why shouldn't this anonymous woman in Tel Aviv have the same privilege, why should she be lashed with furious looks when she peels the wrapping off a piece of candy, with a discretion which drags the annoying noise out endlessly? Hasn't she got the right to make childish sucking noises, with her tender lips begging your pardon? . . . *Sic transit gloria mundi*, with an unseasonable cough in the most tragic moments of the saddest of all the slow movements Beethoven ever wrote, before he transports us into the fourth movement, "Thème russe," that innocent bucolic romp, with all its joyless trills, that folk tune which Mussorgsky did not hesitate to copy in *Boris Godunov*—what had been taken from Russia had to be returned—Russia is silent and apparently resigned to Hitler's acts, but she won't surrender Poland and her control over the Bosphorus—a gesture of goodwill toward Rasoumoffsky, the Russian representative in Vienna who commissioned the quartet, but also a compositional element introduced for balance—since there was no innocent joie de vivre to be found at home, in a nation of pessimistic philosophers, it had to be sought among remote, half-savage tribes, whose love of life had not yet been taught to march step by measured step in a Calvinist procession of virtues, but reveled in instinctual liberty. Like the gypsies, the Hungarians, the Russians. . . . Why else were the French attracted to Africa and China, Rimbaud and Pierre Loti, and the Americans to jazz, whose rhythmic beat, the rhythm of life, takes precedence over melody, which bears ideas on its wings. . . . Rosendorf can't forgive me for my interest in jazz, although it stems from the very same curiosity which made Beethoven write polkas and gypsy rhythms; in his opinion it's nothing but the weakness of a modern writer afraid of missing the latest fashion. . . . Was this acrobatic climb of the first violin to the heights of the E string really the passage of which Schuppanzigh complained that it was too difficult to execute, and received the arrogant, ungrateful reply—after he, Schuppanzigh, had agreed to teach the young musician composition even though everyone said that he was incapable of composing anything in the proper style—"Do you think I worry about your lousy fiddle when the spirit speaks to me?" . . . His Holiness is busy conversing with God and some idiot comes to bother him with the troubles of the poor. . . . In our day and age violinists are no longer troubled by the technical difficulties posed by a Beethoven quartet; anyone who has run his fingers over Paganini will find no trouble negotiating here. . . . But I couldn't help noticing the lack of spontaneous joy in the Rosendorf Quartet—Rosendorf himself played the movement with forced gaiety, like some gloomy Schopenhauer finding himself at an engagement party and forcing himself to raise his beer tankard above his head and stamp his feet mechanically, and not at all like a Russian peasant rushing into a drunken dance on the least excuse. . . . The same attraction to the rustic, the popular, the earthy, the primitive, the healthy, which gave birth to German obscurantism and the Hitlerite movement, gave birth, in more enlightened circles, to the recognition of the rights of remote cultures to exist, and even here, among European Jews of typically Western culture, you find a tendency to borrow from the Bedouin not only their tunes and rhythms, but also their simple, unquestioning attachment to desert and beast, and an attempt to find in the melodies composed on the shores of the Mediterranean Sea some new musical message, which will take its place among the northern melodies singing of their own accord in the ears of the wandering Jew. . . . The rousing Russian melody with its vigorous syncopations wakes the sleepy and does a power of good to the coughing lady, too. . . . And so to the final chord, which unleashes the emotions imprisoned behind the barbed wire of bourgeois manners in a fierce burst of applause, a reassuring noise which immediately puts a stop to the confused stream of thoughts aroused in us by this marvelous work . . .

6/12/39

Lately I've been neglecting my friends and keeping away from the quartet rehearsals, as if to avoid anyone who might ridicule all the vain efforts I'm investing in the piano, but I can't hide them from the good woman who suffers in secret, too virtuous to admit her jealousy. I'm afraid I'll have to find a place to stay—something I've avoided doing up to now, perhaps because of its symbolic significance. Being someone else's guest and having no home of my own means that I'm free to leave whenever the suffocation becomes unbearable, but moving out into an address of my own will mean one step toward accepting my fate. Nevertheless, I won't be able to go on living for long in the home of a woman who loves me while I'm busy day and night thinking about somebody else. On principle I don't find anything distasteful in the idea of a man sponging off a loving, hard-working woman while contributing next to nothing to the household expenses, since this is only the usual convention turned on its head, and as an advocate of the idea of equal rights for women, I respect their right to keep a man they love so that he can dress up to please them and take piano and English lessons at their expense. But I'm not a scoundrel. Respect for myself and others does not permit me to be in love with one woman while slaking my lust in the arms of her sister. True, in terms of conventional morality I have only sinned so far in thought, albeit rather graphically, since my imagination is wilder and bolder than I am, but in my heart of hearts, where my sternest judge is enthroned, I know that the worst betrayals take place in the secret of the soul—and I don't mean the occasional little affairs which detract nothing from the Immortal Beloved, and sometimes even strengthen a weakening bond, but the real betrayal, which consists of the absolute certainty that the one and only love has taken posses-sion of your soul and become so much a part of you that there is no need to reinforce it with the constant discovery of the virtues of the beloved, but on the contrary: in the teeth of the clear conviction that the whole thing is a mistake from begin-ning to end, and that this woman is not only unworthy of your love, but deserves your hatred, for she does not possess a single human quality that you admire, and the more you know her the more you realize how insane it is for a man like you to be in love with a woman like her, and nevertheless. . . . If Staubenfeld had not been the violist of the Rosendorf Quartet she might not have appeared in these pages at all, just as I have ignored other personal matters here—such as the irregular heartbeat which I have accepted in the right spirit of resignation—and I shall only add here that the recent friend-ship between Hilda and Staubenfeld is almost the only sign of my failure to hide my feelings from the woman I have tried so hard to deceive. I am well aware of the dark attraction a betrayed woman can conceive for the one who has robbed her of her happiness, partly in order to dispel the fog of uncer-tainty and partly in order to discover the secret of the attrac-tion itself—an attraction sometimes transformed into an unhealthy kind of love, which Russian literature enjoys wal-lowing in more than we do, and which binds the two women together in an inseparable, claustrophobic alliance. I don't mind pretending, however, to believe in the ostensible reason for the closeness between them, i.e., joining forces to help Litovsky, who was taken in for questioning and only released after Staubenfeld's English boyfriend's feelings had been exploited to the full. Hilda is convinced that it was their plotting and scheming to involve the Englishman in Litovsky's case which succeeded in nipping the affair in the bud, before any real harm was done to the quartet. Litovsky was warned about his connections with a certain shady character, one of those who think that a revolver in the hands of a Jew is more moral than the one used by some ignorant English boy in self-defense, and released after he was found guilty of nothing but being an incorrigibly romantic fool. He never had any intention of actually doing anything. He was content with the kinds of preparations for action that enrich a person's biography. Underground organizations are full of bored people incapable of imagining the consequences of their actions. In any case, he was not responsible for the alliance between the two women. Hilda would have found some other pretext. In the closed circle of our compatriots, who live in the same neighborhood, sit in the same cafes, shop in the same grocery stores, and are addicted to the same forms of entertainment, there are countless opportunities for accidental meetings. And neither of them misses any of these opportunities. They both enjoy the atmosphere of conspiracy. They talk to each other in a code which hides nothing, like the secret languages of children, which anyone can understand once they have discovered which letter of the alphabet is inserted between every two syllables. In their language my name is the extra letter. Every time my fingers get entangled in the difficult passages of the Arpeggione, I can see that penetrating, sympathetic smile hovering before my eyes. Both of them know that this knight errant, who has undertaken impossible missions in order to prove to his ladylove that he is worthy of her, will not be rewarded by her heart on his homecoming, but only by that part of her soul which is generously dedicated to anyone who buys a ticket to a concert of the Rosendorf Quartet.

AUGUST 26, 1939

My Communist friends will have to thread an elephant through the eye of a needle in order to excuse the pact between the eagle and the bear. Dialectics will provide them with plenty of ready-made justifications. Historical necessity will be dragged up again: if the Soviets hadn't preempted their rivals in the West, England and France would have made the pact with Satan. God took pity on a few of my friends and gathered them to Himself before they were betrayed by their comrades. If they hadn't died prematurely, their hearts would have been broken to bits, either by the act itself, or the mental acrobatics of their friends, who call black, white. Even humor, which helps us to accept the world as it is, is not prepared to offer me an ironic consolation this time. My only ever-renewable chance now, to borrow a phrase from our friend Martin, the "Saint of Jerusalem," lies in the blank page in front of me.

Like a nun subduing the agitation of her soul in the painstaking weaving of delicate lace, so I subdue my furiously trembling hands to the exhausting labor of writing my outline. One of my "I's," lower or higher, consistently refuses to complete the work. At a time like this, it is an impertinence to polish a verse or prune prose of redundancies. The form-breakers are perhaps better at describing this reality than we disciples of the clearly formulated sentence. But I cannot force my nature into the fashionable mold. Putting my confusion on display is not enough for me. Writing helps me to understand. If it can't do that, what use is it? Even as therapy it won't do me any good.

In the meantime, the outline is filling up with details, some of them quite spicy. I'm afraid I won't be able to use them though. Rosendorf "disappoints" me. I chose him specifically as a man with nothing but music in his life. But in the course of time I have discovered that he could be the hero of a pica-

resque novel without moving from his chair. Adventures seek
him out and history too has no mercy on him. How ironic it is:
he traveled to a pioneer country in order to escape History,
but she keeps plaguing him with her dark surprises. She has
even succeeded in breaking up his family. He is a closed,
reserved man, almost antisocial, and nevertheless he finds
himself from time to time implicated in love affairs in which
he had no intention of getting involved. Certain facts have
only recently come to my attention. A man in love discovers
fellow sufferers of whose condition he had no inkling before
he himself was infected by the disease.

My outline contains few of those details which the amateur
detective in every writer collects in order to enrich the texture
of a novel dealing with lives of boring people. I omitted the
unhappy love of Hella Becker. I did not think that the charity
dinners which Rosendorf occasionally eats in that quarter, to
appease his hunger, would add spice to my stew. For the
Rosendorf in my novel I shall have to invent a settled family
life, so that I can devote myself to the "Anatomy of a Quartet." I have also left out other banal affairs and routine patterns of behavior, which have no place in my novel except as
metaphors. I shall be faithful to the original Rosendorf Quartet only in including a woman in the players. But my Staubenfeld will play the cello. She will be a woman who sits with her
legs wide apart and protects the source of hope and misery
with a resonant instrument. I need her to bear witness to
music as an emotional pimp.

I shall almost certainly include his landlady's daughter, that
tempting unripe apple with the smoldering eyes. Not because
of the titillation—sexual perversions give a certain depth to
modern literature—and not because I have any intention of
sitting in judgment on the lusts of the characters at my
mercy—I am neither sadistic nor power-mad enough to enjoy
torturing the poor creatures I invent—nor yet because of the
unbearable feelings of guilt which gave birth to some of the

most beautiful movements in the music of the nineteenth century—poor, syphilitic Schubert believed that those exquisite adagios of his were a piece of unpardonable hypocrisy, for what right did a miserable sinner like him have to sing with all the angels?—but mainly because I see an integral connection between the musical personality of this man, who has refined his sensitivity to the extreme limits of human possibility, and his attraction to the bittersweetness of the greenish fruit hanging on the end of a distant bough.

I caught them red-handed. Quite unwittingly. I walked in without knocking, so as not to disturb them in the middle of the lesson. I needed an address in Germany. I caught them at it, nothing sensational, just childish petting, but the intention was obvious—he was standing behind her and showing her the proper way to hold the violin, and his fingers, as if of their own accord, were straying to a very improper place. I could have ignored that, if the pair of them hadn't blushed, and if Rosendorf hadn't found it necessary, that same evening, to pay me an embarrassed visit—luckily Hilda wasn't at home— in order to apologize for his wicked deeds, as if an old sinner like me was sitting in judgment on him, and excuse them on the grounds of true love, and tell me about his distress, both real and imaginary, and his fear of himself, and of the girl's parents, and of the girl herself, of her awakening passions, of his moral standards, which were disintegrating in front of his eyes, and of the need to invent lies at every turn, as usual in a forbidden love, which was true feeling feeding on lies.

The lofty terms he employed to justify the stolen embraces, which did not lead to fulfillment and brought only fear and tension in their wake, were nothing but self-deception. We elevate our low lusts and sordid desires in order to lessen our punishment. He needed to believe that the girl, with her mediocre talent, possessed a rich inner world, to which he had not yet found the key. Kindhearted Rosendorf, who loves those he desires and worships those he has sinned against! Love to him is the magic which purifies ugly deeds. In the end he really will fall in love with the girl to protect his soul from corruption. And he won't have to stray far from his nature to do it.

I have always sensed in him a profound attraction to the moment before fulfillment, to the confusion before maturity. Real grown-ups, it seems, will never be true artists. The tense anticipation of the next note is the artist's most important quality. The promise is more important than its fulfillment, just as the definition of the tangible is not the business of the writer, who captures the indefinable in a net of words like a butterfly hunter, who catches his butterfly first, and only then looks up its name in the Index. The tensest musical moment is the immeasurable interval of time between the note which was and the note which is to come. Art lives its secret life in the no-man's-land between the chord which has already been played and the one which has not yet come into being. Hence Rosendorf's love for Schubert, his inability to discover the full meaning of Bach (he doesn't sing Bach, but declaims him like some exalted speech, every word bigger than the one before), his embarrassment at the nonromantic moments of Brahms— and his reservations about Staubenfeld, who is a finished creature, a mature, defined, disillusioned woman, living behind the fortress of a detached and ruthless beauty.

JANUARY 1955

In the year 1936, in the autumn, as far as I remember, I found myself in Palestine. A penniless refugee. A writer exiled from his country and his language.

I did not go hungry or even feel the pinch. A woman friend of my youth, a great admirer of German literature, took me into her home and gave me everything one person can give another without enslaving him. I made a living by writing articles in émigré journals published in Paris and Zurich, and later on, during the war, I published reviews and other pieces in a local German paper.

I stayed in Palestine until the end of the war, waiting for the acclimatization which would enable me to devote myself to my literary work. Needless to say, God did not give his blessing to the match, and I wrote nothing in those years but articles, which did not count for much with me, and a few essays. I did not have the peace of mind necessary to write a novel. When you wake up every day wondering what will become of you, it is hard to talk prose.

This is not the place to go into my reasons for going to America before I returned to Germany. In any case, I felt a powerful need to subject myself to a renewed encounter with the country which had spewed me out. And the moment I arrived there, I knew that I would never be a writer unless I lived in a place where people spoke my language.

I have no intention of writing an apologia here. I was obliged to leave Palestine for many different reasons. Even the tightening bonds with the woman in whose home I was living made it necessary. There was no point in continuing the ménage à deux any longer without formalizing the arrangement. I felt that I would be untrue to myself if I yielded to her kindheartedness. Her love was deep and pure, and it would have been impossible to detach myself from her by moving to another town. Love can be so tight a bond that in order to loosen it one has to cross the ocean. Love can be a powerful separating force. But it too is not our subject here.

On my return to Israel to take care of the legacy left me by this woman, who remained single all her life—a heavy burden on my conscience—I found among her possessions an outline for a novel, which I had written in those years, and apparently considered unworthy of further development. Looking back, I find in these notes a faithful testimony to my mood during that tragic period. I see no reason not to publish them as they stand, as a kind of literary genre in its own right, not governed by any rules. How can any of us know which of the witnesses we bear will be valid even after we ourselves are gone?

At first the notes were written as a kind of diary, which gradually took on the form of the outline for a novel. The title at the head of the first page ("String Quartet—Outline for a Novel"), which is printed in a clear, firm, self-confident hand, was added later, apparently after a unifying theme emerged from my scribbles. I know this from the pen nib. I bought it in a stationery shop in Eliezer Ben Yehudah Street, on a sweltering day at the beginning of summer, 1937, and the salesman told me that if I didn't break it I would be able to use the nib for the rest of my life.

Human memory is quite mad—I remember a little detail like that, whereas the very existence of the outline itself simply vanished from my memory.

The original title, in my ordinary handwriting—"Diary of an Exile"—was crossed out with one stroke of the pen. The first pages of the notebook are devoted to the reasons for crossing it out.

Since these notes were written in that little Tel Aviv apartment, all the cells in my body have changed about five times over. I am both kin and stranger to the person I was then. At such a distance, I can testify with almost no bias that the man who wrote them tried to write without self-pity. Hence the tendency to sharpen his wit whenever the sadness became unbearable.

The moment I laid eyes on the manuscript I remembered my last meeting with Staubenfeld, the day before the war broke out.

Unlike Rosendorf, I am powerfully attracted to the mature and well-defined, to women barricaded behind their personalities. How else to explain my love for Staubenfeld, which grew even stronger after the disappointment of fulfillment?

That woman succeeded in turning all my standards upside down.

I wanted to love her from a distance, with the yearning for

the inaccessible which is content with a barren romantic dream, in a kind of identification with the poetic lies of the century which gave us the most exalted achievements of German music.

From my point of view, secure in the lap of a woman who loved me unconditionally, Staubenfeld seemed like the crystalline embodiment of an abstract feeling, an expression of the perfectly Germanic, which does not exist outside the imagination of Jewish poets and which gave birth to metaphysical suffering and the yearning for pure, transcendental Teutonism.

It was not I who reached out to pluck the burning ember, but the ember which flew into my hand. With one of those caprices whose unexpectedness gave them a strange charm, she suddenly said to me: "Come on, let's get it over with."

The deliberate coarseness of it was stunning. As if she had observed me from a distance and seen, before I understood myself, that I would not be able to bear it any longer, and had decided to break the spell before it was too late, in the most effective way possible—by the realization of a repressed desire.

Hilda was in Jerusalem. I had intended to go sit in a cafe in Eliezer Ben Yehudah Street after the concert but when we got into the cab she gave the driver her address. When we got out she paid the fare, to make it quite clear who was the host here and who the guest, and then, when I hesitated for a moment, she uttered the above words, which broke a long silence.

"What are you waiting for?" she said when I hung back—it was dark and I didn't remember if there was a step behind the door—"Surely you're not afraid of Sonichka! In any case she's already made up her mind that we Germans are rotten to the core."

When we entered her room she switched on the light and began taking off her shoes. My embarrassment amused her.

"Does the light bother you? I can put it out if you're ashamed of your body."

She spoke in a cold, colorless voice, as if we were discussing some practical problem, as if this were a punishment I had deserved rather than a favor she was granting me. When I didn't move from the door, she smiled to herself and put out the light. For a moment it was completely dark. But the shutter was open, and in the light on the balcony of the opposite house, through the transparent curtain, I could follow her movements. She pulled her dress over her head, revealing long legs as white as the shining bark of a poplar tree.

"Do you intend doing it with your clothes on?"

There was no truth in the impatience of her voice. She wasn't dying for me to hurry up and quench her lust. She chose to speak in that tone in order to put things in their proper light. Her mastery over the nuances of timbre applied to her voice as well as her instrument. I can't remember exactly what I said. Some romantic nonsense, in all sincerity, no doubt, along the lines of: Can the most intimate gift of all be offered without love?

She uttered a short, toneless, muffled laugh with her dress over her head—she probably thought I wanted her to declare some kind of affection, if not actual love, or, at least, single me out among the rest of her admirers, which was exactly what she had no intention of doing—and said that even when she was playing she bared herself. And then she took off her bra and revealed her beautiful breasts. As shamelessly as if she were exposing them to a doctor.

Since I still had not found the strength to move, she asked me with a smile if I was afraid.

I did not reply, although she had guessed my feelings right.

"Would you prefer me to get dressed?" she said mockingly, but made no movement to do so. "Don't you want me?" she taunted me.

I was forced to admit that this was not what I had wanted. I didn't want physical contact alone, without some deeper emotional bond. True, there were such moments in my fantasies, she and I, completely naked, but in my imagination things happened differently—with eyes full of love, with endless tenderness, in utter harmony, and with gentler tones than these. And in them I had never gone all the way. Perhaps I blurted out some such foolishness as a meeting of bodies alone would hurt my soul, or "The flesh without the spirit smells bad," because her reply, which I remember vividly, was: "What on earth do you mean by spirit? If it's not physical it's nothing. Even music is produced by the friction of a horse's tail on a sheep's gut." Her tone was perfunctory, as if she were only talking in order to oblige a man who was incapable of touching a woman before exchanging a few philosophical remarks. "Let me tell you, with a woman the body is the soul. And the more miserable the body, the greater the soul. In the sad places in a woman's body there's plenty of soul. Here you are, see for yourself," and she pulled my hand toward her vagina, but let it drop on the way.

I had no doubt as to the message hidden in this crude, mocking style. The intention was to deprive the sexual contact of any romantic sentiment. She was prepared to put her vagina at my disposal as a simple gesture of generosity, since she had nothing to lose if I enjoyed it too.

"It must be difficult to take your trousers off when your hands are shaking," she mocked. "Here, let me help you," and she grabbed for my penis, which recoiled in alarm at her touch.

She was enjoying my discomfort, and drew the pleasure out by stumbling intentionally over my fly buttons.

It was only when I asked her whether I had to be careful that a note of bitterness crept into her lighthearted, deliberately licentious tone.

"Don't you really know?" she said, with a trace of anger in her voice. "And I thought that in the provinces everybody knew everybody else's business . . ."

Even this most painful story of all she told in the same dry, matter-of-fact tone.

"I'm empty inside," she said. "You can ejaculate as much as you like. A child won't come of it."

In the same tone she told me about the only man she had ever loved. A young composer, by whom she had become pregnant; her family had hired ruffians who beat him to death, even though he wasn't a Jew. Afterward they had forced her to have an abortion, under a false name, in a remote provincial town. The abortion had caused complications. An old story. And now she was liberated from a woman's fears.

The word "liberated" was pronounced with a cynicism so profound, that for a moment I thought that she was trying to ridicule the title of one of my books. But afterward I thought that she probably didn't even know it existed.

Together with her womb they had rid her of bourgeois conventions. Her barrenness liberated her vagina from bourgeois morality. Barrenness can give birth to perfect selfishness and licentiousness without the fear of sin. Without having to fear the consequences, she could flit from one man to another. If she felt like it, she could give honey; if she felt like it—she could sting.

The gestures of her body, the breath of her mouth, and the momentary source of a damp joy were gentler and warmer than her words.

"What more would you like?" she asked, when she sensed a renewed arousal. "Don't be shy to ask. Today is the big chance of your life. There won't be a second."

I was sure there wouldn't. But when she gave herself to me again, and made me feel sensations I never knew existed, I imagined that I saw a determination to realize some ambition on her face, and the only ambition I could think of was the ambition to give me, this one and only time, such pleasure that after it I would never be able to find happiness in the arms of another woman. The cruel enjoyment of a person exempted by nature from responsibility for the future.

I left her, feeling as if I had awakened from a clear dream and fallen into a dark, obscure one, drunk with confusion. The woman I loved had bestowed the final favor on me and given me nothing. Through me she had avenged herself on my sex. She had used her body to murder love. To teach me that the reproductive organs are the seat of morality and responsibility, and it is only in their absence that we are free to bestow happiness where we please.

And perhaps she wanted to say: there is nothing to take and therefore there's no point in giving. The world of our times is a woman whose reproductive organs have been removed. Love is extended egoism. Our actions are absurd. Our failures are pointless. Patriotism is an illusion; language lies. All that exists is music—the last gasp of Western civilization.

I did not stay long in the country. I do not have many friends in Israel. The few people who do remember me criticize me harshly for my return to Germany, which I have no intention of justifying. It's my life and I don't owe anyone an account of my actions. Fanatical enthusiasts who see the Jewish state as the answer to everything are quite capable of crushing a repulsive creature like me without a qualm.

I went there for a specific purpose, to take care of the legacy of Hilda Moses, who had been kind enough to leave me a small bequest, in the touching hope that I would finally settle down in the place where I owned property. I found rare books which she had collected for me from the remains of her many friends, and a few manuscripts, outlines, which I had not bothered to take with me to America because at the time I had given up the idea of completing them. On rereading them, however, I find more point in publishing the outline for a novel, which faithfully reflects the confusion of the creative process. After the total collapse of Western values, there is no point in publishing coherent novels with a solid architectural structure, which is, if anything is, an expression of the belief in these very values. The educated reader of our times will not be angry with me if I offer him broken fragments. He takes more pleasure in sticking the potsherds together than in the beauty of the whole jar.

The Rosendorf Quartet, in its original format, no longer exists. Friedman married a woman who was a member of a kibbutz in the north of the country, and went to teach music there. He put together an amateur quartet from the surrounding settlements, which survived until he was killed in the War of Independence. Staubenfeld married the British officer, who was wounded in a terrorist attack, and is now a violist in the London Philharmonic. Litovsky landed in America, and is now the first cellist in the Minneapolis Symphony Orchestra. Only Rosendorf remained, in contradiction to all my predictions. The war, which took his wife and daughter from him, solved a number of problems between him and his conscience. The pupil he sinned with when she was still a child is now his wife, and she treats him like someone who has earned the right to cast doubt on his honesty and respectability. They have two children, both of whom are apparently endowed with musical talents which will rob them of their childhood. Now, at the age of fifty, he looks to me like a musician submerged in an orchestra. The new quartet he set up is the lifeline which enables him to keep his head above water. The quartet itself has a good sound and flawless technical competence, the second violin is actually better than Friedman, but it lacks the inner tension and the dramatic character of the old Rosendorf Quartet. But perhaps it's only my imagination. I was emotionally involved in the previous quartet; here I am free of obligations. In listening to music, we listen to ourselves.

On the face of things, there are more possibilities now—Europe is no longer barred to Jews and the sky's the limit, as they say in America. Nevertheless, the Rosendorf Quartet's chances of breaking into the international scene are less than they were. Perhaps because in a young country, where everything is new, it is easy to make a man of fifty feel that his life is coming to an end. And perhaps because under the suffocating security blanket of domestic happiness Rosendorf, an eagle with a wounded wing, has resigned himself to his fate and accepted the borders of this country, which were fixed in the armistice agreement, as the boundaries of his world. Only in my ears—there aren't even any recordings—are the moments of inspiration and unendurable tension preserved, when the old Rosendorf Quartet, with stormy hearts, played Beethoven's Grosse Fuge, defying God and man.